I0629131

A Divided Universe

By: H.E. Carl

Edited by: Big Eagle Editors
Cover Design by DMH Designs

All Rights Reserved
Copyright 2018
1-6738034661

Printed in the United States of America
ISBN 978-0-9981101-7-2(Paperback)

Visit us at www.hecarl.com

Books by H. E. Carl
The Last Medallion
The Medallion Gauntlet
A Divided Universe

A Divided Universe

Table of Contents

Chapter One	*Recon*
Chapter Two	*The Assessment*
Chapter Three	*Slave Camp*
Chapter Four	*The Triplets*
Chapter Five	*Lorakits Return*
Chapter Six	*The LuQuarins' Alliance*
Chapter Seven	*A New Pairing*
Chapter Eight	*Temptation and a Trip*
Chapter Nine	*Evil Takes Form*
Chapter Ten	*A Moment of Paradise*
Chapter Eleven	*The Humedlior Intervention*
Chapter Twelve	*A Plea to the Council*
Chapter Thirteen	*The Quest of Evil Takes Form*
Chapter Fourteen	*The Big Delay and a Rescue*
Chapter Fifteen	*An Old Friend, Family and the Council*
Chapter Sixteen	*A Long-Awaited Freedom*
Chapter Seventeen	*Galan*
Chapter Eighteen	*A Final Plea*
Chapter Nineteen	*The Fury of Tenekaris*
Chapter Twenty	*Solaria and New Truths*
Chapter Twenty-one	*Thyons Return*
Chapter Twenty-two	*A Past Uncovered*
Chapter Twenty-three	*Confronting the Council*
Chapter Twenty-four	*Aid for Galan*
Chapter Twenty-five	*Sereptin*
Chapter Twenty-six	*Lanatars Return*
Chapter Twenty-seven	*A Council Revived*
Chapter Twenty-eight	*Elior Prepares*
Chapter Twenty-nine	*Preparation & a New Power*
Chapter Thirty	*The LuQuarin Deploy*

A Divided Universe

Chapter Thirty-one   *The Hologram Deception*
Chapter Thirty-two   *The Battle of Elior*
Chapter Thirty-three   *The Battle Day Two*
Chapter Thirty-four   *Breaking the Stalemate*
Chapter Thirty-five   *The Aftermath*
Chapter Thirty-six   *A New Beginning*

Chapter One
Recon

Alex crawled up the last few yards to the peak of the ridge. Reaching the top, he peered down into the wide valley to the large LuQuarin compound. Fifteen years had passed since the LuQuarin had attacked Elior wiping out eight cities and killing over twenty million Elior. They disappeared after the attack and moved all of their operations to new unknown galaxies until just recently, when several probes the Elior sent out revealed their whereabouts.

The sky was dark but filled with many stars and the light of two full-moons in the distance. He heard slight rustling as Croulac joined him on his left and Matt to his right. They took out their long-range scopes to get a better look at what lay before them. The compound was heavily guarded with numerous shields protecting the structures. They formed a semi-circle in front of the opposite ridge, common for LuQuarin defenses, designed to protect any invasion into the natural structure where their leaders resided with other secrets.

Alex and the Elior had been here for a week, looking for weaknesses, determining what was being protected inside the opposite range. Besides the shields there were numerous weapons and personnel manning the entire length of the top ridge. There were now five levels of shields and entrance into the compound was strictly controlled. Alex and the Elior had used their newest pea sized recon orbs to gain access and see what was inside the structure. It had been a pain-staking and slow process as the recon orbs had to drill through below the surface until they found a gap between the underground shields and the surface shields. The LuQuarin had learned that the Elior could launch special missiles through a planet, up and underneath a structure to destroy it. Four recon orbs were sent, one from each direction and three other groups awaited their return. If successful they would have a complete map and video of most of the structure.

Alex communicated with Croulac and Matt via sign to avoid possible voice or noise detection by the LuQuarin. Finally, Alex saw a small light on his Gauntlet light up, signaling the recon orb was in its' final stages of returning. Another fifteen minutes passed and the recon orb appeared next to Alex. Grabbing it the three made their way back to their own orb quietly and then vaped and ported back to the Admirals ship cloaked in the outer atmosphere.

Back on board the command ship Alex handed the recon orb to a Captain for processing. Two other groups had returned with only one still down on the planet. Alex took the time to go to the Admirals ready room to prepare for the upcoming meeting. Sitting at a table he pulled up a report. It was dated over fifteen years ago, a few days before the attack on Elior had occurred. It was from the Elior space station cloaked in space orbiting Earth, or what was left of Earth. The report read:

Elior space station Earth 4.

While continuing to monitor the 5 remaining underground survival structures still in operation on Earth, our intelligence and subsequent follow up has revealed that all remaining females on Earth are now missing. We suspect they were abducted by the LuQuarin and transported off planet to a LuQuarin hold. Several male humans are also missing, all between the ages of 20 and 40. Based on our surveillance and tapping into the human reports to their leaders, it is estimated that the remaining 8,468 females and 429 males are unaccounted for. Of the females missing 76 were pregnant. All data was subsequently rechecked confirming this data. We are searching the entire planet to verify if there are any remaining females still on Earth. To date none have been found. Should this information hold true, we fear the human population remaining will die off over time as they can no longer re-generate their species on Earth. Additional reconnaissance confirms that all remaining LuQuarin agents have departed Earth.

Alex set the report down. Earths fate was sealed 15 years ago by the LuQuarin. Tenekaris III had purposely abducted them for his own purpose, a human sex slave encampment and later death as a meal for the elite LuQuarins. The planet he just returned from was one of the suspected human camps. He pulled up another report, confidential for only certain members operating under the Admirals command.

A Divided Universe

In it were the details of a special program the Admiral had commissioned secretly outside of the Councils knowledge shortly after the attack on Elior. Since the council had only allowed the Admiral and armed forces of Elior one battle group, the Admiral had formed an intelligence gathering special ops section. With his own scientific team and genetic engineering, an Elior could be transformed into another species. Agents were carefully selected and were sent out with the explorer science groups throughout the galaxies. Over the years they had now infiltrated over 20 species, many of which worked with the LuQuarin in trading alliances. Although the LuQuarin continued to attack and destroy planets, they had also allied with the higher intelligent species on many planets where trade was a better alternative than war. It reminded Alex of the cold war back on Earth, the days of spies and agents. The data they collected since inception had proven valuable in discovering the LuQuarin operations in 3 galaxies. Helped by special programming a map was forming, outlining all LuQuarin locations. Croulac entered the room.

"It is time Alex. We are to meet in the Admirals command center." Alex closed his display, stood and followed Croulac. A minute later they were in the command center where there were 20 others all standing around a giant 3D display of the galaxy they were in. Alex saw Stilzen on the opposite side next to the Admiral. Stilzen was the head of the intelligence agency and reported only to the Admiral. He was a tall Elior 8 ½' and had a presence about him exuding confidence. The Admiral spoke.

"Stilzen just arrived here an hour ago with the latest intelligence updates. That, along with the successful recon of the planet below have now provided us with a much better picture of all LuQuarin operations." The Admiral hit a switch and the image of the galaxy changed lighting up where every LuQuarin site was at and the suspected path or wormholes and star gates they used to travel. It was a sizeable network. The lights were different colors depicting what type of facility on each planet and the names of the species that resided on them. It was the most complete network picture Alex had ever seen of the size and scope of the LuQuarin operations. The Admiral continued.

A Divided Universe

"As we suspected the planet below is a human slave encampment. Other intelligence suggests there are two more slave encampments and possibly one more, which would be Tenekaris III personal one. The three human facilities are quite large and are run by each of Tenekaris III three wives. This is the first one where we have complete details of the site and structure. Our programs point to where the other two should be located, here and here. Where his personal one is at is only a guess at this time but is most likely near his own command center for all operations. The LuQuarin have formed four strategic alliances, one each with the Thornoks, the Blisscrells, the Flemjots, and the Secarios. All four of these species have advanced space travel, but it is limited to within their own galaxy. They also have sizeable forces and weaponry that should be respected. We know the LuQuarin developed cloaking abilities and used them 15 years ago when they attacked Elior. We suspect they have improved on this technology and are capable of building larger star gates. I will now defer to Stilzen." Stilzen continued.

"Our intelligence and programs point to a planet in the next galaxy over to where we have a degree of certainty where Tenekaris III resides. Based on other information, the Admiral has now dispatched several other recon missions to the locations we believe are the human slave facilities, where they may be retaining large groups of their military complex to insure their preservation. It will take a number of weeks, perhaps months before we have the information needed to form a plan for the safe extraction of the human slaves. It is one area the Council of Elders has approved for us to implement as long as it can be accomplished with minimal risk to Elior lives. The recon just completed today provides us the basis to form such a plan but in order to be successful we will need all three-primary human slave camp locations and details of the structures and defenses housing them. I have recommended that the Admiral pull back our forces from here before we are detected to our main base which is a week's travel away. Unfortunately, we need to take a back seat until we have the confirmed intelligence we need to commence operations." The Admiral then spoke.

"I have agreed with Stilzen's assessment and we will travel back to our base camp and exercise patience and come up with a complete plan once all the information is available. Any questions?" Everyone in the room just nodded their heads in approval. The Admiral then ended the meeting and dismissed all participants.

Alex and Croulac headed to the lounge area on the ship. Once there they took seats at the bar and ordered food and drinks. They felt the ship vibrate and knew they were now on the way back to the large base camp and would have a week with little to do. Alex thought about Diana back on Elior where he had left her with his new advanced clone. She wouldn't even know the difference. Alex knew he would be away for a long time and had made the decision for the clone so as not to worry her and the kids. Very few knew that the real Alex was away and would never reveal to others his true whereabouts.

Diana was up early and sitting on the deck watching the sunrise out over the water. Another beautiful day on Elior in the tropical paradise they had called home now for fifteen years. It was her quiet time where visions of her paintings took hold. Her work with painting various scenery were now well respected and sought around the planet. Sipping her coffee, she thought of the day ahead. Soon Alex would be up and go for his long run on the beach, return, change and head out to the military base. The kids would also be getting up. AJ and Xia were in the last few months of their schooling and preparing to enter the academy of higher learning. AJ was almost as tall as Alex but hadn't filled out yet. Xia was a stunning beautiful young woman, taller than her mother by 3 inches and had long flowing golden hair and a body that attracted many a young man. AJ looked out for her at school and the knowledge of who her father was kept the advances on her to a minimum. Both had also been trained by their father and others, in advanced self-defense and martial arts. Diana was comfortable in their abilities, knowledge, and moral conduct they displayed, and they were well respected by their peers. She and Alex had raised them well, and the Elior educational system was far more advanced than anything they could ever have received if educated on Earth. The sun was rising up farther now and well above the distant water line. She got up and went back into the house to prepare breakfast for AJ and Xia.

Olisaria overlooked the sea out and below her home. She would have to get ready soon and attend the weekly council meeting. Being part of the

A Divided Universe

council after her grandfather's retirement had been a fulfilling position. Overseeing the entire human population on Elior had presented a few challenges in the early years but was now flourishing, growing and doing well. Although they had only saved a little more than 3 ½ million from Earths final days, the human species was not just surviving but growing and advancing. The greed, power and evil that had existed on Earth was gone, and a society of intelligent, caring people had emerged. Only a few of those that were saved experienced transitional issues or displayed inappropriate behavior. But with a little intervention by the Elior they too had now adapted to a world and planet that offered endless possibilities for a safe and successful life. Many of the best scientists saved were now integrated with Elior science teams going out into the galaxies exploring new worlds. Her daughter Alett was now a mature young woman of 30 and after finishing her work at the lab with advanced degrees in bio-chemistry and genetics had joined an exploration team and was traversing through the galaxies. She missed her daughter but understood, as she was no different than when Olis was that young. She smiled, remembering the days many years earlier and the excitement of traveling through space and discovering that which was out there. She went inside to prepare for the day and the meeting with the council.

Chapter Two
The Assessment

Alex looked in the mirror in his quaint but small quarters. He hadn't aged a day in 15 years thanks to the Medallion. Even his wife Diana had aged little, the life and purity on Elior had a profound impact on the aging process which they all benefitted from. Dressed in his normal military gear he headed out to the Admirals conference room. A week had turned into a month. News had just arrived from the numerous probes and recon missions. Perhaps today there would be something worthwhile to take action on.

Alex reached the conference room and was soon joined by Croulac, Stilzen and others. They took a seat waiting for the Admiral. A minute later the Admiral entered followed by his officers. After a simple greeting to all, the Admiral hit a switch at a small console and a large map appeared above the table of numerous galaxies. It showed their relative position and many other points in distant galaxies. The Admiral spoke.

"Our recon missions and probes have located a number of LuQuarin facilities." As he spoke the map changed and zoomed to a specific galaxy, and then zoomed further to a sun and several planets orbiting it. The projection zoomed in further to one planet in particular.

"This planet is called Drunora. It is about half the size of Elior and has a climate suitable for many forms of life. The air, water and other resources are abundant and numerous creatures live there, but no intelligent life has yet to develop on the planet. The LuQuarin have set up and established numerous military camps around the planet and here (as he zoomed in closer), is an encampment that imprisons a large population of humans. The defenses are similar to what we recently discovered. A few solar systems down from this planet we discovered another one, similar in nature. It too is home to a large military operation and the third human encampment. With the knowledge of all three, we are only missing Tenekaris III personal human sietch, which we may or may not have the fortune of discovering soon. Thus, I have ordered up our entire battle group to join us and prepare to attack the three facilities and rescue any/all

11

humans. They will be arriving within a week. During that time, we will draw up a complete and comprehensive strategy to simultaneously attack all three facilities. We will only get once chance at this and all three facilities have a large force of LuQuarin protecting them. To reduce risk and loss of life we will need to employ stealth and speed. I will be dispatching all your assignments by tomorrow, at which time you will outline and provide exacting details of carrying these operations out. We have waited a long time for this and if successful can strike a serious blow to our enemy's operations and avenge all those lives lost on Earth and Elior many years ago."

The Admiral opened up the meeting to questions and after a half hour the meeting reached its conclusion. As the meeting broke up the Admiral asked Alex and Stilzen to remain. The room was clear now except for the three. The Admiral looked at Alex.

"Alex, I am setting up a testing area for you on a moon a few planets down from here. I would like you to go there and test your Medallion and Gauntlet against various advanced structures and shields and then report back to me with the results." Alex nodded.

"Stilzen, I understand that Lorakit is returning with important information. For her to leave the prestigious position and being one our best spies among the Secarios is a bit unnerving. When do you expect her arrival?

"Later today Admiral. I will contact you immediately when she arrives."

"Very well Stilzen. I am anxious to hear what she has to say. Alex, I would like you to attend with Stilzen and Lorakit in my private meeting room as soon as she arrives." The meeting ended and Alex and Stilzen left the Admiral and headed to the commissary.

There they discussed the situation and Stilzen filled Alex in on the Secarios as a species and why Lorakit had been sent to infiltrate them. The Secarios by themselves had been a peaceful species and had developed interstellar travel advanced enough to journey between galaxies. Their weakness was greed and they were the earliest group to set up trade and bartering among numerous species and planets. They had a large fleet of ships that transported goods and materials between worlds as agreements were made, and they kept a good portion of the proceeds as profits for their services. A universal monetary system had been set up with gold as the basis and payment for all transactions. The Secarios had grown wealthy over the centuries and had expanded their fleet of cargo ships that now spread to many galaxies. They were a fairly tall humanoid type, large orange eyes and elfin ears with long hair and strong bodies. Their skin was a light cream color but as tough as leather. They dressed elaborately when not traveling through space and were governed by five rulers. They were the first species sought to handle any cargo and were respected by any species that traded through them. Even Tenekaris III used them exclusively to transport materials to those he had allied with and others to gain those materials he needed to continue to build his war machine. The Secarios had excellent weaponry and defenses built into each cargo ship and also very advanced escort fighters that traveled with each shipment. Even Tenekaris III respected their fighting abilities.

Lorakit had been with them now for 14 years and was highly sought because of her beauty and physique, using her looks, intelligence and sexual prowess to move up in the hierarchy of power. Her Elior training and skills as a fighter had been most useful in achieving the desired effect to gain access to a wealth of information in the Secarios network and other species including the LuQuarin.

Stilzen continued to brief Alex in more detail on their spy network and other species they had infiltrated to get a better picture of what the LuQuarin were up to. All of it suggested a massive military buildup for yet some unknown purpose. With his other alliances now well in place Tenekaris III held tremendous power which could be unleashed in several galaxies. Many species had simply capitulated to his demands to avoid annihilation, while the LuQuarin and their allies got stronger and stronger. Stilzen continued to brief Alex for another hour and then excused himself to attend to other matters, but would contact Alex when Lorakit arrived. Alex decided to vape and port to a special zone set aside for all personnel.

A Divided Universe

Arriving a few moments later, he stood at the entrance of the need fulfillment center. Walking in he was greeted by a female Elior and directed to a terminal where he could select a clone mate to be with and fulfill the physical desires that had built up over the many weeks being away from his true mate Diana. He thought of his clone back on Elior and how he would be having intimate relations with her while he was away. Diana's sexual appetite had remained strong over the years reminding him of the days when they were first together. He smiled, knowing how fortunate he was to be her husband and missed her and the kids. But his physical needs for sex were strong and a couple hours with a clone would take care of that. He sat at the terminal and decided he wanted an Elior female versus a human. He went through the choices and programmed her exacting features, clothing, abilities, traits and knowledge. Once satisfied with all the details he activated the terminal. A minute later she was standing next to him. Smiling she took his hand and together they vaped and ported to a private area.

Alex was lying next to his playmate when a messenger disk appeared above him. They had spent the last three hours together in an exhilarating experience. She saw the disk and knew their time was up. Standing she said, "I hope you enjoyed our time together Alex. Perhaps you will call upon me again one day." She smiled, bent over and kissed him and then poof, she was gone.

Alex dressed back into his military uniform, read the message from Stilzen. Lorakit had arrived and he was requested to report to the Admirals conference room immediately. Alex exhumed the Medallion from his chest so it appeared outside his uniform, put on his dark glasses, vaped and ported as instructed.

Arriving just outside the Admiral's private conference room, he was immediately ushered in by the guard, the door closing behind. The Admiral was standing at the head of the oval table and seated were Stilzen and Lorakit. He had seen pictures and videos of the Secarios but had never met one in person. Lorakit was dressed in Secarios uniform which covered her 7' stature in a golden yellow with dark green trim worn by the high level of the species. Although an Elior, she had yet to convert back to her true identity. Alex was thankful he had his glasses on as her beauty was almost blinding. Despite the uniform her immaculate female form was ever present. Her long golden-brown hair with streaks of yellow fell to her shoulders. The bright orange eyes above a small petite nose and a set of perfectly curved lips. Her elfin ears barely showed through her hair. She looked at Alex and he could sense a presence about her, like that of the Admiral and Stilzen. The Admiral gestured him to sit as he exchanged a greeting nod with Stilzen and Lorakit. The Admiral spoke.

Thank you, Alex, for coming so quickly. As you can see Lorakit has returned and I wanted you to hear first-hand what she has to say to all of us. The floor is yours Lorakit." When she spoke is was a soft, pretty voice but projected with strength and confidence.

"Thank you, Admiral. It took me over three weeks to get here. As you know I have been the Mistress of Kokolaris for the past three years. He is what you might describe as the Director of inter-galactic transportation governing seven galaxies. In the past year a majority of the shipments have been for the LuQuarin, many secretive and most likely military in nature. They also added LuQuarin guards to accompany almost every shipment, of which I suspect a number were also spies for Tenekaris III. My rise in stature among the Secarios came under their scrutiny six months ago, and I know I have been followed and watched closely during that time. In order to gather more intelligence and information, required that I take some risks. Recently Kokolaris asked me to be more than a mistress and to become his one and only. I was able to deflect and defer his request at the moment but knew my time was growing short. He was leaving on a week's long mission to deliver something very important for Tenekaris. With the surveillance on me getting tighter in his absence, I elected to hack into the main systems and retrieve as much data as I could, and then I staged my own death using my exacting clone, and went into hiding until I could stow away on a ship heading this way. By now Kokolaris has discovered my death and there will be hell to pay for how I staged it." She paused, took a few sips of a restoration drink and then continued.

"After Kokolaris had left on his mission I retrieved my exacting clone out of hiding and put her in my place. There were always three guards watching over and protecting me in Kokolaris' absence. It was common for me to bring them drinks and food when I resided in my private area. The real me had spiked their drinks with a special narcotic and my clone was dressed in a very provocative manner and left the doors open to her most private room after parading about in a most enticing way. The drug soon took affect and the three guards soon followed my clone into her chambers and proceeded to pin her down, rip the scant garments from her and then ravage her repeatedly for a long time. I was in my pea size orb in the room and had activated all the surveillance videos. After they had each raped her a number of times the drug began to wear off. I then used my special shooter from the orb and shot and injected the three with the antidote which also made the drugs untraceable and left behind a common toxic beverage which many Secarios drink."

"As they came to their senses and realized what had happened, the lead guard pulled out his long-sheathed knife and came over and slit her throat. They then proceeded to take her body and sneak it out of the home and disposed of it in a landfill. Again, all of this was recorded and left behind for Kokolaris to view when he returned. The three guards then left the area and disappeared. I left soon after and began my escape route." She paused and took another drink before continuing.

"We all have been trained to have at least a couple escape routes and when I ran into trouble on the first, I had to change and use my secondary route. I finally made it to a remote outpost where I had a small ship hidden. I disabled their tracking systems for a few minutes making it appear as a glitch in the system and was able to take off and make my way out of the solar system. Although not a fast ship it had cloaking abilities and within a week I was out of that galaxy. I finally made it to our secret outpost in section 18, where they were able to put me on an SSSTS to get back here which arrived just an hour ago." She paused and took another drink. Stilzen looked at her and knew there was more. They all waited until she finished her drink. The Admiral asked.

"Would you like another, Lorakit?"

16

A Divided Universe

"No, I am good, but to be honest I am looking forward to transforming back into my Elior body. It has been so long now." The Admiral looked at Stilzen knowing too there was more. She spoke.

"Admiral, Stilzen and Alex. I would not have left my situation had I not discovered something I felt needed to be heard by you. In just my last month there before I faked my death I discovered that the LuQuarin have formed yet another alliance. This one scares me as it is with the Lycoats. They are as dangerous as the LuQuarin and have vast numbers and a military almost equal to the LuQuarins. Tenekaris III I suspect met with their leaders and subsequently provided them with vast amounts of materials, most of which are used for weaponry. They too have intergalactic capabilities and the meetings were set up by the Secarios to form the alliance. Together they have the military might to control or destroy almost anything. I have as much information on them as I could pull from the main system. Such an alliance would make it possible for Tenekaris and his allies to seek out and destroy the Elior and all those other species which we protect. I fear an inter-galactic war on a huge scale coming soon. If the Elior and others are not prepared it could result in the destruction of many planets and species including our own. That was why I chose to leave and get to you as quickly as possible." She sat back indicating she was done talking. The Admiral spoke up.

"We are reviewing all the information you brought back to us. It is substantial and will take some time to go through it all. Since you no longer can serve as a spy among the Secarios you may change back into your Elior form at any time. We have a unit here on our base that you can use to make the change."

"Thank you, Admiral."

"Is there anything else you would like to add, Lorakit?"

"No, sir. There are small details in my master report, but to be honest I am very tired and could use some rest once I transform back into Elior form."

"Very well, Lorakit. You are free to go, transform and take some time to eat and rest. I will summons you if something important comes up."

"Thank you, Admiral." She stood up, nodded to Stilzen and Alex, then departed the room. The Admiral was pacing back and forth. He then hit the intercom on the table to the bridge.

"Is Major Croulac there?"

"Yes, sir."

"Please have him come to my conference room."

"He's on his way, Admiral." The Admiral turned off the intercom and resumed his pacing. Within two minutes Croulac arrived and was ushered inside.

"Thank you for coming so quickly, Croulac." Croulac nodded.

"How are we doing with the information disk Lorakit brought us?"

"It's two Zettabytes of data sir, it will take time to go through it all."

"How long?"

"We have all available personnel working on it, but it could take weeks, sir."

"We don't have weeks, Croulac. Can you get any more of our people on it?"

"I will try and find more, sir, but I doubt we have available here the kind of expertise we need to do it any faster."

"Hmmm. Ok do the best you can and if you discover anything of importance get it to me immediately."

A Divided Universe

"Will do sir." With that Croulac departed the meeting. Stilzen spoke up.

"Admiral, if I may speak?"

"Yes Stilzen, please do. The news from Lorakit is most disturbing."

"Admiral, if what Lorakit has told us is true, then the threat to the Elior and others has never been greater. I suggest we get messages to all our agents in the field immediately to report and update us if possible without risking their position."

"I agree Stilzen."

"I will also suggest we get word back to Elior on these latest developments in order that they have the opportunity to prepare for a possible attack, and also send warnings to all our allies so that they may prepare as well. With the time we have lost here doing recon and the three weeks it took Lorakit to bring us the information, we may have little time left."

"Yes, that is true Stilzen, but we will need more than just Lorakit's word to convince the Council into action. We need the data she brought back that could clearly demonstrate the threat. Alex, you have been quiet. What is your assessment?"

"Admiral, we have a serious dilemma on our hands. Here we are a week away from launching a rescue mission to save the humans from the sex slave encampments. On the other hand, if just half of what Lorakit brought us is true, the threat to the Elior and all those we protect is at risk. With the size and scope of our enemy and his allies even with our technological superiority, we would be in jeopardy with the numbers they could mass against us. You have only one battle group active, which I fear, could easily overrun at this point. Although we would inflict serious losses to the LuQuarin and his allies, their sheer numbers would eventually defeat us. Granted Elior has a complete neural net around the planet, that also can be turned into an impregnable shield, it is still vulnerable to their star

19

gate technology. They did it once as we all know without us detecting it, so what is to say they couldn't do it again and this time pour millions of their soldiers and ships through. All life on Elior would be in harm's way. With the Councils decision to stand down 15 years ago our armed forces are down to six million. Granted we furnished the eight other planets with a million clones of our best soldiers and weaponry, I fear that too would not be enough to adequately defend those worlds." The Admiral spoke.

"You paint a grim picture Alex. One that is hard to fathom. We must find a way that such a sequence of events does not come to fruition."

"Yes Admiral. We will need to find a way and the means necessary to thwart their actions and give them cause not to seek out and destroy all that we know and love. We first must get the information that Lorakit brought to us, at least enough to bring to the council so appropriate steps could be put in motion."

"Yes Alex, I agree. I am going to see Croulac and get a progress report. Perhaps you and Stilzen can begin to develop a plan as to how we may meet this seemingly impossible challenge."

"Yes Admiral. One more thing. I think you should call off the mission for the slave encampments. As much as I would love to see my fellow humans rescued from such a life, there is more at stake here and our resources are limited. If anything, such a mission would only antagonize our enemy and could possibly bring a massive attack on us sooner, before we have a chance to adequately prepare."

"Yes Alex, I had the same thoughts. When our battlegroup arrives, we will need to redeploy them for what we fear is coming. Rescuing the humans will have to take a back seat for now." With that the Admiral walked out seeking Croulac. Stilzen looked at Alex.

"Alex, we are going to have to come up with something that evens out the odds against us."

A Divided Universe

"Agree Stilzen. While we are waiting for the details on the information Lorakit brought to us, the first thing that comes to mind is that we need to disrupt their supply lines and quickly. If Tenekaris is not ready, we can disrupt his operations and at least buy some time."

"True Alex, but that would mean taking out the Secarios ships and their personnel, only inflaming them to join with Tenekaris."

"Yes Stilzen, but in truth they are already a part of his armada providing the means to build up many forces. They are as big a part of it as his newly sworn allies. But if we took out enough of the transport ships and materials we may be fortunate enough to disrupt the process. Tenekaris portals are not yet large enough to move large items or materials being used. He relies on the Secarios transports for that."

"From what we know they are well protected and have good defenses. It will not be easy to take them out."

"Yes, that is a bit of a problem Stilzen and one we must try and overcome. Are any of our long-range space probes equipped with any weaponry?"

"No Alex I am afraid not, as if they were equipped with any weapons they would lose their stealth and cloaking abilities and could be easily detected."

"Damn!"

"Alex, there is little we can do until we have more information from the disk Lorakit brought us."

"I know Stilzen, that is the frustration. I need a drink. Let's go to Officers' Club for a bit if that's Ok with you?"

"Sounds good, Alex."

A Divided Universe

Chapter Three
Slave Camp

She looked down into the well which was their drinking water and saw her reflection. The lines on her face had aged and her hair was a long mop in disarray. Her eyes had dark circles underneath, a by-product of the many years of enslavement. She tried to muster a small smile but could not manage it as there was nothing to smile about. She lowered the bucket in and filled it up. Pulling it out she turned and headed back to her cell, passing by two LuQuarin guards that snickered as she made her way. On her arms were numerous tattoos, each representing a child she had given birth to. Her left arm had eight and her right arm had four, signifying eight girls and four boys. She shuffled by other humans coming and going, the blind stare emanating from their eyes. She reached her cell and set the bucket down and then took a seat on her basic bunk. Across the cell on the other side another woman was lying down and sleeping. Lying down on the flat canvas, she stared at the rock ceiling wondering when the nightmare would end. Closing her eyes, she relived the experience that had brought her here.

The last thing she remembered before the hell started, was walking down a hallway in the Pentagon's underground bunker after Earth had gone through massive destruction. Being one of the General's aids she had been evacuated to the large underground facility. As a Lieutenant, she had been serving in the Pentagon for two years following a distinguished young career in the armed services. She had been a logistics genius and spoke three languages and had come highly recommended to the general. A young and pretty woman of just 26 she was learning to survive the aftermath. She remembered walking into the ladies' room with a co-worker, her last memory of being on Earth.

The next thing she remembered was waking up in some strange cave.

She had been bound and gagged and her clothes ripped off down to just her panties. Next to her was the woman from the restroom. She saw numerous other women and a few men, bound as well. Looking up she saw a most hideous creature speaking in an unknown language and barking

23

orders at other hideous creatures. One by one the creatures placed them on a stretcher and walked them up to a brightly lit portal perhaps a 12' circle. The stretchers were set on a type of conveyor and slid through the gateway. Poof they were gone. She watched as the process continued until it came to be her turn. At first, she tried to struggle sensing danger but was bound tightly. As she slid through the gateway a flash of colored lights surrounded her. She could sense she was travelling fast, the lights changing with twists and turns along the pathway. This went on for almost an hour before the sensation of speed slowed down and she slid through another gateway.

As her stretcher exited she was met by two more of the hideous creatures. Her feet were unbound and she was forced to stand. The creature grabbed her panties and ripped them off leaving a mark on her thigh from his long nails. She winced but was forced to walk down a corridor behind other women. The floor was a mixture of sand and dirt, lit along each side with strange lights that hung near the ceiling. Soon it opened up into a larger room where many humans were gathered. At the head of the room up on a rock was a female human, surrounded by creature guards, some carrying weapons. As she entered the bigger room another creature cut her hand ties. Looking up she spit in his face and was immediately backhanded on the face almost knocking her down and leaving a welt on her cheek. The creature just snickered and pushed her farther into the room. Looking around she recognized several people, all from the underground compound on earth. She had no idea where she was and saw looks of horror and shock on almost everyone she met eyes with. There were more guards around the room watching closely. A man spoke up.

"Is anyone in here above the rank of Captain?" No sooner had his words been spoke when a guard lashed at him with a prod sending an intense electrical shock into him. He fell hard to the ground. The guard stepped back as others helped him get back to his feet. One guard used his finger and motioned with it by his mouth indicating that silence was the order. The man nodded as did others and the room went silent. More humans were shuffled into the room. Finally, the woman on the rock spoke.

A Divided Universe

"I am a human as you are but my body and mind are controlled by your captors. You are all prisoners now of the LuQuarin. I strongly suggest you obey every order given or you will suffer greatly. You are no longer on Earth. You have been transported here by their advanced technology and there is no escape. Simply obey and you will be treated well. You will go through the journey process a few more times until we have reached the destiny chosen for you. There, you will be imprisoned and given orders upon your arrival. Do not resist, I beg of you, or you will suffer great pain and hardship. Make this no more difficult than it already is, and you will live for many years to come. You will never return to Earth. Earth is in total ruins now anyway, there is no longer any life on the surface, just a few remaining survivors in underground shelters. Earth has entered an Ice Age which will last for thousands of years and those few remaining will perish in due time. In a way you are fortunate and will have a new life, and although imprisoned, is better than the fate you would have faced on Earth. There will be no questions. You will now follow the guards to the next platform to be transported. If you must use a bathroom there are troughs set up in the next room. Understand all your rights to privacy no longer exist. Make the best of what you have. The woman stepped down from the rock and two guards ushered the people through an opening at the front of the room. Like cattle they all moved forward into another corridor. Soon they reached a platform and another 12' lighted circle was visible. One by one they were forced to walk through it.

The last journey through a gateway opened up into a large brightly lit dome. They were split apart into two lines, males from females, of which there were many more of. They came to a white tunnel with a moving walkway. Again, one by one they were ushered through. As she put her feet onto the conveyor it moved her forward. At a point, she was hit with jets of spraying water, dousing her entire body, washing away the dirt and dust. Then another set of jets, but this was more than water and had a strange scent to it. Last was what one might describe as a wind tunnel blowing the moisture from her body. She had to close her eyes until the conveyor took her past the wind and out of the unit. She was ushered into another line.

A Divided Universe

At the head of the line was a table and the female that had spoken to them back in the first cave. Next to her was what appeared to be a female version of the creatures, LuQuarin I believe is what they were called. She watched as the first female came to the table and was forced to lay down on it. The female creature waved a wand over her body, a scanner she guessed. After two passes the female creature used a marker and put a symbol on her forehead. The process continued with the next. Across the room the males were going through a similar process. When it was her turn, Karen laid down as instructed and felt the scan go through her body. Complete, she stood up and had a mark put on her forehead. She then followed where the others had been led out. She walked down a smooth sidewalk, and looking up could see sunshine outside of the clear dome. After ten minutes of walking she was ushered through a steel gateway, inside were numerous cells like those of prisons on Earth. As she passed some cells she could see there were two women per cell, and some were being forced to do sexual acts with some of the guards. She was forced to continue to walk forward until she was stopped and directed into her cell. She was dreading the possibility of what she had witnessed going on in other cells. Her guard just gave her a sly grin and pushed her in. He did not follow and she took a seat on one of the two cots. She was shaking fearful of what may come next. The horrors of what she had heard about prisons entered her mind.

A few minutes later another woman was ushered into the cell, her roommate no doubt. She had a different mark on her head and a guard followed her in. She turned her head away, she couldn't bear to see what was happening. A few minutes later the guard left and the cell door closed behind locking them in. She rolled over and saw the other woman in a state of shock, watching her lie down and curl into the fetal position crying.

The next day Karen was led from her cell to another room farther down the corridor. When she reached there, she found herself in a room with two other females and six men. The spokeswoman was there.

"The LuQuarin feel it is important that the human species survive and go on. You will be bred as ordered. Karen noticed there were three make shift beds in the room. The spokeswoman continued.

26

"You have a choice, cooperate and do it naturally or you will be forced to do it. The scan you went through did a number of things. First the LuQuarin now know your complete genetic make-up. Second the scan showed you three as ovulating right now and is a good time to impregnate you. For the next three days, you will copulate as ordered, twice each day with two males here, the succeeding days with two more until all six have been with you. If you become pregnant you will be moved to different quarters. Please nod if you understand." They all nodded.

"Good, now ladies each of you get on a bed." Karen and the other two did as they were asked. A male counterpart was selected and put with each.

"You will not have privacy and as you can see there are three female LuQuarins here to make sure that you do as you are told. Remember this is for the survival of your species and you should honor that you have been selected." With that the spokeswoman left and the three LuQuarin females motioned them to get busy.

The first man she was with whispered in her ear he was sorry but had been given no choice. It didn't last long and a few minutes later she was engaged with a second male who said nothing. One woman resisted and was immediately tied up. In the end, she too had been mounted twice. The males were led out of the room and the women escorted back to their cells. The next two days were the same. Karen realized even if she became pregnant that she would not know who the father was and assumed that was by design. Two more days passed and Karen had morning sickness and a female LuQuarin examined her with a scan. Smiling the LuQuarin female led her to a different section of the compound. There she was finally given clothing and better food. Getting pregnant seemed to have some value.

Now twelve children later she was in a different section of the compound, one where any woman that had given birth to at least ten offspring was sent to, evident by the tattoos that they bore on their arms. She could only guess at how many years had gone by and seen none of her

A Divided Universe

children once they had been weened after 8 weeks of nursing. Being versed in languages she had learned enough of the LuQuarin language to understand and speak well enough to have gained respect among her captors. She had endured many horrors along the way and blocked them from her mind. As hard as it was, she was still alive and prayed each day that the hell would end. She had thought about suicide often but the LuQuarin had a close eye on them and made that impossible. Those that tried suffered great punishment. There was simply no way out of the horror they all lived.

Chapter Four
The Triplets

Thyon sat back in his captain's chair aboard the ship he directed with his sisters Kira and Tira. The triplets had departed Elior fifteen years ago and had traveled the universe, visiting many planets in several galaxies. This was their newest ship which was faster and more capabilities than the previous ones. The first year after departing Elior they had visited the Kinorians on Norkar, the creators of the Medallion, which was responsible to a great extent of what they were now. A byproduct of the Elior and human race infused with an extreme power source contained within the Medallion that their father Alex had been wearing during conception with their now deceased mother Kate. The visit with the Kinorians had been interesting. Even they were surprised at what the three had emerged into. They were now known as a new species, the Humedlior, and possessed powers greater than Norkar or the Kinorians ever imagined possible. They were apprehensive and fearful of Thyon, Kira and Tira. When Thyon requested them to provide the information of all of their advanced technologies, the Kinorians quickly abided. They had left soon after in what was their second spacecraft and began their travels.

To the right of Thyon and laying on the floor was a rather strange looking creature. It was a Darkin, resembling a cross between a large dog and an eagle, with smooth short hair, three front legs and 2 hind, with wings tucked into the sides and a twin tail. The head was a blend of a lab with bat like ears and twin rounded beaks, that held sharp sets of teeth beneath. Thyon petted the head of his Darkin, smiling as he had been a good companion now for many years and one he could communicate with telepathically. More than once the Darkin had earned his keep as a protector and scout on planets of unknown terrors.

Kira and Tira were in front of him in the command center of the ship watching their displays as they orbited yet another planet that contained an intelligent humanoid species known as the Brepnids. The planet was rich in resources and abundant life in many forms. The Brepnids had engaged in trade with the LuQuarins, Thornoks, Blisscrells, and the Flemjots with the transportation of material being provided by the

A Divided Universe

Secarios. At first the trade had gone well, but demands from the LuQuarins' and the others had been increased with no additional compensation or return of goods in trade. When the Brepnids refused to comply, they were given an ultimatum. Either furnish the requests and demands made or they would be invaded and face annihilation. It was the prelude to a war. The Brepnids quickly prepared for an attack on their world and awaited the once trade partners now turned enemy. Tenekaris III in his quest to dominate the universe had assembled a large force with troops and equipment from his allies to conquer the planet.

That day had come and the planet was now surrounded by massive military forces of LuQuarin and allies. There were thousands of ships and millions of troops now approaching the planet. Kira spoke to her brother.

"Brother, our screens display an incredible force approaching Brepnid from numerous directions. They are LuQuarin, Thornok, Blisscrell, and Flemjot military ships and behind them are many more Secarios transports. We estimate an invasion and attack force of over 50 million closing in on the planet. With their technology, the Brepnids have little if any chance of surviving."

"Yes, I know my dear sisters. Tenekaris III march to conquer all continues. The planet is so rich in resources to feed his ever-growing military machine that the Brepnids will suffer greatly if they choose to fight, and if they don't they will simply become another slave planet and species like so many others."

"Thyon, I know that we chose a position of non-interference and have watched many a planet and species consumed by the LuQuarin, but to continue to let this happen is most disturbing. Is there nothing we can do brother?"

"We have all studied war, conflicts and the underlying causes that created them. Even nature herself which promotes survival of the fittest. To no end, intelligent life still has much to learn if the universe is ever to have peace. We have debated this to a great extent but to no avail. Even if we interfered with the powers we possess we would do little to change the course of that which is in motion. The only race with the means and technology to face up to the LuQuarin and her allies are the Elior and her allies. But they chose a state of isolationism fifteen years ago, leaving the door wide open for Tenekaris III and others to expand their conquests. In time Tenekaris will go back after the Elior and others with overwhelming numbers and his conquest will then be complete. Unless there in another race or species out there with the capabilities to stop him, there is little hope."

"You paint a bleak picture brother. We must do something. We are blessed in so many ways and have powers that we have yet to find anyone can rival. Is it not time to use our powers for a greater good and seek to find a way to stop this madness from engulfing every living thing?"

Thyon rubbed his chin as both his sisters looked up at him. The screens on their monitors lit up. The first wave of the attack on the planet had started. Safe in their ship miniaturized and cloaked so they appeared to be just a small particle or a rift in space they had nothing to fear and could watch, track and monitor both sides of the conflict now underway. The Brepnids had erected shields over many of their cities and compounds. The first wave of the attack with thousands of ships was blasting the shields down all over the planet. The Brepnids were returning fire. Thousands of missiles and lasers were being shot at the intruders, some finding their marks. A second wave entered the atmosphere and the onslaught of weapons unleashed from the invaders was devastating, blowing up the defenders' armaments, buildings, killing thousands with each passing minute. The Brepnids defenses were being wiped out. The larger LuQuarin battleships now entered the atmosphere and unleashed a mighty barrage on all the major cities supported by smaller flying aircraft. The cities were soon on fire and crumbling from the attack. The Brepnids had little return fire and were being exterminated. Large transport ships now entered filled with millions of troops and would descend to the surface and take out any remaining resistance. Millions of Brepnids had perished and many more would suffer the same fate before the day was out. Thyon could no longer watch and ordered his sisters to get away from the planet. Kira and Tira did as he asked and turned their ship around and jetted away from Brepnid, the scene behind a holocaust of epic proportions. Once far enough away and out of the solar system they uncloaked the ship, restored it to its natural size. Safely away from any detection Kira asked,

"Where to, brother?"

"I think it is time we go back and visit our father. My internal senses tell me he is in this Galaxy here on the map. Set a course and heading to get us there. Once we are closer I will be able to identify which solar system he is in." The twins nodded and set the course. A moment later they were traveling at an incredible speed. They looked at each other, a small smile ensuing. It would be good to see their father after all the years gone by.

Chapter Five
Lorakits Return

Alex and Stilzen had been at the club for two hours when a message disk appeared for them. It was from the Admiral. Croulac had retrieved useful information from Lorakits work. It was a request for them to meet with the Admiral with all due haste. They arrived at the Admiral's command center and were ushered into a conference room. The Admiral and Croulac were at the front of the table with a large monitor behind. They exchanged greetings and then all but Croulac took a seat as he spoke.

"Lorakit's mass amount of information has revealed all of their supply routes and what was contained on many of the transports. It appears as if they have amassed a huge military operation and plan on attacking the Brepnids who refused to comply with the outrageous demands that Tenekaris has made. Based on the dates of this information the attack has most likely already taken place. What little we know of the Brepnids we learned from the reports, if true, they have little chance of survival. Their technology is not advanced enough to endure such an assault and we must presume the planet is now in the hands of the LuQuarin and their allies. The planet was rich with resources and will only fuel their conquests to greater heights. We also now know of numerous other supply routes that are being used through three different galaxies. They also suggest additional attacks and conquests in the near future. The estimated size of the enemy forces is beyond anything we have surmised thus far. They now have a billion active soldiers with tens of thousands of ships and military equipment, many of which have advanced from previous known reports. We are sifting through the rest of the information Lorakit brought us, but thus far it paints a pretty grave picture for anyone or anything standing in the LuQuarins' path. I will now pass it to the Admiral." Croulac took a seat as the Admiral stood up.

"Alex, Stilzen. This is worse than anything we expected at this point. The size, volume and might of the enemy puts an extreme risk to any peaceful species in any galaxy. Those that lack technology are most vulnerable and will face a genocide if they do not comply, or if they do, will be subject to a form of slavery for the rest of their existence. We are now breaking down their specific military capabilities and weaponry in order to understand what tools we have to combat them with. They have advanced a great deal in the last 15 years and with the addition of their allies and even more troops and equipment pose an imminent threat to the entire universe. I am having a copy of all this information made, adding summary reports, and will send it back to Elior and the council shortly. I am afraid even with all our advancements, the sheer numbers they have would be an overwhelming prospect to Elior if they elect to attack us and our friends. We may not have much time, gentlemen. Elior must prepare for the worst should it come, and do so quickly, as well as all of our allies and friends. If we cannot meet this threat and put up a viable defense then the fate of the universe may fall into the LuQuarins' hands". The Admiral continued.

"Thus far in sifting through all the data we have yet to discover any information on their star gates or portals and whether or not they are using them in their master design of conquest. Brepnid also had the resources to feed their entire military for many years and if managed properly could provide an indefinite supply. We are in the early stages of discovery of two additional planned future operations, one in the same galaxy and a second in the galaxy adjacent to it. Stilzen, have you sent out the coded messages to all of our remaining agents in the field?"

"Yes, Admiral, but it may take weeks before we get anything back. I also instructed them that if they feel they are in jeopardy to get out and return to their designated retrieval points."

"OK, good Stilzen. Hopefully they will be able to add to what we have just learned. I expect we will have enough information to send it back to Elior within two days or less. I must remain here but will need someone that has the ability to persuade the Council of the seriousness of the situation so that they begin to take action. The days of isolationism are coming to an end, and quickly. Alex, I feel you are our best choice to go back to Elior for this task. Will you do it?"

"Yes, Admiral. I will need as many of the summary reports as possible so I can adequately prepare to present to the Council."

A Divided Universe

"You will have that and all the supporting details as well. You will be able to read through it while traveling. I would like to meet again in six hours to update you. Lorakit and a few others will be joining us. We will meet in the larger conference room. That will be all for now, you are dismissed, but please be prompt at the appointed time." With that the Admiral left the room followed by Croulac. Alex and Stilzen followed them out and headed to an off-base establishment that served food and drinks. After porting they grabbed a table, ordered up from a fine young Elior female and stared out the domed establishment of the planet they were on. The sky was a mixture of sunlit colors cascading down and across a set of mountains in the distance. Background music played light jazz. It was a fairly large place with a long bar and numerous tables of which perhaps one third were filled with other patrons. Alex and Stilzen continued their conversation about their enemy and what other possible measures could be taken. They were on their second drink when an unusual orb appeared near their table. It was a grayish black orb with speckles of gold. A moment later three vapes formed below it and formed into one male and two female beings. With the formation complete Alex stood up not believing his eyes. There a few feet in front of him were Thyon, Kira and Tira. Thyon smiled and spoke.

"Hello, father."

"Thyon, Kira, Tira. Damn you're all grown up and so tall."

Kira smiled and came over and hugged her father, then Tira. Once the embraces were finished Thyon came and shook his hand with a half hug. Thyon was well over nine feet so it was a rather awkward embrace. The girls likewise were over eight feet tall and beautiful, dressed in one-piece uniforms that hugged their bodies. Kira was in a light blue uniform and had long golden hair. Tira was in green, her hair slightly darker, but there was no mistaking they were identical twins. Thyon had the build of a gladiator warrior and was dressed in a silver uniform lined in black. Alex introduced them to Stilzen and all five sat at the table. Thyon started the conversation.

A Divided Universe

"It is good to see you father, after all these years. My sisters and I have been traveling the universe, visiting many galaxies and discovering many new worlds, some with life in various stages of development and others where intelligent life exists, some having progressed quite far. As you know when we left, we chose a life of non-conflict or interference with the ongoing dispute between the Elior and her Allies and the LuQuarin. But over the past couple of years we have witnessed the continued onslaught of Tenekaris III and his LuQuarin forces to where we can no longer maintain a neutral position. We just came from Brepnid and were there when the LuQuarin and her allies attacked the planet. We were cloaked in space and witnessed first-hand the invasion, destruction and slaughter of the Brepnid people. It was a horrifying sight."

"This is not the only instance we have witnessed over the past few years. The evil, greed and power has reached an extreme and no planet or species is safe anymore. That is why we are here now, to assist you, the Elior and others to put an end to their conquests. On our way in we noticed your Admiral has established a large military base here and the rest of his fleet will soon be here. Although you may have as many as a million soldiers and equipment, the LuQuarin and allies have two hundred times that just in two galaxies we know of. We suspect their armed forces now reach over a billion and their technology has advanced a great deal in weaponry and tactics."

"Yes, we know my son. We are trying to develop a plan as we speak. We just had one of our best undercover agents return after fourteen years with the Secarios, and she brought us an entire database of information which is in the process of decryption and decipher. What we have learned so far suggests exactly what you are saying, that no planet or species is safe. We fear they will attack Elior as we have been the only force that has been able to defeat them in the past. But if the numbers you suggest match what we are discovering, even with our technology, the sheer numbers they may attack with would be overwhelming. If the Elior and our friends were to fall, there would be nothing to stop Tenekaris from ruling the entire known universe."

"You say you acquired the entire Secarios database?"

A Divided Universe

"Yes, our agent Lorakit had made her way high up into the Secarios system and risked her life to bring it to us. But it is a painstaking process to extract the information that has advanced encryption."

"Maybe we can help father. Kira, Tira and I have exceptional talents in that area as well as many others. Perhaps we can speed up the process?"

"Yes. Let me send an urgent message to the Admiral about your arrival, discovery, and your ability to assist." Alex pulled out a small disk and quickly dictated information into it and then sent it in a flash to the Admiral. "He will have it in hand in a moment and we will await his answer. Take a few minutes to get something to eat and drink." They all nodded and ordered. A maroon orb appeared nearby and out vaped Lorakit. Once formed she smiled and walked to the table where Alex and the others were sitting. Alex and Stilzen stood up as Alex spoke.

"Hi, Lorakit. Please join us." Thyon looked up and his eyes glowed as Lorakit approached. She was the most beautiful female he had ever seen. Tall, dressed in a tight-fitting silver body suit, her long maroon hair tied back that had a few streaks of blonde within. Thyon stood up as she reached the table. Alex continued.

"Lorakit, this is my son Thyon and my daughters Kira and Tira." The girls smiled and giggled a little as they saw the look on their brother's face. He was apparently very smitten with Lorakit's beauty. They exchanged greetings as Thyon added a chair next to his. Lorakit was impressed with Thyon's size and physique as she sat next to him. An attendant was there and took Lorakit's order. They engaged in idle chat for a few minutes as the group simply enjoyed the food and beverages as they arrived. Stilzen then led the conversation.

"Lorakit, Thyon, Kira and Tira have just come from Brepnid, where the LuQuarin and others annihilated the planet and inhabitants. They have come to assist us with the data you brought. We expect to hear from the Admiral at any moment." Lorakit looked at Thyon.

A Divided Universe

"How bad was the attack on Brepnid?"

"It was bad enough that my sisters and I decided to use our talents to try and put a stop to their seemingly endless conquests to control the universe. The threat to all has never been greater." Lorakit had heard the stories about the three children of Alex and Kate and that in reality had been classified as a new species, the Humedlior and that they had extreme abilities and powers. Thyon continued.

"I understand you brought back the entire Secarios database?"

"Yes, but it seems it is very well encrypted."

"My sisters and I should be able to help alleviate that issue." As he finished his sentence a message disk appeared next to Alex. He opened and read it.

"OK, we all have been summoned to be at the Admiral's command center in fifteen minutes. So, let's finish our meal and then head over there." They all nodded in agreement and returned to eating quietly. The time passed quickly and they finished eating, retrieved their orbs, all porting to the Admirals designated area.

Upon arrival and vaping out of their orbs they stood in front of the command and ops center. The Admiral and Croulac were at the entrance with two armed guards to greet them. After a brief introduction with Thyon, Kira and Tira, they were led in, following the Admiral to a special operations room. There, inside the room were a couple hundred Eliors attending to monitors and equipment. The Admiral went to the center where a table and three additional monitors had been set up. Croulac explained briefly where they were at in deciphering the vast amount of data that Lorakit had brought and the difficulties they were having in getting past the encryption codes to access the data. Thyon, Kira and Tira each took a seat in front of the monitors and began the work. It was fascinating to watch how fast they worked and Alex could tell they were communicating telepathically. Thyon paused, turned to the Admiral and spoke.

38

A Divided Universe

"Admiral, we should have access to all the data in a few minutes. We are very close to finding the master key and primer." True to his word as he and his sisters worked at an incredible speed the screens changed appearance, the data now accessible. Croulac exclaimed,

"Damn that was fast. I've never seen anything like that. I do hope you will share what you did with my people."

"No problem, Croulac. Now let's see what they are hiding from us." He looked at his sisters again communicating telepathically and the resumed the work. A minute later Kira spoke.

"Admiral, we have now partitioned the data into more manageable groups which you can divide among all your technicians. Croulac, take a look please." Croulac bent down looking over Kira's shoulder at the large monitor. "I created a database management list here for you and divided the information. Tira is writing advanced query and algorithms' now for you for each partition, so you can do accurate searches for whatever it is you wish to learn. Kira felt the warmth of Croulacs' presence right behind her and experienced a new feeling within. She turned and smiled as his eyes turned from the screen to hers. For a moment they just looked into each other's eyes, a glow emerging in both, and Croulac caught a light scent of her pheromones.

"This is amazing, Kira. Can we spool each of the groups to one of our other stations here so I can assign the appropriate staff members to start the digging?"

"Sure. Just tell me how you want it divided." Croulac pointed to one then the next set of data groups and advised Kira where to send it. He went through 30 groupings, then stood up and made an announcement to the room, so everyone could hear.

"OK, my fine technicians. Each of you will be receiving a set of data, which I want broken down and detailed as quickly as you can. The entire database is now accessible. I want you to report to me with anything you find and deem is valuable to understanding what the Secarios were doing.

Understand?" The room was filled with nods of acknowledgement and the technicians all began the work.

Thyon turned, stood up and looked at the Admiral and Croulac.

"OK Tira has written the code for the advanced query. Tell me Admiral, what would you like to know about first?"

"Well Thyon, how about a listing of their shipments, origin, contents and destination with time frames. That would provide a most useful picture of what the Secarios are doing for the LuQuarin. Also, any reference to the LuQuarin or Tenekaris please."

"Consider it done, Admiral. Croulac, take my seat and I will show you."

Croulac sat down and was right next to Kira. Thyon had noticed how they had looked at each other and smiled. After showing Croulac a few things, he nodded and understood how to mine the data in the most efficient matter. Tira had created an AI program that would speed up the process. Thyon turned to the Admiral.

"Admiral, my sisters and I had a fast but hard journey to get here quickly. If possible, we would like to return to our ship to rest for a while."

"Yes, Thyon of course. Your help here today is invaluable and it will take us at least a number of hours to put together a complete picture. Feel free to leave and just send me a message when you are ready to rejoin us." Thyon looked at his father, Stilzen and Lorakit. He shook his father's hand, then Stilzen. As he looked at Lorakit he saw a slight face of disappointment. But he had read her mind earlier, and now, so he elected to give her a telepathic message.

"Lorakit, you are the most beautiful female I have ever seen. I would consider it an honor if you would join me on my ship a little later and we can dine privately." Lorakit smiled and returned his thoughts.

"Yes, that would be nice. How about in an hour or so?"

"Perfect, here are the coordinates you will need. Until later then." He shook her hand, then turned to his sisters.

"Ready, my dear sisters?" They were both standing, said their good-byes, then all vaped and ported away. After they left, the Admiral asked Alex to join him in his office, leaving Stilzen and Lorakit with Croulac. Once in the Admiral's office he took a seat at his desk and motioned for Alex to sit down.

"Alex, I have the SSSTS standing by once we have the information we need for you to go back to Elior. I can't impress upon you enough how important it is for you to persuade the Elders to activate all our forces and resources to meet this threat. The numbers we have seen so far of the LuQuarin and their allies are overwhelming and will require our entire population and our allies to have a viable chance of survival. Your son Thyon and daughters were most helpful today. Have you had a chance to talk with them and learn what their capabilities are other than what we witnessed?"

"Not really Admiral, but I suspect they have great powers and knowledge of the universe we do not possess. I am just happy they returned and are willing to help us meet this threat."

"I agree Alex, but if you have a chance before you leave, it would be nice to know what other types of assistance they may be able to offer."

"Will do, Admiral."

"For now, we just have to wait until Croulac's team has what we need. Why don't you take some personal time for a few hours? I will summon you when we know more and are ready to take action."

"OK, Admiral." Alex stood up made a short bow to the Admiral and departed the room. Stilzen and Lorakit had left and Croulac was busy running around various stations as new information came to bear. Alex walked out of the command center, stood and looked out into the early evening sky. There were a few clouds partially blocking the remaining days sun, providing a most colorful view. He ported to the club to have a drink or two before heading back to his quarters.

Chapter Six
The LuQuarins Alliance

Tenekaris III was pacing back and forth at the front of the great hall of his newly finished compound. He had called for a meeting with the leaders of all his new allies and a celebration for the conquests made. The Emperor of Blisscrells arrived with his consort and would be the first one he would meet with. The others would soon arrive. Eftar entered the room and approached his master.

"Master, Emperor Kirkra will be here shortly. Is there anything you require for the meeting sir?"

"No Eftar, show him in as soon as he arrives. I will be here on my throne with my personal guards nearby. But have a few additional guards escort them in here and have them remain at the sides of the hall. We don't know all of his consort, so a little precaution is in order."

"Very well Master." Eftar left the room. Tenekaris sat on his throne made of gold and rubbed his chin thinking about his new ally. The Blisscrells were a dominant species in the quadrant of the galaxy they came from when the two species had first met. The LuQuarin had a team on a mining expedition of a planet they had discovered rich in resources with little life of a prehistoric nature. The Blisscrells were already there and mining when the LuQuarin had arrived. At first it appeared as if it would break into a conflict but the leader of the LuQuarin team had been smart enough to negotiate a peaceful coexistence whereby both species could extract materials from the planet and not be in competition. Tenekaris had sent additional personnel to the planet and incorporated infecting the Blisscrells with his agents taking over their minds and bodies as he had done on Earth and other planets. Within a short time, this manipulative approach had proven to be invaluable as more and more of the Blisscrells were infected with LuQuarin hosts. In the years since, the LuQuarin had assumed control of enough of the Blisscrells that an alliance was formed in resources and military without the Blisscrells' knowledge.

A Divided Universe

The Blisscrells were stout in appearance averaging seven feet in height, had heads slightly larger than most humanoid type species, with pointed ears. Their complexion was a variety of purples with eye colors that varied. The leaders dressed impeccably with colorful suits and jewelry. Likewise, their military leaders wore their medals with pride on their fitted tan and blue uniforms. Their females were attractive, at least the ones Tenekaris had observed, with nice figures and only a little shorter than their male counterparts. The males usually had dark hair, but short and neat. The females' hair length varied, as well as the colors. They were usually dressed in long tight-fitting gowns, draped with a cape.

The doors to the great hall opened and Eftar led in the Blisscrell procession followed by more LuQuarin guards who took station on both sides. Twenty Blisscrells were led in by Emperor Kirkra. Tenekaris stood up and walked to great him. Smiling they shook hands.

"Welcome, Kirkra, it is good to see you."

"Thank you, Tenekaris. Congratulations are in order for the conquest of Brepnid."

"Indeed they are, Kirkra. My reports show your military performed very well with few casualties."

"As did yours and the others Tenekaris. It was a swift and decisive victory and mining and harvesting operations are well under way."

"Excellent. Eftar is going to take your procession to the wonderful accommodations we have set up for you and let you all get settled while we wait for the other delegations, if that's ok?"

"Yes, that would be fine." Tenekaris spoke to Eftar and the group as they turned and filed out. He then turned to Kirkra.

"If I may have a short private conversation with you, Emperor?'

A Divided Universe

"Yes, of course." The delegation had left and Tenekaris had dismissed all of his guards. Only the two remained in the large room. Tenekaris moved back to his throne and gestured for Kirkra to sit in one of the three other fine seats that were there for his Queens. Now seated Tenekaris spoke.

"Kirkra. How are your people and home planet doing?"

"Master Overlord Tenekaris III. Since our alliance began and through your generosity my people and home world have never been better. Our entire society now flourishes and has grown and developed faster than I could have imagined. Granted there have been a few that spoke out about how this has been achieved, but they have been silenced. The masses don't seem to care and we keep them ignorant as to how we have gained the prosperity they now enjoy. Our military has continued to grow and become stronger with the incentives provided and more volunteer each day. With the training and equipment now available our military leaders assure me that we can control vast areas within our galaxy and beyond should we so desire. Of course, we will always work in tandem with you and the LuQuarin on any quest. Your forces and technological aid have given birth to the finest alliance and military forces ever achieved in the universe. Along with our other allies I see no reason that we can't eventually gain control of all the galaxies with the rewards and riches that exist."

"True Kirkra. But one obstacle still remains."

"Ah, yes the Elior."

"Yes, the Elior. As long as they remain with their allies they will pose a threat to our expansion and control. We near the time when we will have to change that. They have technologies that we do not, and a fine military but small in comparison to ours. When the others get here and after some celebration we will all meet and finalize a plan that will change the course of history. Then the universe will be ours. For now, my friend, let us just celebrate our latest victory of Brepnid. The others should be here soon and we will gather later this evening and enjoy a feast and celebration. So, for now join your delegation and enjoy the hospitalities I have set up for you. Eftar will see to any and all of your needs or requests." Kirkra stood up as did Tenekaris. They shook hands and then Kirkra turned and departed. As soon as he was gone he summoned two of the guards. Together they walked out of the great hall and headed to another chamber deep underneath the compound.

Tenekaris and the two guards traveled down several levels below the compound. Finally reaching the lowest level and walking through a tunnel they reached a door where two more guards stood at attention. Seeing Tenekaris they opened the door to let him in, his two guards following. The door closed behind in a dimly lit room Tenekaris walked over to a desk where one of his scientists was sitting at a terminal. Beyond him on a wall were four naked prisoners chained to the wall. One was a male Blisscrell. The next a female Flemjot, a male Thornok and then a female Secarios. He asked the scientist,

"Well, have you been able to obtain any information yet from our prisoners?"

"No, my lord. They have been resistant to every form we have tried to extract information to tell us whether or not they are truly spies. It is strange my lord, as in testing them, it appears as if they are genetically perfect. That simply does not occur with any of these species."

"Have you employed any forms of torture yet?"

"Only through chemicals which have nasty side effects, but to no avail. Their stories have all been validated and we have no real strong evidence they are spies, only supposition and suspicion."

"I am telling you they are spies, and the Elior are behind it with their master cloning and genetic abilities. My men followed each of them for weeks and months collecting data which implied they were either communicating or aiding our greatest enemy. Perhaps a little demonstration of torture would loosen their tongues?"

A Divided Universe

"What do you suggest my lord?"

"First of all, did you complete the task of gathering the information to create a guilty plea from all of them?"

"Yes, my Lord. When they were first captured and interviewed we collected all their voice data and gestures from which we could compile a complete video of them confessing to be Elior spies. It is in the final editing process now and we should have it for you within a day. No one will be able to tell that we created the entire thing."

"Excellent, I will be needing that for the upcoming meeting with our allies. If you're confident that those guilty pleas will pass without exception, then I want you to proceed with a bit of torture. Start slow and then move on until you get a true confession and video it all for me. Now I will speak to them before I leave." Tenekaris III walked over in front of the four prisoners chained naked to the wall above the ground. Their heads were lowered in a state of exhaustion. Being ten feet tall Tenekaris stood in front of them. He grabbed the first one by the chin and raised his head. The prisoner's eyes opened as he spoke.

"I know you are an Elior and you will confess to me or suffer greatly." He raised his voice so all four prisoners could hear.

"Listen up, Elior scum." They all raised their heads up.

"The days of the Elior will soon come to an end. Choose as you will to continue to bite your tongue, but I know who you are. You will regret the task you have undertaken to spy on the LuQuarin and our allies. You will have one last chance to speak and I will spare your lives. If not, you can kiss good-bye your life as an Elior and the chance ever to return to your people." He looked each one in the eyes which stared back at him in a lifeless answer. The Secarios female spit at him but missed. Tenekaris walked over in front of her and put his hand over her mouth.

A Divided Universe

"A defiant one, are you? Too bad, and such a beautiful creature." He grabbed her by the throat tightly causing her breathing to be interrupted as she gasped.

"It is up to you pretty one. Speak now, confess and tell us what you know and I will spare all of your lives." She continued to gasp as he clenched her throat, releasing when she turned color in the face. He stepped back as she caught her breath, looked at him with a sense of hate yet said nothing.

"So be it you Elior fools, enjoy the pain that awaits you." Tenekaris turned, motioned to the technician and walked out.

Tenekaris III spent the rest of the day greeting the four other delegations as they arrived, meeting with the leader of each for a brief few moments. They had all been escorted to lavish chambers to rest prior to the beginning of the celebration. As he walked to his personal chambers to get ready for the festivities a sheepish grin crossed his face. He thought. "Soon, very soon now, I will eliminate the Elior and the conquest of the universe will then be mine for the taking."

Chapter Seven
A New Pairing

Thyon was looking out the window from his private quarters on the ship. He had changed into comfortable clothing and awaited Lorakits arrival with a sense of excitement within he had never experienced. The attraction to her was overwhelming. Understanding what it was, he pondered how the evening would progress. He had set up a quaint dining table and two chairs with candles. On board the ship, there contained lavish foods they had gathered from many planets and he prepared several them to share with her. He added soft background music and simply waited for her arrival. Anxious was a new feeling and the minutes seemed longer in anticipation of what may follow. He laughed to himself, wary of what he was experiencing.

Her orb appeared inside the entrance to his quarters and a moment later Lorakit vaped out and stood before him. Turning he watched the final formation as she came to life across the room. He stared across looking her in the eyes with a glow within. She had changed her clothes and was wearing tight fitting white slacks with short black boots. Her semi-sheer black top was a V-neck crop style three-quarter sleeve, which displayed her firm breasts pressed in tight and an open area displaying her naval. She wore a platinum chain around the neck. Her maroon hair with streaks of blond had been combed out with half in front that partially hid her cleavage, and the rest streaming half way down her back.

Smiling she spoke. "Good evening, Thyon."

"You look very beautiful, Lorakit. Please come in and have a seat." He gestured over to a couch near the window. "May I get you something to drink?"

"I will have whatever you are having, Thyon." He walked over to a small kitchen like area, went to a silver unit and keyed into it. A moment later two unique glasses appeared. There were four prongs at the base that held a cylindrical tube that rose up and at the top expanded out into a martini shaped glass. Inside was a mixture of blue and yellow with a glow to it. He brought the two glasses over and handed one to Lorakit who had taken a seat on the couch. "I call it Aquasun. It is made of natural ingredients. I hope you like it." He toasted. "To your beauty." and they both drank.

"Mm mm. That is delicious, Thyon. Thank you."

Kira and Tira were on the bridge of their ship. They had noticed on a display that an orb had boarded in Thyon's quarters. They both giggled. Their brother had company and they knew who it was. They were discussing Croulac and Stilzen and how they too were feeling new urges to have a companion. Although only 15 in standard years all three were very mature and not a reflection of the time of existence. It was a new and wonderful experience they were feeling. They continued to talk, exploring how they could bring these feelings into a reality of actions and how/when they might meet up with the males of their desires.

Chapter Eight
Temptation and a Trip

Alex was sitting at the bar in the club sipping on a beer after finishing his meal. Looking out the window across the room the early evening had given away to night. The female tending the bar, Mora, came up and removed his plate. "Is there anything else I can get you, Alex?" He turned back towards her and smiling.

"I wish there was, Mora. Perhaps a cup of coffee and a Sambuca would be nice."

"A good choice, Alex. I will bring it to you in a minute. We're brewing a fresh pot." She walked away with his plate taking it to the kitchen. A minute later she returned with his coffee and a glass of Sambuca with three beans in it. Setting it down she looked at him again.

"Alex, you seem troubled. What is it?" He realized his expression had given a sense of despair that Mora had picked up on.

"Nothing really, just a lot on my mind at the moment."

"Would you care to share? I get off in twenty minutes and could use a drink myself." He looked at her and realized how pretty she was. Since his arrival he hadn't paid attention to anything, his mind adrift with the threat the LuQuarin now posed. She spoke again.

"Alex, we all know you are the bearer of the Medallion and married to a beautiful woman back on Elior. At least have a drink with me when I get off."

"OK, Mora, that would be nice."

"Good, it is settled then. Enjoy your drinks as I have to begin to close out my shift to hand it over to the next attendant. I will join you shortly." AS she departed he watched her walk away, noticing her tall Elior figure from behind. Realizing he had been alone most of the journey a little female company might be a good thing as he awaited the Admiral's message. He sipped the cordial and followed it with the black coffee feeling the warmth of the two drinks flow down his throat. He returned to looking out the window into the clear night sky, now lit with stars and a half moon. Before he knew it, there was Mora standing in front of him, all seven feet of her, smiling, a drink already in hand. He gestured for her to take a seat next to him. She had removed the apron she had been wearing revealing a low-cut blue blouse that flowed down below her waist, a pair of tight-fitting gray pants neatly tucked into her black boots. She had removed the two hair clips that held her teal hair up, which now feathered down one side to her shoulder. She was one of many Elior females that had elected to have hair. Realizing he had been staring at her, Alex spoke.

"Sorry Mora. So, what are you drinking?"

"It's a rather new drink called special tropical paradise, and quite refreshing. It is made of natural ingredients but does have an alcohol kick to it. Care to try one?"

Alex had finished his coffee and drink so he agreed to try one. Mora signaled the new attendant and a minute later there was the new drink in front of Alex. He picked up the tall glass and gestured to Mora. "Cheers." She replied in kind and they both took a long sip from their drinks.

"Damn, that is good."

"Glad you like it."

"So, Mora do you just tend bar or have other duties like most stationed here?"

"Yes Alex, I just do this part-time a few days a week while we are waiting for the rest of the fleet to join us. I normally work with the propulsion and weapons systems for our fighters which I have come to learn that many will be here within a day. Then it will be twelve-hour days or longer to make sure they are all in good order. I was promoted to Lieutenant when I arrived three years ago."

A Divided Universe

"That's impressive, Mora. You seem very young to be in such a position."

"Not really, Alex. After completing my studies in advanced propulsion and weaponry at the academy, I put in to be part of the military and join the Admiral's group. I lost both my parents and younger brother back when the LuQuarin destroyed the city we lived in. Had I not been in school I to would have perished that day."

"How old are you?"

"I am 26 by your standard years and was 11 when the attack occurred. It was very difficult at first but with help I was guided into the academy and took an interest in understanding how our military ships work. I hope one day to be a fighter pilot and have put in the request to attend the training program." She downed her dink and ordered another.

"So, Medallion Alex. I know you really can't talk much about what you do, seeing as you report directly to the Admiral and the Council. But it would be nice if you could just spend some time with me and share what you can." Alex smiled.

"What would you like to know?"

"Most humans I have met are shorter than you and not as well built. Is that normal?" Alex laughed.

"Yes, on Earth I was on the taller side of average, but since my involvement with the Elior at times I feel rather short and it's taken some getting used to having to look up most of the time." Mora giggled.

"True, we are quite a bit taller. Tell me, Alex. There are stories of your heroics that float around about a battle with the LuQuarin to rescue many humans from enslavement. Are those stories true?"

A Divided Universe

"I was involved with that rescue mission, but there were many that day that put their lives on the line, mostly Elior. It was a group effort that made that mission successful."

"It is said you have great powers."

"I am blessed with certain abilities, but to be honest it is not something I share or care to talk about."

"OK, Alex, I understand. It must be difficult for you at times. Elior lost eight cities fifteen years ago. You lost an entire planet."

"Yes, Mora. If not for the Elior intervention, I doubt that any Earthlings would still exist. Only a very small percentage of humans were saved from the LuQuarin holocaust on Earth. So, tell me Mora, have you found yourself a suitable mate?"

"Well, sort of, I guess you could say. There is a handsome pilot I have had my eye on for some time but he has been away now for months, but should be returning with the rest of the fleet. I was hoping to be able to get together with him when they return, but I have my doubts as we will all be very busy. I suspect we will be mobilizing our forces soon. The Admiral's fleet never stays in the same place for very long and is usually dispersed. This will be the first time I have ever known that all of our battle group will be together in one place."

"Yes, the Admiral does keep things moving, that is for sure." Alex noticed Mora had shifted in her seat, downing another drink and then looked back into Alex's eyes.

"Do you think I am attractive Elior female, Alex?"

"You are quite beautiful, Mora." Alex had realized that Mora was trying to seduce him. She was very attractive and the thoughts of being with her had entered his mind. Being away from Diana was hard, and knowing his clone was satisfying her desires only made it worse. Mora was unaware of the advanced cloning privileges he and select others were privy to. He felt her hand on his knee and felt the tension growing. He looked her in the eyes as she spoke.

"Alex, I know you are married and a good man, a hero and legend among the Elior." She took her hand and put it on his chest, then grabbed his hand and brought it to her breast holding it there so he could feel her now erect nipple. The temptation was becoming overwhelming as he caught the scent of her pheromones. She moved her legs bringing her knee gently up into his groin. Her lips were slightly parted with a touch of moisture as she moved her mouth just inches from his, the deep emerald eyes glowing as she stared into his. She guided his hand inside her blouse, their closeness hiding the gesture from other patrons. Her breast was firmly in his hand the hard nipple in his palm. He sensed the attendant close by and withdrew his hand as she approached.

"Would you two care for another drink? We will be closing soon."

Alex turned. "Yes, another round of drinks would be good, thank you." Mora pulled back removing her knee from his groin and seated herself back in a normal position. Alex elected to read her mind. Just then a message disk appeared next to Alex. He recognized it being from the Admiral. He broke off the mind reading. "Excuse me Mora, seems I have a message. She sat back and took a sip of her drink as he opened the message and read.

"It seems Mora that I need to leave. The Admiral wishes to see me immediately. A little advice Mora. Take that kindred seduction you have and use it on that pilot you are chasing. I have no doubt you will be together in short order. Thank you for the evening and I wish you well, but I must depart and hope you understand."

"Yes Alex, I do. Thank you for a wonderful evening and spending some time with me. I wish you all the success as I fear we will soon be at war with our enemy."

"Take care, Mora." With that Alex stood, pulled out his orb, vaped and ported to the Admiral.

A Divided Universe

Back at the command center Alex walked into the large room where all the technicians were still busy working on the data. He saw the Admiral and Croulac at the center and made his way there. The Admiral looked up.

"Sorry to bring you here in the middle of the night Alex, but we now have enough data and evidence that needs to get back to Elior post haste. I have the SSSTS ready for you and within a half hour Croulac will have all the information copied as well as the briefs and summary reports. You can read them on the way in order to prepare for the Council."

"Can you give me a synopsis of it, Admiral?"

"Yes, Alex. Basically, we now have all the details of how the LuQuarin and the others set up and massed the attack on Brepnid, as well as a few other smaller exploits. In addition, we know the routes that are used to transport vast amounts of equipment, supplies and personnel through 3 galaxies. The routes and movements suggest they are in the final stages of planning an attack on Elior, and then on our allies. Croulac, pull up galaxy trans image number six." Croulac hit a few buttons on the display panel and a second later a 3D image appeared above the large table. It outlined the galaxies and the routes the LuQuarin and allies were using, providing scope and direction.

"Alex, look over here at the galaxy two distant from where we are at. There are three primary routes they are using that head in the direction of Elior. Within the manifests we found massive amounts of military equipment and supplies as well as troop transports. They are beginning to stage here, here and here which would form a three-prong attack once in place directly towards Elior. They are setting up huge encampments at each location from which if the Secarios supplied them with the transportation they need, they could be within striking distance of Elior within a couple of months. The estimates of manpower and equipment they are moving or will be shortly is unlike anything ever before. They could have a fighting force of over a billion in place with excellent technology and the odds against us would be overwhelming. We must get the Council and Elior to immediately prepare for this massive assault and pray it is not too little too late. You must convince the Council to take immediate action. I am working with all my Generals to formulate a plan to see if we can at least disrupt their operations and slow them down. But with only a million in our fighting force I am uncertain of how much we can accomplish. So, as soon as Croulac hands you the information get on the SSSTS and get back to Elior. It will take you two days to get there. Formulate your presentation to them well, as Elior's fate may rest in your hands. I trust no one more than I do you, Alex, to accomplish this task."

"I will do my best Admiral."

"Thank you, Alex. I am going to rest for a few hours as I haven't slept much now in days. Last thing, once you have word from the Council as to what they have decided, please dispatch a message to me and send it back in the SSSTS. Take care Alex, and have a swift and safe journey."

"Thank you, Admiral." The Admiral left the room. Alex looked for Croulac who was a of couple stations down and packing up the data disks in a special pouch. He closed it up when the last disk was securely in place and walked over to Alex.

"Alex, here is the information. I have included all the summary disks for you as well as all the supporting data, and a program that will assist you in assembling it in an order that you feel would be the best way to present to the Council. It's a ton of data Alex, so don't let it overwhelm you. Take it in pieces and learn as much as you can. With two days of travel you should be able to put it together in such a manner that presents a strong case for a call to action. Good luck, my friend. I hope to see you again very soon with good news. I too need some rest. My assistant will take you to the SSSTS now." Croulac shook his hand then turned and walked out of the room. A young assistant was standing by and motioned for Alex to follow. Within ten minutes he was in the launch room for the SSSTS and went through the preparation routine, then was miniaturized and boarded. He was greeted by the pilot of the ship and a second officer that would accompany him back to Elior. A final checklist was gone through by the pilot and then the signal given to launch. A minute later they were speeding through space at an incredible speed on their way back to Elior.

A Divided Universe

Thyon was standing and looking out the viewing window from his private quarters. The sun was just rising in the distance on the other side of the planet with his view from space. His ship was in a slow orbit well above the Admiral's compound on the planet below. He was still waking up after experiencing an intimate night with Lorakit. Although he had empirical knowledge of sex and intimacy, it was the first time he had experienced such pleasures. He looked back to the large bed where Lorakit was still sleeping peacefully. He returned his gaze out and to the planet below as thoughts of the challenges that lay ahead entered his mind. Dressed in only a pair of shorts he walked over to the dispensing unit and ordered a warm beverage, a specially blended tea full of nutrients that would assist in the waking up process. Staring back down to Lorakit on the bed, thoughts of rejoining her for another interlude set in. He now understood the appeal that went with the physical intimacy that two could share. He smiled as he watched her sleep and envisioned more of what the nights experiences had provided. As the tea took effect his mind returned to the tasks at hand. There must be a way to slow down the LuQuarin onslaught on Elior, his birthplace and all of its' inhabitants could very well perish. He returned to the viewing window, took a seat in a plush chair and looked out into space where thousands of stars glistened in the distance and the moon of the planet shone brightly.

Lorakit stirred in the bed, slowly opening her eyes and gaining consciousness. She sat up and saw Thyon sitting across the room with a cup in his hand and staring out the viewing window. She got out of bed, still naked from the night and walked over to him. Looking up, smiling, he set the cup down and gestured for her to sit on his lap. She kissed him on the forehead and nestled into his awaiting arms. She joined his gaze out into the stars.

"Good morning, my young lover." Thyon laughed softly hearing her words.

"Young, am I? Seems a cougar seduced the innocent."

"Call me a cougar? I kind of like that. Young may you be in standard years, but you seemed to have the experience, that of a well-versed lover."

A Divided Universe

"It was a magical night, Lorakit. One I will never forget, and hope to have many more in the days ahead."

"That I can promise you will, dear Thyon. We could start again now if you wish."

"True Lora, the thought has crossed my mind and I would like nothing better, but alas my mind is now plagued with the threat we all face, and I must find answers to this dangerous situation, and quickly. I have already sensed my father has departed back to Elior. It will take him two days to get there, and then who knows how long or if the Council will react. We do not have the luxury of waiting. From the data I absorbed, taking immediate action will be necessary. If nothing else we must slow down the enemy and buy the time needed to assemble the forces necessary to meet the evil that threatens all the universe." Lorakit could see his mind was churning and it was not the time to re-engage in the world of physical pleasures.

"How can I help Thyon?"

"I know you are well trained in weaponry, flying crafts and more. This ship that my sisters and I built has many capabilities which may prove useful should they be required. I would like to show you what this ship can do and perhaps employ your talents in taking on our enemy."

"I will help you in any way I can Thyon."

"Excellent. Let us freshen up and get ready for the day. A plan is forming within, and we will need to see the Admiral. When my sisters awake I will discuss the idea with them, and if they are in agreement, we all will see the Admiral. Now get that pretty ass of yours up my cougar."

She laughed, kissed him on the forehead again, got up and headed to the shower. She felt a little slap on her ass as she walked away. Smiling, she turned. "Be careful my lover, or I will drag you back into bed." Thyon laughed as she continued to walk away. He then heard.

A Divided Universe

"What's the attire for today?"

"Military." Thyon then drafted a message and sent it to the command center for the Admiral.

An hour later Thyon, Kira, Tira, and Lorakit were all sitting at a quaint dining table in the hull of their ship eating a hearty breakfast. Thyon had explained the plan to them which he would present to the Admiral when he was available. They had just finished eating when a reply was received. Thyon read it out loud for all to hear. They would be taking their ship down to the planet and land near the command center within the next hour. The three siblings headed for the bridge while Lorakit cleaned up. A few minutes later she joined them on the bridge as the ships systems were coming to life. She took a seat at the back and watched the three put the ship in motion and maneuver it as it made its' descent down into the atmosphere. With the viewing window open Lorakit looked out as the planets' surface came to form, the stars disappearing behind them and the light of the day shining down. Kira made a few adjustments to the descent and angle. A minute later the command center was in full view with a landing area next to it.

There were several smaller craft, fighters lined along the main building with Elior technicians scattered about watching as the ship did the final approach. Kira did a last maneuver and the ship came to rest on the surface. They shut the systems down as Thyon led the way out through the back, the exit door opening with a down ramp in motion flowing out from the hull for easy passage. Lorakit was the last to come down the ramp and followed the others. She looked back at the ship and couldn't believe how big it was, the design unique to anything she had ever seen. Its' silver metallic body glistened in the early daylight and was as large as an Elior battle cruiser. She returned her gaze back to the three others who were farther ahead and ran to catch up to them. The entrance to the command center had two guards and a Captain there to greet them and lead them in. Once inside the compound they were led to the Admiral's private conference room. The Admiral was waiting with Croulac and Stilzen. They exchanged greetings and then the Admiral spoke.

A Divided Universe

"Thyon, thank you for coming. So, you have a plan you wish to share with us to thwart our enemies progress?"

"Yes Admiral. Do you have the displays ready that I requested?"

"Yes. Croulac could you bring up the maps Thyon asked us for?"

Croulac went to the display board and keyed in some information. A large 3D large map came to life in the center of the room showing two adjoining galaxies. He zoomed into one area on the more distant of the two. Thyon then asked,

"Croulac, show the three origin points where they are assembling all their ships and equipment." Croulac complied as Thyon walked closer to one of the locations being displayed.

"Here is the first major area on this planet where they have been bringing in supplies, weapons and troops from numerous resources. Based on the manifests and their outlined time frames, this process is near or at completion as are the other two in the other part of the galaxy. From there we know the routes they will take with thousands of ships to the next galaxy which is only one away from the one Elior lies within. Each will have a large contingent of military escorts when they enter hyperspace for the trip." Croulac added a few more commands to the display and all three routes were outlined from beginning to end. Thyon continued.

"They will have to come out of hyperspace here, here and here. They will only be a few solar systems away for the designated final staging areas. Once there, when they have amassed all their forces, they will head towards Elior. We know from the estimates that the numbers are staggering and would outnumber the Elior by over 500 to 1." Thyon had brought a backpack and went into it and pulled out a circular object. He handed it to the Admiral.

"Admiral, this is a new disruptor disk. It can be fired from our ship and attach itself to their transport ships. It will only be activated at a time of our choosing. I have the plans with me as to how you can make them. We will need thousands of these and quickly. When their ships come out of hyperspace we can be there waiting and as each becomes visible we can launch them from our cloaked position. They are small enough that they will not be detected and basically act like a mudball when they hit their target. We can attach one of these to every transport ship as they pass before they put up their shields, which is highly unlikely they would do so anyway."

"The escort ships, however, pose a different problem. Their protocol is to immediately activate their shields as they come out of hyperspace to insure they are protected as they protect the massive amounts of cargo. Once all of the transport ships have the disruptors attached, I will pull a main switch and activate them all at once. The disruptors will interrupt their propulsion system and they would come to a halt and just be floating in space. It will also deactivate their defense systems. Only basic life support will still be intact. Since this is an unknown technology to them it will take quite a while for them to figure it out. They could be stuck in space for weeks or have to be towed to their destination and will be completely vulnerable."

"The only problem I see is we don't know how the military escort ships will react. I expect them to take up a defensive posture around the transports and seek out that which caused this huge phenomenon to occur. With that many enemy fighting ships, even I would not wish to engage them at that time, although I feel many could be destroyed by the weapon systems my sisters and I have developed. Remaining cloaked we can slip away quietly. Since our ship can be divided into three fighting ships and armed with the disruptors we would be able to attack all three main routes." Thyon paused as the Admiral and the others had been listening intensely to Thyon's words. The Admiral was turning the disruptor ball over in his hand as he spoke.

"So, this little ball will incapacitate and entire transport ship?"

"Yes, Admiral, and it could do the same to a fighter if its' shields were down. I will be happy to demonstrate it for you. My sisters and I have already successfully used it on a few rogue pirate ships that are outside the realm of our enemy or the Secarios. Here are the plans and what you need to make them as well as where to retrieve the materials if you do not have them available."

"Captain," the Admiral continued, "Take this sample and the plans and get it to our Engineering group, priority one. Have them pull all manpower and resources to get these made as quickly as possible. Report back to me when you have an estimate on time."

"Yes, sir." The Captain took the sample and disk with the information and hustled out of the room. The Admiral then spoke to Thyon.

"We have a few older cargo ships we recently replaced that are still functional that you could provide a demonstration for us all. I could arrange it for this afternoon."

"That would be fine, Admiral. One other thing. Since I will be dividing our ship into three separate ships so we can attack all three routes I will need to have a second with each one. I would like to take Lorakit with me. I am asking you if Croulac can go with Kira and Stilzen with Tira as they have the skills and experience we will need for the mission."

The Admiral rubbed his chin. He too had noticed the attractions going on and disliked the idea of letting either one of two of his most valuable men go. "Let me think on that, Thyon, for a bit if I may. How long would you be gone?"

Admiral, our ship is as fast as your SSSTS if not faster. Looking at the maps here we could be in position in 2-3 days if not less. From there it depends on when our enemy arrives. The operation will go quickly and then the return trip barring any unforeseen circumstances. Based on what we know, intercepting them on their schedule will depend on whether you can have the disruptors ready for us. As it stands now, you have only two or three days to have them made."

"Very well, Thyon. We will find a way to get you all the disruptors you need, and you can have Stilzen and Croulac to assist your sisters. If your plan works that could buy us the time we need to mobilize our other Elior forces, if the Council willing, and perhaps have a chance of survival."

"Yes, Admiral. I would also like you to consider forming three attack groups to send and hide near where our enemy will come out of hyperspace. With their Transport ships disabled and without a complete fighting force, you may be able to take out many of fighting escorts that are with each group and decide then whether or not to destroy all the transports as they would be sitting ducks. That would be a serious blow to the LuQuarins plans."

"I will look into that as well, Thyon. Thank you for the input."

"Admiral, with the demonstration this afternoon, I would like to take Croulac, Stilzen and Lorakit with us this morning so that we can begin preparation on our ship and train them in its' operations."

"Very well, Thyon. I will attend to the disruptors issue and planning the possible attacks. Croulac, assign Major Karess to take over your duties for the time being. Stilzen, have your next in line report to me later today. We will meet here after lunch to review where we are and then proceed with the demo." With that the Admiral dismissed everyone.

Croulac and Stilzen excused themselves to attend to the change in command and debrief their successors and would catch up with Thyon and the others at their ship as soon as they could. Thyon led the way out and back to the ship to begin the preparations needed. It would be a busy day.

An hour later Croulac and Stilzen joined them at the ship. Kira took Croulac and Tira was accompanied by Stilzen. Inside the ship they were given a brief tour and shown how the ship would divide into three equal sections becoming a ship of their own. Thyon, Kira and Tira would be piloting and controlling the main systems, while Lorakit, Croulac and Stilzen would man the disruptor discharge systems. There was an ample supply for disruptor charges on board each section for the upcoming demonstration. Thyon had received a message from the Admiral that three large cargo ships that had recently been decommissioned and replaced by newer ones would be used for the demo and were being prepared. The training continued filling the rest of the morning into early afternoon. Thyon, satisfied that all three were now ready suggested a lunch break. They would launch into space thereafter and await the Admiral.

They were eating lunch in the main canteen and discussing the upcoming demo when the Admiral joined them at their table. He ordered a quick bite to eat and asked Thyon a few more questions. With lunch complete they all headed out to the mighty ship. Thyon spoke.

"Admiral, I want you to join me and Lorakit in the middle section. You will be able to observe the entire operation from there. We have a direct communications link set up with your people here on the ground."

A few minutes later they were all in position on board as Thyon, Kira and Tira fired up the ship, lifting off and heading out into space. Once clear of the atmosphere in orbit Thyon gave the command. The ship was separated into three individual fighting ships now, Kira on his left and Tira on his right. Lorakit, Croulac and Stilzen were also at their consoles preparing the disruptor units. The Admiral signaled to the ground and the three unmanned cargo ships were launched into space. The three warships moved farther apart to lay in intercept courses to the three cargo ships now entering space taking different courses, heading deeper into space.

Thyon gave Kira the order and she cloaked her ship and then maneuvered out in front of the first cargo ship. Once their she told Croulac to fire. A minute later a small flash appeared on the rear section of the cargo ship and it stopped dead in its' tracks. The Admiral spoke to his ground crew that were piloting and monitoring its systems. He heard the ground crew reply that all propulsion systems had been incapacitated, as well as all other major systems. The only systems still working were for life support. They were taking readings and had no explanation why all the systems were down and inoperable.

"Quite effective, Thyon." The Admiral continued. "OK, try another." Thyon gave the order to Tira and as her sister had done she cloaked her ship. Although the Admiral couldn't see Tira's ship he figured she was taking up position. Again, a flash appeared on the cargo ship and it came to a full stop. The report from the ground was the same.

Thyon then moved his ship, cloaking it and quickly getting out in front and above the last remaining cargo ship traveling on a course farther out. He gave the order to Lorakit. The disruptor charge was fired and splashed down into the hull. Had it not been for the video cameras Thyon was using with extreme zoom, the Admiral would never have seen it attach itself to the hull. Thyon nodded and Lorakit hit a switch. The disruptor flash followed and now the third and final test ship lay still just floating along. The Admiral received the final report and turned to Thyon.

"Quite impressive, Thyon, I must say."

"Thank you, Admiral. Now the only question is whether you will have thousands of these disruptors made and ready for us; the sooner, the better."

"We have the production facility almost built, and the raw materials are starting to flow in. We hope to be able to begin production later tonight and have what you need within another day or so."

"Excellent, Admiral. Now I am going to have the three sections of our ship rejoin and then head back to the surface." Thyon spoke to his two sisters, and with all three sections now uncloaked they repositioned the ships in orbit, bringing them back together as one. Once locked in place, Thyon took over all the controls and they flew back down and landed on the surface. Thyon explained to the Admiral that he wanted to head back out into space for more training with the three newly added personnel and they would return the next morning. After the Admiral departed the ship, it took back off and was quickly out of the atmosphere and into space. The Admiral smiled, remembering his days of youth when he had first met his now deceased wife.

Thyon telepathically spoke to his sisters, both smiling, then hit the controls launching it to an incredible speed into the stars.

Chapter Nine
Evil Takes Form

Tenekaris III sat at the head of a long conference table. On one side were his twelve Overlords and the other side the leaders of the Blisscrells, Thornoks, Flemjots, and Secarios.

Two nights and a day of lavish celebration had ended that were filled with endless, food, spirits and entertainment, some of which was decadent in nature. Now that his guests had their fill of fun, it was time to be serious and lay out a final plan to destroy his longtime nemesis, the Elior. The idle chat from the table subsided as Tenekaris III stood up.

"Welcome to all of you. I take it you have enjoyed your stay here and been able to celebrate our most recent victory over Brepnid along with the many others we have achieved in the last few years. Our alliance has never been stronger and our forces have grown, our technology greatly improved and our resources more than enough to sustain all operations for many years to follow. The time has come now when we need to address the only true threat to completing the conquest of all the galaxies, the Elior and their few friends. But over the past fifteen years they have become weak and complacent, taking a position of isolationism except for one rogue Admiral who is on an endless search to seek us out and destroy us with his meager forces. Together we now have a combined fighting force of over a billion, well-armed and ready to take out the remaining thorn in our side. Each of you have been provided with the means, manpower and resources necessary to accomplish this task and we are well underway in positioning these resources for the final attack on Elior. Even with their superior technology and defenses they will be no match for what we will bring down on their planet. Once we have destroyed them it will be an easy task then to take out their allies and gain all the riches and resources those planets can offer. My twelve Overlords have been working closely with all of you and in turn you have come forth furnishing your own resources, personnel and technology in meeting the challenge of this quest." Tenekaris III pulled up a giant display behind him at the front of the room.

A Divided Universe

The display showed an overview of three galaxies. He used his controller and brought it down to one, zooming in farther and farther until they could see a few solar systems and recognized as the origins of their military and resources. A path then illuminated connecting the resource planets into one larger path that led its' way out of the galaxy. Tenekaris did this sequence two more times until three paths had been created and emanated out of the one galaxy to the next. There the large paths once again subdivided and stretched down onto several planets, or moons of planets. This was the staging area where all the resources would be brought to prepare for a final three-pronged move to the final galaxy, the one where Elior lay. Tenekaris explained what resources were already in place and went on to explain how the rest were now in motion, or soon would be. Thousands of Secarios transport ships were at the origins loading up all the equipment, weapons and supplies that would be needed to sustain such a large force. He handed out a disk to each of his overlords and allies that provided the details that comprised the big picture he was displaying. Each had specific assignments, all the pieces that would fit together and soon be in place. Their mission was to insure the details were carried out on time. Finally, he addressed the group on two other matters.

"I must bring to your attention that we suspect the Elior have planted spies amongst us. In fact, I know this to be true as my agents were able to track down and capture four of them. I have their confessions for each leader to see. Make no mistake, they are here and will try and discover what we are about and may make an effort to thwart our plans. I suggest you take careful watch among your own people to insure our plans are not leaked to our enemy. I doubt it will make much of a difference in the end as our forces are the most powerful in the universe and our numbers much greater. But I do not want anything to slow us down at this point."

All the leaders nodded in agreement, and Tenekaris III continued.

"I am also going to employ our stargates in a number of systems and send in a contingent battle group through each with our new cloaked two-man fighters. They will be deployed and put into action on some of the Elior allied planets simultaneously. In doing this we achieve two more things. First, they will not be able to assist Elior when we attack. Second, if

68

A Divided Universe

Elior elects to send their resources to any of these planets they only weaken their own forces making it easier for us to overwhelm them on their home planet. Now I want you to take the information disks and meet with your military leaders and go over all the details. I wish to meet with you again here tomorrow at the same time with any questions, concerns or suggestions you may have. From there we will finalize the plan and put it into its' final phase. Good day, gentlemen." Tenekaris turned and disappeared through a door behind him. He made his way down a hall that led to the throne area seeking to find Eftar. At the chambers entrance he found him.

"Eftar." Eftar saw his Master and quickly was in front of him bowing.

"Yes, Master?"

"Find Overlord Kwindat, and have him meet with me in the underground planning room. And find our leading weapons scientist and have him join us there, and do it quickly."

"Yes Master." Eftar immediately left the room to do his masters bidding. Tenekaris made his way to the underground planning room where he found a few technicians working on the equipment. He dismissed them and awaited the two he had summoned, leaving only two guards at the outside entrance. His mind was turning rapidly. It was time to throw a few twists into the overall strategy. He was pacing back and forth, impatiently waiting. Ten minutes or more had passed before the door finally opened and Kwindat was ushered in, followed by the scientist and Eftar. Kwindat bowed and remained silent. The scientist also bowed in unison with Eftar. Then Eftar spoke.

"This is our leading weapons scientist, Master. He goes by the name Leffe."

"Thank you, Eftar. Please remain as I speak to these two. Kwindat, thank you for coming swiftly. I have a new task to add to your others."

"Yes, Master Overlord, whatever you wish."

A Divided Universe

"You had a previous Lord named Lanatar that worked with my wife Vivacious and both perished at the hand of Alex, the Earth Medallion bearer." Kwindat waited for Tenekaris to continue.

"I understand he bore many children, but one, his firstborn male now known as Lanatar II."

"Yes, my Lord that is so. He is a fine young warrior following in his fathers' footsteps. He has grown through the ranks and now holds the same position his father used to have under my house."

"Where is he now, Kwindat?"

"He is with one of the battlegroups preparing for the attack on Elior."

"Not any longer, Kwindat. I want you to pull him from those duties and find a suitable replacement. I have a special mission I want him to carry out."

"Yes, Master. What do you want me have him do?"

"Send him to Nephron station 1. I will have a small battlegroup there waiting for him. He is to use the Stargate portal there and lead the group through it to Galan. We still have a portal there which is being upgraded now to accommodate our two-man cloaked fighters. He will be attacking all the main villages. Leffe, as our leading scientist tell me about our biological weapons."

Leffe cleared his throat. "Master Overlord. We have many biologics, some of which are very deadly and spread rapidly when dispersed from our short-range missiles. What type of biologic are you asking for?"

"The kind that will kill the Galanian people quickly."

A Divided Universe

"Yes, we have a very deadly biologic specifically designed to act quickly on them, their immune system, cardio-vascular system and nervous system all at once. Death comes within a matter of minutes after contact."

"Excellent. And how large an area could we infect with each missile?"

"Unfortunately, Master, the nature of the biologic and how it spreads is limited and would only infect a square mile or so. The climate on Galan is not conducive to it spreading much beyond that. It also has a short life span and would infect only those directly in its path, and will dissipate and not have any impact after just a few minutes."

"I see, Leffe. Are there other agents we could disperse at the same time with greater impact?"

"Yes Master, we have others as deadly but work slower and could be spread over wide areas much easier. The symptoms would not be immediate but within a few days if not treated would create a slow painful onset within their bodies leading to death a week to ten days later."

"Is there an antidote or cure for it?"

"Not that I am aware of, Master. It is why we keep it very secure as it would have the same effect on us as our enemy."

"Thank you, Leffe. How much of this second biologic do you have available?"

"If dispersed properly it would cover many geographic miles with each missile exploded. Our inventory is ample enough for 100 or more missiles."

"Very well, Leffe. Prepare both agents in a secure manner and see Eftar when you have them ready for transport."

"Yes, Master. I will attend to it immediately." Leffe bowed and left the room.

71

Eftar spoke. "Master, the Galanians have many festivals where they use fireworks as part of the celebration. Instead of launching missiles perhaps our cloaked ships could place a number of explosives in hiding by each village, then retreat to the portal. Add a timing mechanism to each to go off at the same time the fireworks do. That way there will be nothing seemingly out of normal and the Galanians will be infected as they party on. No alarms will be raised and our troops would be in and out without any losses."

"Eftar, you are a genius and I like your way of thinking. Have the chemists draw up a plan and our engineers design something inconspicuous that would fit in well with the Galan habitat. See if you can find out when the next festival is. If soon we will take your approach, if not we go in the other way. One more thing Eftar, please arrange to have all the Overlords dine with me this evening. I have a few more plans I want to invoke on them."

"Yes Master, I will find out and also make the arrangements for dinner tonight." Eftar departed, only Kwindat remained.

"Well, Kwindat what are you standing there for? You have your orders, so get to them."

"Yes, Master." Kwindat bowed and withdrew the room as quickly as he could.

Tenekaris formed an evil grin as he rubbed his chin. "The Elior will be quite upset when their rotund friends the Galanians begin to perish." He laughed out loud and then headed to his own personal chambers for some afternoon entertainment.

Chapter Ten
A Moment of Paradise

Thyon had raced their ship for an hour into a little known solar system. Lorakit was next to him at the controls while the other four were relaxing in a lounge area just behind the bridge.

"Where are we going, Thyon?"

"There is a nice little planet we found years ago that we visit from time to time when we are in this galaxy. I think you will enjoy it." Thyon worked the control panel as they were about to come out of hyperspace. The ship went through a series of slowdowns until it was finally traveling at less than the speed of light. Thyon opened the viewing window and the stars in the darkness came to life. There were hues of yellow and pink with blues in the distance mixed in a cloud-like formation. It was an impressive sight. He felt the other four walking onto the bridge and taking in the view. He steered the ship left and headed to a small solar system becoming visible in the distance. A few minutes later they were passing by a large planet leading to others.

They passed four more planets when Thyon slowed the ship again. There in front, lay a small planet with beautiful colors of blues, greens with some land masses in browns and grays. It grew in size in the view as they approached the outer atmosphere. He slowed the ship one more time as they descended into the atmosphere and the details below emerged. He steered the ship again as it descended. A large land mass was surrounded by water with smaller islands surrounding it. The sun was shining down and the water below looked rich in life. It was a tropical paradise surrounded by calm seas, reefs, inlets and bays. A last maneuver and the ship made a final approach to a large beach area where Thyon landed the ship. He hit another switch and a large dome emerged over the entire area. The dome would act as a cloaking device and covered a few miles in all directions. From space no one would even know they were here. With the ship stable on the surface Thyon shut down all the other systems.

A Divided Universe

"Welcome to paradise." The sisters laughed and led Croulac and Stilzen out the back of the ship and down the ramp to the sand below.

"Lorakit, go down to the beach, I will be with you in a minute. I need to get something first." Lorakit made her way down the ramp, reaching the sand and looked up into the island walking slowly taking in all the beauty before her. She walked a hundred yards to where the tree line and shrubs started. Kira and Croulac were to her left fifty yards away and Tira and Stilzen to her right. She watched as Kira pulled out an orb, a few seconds later she and Croulac had vaped and disappeared. She looked to her right but Tira and Stilzen were already gone. She looked back towards the ship and saw Thyon walking out of the ship with a large dog-like creature with a pair of twin eagle beaks as a mouth. The animal, obviously his pet, walked in tandem with Thyon as they approached her.

"Lorakit, this is my Darkin. He has traveled with us for two years now. I had him in hibernation the last few days as it is better for him when we travel at great speeds. This is his home. Lorakit bent down and petted the strange but beautiful looking creature. It welcomed her gesture and sat back on its' hind legs. The Darkin looked up at Thyon apparently telecommunicating with him. Thyon petted him a few times, then the Darkin got up, walked a few steps, stopped look back at Thyon and spread the wings from his sides and took off in flight. He soared up high and was gone over the trees heading inland and quickly out of sight. Thyon spoke.

"I wanted to bring him back here where he belongs, especially since we will be traveling a great deal and even perhaps heading into harm's way. It is also the season the Darkens seek and find a mate which is for life. He deserves no less and has been a good companion and protector these past two years." Lorakit looked at Thyon.

"He is a beautiful creature Thyon. It is a bit warm here to be wearing our military uniforms don't you think?" Thyon laughed.

"Yes, it is. I can fix that." He pulled out his orb and handed Lora a bracelet. Together they vaped into it and poof, ported away. A few seconds later the orb stopped and they vaped out. Lorakit's eyes opened

74

wide. She was standing in front of a large tropical hut that overlooked a lagoon, a waterfall on the opposite side rolling down a cascade of rocks, the water splashing down. The lagoon was surrounded by a myriad of plants, flowers and trees. It was unlike anything she had ever seen. Thyon had taken off his top tunic and bare chested walked into the thatched roof hut. Lorakit followed. Inside was a plush setting of furniture, the wood floor laden with a large throw rug, and artifacts from other worlds on tables and shelves. Thyon tossed his top on a chair, then took his boots and pants off, leaving only his briefs on.

"No one will bother us here, Lorakit."

"Where are the others?"

"My sisters each have their own place, not far from here, but isolated for privacy. When we come here we all just relax in our own way, or explore the planet at our leisure. Most of the time we run around naked as the temperature and humidity are near perfect. We can message each other telepathically when required and get together at times to share meals or exploration. My sisters are very happy at present and I believe in lust. This will be their first experience with a male counterpart as my experience with you was last night. It brings me joy to see them so happy. Now Lora, might I suggest a swim in the lagoon after which I will gather some of the most delicious fruits you will ever taste." Thyon took off his shorts and walked outside to the lagoon, Lorakit's eyes lavishing over his immaculate body. She quickly stripped down and followed him out. He was already in the water waist deep and striding towards the waterfall. As she stepped into the water she felt its warmth and walked in deeper feeling the soothing pleasure that ran over her skin. Thyon had reached the waterfall and stepped right into it, the water cascading down his head and over the rest of his body. She joined him, closing her eyes as her head breached the falling sheet of water. It too was warm and felt as if she were standing in a warm shower at a spa. She felt his arms grab her waist and pull her behind the waterfall. Now in an embrace she looked out through the sheet of water to the hut on the opposite side and then up into his eyes as they embraced.

A Divided Universe

The day passed quickly on the island retreat. Thyon sent his sisters a message that they should all dine together that evening and then have a bonfire on the beach. They would be departing early the next morning to return to the Admiral's command center.

Chapter Eleven
The Humedlior Intervention

The Admiral was pacing about. He had awoken an hour earlier to a new day after only a few hours of sleep. Overseeing the production of the disruptors with his newly in charge Crystal who he had promoted the day before from Captain to Major to replace Croulac. She was a highly capable officer and deserving of the promotion. The production had gone well during the night and he expected to have a few thousand ready for Thyon, Kira and Tira when they returned. He had also planned out possible attacks on the enemy once the transports were incapacitated. There in was the problem. His orders and guideline from the Council of Elior did not allow him to make a first strike against the LuQuarin or any other force. Unless he was attacked he could not assume a first strike approach. The only exception was if it was in an effort to rescue the humans from the LuQuarin slave encampments. If he violated the Councils orders he would be committing a criminal act of starting a war without authorization. He paced about his quarters and stared out the window which showed the sun coming up over the horizon. He prayed that Alex would succeed with the Council and that new orders would follow allowing the attacks. He switched his thoughts and wondered when Thyon and the group would return. He was well aware of the emotions the younger ones were experiencing reminding him again of the days with his wife. It seemed so long ago as the pain of her loss filled his mind. He stared out again, the sun now peaking its way higher into the sky and shook his head to return to the task at hand. It was time to get dressed and see how the production was coming along. It also was the day the rest of his battlegroup would be landing. A busy day indeed lay before him.

Thyon piloted the ship with Lorakit next to him. The four others were in the lounge area having a warm morning beverage as they made their way back to the Admiral's command center. They were all refreshed and feeling good from the short break on the small planet island getaway. Lorakit rested her hand on Thyon's forearm, a warm gesture of the time they had just spent together. Thyon looked at her and smiled, his feelings for her growing, the human emotional side of his being emerging. He started the first series of slowing down the ship which was faster than even the SSSTS the Elior had. It was time to change focus. Had the Admiral achieved making the disruptor charges they would all soon be back in space heading in three different directions to intercept the enemy. The plan seemed simple, but Thyon knew few things in life were and he contemplated all the possible contingencies they might come across once engaged with the LuQuarin and others. The ship landed near the command center in the same spot it had previously. Minutes later they were in the compound in central control approaching the Admiral and others. After brief greetings the Admiral spoke.

"Thyon, we have been working through the night and have almost 10,000 of the disruptors made. I know you asked for a minimum of 15,000, 5000 for each ship which we should have completed later today. They are being packed in the special tube design you provided and we can start loading whenever you're ready."

"Excellent Admiral. Croulac, Stilzen and Lorakit have all been trained how to load them on each portion of the ship". He looked at the three.

The Admiral looked over at three officers standing nearby and ordered them to make the arrangements to load. Thyon continued.

"Admiral, have you been able to draw up the plans to have your fighters near the attack zones we will be in to come in once we have disabled all their ships and take out their escorts?"

The Admiral displayed a grim face before answering.

"Thyon, we will not be able to formulate or carry out an attack at this time. As you know, I still answer to the Council and if we were to attack without their approval it would be considered an act of war, precipitated by our actions. Disabling them borders that same principle but you will be carrying that out providing me with the gray needed in order not to violate their current position with respect to our enemy. The Council has remained in a defensive peace posture and unless the Elior or our allies are attacked, I doubt they will approve the use of force or offensive measures. The only exception we have at present is if we can rescue/save the human colonies that are enslaved by the LuQuarin, and even that has to be carried out with a minimum risk to loss of life. In order for me to order an attack we need the Councils approval. That is why Alex's mission is so important to convince them and return quickly in order for us to execute." He looked at Thyon and the others awaiting a reply. Thyon rubbed his chin.

"Perhaps there is another opportunity we can exploit, Admiral. One within the bounds of your directives. Where are the human encampments?" The Admiral pulled out a 3D map on a huge display behind them.

"Here, here and here are the three we know of and have done preliminary work and a detailed plan to extract them. We know there is a fourth most likely close to Tenekaris III which he keeps at the ready for his personal use." Thyon walked around the huge map of the galaxy selected.

"Admiral, now pull up the three points we are going to use to disable the transports and convoys." A moment later those three routes were displayed and the points of interception. Thyon again walked around the map calculating the distances and time frames in his mind as only he could do. They all watched as Thyon added a few lines to the maps.

"Admiral, this looks possible, but will require your assistance with the slave compounds."

"What is your thinking, Thyon?"

We can carry out our original plan and disable the three convoys, then leave them floating helplessly. Then we can reroute my three ships to the three encampments. There are planets nearby all three where you could have your rescue/assault teams at the ready for extraction. You will need to bring more disruptors with you. We would then join your forces at the designated point, reload our disruptors, then go in cloaked and apply them to all the LuQuarin forces that protect these compounds. With their defenses disabled, if timed right, you could execute the rescue missions and get the humans out. We will need to work out the exacting details and timing but the opportunity exists to slow down our enemy's quest to conquer Elior and save the humans from their horrible fate."

The Admiral now walked around the maps taking in Thyon's vision of the two-fold plan. The rest remained silent as the Admiral walked around the map again. Turning to Thyon.

"Thyon, yes I do believe this is possible. Let me get with my commanders and get the details we need and draw up a complete plan. We should be able to have it ready by the time your ship is loaded with the disruptors."

"Very good, Admiral. For now, my team needs to return to our ship to oversee the loading and prepare our flight plans for you to coordinate the timing. We need to check the details of the convoys to insure when they will come out of hyperspace when close to their arrival points. Any real deviation from the timing could present problems to the plan and contingencies need to be drawn up as well. We can meet this afternoon when the loading is near completion and finalize the plan."

"Yes Thyon, agreed."

"Until this afternoon then, Admiral." Thyon turned and led his small group out of the command center heading back to their ship.

The day was filled with the activity of preparing the ship to disembark. The loading of the disruptor charges in the three holds of the ship proceeded while Thyon and the five others laid out the detailed plan for the three intercept points. The manifests acquired showed the three convoys were already on their way and would be reaching their destinations within two to three days which barely gave them the time they needed to get there prior to them coming out of hyperspace. The last part of the journey was the staging areas the LuQuarin, Blisscrells, Thornoks and Flemjots would set up in the galaxy next to the one Elior lay within. The number of transport and cargo ships in each group numbered in the thousands with a heavy escort of fighting ships to protect them. It would take hours of rapid deployment of the disruptors dispersed and attached to all the ships before the final switch could halt them in their tracks simultaneously. Then to rendezvous with the Admirals troops for the rescue mission would take another day of rapid flight, reload and prepare the rescue and assault on the slave encampments. The Admirals elite forces would do the extraction once the LuQuarin military forces were neutralized and would not be able to assist.

Thyon estimated his ship and his sisters would need only an hour to be in place but the Admirals forces and ships were much slower and would be seven hours behind. They would wait for the rescue teams to be in place and utilize the tunneling that was already set up with larger orbs to hold the rescued slaves at the ready. When the signal was given Thyon would use the disruptors on the bases where most of the enemy troops were located. Then the final assault into the compound would take out any resistance and gather the humans into the orbs, safely porting them to the awaiting ships in cloaked orbit. The timing had to be precise and any number of things could go wrong, but it was as good a plan as possible and there would be no turning back once it started. Pleased with their work the group headed back late in the afternoon to meet up with the Admiral and his commanders to come to final agreement.

The meeting lasted over two hours as every detail was scrutinized by Thyon's team, the Admiral and all the commanders. The special Ops forces leaders were also present. Now in agreement Thyon and his team would need to leave within two hours to reach the desired positions in time and await the convoys. The Admiral had set up a dinner to accommodate them all prior to the departure.

Seated at a large dining table the group mostly ate and drank in silence, each preparing for the mission in their own way. Idle chat could be heard among the large group and a splash of laughter here and there to loosen the mood. Croulac displayed a very humorous side which broke up the tension felt in the room. The dinner approached its' end when the Admiral stood up raising his glass to the others. They all stood.

"I wish you well on this mission, that it can be carried out with great success and that all of you return safely. This marks a day when the Elior and her friends embark to preserve the sanctity of our heritage, our people and all those civilizations that live in peace. May we keep them all from harm's way, and bring peace to this universe and all living creatures. I salute you for your commitment and bravery to this cause." A resounding "Here, here," echoed through the room. They all drank from their glasses and dispersed.

Thyon, Kira, Tira, Croulac, Stilzen and Lorakit were now on board the mighty ship. Inside at the main bridge Thyon huddled with his two sisters as the three touched heads. Telepathically Thyon spoke to them.

"My dear sisters. We are the three who can make a difference to end this struggle and bring harmony to all the galaxies. I know you are both strong, talented and have skills that no others possess. Be safe and let us all rejoin in a few days, for I know not what I would do if I lost either of you." The two answered in kind.

"You be safe as well our dear brother, as we have and always will work as three in one." Their heads parted. Kira and Croulac headed to the left ship attached, and Tira and Stilzen to the one on the right. Once all were settled into their respective command consoles Thyon initiated the take-off sequence. A minute later they were up and out of the atmosphere where the fastest starship in the universe split into three separate ships. They bade their final good wishes and then the three ships each took off in different directions and jettisoned into hyperspace.

Lorakit was at the console next to Thyon's as the ship was now traveling at an incredible speed towards the objective. It would be two days of hard and fast travel. Satisfied with the settings and coordinates Thyon set it to autopilot and stood up.

"Well, my dear, Lora, we have almost two days now to do as we wish."

Lorakit stood up and walked over and embraced Thyon.
"I have a few ideas as to how we can spend that time my young lover."

Chapter Twelve
A Plea to the Council

Alex woke from a deep sleep. Wiping his eyes, he took a drink from the cup held in his console chair. He looked at the time. He had slept four hours, exhausted after going through the information and preparing for the arrival on Elior and the meeting with the Council. It had been a rough two days traveling on the SSSTS, but they were getting close to coming out of hyperspace and making the final approach to Elior. He heard the Captain on the intercom letting him know they would be slowing down shortly and be in the solar system next to Elior and would be landing in less than an hour.

Alex sat up, turned his monitor back on to go over his presentation for the Council one more time. Convincing the Council into action was paramount and he felt the pressure and weight on his shoulders to do just that. Deloria was now the head of the Council after Ezmull's retirement and Olisaria had filled the vacant spot. As he finished going through the presentation he felt the ship shake, then slow down. They were coming out of hyperspace and would be landing soon. He shut off his monitor and pulled out the disk he would need. The front viewer opened up and he could see over the pilots shoulder the solar system they were in. As often as he had flown in space, he was still in awe of the sights that lay before him. Within ten minutes they hand landed and the disembarking procedure started.

Now back to normal size and out of the SSSTS and changed into his military uniform, he was met by an officer on the platform. The officer recognized him.

"Alex, welcome home. We did not expect you for some time yet."

"Officer Meld. I am back on an urgent matter and need to get a message to the Council immediately."

"Yes, Alex, please follow me and we can get the message off in just a few minutes." Alex followed Meld into a control room. There he transcribed an urgent encrypted message to the Council and sent the message disk on its' way. Meld spoke.

"Alex, being late in the evening, I doubt the Council will answer you until the morning. Are there any arrangements I can make for you?"

"No Meld, I can make my own arrangements, thank you." Alex pulled out his orb, said goodbye, then vaped and ported away. He was standing outside his house a minute later and sent a signal to his clone which was unique and undetectable to others. He needed to meet up with his clone to get all the updates of occurrences in his absence before taking his place and putting the clone into hibernation. It was late on the star bright night. Alex walked on the beach awaiting his clone. Staring out and over the waters of his beach home he waited patiently. His clone would need to quietly slip out of the house without being noticed, yet alone followed, or the ruse would be up with his wife Diana. This was always the tensest moment, changing back the clone for his real self. An hour passed before he saw the Alex clone approaching him on the beach.

Once they were together Alex extracted all the clones' life data history since he had departed. It took only a few minutes and when complete he vaped and orbed his clone to the secret place designated for his storage. He had assumed matching every element the clone was last seen in. Breathing heavily after the nervous exchange he walked back to the house where Diana, AJ and Xia were sleeping. He hadn't seen his house in months and noticed the changes Diana had made that his clone had transferred to him. Everything looked in order and was quiet as he made it to the deck. He was aching to be with his wife but would have to wait as his clone had been intimate with her twice earlier in the night and it would be necessary to refrain from intimacy to insure Diana didn't grow suspicious. Trying to act normal with the information he had and the urgency of the situation would be difficult to hide from her.

He sat on a chair on the deck and ordered a drink from the dispensing unit. Looking up into the night sky, his mind was a whirl of the places he had just been, wondering what had transpired since his departure. Thyon, Kira and Tira had come back and now joined the fight against the LuQuarin.

A Divided Universe

As powerful as his children were, he worried about their safety as only a parent can do. He heard the sliding door open, looked back and saw Diana in a nightie come out on the deck. She came over and sat on his lap curling up for warmth. He hugged her, taking in her scent and kissed her on the head. When she spoke, the words stunned him.

"Welcome home my beloved. I was wondering when you would return."

"What are you talking about?"

"Seriously Alex, you're going to play that card. Your clone is good, almost perfect, but a woman knows her true husband and I am happy you are back and safe." Alex didn't know what to say.

"It's OK, my dear husband. I know you carry the Medallion and need to serve the planet and all the people. You have unmatched powers and are using them to insure our safety."

"How long have you known?"

"It hit me two trips ago after you left. Somehow my instincts told me that the man I was with was just not my true Alex. Don't get me wrong, he acts like you in almost every way, even the intimacy we share. So, I just made the best of it, going along as if all was as it should be. Our life became so predictable and your routines never varied confirming my suspicions."

"If anything, Diana I was envious that he and not I was the one sleeping with you, and all the other things we enjoy doing together. Do the kids know?"

"No Alex. They are so busy being almost adults with all that goes with that. They just saw you as the same old dad, never wavering. I think it best if we keep it that way. They are both doing so well in their studies and achievements that knowing there are two of you would only confuse and upset them. We will keep it just between us."

"OK Diana, you would know best on that subject."

"One thing I ask from you Alex?"

"What is that my loving wife?"

"The next time you are going to leave and send in your clone, I would like to know ahead of time. If possible, tell me where you are going and for what purpose."

"I will tell you what I can."

"See, this won't be difficult. But my dear husband I do see one problem."

"What's that?"

"Seems you have a bulge in your pants that needs a bit of attention."

Alex laughed then pulled Diana into an embrace and kissed her. He was a lucky man to have a wife, woman and best friend as Diana.

Sipping his coffee, Alex watched as Diana was preparing breakfast for AJ and Xia whom had just sat down at the table, dressed and ready to head to the academy after eating. The usual good mornings had been exchanged. The sun was up with clear blue skies setting the stage for another beautiful day on Elior. Alex looked at his children realizing they were now young adults. Xia looked a lot like Diana but was taller than her mother now and carried a demeanor of confidence. AJ too had grown and was nearing the same height as Alex but had yet to fill out. They engaged in idle chat about the studies at the academy and what the day before them held. Alex simply listened, cherishing the moment as the four sat together as a family. The time passed quickly as AJ and Xia finished eating. Xia came over and kissed her father on the head, then her mother, vaped and ported away. AJ kissed his mother, patted Alex on the shoulder and was gone a moment later. Diana sat with Alex seeing the smile on his face. It was obvious he had missed them dearly as he had missed her. His passion during the middle of the night was more than she had experienced with him in quite a while. She sipped her coffee and continued to watch Alex staring at nothing. His smile turned to a grimaced look, his mind whirling away. She had seen this look before, realizing that whatever he was thinking was of grave importance.

"Alex, dear, what is it?" He turned to face Diana and realized she had been watching him, knowing he was troubled about something.

"I need to see the Council as soon as possible."

"About what, if I may ask?"

"There are changes taking place in other galaxies which they need to be aware of is all I can say at this point my love." Diana had heard that tone before and knew that changes usually meant something was wrong.

"But good news, my wife. Thyon, Kira and Tira stopped by our base and visited with me for a bit."

"How are they doing?"

"They are doing quite well, and have been traveling through many galaxies. They have developed their own spacecraft which is faster than anything the Elior have. Thyon is well over nine feet tall now and built like a gladiator. The girls are also very tall, perhaps eight and a half feet, incredibly beautiful with long flowing hair, sparkling eyes and a body that any female would envy. All three have developed their powers, although I am not sure of what they all are, as we did not get to spend that much time together." Alex looked at Diana with a smile seeing the woman he had been with now for twenty years. She was as beautiful as ever and had aged little in the time spent on Elior. Although forty-five now, she had the appearance of a thirty-year-old.

"So how are your paintings coming along?"

"I just finished my latest one and had it put into the art museum of the human colony where Derek resides. It is one of my best pieces yet."

"Although my clone passed the image to me, I must go see it for myself when I have the chance."

"Thank you, sweetie, that would mean a lot to me." Alex stood up, and grabbed a new cup of coffee from the dispenser unit.

"I am going to sit on the deck for a bit."

"OK. I need to change and have plans to take my parents to the new library that was just completed. It contains the entire written history of Earth and is supposed to be spectacular. You should come with us if you can."

"I wish I could, but I must see the Council."

"From what I understand, the Council does not meet as often as they used to. With Elior doing so well, they have little to govern or get involved with."

"Then I must see Olisaria."

"I am sure she would love to see you as well. Your clone never visited her and I suspect she is aware when the real Alex is gone. That was another big clue, my love. You should send her a message."

"Yes, I will. I hope she can see me as soon as possible." Alex pulled out a message disk and when completed sent it to Olis.

"Now take your coffee and go relax on the deck for a bit while I get changed." Diana left the room. Alex headed for the deck, took a seat in a nice tall lounge chair and looked out to the beach and waves rolling in. A half hour passed, Diana had returned, kissed Alex good-bye and was off to her parents. Alex paced back and forth on the deck, eager to see Olisaria and the Council. The waiting was killing him. To pass the time he went back into the house to change into his best uniform to be ready the minute he heard from the Council or Olis.

Back on the deck and dressed impeccably, Alex resumed his pacing as it was mid-morning and still no word. "Damn it! Why don't they answer?"

Feeling frustration setting in he went to the dispensing unit and ordered a drink. Although early in the day he needed something to calm down. Chugging the drink, he set the glass down and headed to the beach for a walk, going over in his mind what he would say to the Council when the chance arrived. It was a cool day with a light breeze, the temperature warm but mild, the sun now high in the sky. Another hour passed and now back on the deck he had a second drink and put on music to fill the empty void of sound. A disk appeared and he recognized the color. It was from Olisaria. He quickly read the information.

"Alex, it is good to hear from you. Why don't you join my grandfather and me at my place for lunch at around noon?" It was signed Olis.

Noon. Shit, another hour to burn before he could go. He had a third drink, knowing the Medallion would offset any intoxication, and sat back down on the lounge chair. Lunch with Olis and her grandfather Ezmull, the previous leader of the Council. This might be good he thought.

Noon arrived and Alex vaped and ported to Olisaria's home and stood at the front door. He rang the doorbell and waited. A few seconds later the door opened and there stood Ezmull.

"Greetings, Alex. It has been a long time. Please come in."

"Thank you, Ezmull. You are looking well."

"Yes, retirement has been good to me, but to be honest I get bored at times. Olis is out back. We are going to have lunch on the veranda."

A Divided Universe

Alex followed Ezmull through the house and out onto the veranda. Olis was seated at a table dressed in a tan blouse and a pair of white shorts. She stood up as Alex approached, giving him a hug.

"Please, have a seat Alex. Lunch will be served shortly." They all sat down, Olis ordered a round of drinks for them and levitated the three glasses to the table. They held their glasses up as Olis made a toast.

"To our Alex, returned safely back to Elior." The three took a sip of their drink, then Olis continued.

"You have been gone a long time my friend, traversing through the galaxies with the Admiral I take it?"

"Yes Olis. I have returned to see the Council on a most urgent matter."

"Yes Alex, I saw your request to the Council after your landing on the SSSTS last night. What is so urgent for this hasty request?"

"The Admiral asked if I would personally deliver a wealth of information we obtained directly to the Council. Our enemy the LuQuarin and their allies are more dangerous than ever and threaten to take over every planet and species that is in their path, including the Elior."

"Alex, we have read the Admiral's monthly reports as he has been running about the galaxies and solar systems in the hunt for the LuQuarin and the human slave colonies. What makes this so different? The LuQuarin have distanced themselves from us and have posed no threat now for fifteen years. Even with the new alliances they have made, the Council still does not see this as any real threat. Our planet and our friends have enjoyed peace the entire time. We cannot be the police to all planets and species Alex, they will need to fend for themselves as best they can."

"Olis, this isolationism approach may have worked well up to now, but it will not last much longer. The LuQuarin and allies are amassing for a huge assault on Elior and their numbers are beyond anything we have ever surmised in the past. The threat is imminent and I fear it will be here soon if we do not take action." Ezmull spoke.

"Alex, the Council will need hard evidence before they will even consider taking action."

"I have the evidence with me Ezmull, and will gladly show it to you here and now." The sound of Alex's normal calm voice had changed to one to desperately be heard. Olis looked directly into Alex's eyes and saw the tension within.

"OK Alex, show us what you have."

"I will need a 3D display Olis." Olis pulled a small remote from the pocket of her shorts. A large display appeared behind her and Ezmull with a small box on the table where Alex could insert a disk. Alex pulled out the disk.

"This is what I want to present to the Council." He inserted the disk and the display came to life.

"This first part is from a video Thyon took while cloaked with his sisters above the planet Brepnid." The film started. Olis and Ezmull watched as there were multiple cameras and views which displayed the massive attack on the planet and its' inhabitants. The video was twenty minutes long and had captured the attacking LuQuarin, Blisscrell, Thornok and Flemjot warships entering the atmosphere and attacking all the major cities on the planet, wiping out the Brepnid defenses and destroying the cities down to rubble and ash. Then hundreds of large transport ships came into view landing ground forces to wipe out or capture any remaining resistance. The film ended there as Thyon had seen enough and left the planet. Olis spoke.

"Alex, the Brepnids had no chance. I have never seen such a large attack on any planet such as this, but the Council will need more."

A Divided Universe

"Olis, that is nothing compared to what they are planning for Elior. We had one of our agents capture the entire database of the Secarios, whom as you know handle all the transportation and cargo for the LuQuarin and the others. That information provided us with all the details and manifests of what they are in the process of doing. Let me show you."

The video started again and this time showed the adjoining galaxies and the convoy transports from initiation points to where they consolidated, and then the paths to be used to stage the equipment and personnel just outside the galaxy that Elior lay within. It showed the volume of equipment and supplies, mostly military, and the manpower included. When the video stopped Alex added.

"Olis, Ezmull. From the data we collected there will be a billion soldiers, equipment and fighters in place very soon just outside our galaxy. Their technology has improved and the speed they can move is faster than in the past. Even with our advanced Elior technology and defenses the numbers will be overwhelming. We will be outnumbered 500:1. You know Tenekaris III has always wanted to destroy the Elior, and if successful there will be nothing to stand in his way to become ruler of all galaxies." Olis stood up and took a few steps away from the table, then turned and walked back.

"A billion soldiers, Alex?"

"Yes, and tens of thousands of warships and transports. They don't even need to use their stargates anymore."

"What is the Admiral doing about this?"

"Olis, you know his hands are tied and he is not allowed to initiate or start a war without the Council's permission. At present he is trying to figure out a way just to slow them down and buy Elior the time it needs to properly prepare and defend itself." Olis looked at her grandfather who had a look of real concern on his face.

A Divided Universe

"OK Alex, I will send an urgent message to the Council to see how quickly they can assemble and meet with us."

"Thank you, Olis." Olis left the veranda and went inside. Ezmull and Alex sat in silence, each thinking about what was evident and the real threat it carried. Olis returned a few minutes later.

"The message has been set. I called for an emergency meeting and we should hear back before the day is out. Now I suggest we take a little time to have a nice lunch and discuss this more."

A Divided Universe

Chapter Thirteen
The Quest of Evil Takes Form

Tenekaris III sat at the head of the long dining table. On each side there were six of his Overlords, all twelve present. There were additional tables set apart and to the sides where numerous Lords, and the heads of the scientific groups. Tenekaris ordered up one of the favorite dishes, a slow grilled pit BBQ human which he had reserved for such a meeting. The human must have been huge, and Tenekaris paid homage to his chef for selecting such a fine fair for the evening. LuQuarin grog filled many pitchers at each table with silver flasks in front of every one sitting. There was also entertainment. Many females from other world species they had enslaved, barely clothed, were dancing in an erotic manner to music that played from a small ensemble. To insure there were no outbreaks from the dancers, Tenekaris ordered they be drugged to cooperate fully and provide the type of entertainment his Overlords and Lords enjoyed. Drinks were being had in liberal fashion and the LuQuarin were getting louder, laughing and being obnoxious with lude remarks to the dancers, who all glass eyed seemed not to notice or smiled at their captors as if they were enjoying themselves. The Master Overlord laughed to himself as he ate and drank the grog. He would let them enjoy the night and all the pleasures it held, but before he turned them loose he would speak to them when they were done with the main course before they lost control.

Tenekaris took his last bite of the tasty meal and looked around to see most others had finished as well. He stood up and raised his flask to the room.

"My Overlords, Lords, and guests. Tonight, we celebrate. Tomorrow we begin our final quest to rule all galaxies and the universe. With our strong alliances now well formed, technology advanced thanks to our scientific group and a fighting force larger and more powerful than anything ever created, there will be no force or opposition that can stop us, not even the Elior and their friends. To our upcoming victory!" the whole room had raised their flasks.

A Divided Universe

"To victory!" They all cried out. After the toast Tenekaris sat down and let the rest of them finish their dinner. He then had Eftar speak to Overlord Seldon to meet with him in his conference room and to bring any of his Lords that were attending the dinner. Tenekaris left the room and went to the conference room awaiting Seldon. Two minutes passed by before Eftar opened up the door and ushered in Seldon and two others, apparently two of his Lords. Tenekaris dismissed Eftar as he told them all to have a seat. Tenekaris paced at the front of the room, his hands clasped behind his back as the three awaited in silence.

"Seldon. You have been the Overlord of your house now for over 200 years."

"Yes, Master."

"Yet in that time your house has been the worst performing house of all my Overlords. Can you explain why?"

"No sir. We have always tried to follow your orders and carry out the missions to the best of our ability. I didn't know we were failing you so badly."

"Not failing Seldon, but underperforming. Your Lords and men seem to always fall short of the expectations I had, be it mining, extracting food resources or maintaining control of the inhabitants enslaved on the planets you control. I have seen that there have been five uprisings on those planets you are supposed to be in control of. Perhaps it is time for me to find a new Overlord."

Seldon was shaking as the last words permeated the room. His two Lords also appeared to be nervous.

"I will give you one more chance Seldon to prove your worth."

"Yes Master, whatever you need, we will do it."

"That remains to be seen."

96

A Divided Universe

"What is it you wish of us?"

"I will be sending you and some of your troops to Cryplas. You will use the stargates there which will be updated to our newer larger version. We need more Plastasious quickly as our supply is running short and we need it to build more of our cloaking warships. Get through the stargates with your men, secure the mining fields and protect them with your forces. There is no need to attack the Cryplasians. Get your mining equipment working fast, extract the material and get it through the stargate as you mine it. As we receive it at the other end it will go straight to our production facilities. I expect two to three tons a day through the portal and we need at least one hundred tons to meet our immediate requirements. Do you understand?"

"Yes, Master."

"Good. Now take your two Lords here and get started immediately, as your fun is over for the evening. Assemble the resources you need and give me a report when you are ready to start. Do not delay or I will find your replacement. Now get out of here, you have your orders, and do not fail me."

Seldon and his two Lords rushed out of the meeting room. Tenekaris laughed. He doubted that Seldon could extract that much in such a short time, and in reality, the existing stockpiles were more than sufficient. Just another ploy to attract the attention of the Elior. Seldon's forces would not be missed for the larger battle to come. He summoned Eftar. Eftar entered.

"Yes, my Lord."

"I want you to take the four spies we have in custody, bring that Secarios bitch to my chambers, then slice up the other three into a few large pieces, but have the pieces wired together so they still appear to be whole. Then send them in an unmarked cargo ship bearing a white flag so to speak, to where the Elior Admiral is, or at least one of their outposts if we don't have his exact location. On each of their foreheads burn in my symbol. Then have our agents keep a close eye on all their suspected agents. If I am right, the Elior will give them the order to get out and when they do run, apprehend them. They may prove useful to us down the road."

"As you wish, Master. Is there anything else?

"No, just bring the Secarios bitch to me first."

"Very well, Master." Eftar hustled out of the room to carry out his orders.

Chapter Fourteen
The Big Delay and a Rescue

Thyon sat at the center console looking out through the viewer at the planets and solar system directly ahead. With his ship cloaked, he was waiting for the convoy to come out of hyperspace. With only minimal systems activated they would be undetected when the first ships emerged which he anticipated being escort warships. He and Lorakit arrived just hours earlier of the anticipated time when the convoy should appear. Lora was resting after the two hard days of travel mingled in with intimacy. Thyon had his long-range sensors finely tuned just in case the convoy emerged from a spot different from the one slated to be used. He thought of the time he was spending with Lorakit, and how well they seemed to be a perfect match. Her beauty was only exceeded by her skills and talents. A fast learner, she had grasped all the major concepts and controls of the craft with the minimum of Thyon's training and guidance. They should prove to be a worthy team and match for the expected enemy when they arrived. Thyon rechecked all his instruments, then retrieved a restoration drink. He wanted to be at full alert when the time came to engage the enemy. He sat back down at his console sipping his drink. He heard the soft footsteps of Lorakit behind him and a moment later she was sitting at the console next to his.

"Did you rest well, Lora?"

"Yes, I feel much better now. This traveling at such high speeds is a bit taxing."

"Good, because I don't think we will have to wait much longer and then we are going to very busy."

"I am ready Thyon, time for some payback to these bastards for all they have done to Elior, Brepnid and so many others."

"Easy, my dear. We just want to incapacitate them for now. I suspect that the killing won't be too far behind. We disrupt as many or all of the transport ships, then we scoot to our rendezvous point to prepare and rescue the humans from the camp. We only open fire if we are discovered and even then, we still get the hell out of here. Understand?"

"Yes Thyon, I know, but it would be nice to wipe out a few of their warships."

"Hopefully my father convinces the Council into action and they send us some of that Elior might. For now, we buy our home planet as much time as we can."

Thyon's short range sensor flashed. This was it. The ships would be emerging from hyperspace right where they were expected. Lorakit quickly turned on her control panel and was ready to activate the weapon to disperse the disruptor charges. Their ship would remain cloaked and Thyon would steer above and in front of each ship as it passed. A small tube would emerge from the aft of the ship where the charges would eject from, find their target and stick to the hull near the engines. They would remain cloaked and the ejection would not be noticed or picked up by any scans the enemy might employ. Even if it picked up the small projectile, it would appear only as a small piece of space debris and be ignored.

"Lorakit, get ready. We have practiced this in simulation, but this is the real deal now."

"I know Thyon. I have never been more focused than I am now. Just pilot this ship like the genius I know you are and I will do my part with the disruptors." Thyon looked over at Lorakit and smiled.

"I have no doubt of your abilities, my love." Lorakit turned back and looked at him.

"So, I am your love now?"

"Yes, if you will have me?"

"Let's get through this first and then you will have my answer."

A Divided Universe

The first ship to appear was a LuQuarin destroyer which moved ahead activating its' shields. It was followed by two more destroyers that panned out to the right and left of the first one. Then two more appeared and took up flanking positions. They moved ahead slowly their scanners active looking for anything that may threaten the convoy. Now leading out and away two Blisscrell cruisers appeared and stationed themselves to the left and right of the pathway. Several smaller fighter craft emerged from the cruisers and deployed above and below forming a protective tunnel.

When the first Secarios transport appeared Thyon's eyes opened wide. It was a mammoth ship, larger than anything he had ever seen and based on its' size could hold a great deal of equipment, supplies and troops. Thyon silently positioned his ship just beyond and above the huge cargo ship. Lorakit lined up the firing mechanism and then ejected the disruptor. Within a few seconds it was attached to the hull of the craft. Thyon kept his position still and awaited the next one. Slowly they emerged from hyperspace and one by one Lorakit fired the disruptors. Twenty more passed by and were tagged. Then two more destroyers appeared, one close to Thyon's position. They passed and then the next series of transports emerged, again one by one. This went on for hours, Thyon keeping track of how many and what type of ships passed by.

As anticipated the warships protecting the convoy immediately put up their shields and were on full alert, ready to strike down anything that may interfere with the precious cargo. The procession and tagging went on for ten more hours, the number of transports numbering over 1200 before the last few emerged and flew by, followed by more warships. The entire convoy was now spread out over a few thousand miles. Satisfied that the last of the ships was through and past them, Thyon steered his ship slowly above and towards the center of the convoy. As their speed was relatively slow compared to his craft, he traversed halfway into the long line of ships. Looking at Lorakit he gave the signal and she hit a main switch.

It only took a few minutes as the transport ships all had a brief flash on their hull and then stopped dead where they were just floating now in space. Thyon didn't wait for the escort warships to begin to maneuver sensing danger. He lifted the ship up and away from the convoy, slowly maintaining the invisible posture. Soon the size of the transports shrank in the distance. Thyon saw several fighters flying about seeking the invisible enemy that had stopped the wagon train. Thyon continued to ease farther away as numerous scanners were being deployed trying to seek him out. He dared not to start up the main engines as it would give them away, and although he knew he could outrun the enemy, stealth and silence would serve them better to confuse the enemy.

Lorakit watched through the viewer as the ships faded away, just dots now in the distance. Thyon continued the slow retreat for another hour until satisfied that enough distance was between them. Turning the cloaked ship around he activated the first set of thrusters with a low signal ratio, and moved away faster and on course to the rendezvous point. Now four solar systems away he decloaked the ship, activated the main propulsion units and engaged full power. The craft was a blink of light and gone, now speeding through the galaxy. He looked at Lorakit.

"Damn that was a lot of ships to tag, and the size of them."

"Did you film it all, Thyon?"

"Yes, the whole thing. We can use the video to study all the ships better, especially the warships."

"I'm hungry babe. How about you?"

"Yes, I am starving. So, you have an answer for me?"

"Yes. I will be your love, Thyon." They both smiled as Lorakit made her way to prepare some food while Thyon piloted the ship, making sure they were not being followed. He thought, "I hope my sisters do as well as we did today."

Chapter Fifteen
An Old Friend, Family and the Council

The lunch with Olis and Ezmull ended and Alex had conveyed more information that would be presented to the Council to give them a complete picture. The day drifted on into late afternoon. Still no reply from the Council. Olis suggested Alex take a break and perhaps go visit his old friend Derek. She would send him a message the minute she heard from the Council. The idea sounded good to Alex, so he bade his good-bye to both, then vaped and ported to the town where Derek lived and ran the local saloon for vets. Olis looked at her granddad.

"Grandfather, if just half of what Alex has shown us is true, the Elior and all our friends could be in jeopardy."

"Yes, granddaughter I know. The days of isolationism and peace have served us well, but on the other hand may have marked the beginning of our demise. It will take a great deal of effort and a bit of luck if we are to survive.

Alex arrived in the town where Derek lived and vaped out of his orb in front of the saloon. He had known Derek since first arriving on Elior over fifteen years ago. Derek had been a Viet Nam vet that the Elior had taken off the streets of despair on Earth, repaired all his medical conditions and eventually transported him to Elior. He was in charge of looking out for all the veterans now on Elior under Olisaria's guidance. Alex walked into the saloon hoping Derek was there.

True to form he saw Derek sitting on the far side of the bar chatting with a couple other vets. Alex made his way down the bar. Derek looked up from his conversation and saw Alex.

"Alex, long time no see. Welcome."

"Hello Derek, it is good to see you my old friend."

A Divided Universe

"Have a seat. These two old sods were leaving anyway. They both run similar saloons in other towns." Alex shook each of their hands as the two others greeted him before departing.

"Sit Alex, tell me how you have been." Derek ordered two beers and shots.

"I am well Derek. I just returned from many months of service under the Admiral."

"Still chasing the bad guys eh?"

"I guess you could call it that."

"Any luck?"

"That remains to be seen, my friend. The LuQuarin are very resourceful and elusive." The beers and shots arrived as the two men toasted, downing the shots and following them with a hefty swig of their beers.

"Damn, been a long time since I did one of those. I think the first time we met we did these in Ventura."

"Your memory serves you well, Alex."

"How are your ladies and children, Derek?"

"They are well and growing up fast. My son from Sirianna is almost fifteen now and my daughter from Chunhua only a month behind. I had a second child with Chunhua, a boy who is now twelve. They call me uncle, but are of an age now where they know I am their father, but honor their mother's lifestyle. It has all worked out well."

"So, fatherhood/uncle suits you well then?"

A Divided Universe

"Yes Alex, it has been a wonderful experience and they're all great kids. So how are your kids these days?"

"AJ and Xia are entering the academy and recently turned eighteen. Thyon, Kira and Tira just recently visited me when I was at the Admirals command center. They have been galivanting around the galaxies since they left Elior."

"Jesus, that's right. They left when they were but six months old or so."

"Yes, my friend, but few know of their existence or their powers. It would scare to many if they knew the truth." Alex shifted in his seat and ordered another round for them. A minute later they arrived and Alex took his shot and downed it, followed by chugging half of his beer.

"Damn Alex, take it easy lad." Derek saw that look in Alex's face he had seen before and knew something was troubling his much younger friend.

"What is it Alex, what is bothering you?"

"I have a question for you."

"Sure Alex, shoot away."

"Life here on Elior is like a dream come true, is it not?"

"Yes, Alex it is. There is peace and harmony among all, there is no disease, no pollution, no conflict, need I go on, you know all of this. Why do you ask?"

Alex shifted again in his seat, uncertain if he should tell Derek about the impending peril that could destroy all life on Elior.

"Derek, what would you do if the life here you know was threatened and could possibly disappear?" Without hesitation Derek answered.

A Divided Universe

"If anything, ever threatened this world or our people I would stand up and prepare to fight and give my life if necessary to defend it."

"I have no doubt of that my dear friend."

"Is that something I should be concerned about?"

"It is now a possibility. The years of isolationism and a strictly defensive posture have made us vulnerable."

"I don't see how Alex. We have the entire planet covered in a neural net and our defense technology is better than any known enemy. Every major city and town has a shield that can be put in place in just a matter of moments. Our military is very strong, although much smaller these days. What could possibly threaten our planet?" Again, Alex shifted in his seat, uncomfortable that he had opened the door and now had his friend worried.

"Alex, whatever it is you know, I hope you will share it with me. If you ask I will keep it just between us, you have my word."

"Thank you. It is a very complicated situation and that is why I have returned. I am waiting for a meeting with the Council to bring them up to date."

"Is it the LuQuarin?"

"Yes, and more. We may have little time to prepare before an attack may occur. I can tell you more after I meet with the Council and see what they may or may not do. Forgive me my friend for keeping you blind to the details. Perhaps there is a solution to this matter that will alleviate this concern for all. I do not want to be premature and cast an alarm if it is not justified."

"OK Alex, I understand. Let me tell you this. There are over 50,000 veterans on this planet from many nationalities. Some of us were enemies at one time and have all experienced the horrors of war, killing, seeing our brothers and sisters die for a cause we believed in at the time. The Elior gave us a new life, healed our wounds, both physical and mental. We educated ourselves to understand that we were puppets doing the bidding of others, their greed and lust for power. Now those that used to be enemies are friends and we live united as once race which we call human. I can speak for all veterans here on Elior. If Elior was ever threatened we would unite and fight to defend our freedom, liberty, families, friends and a way of life that all should have. We range in age from forty to over ninety now, but the life here makes us younger than our age may show. If necessary we would gladly take up arms again to defend this life and the preservation of our species and others."

"Thank you, Derek, I know you would. Let's hope that it doesn't come to that." He smiled at Derek and patted him on the shoulder as soldiers do.

"You must keep this to yourself. I will return and see you after I have met with the Council and perhaps I can share more with you at that time. Let us just enjoy each other's company for now, and talk about more pleasant things, if we may."

"Of course, my friend. How about another shot and beer for old times' sake?"

"Sounds good. How often do you meet with Olis?

"Only once a month now, as there are few matters that need attention, most of which are trivial in nature. They did approve the veterans to have a 12" slow pitch softball league. There is one for 40-55 and another for over 55. We had one stadium built and it's a hell of a lot of fun. We draw quite an attendance. The Elior seem to enjoy watching a bunch of old humans' whack a round object around with a stick." Alex laughed.

"How is Olisaria's daughter Alett?"

"She hardly sees her anymore as Alett has been on tour visiting all of our friends' planets. I understand she is part of a team to shore up their defenses against biologics, chemical or nuclear weapons as part of a precautionary design the Council approved. Alett is a genius in biochemistry and you know she completed all the work that Kate was involved with."

"It is good to hear the Council approved such measures."

"They felt it prudent after what happened on Earth and then the attack here. I also understand they expanded the clone armies on all the planets, something like two million of our clone soldiers are now active at each with only a few real personnel to command."

"Seems the Council has been doing more than I was aware of."

"Alett sends her mother a long message every few weeks or so as she bounces from one planet to another. Last I heard she was heading to Galan for her final stop before returning to Elior."

"Galan is such a nice planet and the people there are fun to be with."

"She timed it to be there when they celebrate a worldwide holiday. You know the Galanians love to celebrate."

"That they do indeed." Alex laughed. They continued to talk for another hour. With the dinner hour approaching Alex headed home to eat with Diana and the kids. He bade his friend good-bye and headed home still wondering when the Council would summons him.

At home he found Diana sun bathing on the deck in a skimpy bikini. He approached her, bending over and was met with a warm kiss.

"Hi sailor, was hoping you'd come home for dinner." Alex looked at her and felt the stirrings within. She saw the look on his face.

"How about a quickie, my husband, before the kids come home from school? I need to get the oil off my body and perhaps you could help me in the shower?"

A Divided Universe

"Lead the way, my love."

Alex emerged from the bedroom forty-five minutes later in his cargo shorts and a tee. He found AJ and Xia sitting out on the deck and surmised they had come home a little early and discovered their parents were involved in the bedroom. He walked out as if nothing had happened.

"How about we grill down at the beach and have a big bonfire tonight? Your mother has invited her sister and their tribe as well as your grandparents. If you want, call up some of your friends and have them join us."

"Sounds good, dad." Replied AJ. Alex saw his daughter chuckling.

"What is it, Xia?"

"You and mom amaze us."

"How is that?"

"I know you're not old dad, but you and mom have more amorous activities than any of our friends' parents. It's all good dad, don't get me wrong." Alex laughed.

Go call your friends and let's all have a wonderful dinner and time at the beach tonight." They both nodded and sent messages to their friends.

Alex and Diana set up the portable tent, table, and chairs with glow light so they could enjoy dinner near the beach. Alex orbed out a giant BBQ grill they kept in storage for such occasions. Alex then added a large bonfire pit out on the sand which looked like real wood burning but was simply just another Elior technological wonder. Diana set the table, adding a tray of fruit and seafood to go with the fish Alex would be grilling. Her sister, husband and their two kids arrived, followed by Diana's' parents. A few minutes later AJ and Xia returned each having two friends in tow. Diana added a portable music player now emitting tropical island music. The sun was setting in the distance as Alex lit up the torches around the tent. Everyone was talking and enjoying the impromptu mini dinner beach excursion. AJ, Xia and their friends were out on the beach around the bonfire as Alex retrieved the fish filets for the grill. It was a perfect setting as Alex took in what was around him, smiling and relishing the moment. Diana and her sister did the final touches of displaying various foods, laughing and giggling as sisters do. Her parents were sitting in beach lounge chairs and sipping on tropical drinks.

The evening progressed as they all enjoyed the food, drinks and now a starlit sky. The bonfire was blazing with the young adults sitting around and playing music. Xia's friends brought their wooden instruments and played for their enjoyment. After dinner Alex had taken a seat next to Diana at the edge of the tent just listening to the younger ones continue to play with one girl singing a sort of blues folksy song, her voice captivating and beautiful.

A small messenger disk appeared next to Alex. Diana frowned as he opened it. It was from the Council. They had set an emergency meeting to meet with Alex at midnight and provided the coordinates. Alex closed the message and looked at Diana. She knew the look and returned it with sad eyes.

"I will need to get ready in a half hour and don't know how long I will be gone."

"I understand. Am glad we could do this tonight. Everyone is having a good time and we are all together."

"Yes, my dear wife. These are the moments that bring true meaning to our lives." Alex grabbed Diana's hand and just held it as they sat and looked out on their children and the others. As they held hands Diana could feel Alex was making the mental transition, from father and husband to soldier and bearer of the Medallion. She could feel his anxiety and concern and wondered what could be so troubling to make him feel this way. The time passed quickly and Alex stood up, walked out to the bonfire and said his good-byes to AJ, Xia and their friends. He came back to the tent area and did the same with Diana's sister, husband, kids and grandparents. Last, he embraced and kissed his wife, no words needed to be spoken. Turning, he headed to the house to change and then port to the coordinates he was given.

Arriving at the coordinates, now vaped from his orb, Alex sensed he was deep underground. An arched hallway lay before, twelve feet tall and only six feet wide, paved a path twenty yards distant where two guards stood in front of a doorway. Alex smiled knowing the arched hallway was an advanced scanning device he would pass through to ensure that it was truly he, Alex. He walked down the pathway and was in front of the guards. They nodded and opened the door to let him in. As he entered the door closed behind him and opened up into a large conference room. The nine Council members were seated at a curved table, Deloria the head of the Council at the center. On the far right was Olisaria. He stepped in front of the table, bowed and greeted the Council. Deloria spoke.

"Alex, it is good to see you as it has been many months since you were last with us here on Elior. We have agreed to meet with you based on Olisaria's message."

"Thank you."

"You may present to us if you are ready."

"Yes I am." Alex took his information disk and stepped back, inserting it into the control panel on a small table with a chair next to it. He started the program and a large video came to life in front of the Council.

"This first part is Thyon's' ship cloaked in orbit of Brepnid." The video began. It showed the hundreds of LuQuarin, Blisscrell and Thornok warships descending down to the planet and opening fire on numerous Brepnid cities. There was return fire but it was short lived as all the Brepnid defenses were taken out. The Council watched closely as Thyon used several cameras that zoomed down towards the surface and showed the gripping details of the massive destruction the offenders were inflicting on the planet and the Brepnid people. Twenty minutes into it the Flemjots with Secarios transports entered the atmosphere dispersing the millions of ground troops for the final invasion. The video ended. Alex continued.

"It was the invasion of Brepnid that was the deciding factor that Thyon, Kira and Tira would no longer remain neutral to the ongoing conflict with the LuQuarin, their allies and the rest of the known galaxies. After Brepnid they sought me out. They have some type of advanced sensory abilities that they can locate me should they choose to do so. They caught up with me only two days after the attack at the Admiral's command center. Deloria spoke.

"Alex, such sensory abilities are well beyond anything we have ever known. What other abilities do they possess?"

"I did not have enough time with them to learn those details, but I suspect they can do all of the things I can with the Medallion, Gauntlet and more." They have exceptional computer, math, encryption skills, and a large space craft which is faster than our SSSTS. It was their encryption abilities that aided and sped up the process of the information captured by one of our agents that was living among the Secarios. She risked her life to get it to us."

"Hold on, Alex." Deloria continued. "You said one of our agents living among what we now know as part of the enemy?"

"Yes."

"For how long?"

"She was living among them for fourteen years disguised as one of them, and had worked her way up high in the social system providing access and privilege to many things." Deloria stood up.

"Damn that Admiral. When he asked us permission to set up a division for special agents, we denied his request. Apparently, he took matters into his own hands. This is a direct violation of the Councils orders. Who is running this agency for him?"

A Divided Universe

"Stilzen."

"I see. We should have known he would defy our directives. The Admiral has been running around the galaxies for fifteen years now. We have sent him supplies, new ships, and replaced many of the troops over that time. How are we supposed to listen to one of our leading military men now when the interests of this Council and planet are not adhered to?"

"Deloria, if I may continue, I think you will find that the Admiral acted in the best interest of the Elior and all peaceful species." Deloria took a few paces back and forth, her anger evident. Finally, she sat back down.

"All right Alex, we will let you continue, but be careful where you tread with this. This Council elected to take a position after the attack on our planet and we have lived in peace since that day. We elected to only maintain and assist those planets and species from the past and would no longer act as the police force or enforcers of peace to all planets and galaxies. The logistics to do so was simply not possible. Yes, we feel a sadness for the Brepnids, and others out there who may have suffered the same fate, but Elior comes first. Do you understand?"

"Yes, Deloria." Alex reactivated the disk and a new video appeared of three adjoining galaxies. As the video played Alex talked, walking around to explain each part, pointing out enough details to paint the picture of what was occurring. The Council watched intensely as the LuQuarin plan unfolded, the size, scope and depth of all the resources being put into position and would soon bear down with the destruction of Elior as the end goal. Alex took over an hour before the video ended. The room was silent. Alex, now standing before the nine-member Council continued.

"From what we now know the LuQuarin and others already have in place some of the resources destined for an attack on Elior with more in transit as we speak. The Admiral, his fleet and with the aid of Thyon, Kira and Tira were working on a plan to at least try and slow them down to give us time to decide what course of action would be best. The Admiral knows he cannot take an offensive position or initiate a war, that he has held true

113

to. I don't believe any of us wants a war, but the facts suggest we may not have any choice soon. We all have enjoyed the peace and wonderful life here on Elior and our friends on many planets have enjoyed the same. It is most unfortunate that the forces of good are once again being threatened by all that is evil. I fear if we do not act swiftly and with haste that Elior's fate may be sealed. If Elior were to fall, there would be little to stop the LuQuarin from conquering anything and everything that stood before them. Understand this; the LuQuarin do not want to conquer Elior, they want to exterminate us and any others that align themselves to our cause. This Council and its' members hold a great responsibility and have always acted in the best interest of Elior and many others by fighting the LuQuarin and restoring, preserving peace and harmony. The days of isolationism are coming to the end. Whether you choose to fight now or wait is for all of you to determine." Alex sat back down in his chair. Deloria spoke.

"Alex. This Council will continue this meeting and discuss what you have presented to us this night. No doubt the Admiral is looking for an answer as soon as possible. Let us talk among ourselves. We will summons your return when we have an answer. We are thankful for all your service, your unique powers and abilities and know that you are dedicated and loyal to the Elior way of life. Go now and get some rest and spend time with your family." Alex stood, the meeting over. He bowed to the Council, turned and left the room. He ported back home and went out onto the deck with a beer and a bottle of Southern in his hands. Sitting down he looked up and out to the night sky over the ocean and pondered whether had he done enough with his presentation to the Council to convince them into action.

Chapter Sixteen
A Long-Awaited Freedom

Thyon sat at the command console looking out the front viewer now that they had exited hyperspace and were approaching the rendezvous point. It was on a small moon of the planet just one solar system away from the human slave encampment the LuQuarin had. He landed his ship on the base where the Admiral had sent the rescue team and forces they would be using for the mission. Departing the ship with Lorakit they made their way to the small command center used to finalize the plans. Inside they were met by a Major Lindor and his team.

"How did it go, Thyon?"

"Perfect, we tagged and immobilized the entire convoy of transports without incident. They are floating around useless for the time being to our enemy." Thyon heard a familiar voice.

"I would expect nothing less from my nephew." Thyon turned and saw his Uncle Matt, who was the Commander of the special ops team that would be going in on the rescue mission.

"Uncle Matt, it is good to see you." They shook hands.

"Damn Thyon, you are quite the sizeable man."

"Good genetics, Uncle."

"Your mother would be proud of you."

"I hope so uncle, she was a fine woman that gave my sisters and me life. It was sad when she perished on Ventura. I wish I could have known her better."

"She is within you Thyon and a part of you and your sisters."

A Divided Universe

"So, uncle, you will be leading the sniper team to take out all the guards when we attack to create the diversion we need?"

"Yes Thyon, as soon as you disable all their warships and our underground orbs are all in place. We have 200 transport orbs which can each hold fifty humans. As long as there are no more than 10,000 prisoners to rescue we should be good. Once the ships are disabled my teams will take out all the surrounding guard towers and defense systems protecting the shields. We will bombard the shields even though we will not be able to penetrate past the third level but should keep them occupied. Our underground orb teams already have the tunnels built and will first enter the compound on all four sides simultaneously and take out any guards or resistance quickly. We will then send in the larger rescue orbs to begin to assemble the prisoners, put bracelets on them and get them in the orbs. Our recon teams will then seize and take down the shields from the inside control room. That will provide a clear path up and out of the compound for all the orbs directly to our ships in orbit. With no available ships to transport their troops the LuQuarin will not have the time or ability to launch a counter attack. We should be able to get in and out quickly with minimum risk to loss of life."

"Excellent, uncle. Major, when do we begin the assault?"

"In just under four hours, when it is the middle of the night there and they keep only a minimum force on duty. Our transport time to the planet is only a half-hour. Once we return back here we have been ordered to shut this base down and get all the evacuees back to our main base. There we will have transport ships standing by equipped with medical facilities to transport them all back to Elior. We have consoles set up on the command ship to stream live every aspect of the operation. Our command ship will have eyes on the encampment and all the LuQuarin forces. Matt's group will also be streaming, and the four rescue teams will be providing real time video. I would like to add a set of consoles on your ship, Thyon, so you can see what is going on as we see it. If you could stream back to us we should be able to view the entire operation and make any adjustments to our plan as needed."

116

A Divided Universe

"I agree Major, please have them installed on my ship. I will need the additional disruptor charges if you have them. We burned up a majority of the supply we had on board." Major Lindor spoke.

"Yes, Thyon we have them here for you and I will have my men get them to your ship right away and install the monitors."

"Thank you, Major."

It was the middle of the night and Karen, sitting on her cot, wide awake after returning from the bathroom. She thought of her home when she was just a teen back on Earth. The memories brought a smile to her face. "So long ago." She whispered.

There was a sound down at the end of the corridor and then a few flashes of light. She stepped up to the bars on her cell to see better and listened. More strange sounds and flashes, then two thuds. She saw lights rushing down the corridor and the sounds of cells being opened up and hushed words, human words being spoken. More lights and people running, talking. Since she was at the far end of the corridor she still could not see what was going on, just lights flashing, cells opening and hushed talking. Her roommate had woken up and was standing next to her.

"What is it, Karen?"

"I don't know." She looked at her cellmate and saw fear in her eyes. Their hearts were racing, uncertain of what was approaching. They heard the cell next to them open and a human voice.

"We are here to rescue you, please remain silent and do as you are asked. You will be out of here and safe within a few minutes. Put these bracelets on, quickly." Karen heard another strange sound, a slight buzzing followed by a vapor cloud forming and then disappearing. Suddenly a human combat soldier stood in front of her cell, unlocking the door. He smiled and repeated what they had just heard. With the door open they stepped outside and were handed a bracelet.

A Divided Universe

"Put them on, quickly, we don't have much time." Karen put the bracelet on her left wrist and felt the soldier's hand touch the center of it. A strange sensation immediately entered her body and in the blink of an eye she found herself inside a large round object with many other prisoners standing all around. A second later her roommate appeared next to her. They all heard a voice.

"Please sit down on the floor and grab one of the handles there. We will have you in a safe place in a minute." Everyone sat down, and as they did she saw a tall humanoid creature at the front of the circular room at a control panel. She heard him say,

"OK that's fifty, I am out of here." The room vibrated and a second later she could feel the sensation of moving fast, a kaleidoscope of colors enveloping the outside part of the structure. It lasted only two minutes and the vibration and sense of speed stopped.

"OK, you can all stand up now." Everyone rose to their feet, all were female.

"Now listen and do as I ask. Once you do, you will find yourself outside this ship and in a medical receiving facility aboard our transport ship. There you will be greeted and attended to. I know this is all very strange, but you are safe now and out of the LuQuarins control. Each of you is wearing a bracelet. On the one side of it you will feel/see a very small circle protruding out slightly. Press on it two times whenever you are ready."

One by one the women did as he asked, and Karen saw them vaporize into a small cloud of energy and then disappear.

What the hell, why not." She heard herself say. Again, the strange feeling and she reappeared in a large area of what seemed to be a huge spaceship. The other women she was with formed around her, they appeared in small clouds of dust and energy. She could see the looks of shock and awe on their faces. Up on a platform above the group stood a human female dressed in a military uniform. They all looked up at her as she began.

"I am Captain Alianna. You are safe now and aboard a ship that will take you to a new home, free from slavery. I know you are all scared and don't realize what has happened. Simply put you have been rescued by a friendly race and humans from Earth that assisted us. If anyone needs immediate medical attention let us know. There are many here that will help you. Don't be alarmed by their size, they will not harm you in any way. They are known as Elior and are the best friends any human could ever ask for. Are there any children among you?" A woman in the front cried out.

"We all have children, many of them, but they are taken away from us as soon as they are weened. We never get to see them after that."

"OK." Alianna said. "We will find them if they are there, and bring them to safety. Now, if you are not hurt or need any medical attention please move forward and to the left in a line. We need to get your names and run you through a decontamination tunnel. It will be like taking a nice warm shower. At the end of the tunnel you will be provided towels and clothing of your choice, which I think you will discover to be a nice experience. After you are clothed we will be providing food and beverages in a large cafeteria style setting. Please show a little patience as we have a lot of you just rescued today, but I can assure you that you all will be well taken care of. After you have eaten, we are asking you to come to an auditorium and watch a brief film which will explain what has happened and where you will be going. This is a day of joy for all of us, now that you are free from the LuQuarin. There will be additional attendants available to address any specific needs you may have. We will be setting up sleeping quarters for all of you before the journey to your new home. So, unless you are in need of immediate help please move forward and to the left. You will be guided through the entire process." Alianna stepped off the platform and retrieved her headset.

"This is Alianna on the first rescue transport to command central."

"Go ahead, this is command central."

"We have just been informed that there are hundreds of children somewhere down there."

"Very well, we will inform the rescue teams and advise."

"Thank you." She clicked off her headset.

Karen could hear several women talking quietly as the crowd moved forward. A line was formed at the corner of the room and a tall Elior female speaking perfect English, Spanish, Chinese or whatever the native language was for that human, guided them through the entrance one by one after getting their name. There were at least five hundred in the crowd, almost all women from many cultures back on Earth. It took a half hour before Karen had reached the front of the line. The 7' Elior female was in a tight-fitting body suit of teal, bald, with a beautiful face and features and glowing emerald eyes. Karen gave her name when asked and added her rank and previous position before being captured on Earth. The Elior female thanked her, then directed her to step on a moving conveyor walkway. As Karen stepped onto it moving forward she reached an entrance to a white tunnel. There she was asked to strip down. She had little clothing on as it was, which smelled from many days of wear, so without hesitation she ripped her clothes off tossing them into a barrel, then back on the moving walkway leading into the tunnel. True to form it was like taking a nice hot shower, all the dirt and grime she had grown accustomed to was washed away. By the time she reached the end she felt cleaner than she could remember, totally refreshed. Even her long hair was clean and without tangles. She was handed two towels and led into a sitting area where there were at least twenty attendants at consoles, each having a human sitting next to them. Taking a seat on a bench with others waiting, she watched in awe as they selected their clothes on a monitor and a minute later were wearing what they had selected.

"Matt and his men had taken out all the guard posts outside the encampment and then had gone in to assist with the rescue. He had just put the bracelet on the last woman in the section of the compound, vaped and ported her with the others. He heard on his headset that another team had taken control of the enemy's' communications center and shield controls. The defensive shields now above the compound had been lowered making it easier for the extraction orbs to leave. His team moved farther into the complex, killing more LuQuarin guards. Now in front of a large door that was sealed he gave the order to blow it open. A small charge was placed on it and seconds later the handle and lock had been blown off. Two of his men entered. The sounds of laser fire were heard as Matt followed, his weapon at the ready. Two more LuQuarin guards were down just inside the entrance to a large cavern that was dimly lit. His men had five female LuQuarin attendants who had raised their hands to surrender up against a wall and were binding their hands behind their backs. Matt's jaw dropped. The left side of the room had numerous chairs, and he counted eight human females nursing their babies. In the middle section were rows and rows of cribs containing more infants, some now crying. Farther in were more pens and children perhaps eight months and older. Beyond that were more children from the ages of one to four or five. His men secured the area and bound up more LuQuarin females. Matt proceeded down to the right, finding cots with children five on up to fourteen or so in age. Many of the younger ones were crying, others in shock and a state of fear. Matt got on his com-line to the command ship.

"Give me the Major please."

"This is the Major, go ahead Matt.

"You're not going to believe this but we have hundreds of children down here, from newborns on up, and mothers nursing babies. Transporting them is a problem. Please provide instructions as to how we should extract."

He heard the Major say. "Holy Shit. Get me our senior medical officer, stat. Hold on Matt, will advise in a minute." His six-member team was positioned around the room, now noisy with crying. A minute later he heard,

A Divided Universe

"Matt, I am sending down our medical officer and her team to assist you. Give me your coordinates." Matt complied. A minute later four light blue orbs appeared and the medical team vaped out. The lead medical officer was named Rose. She quickly assessed the situation and gave her team instructions. Then to Matt,

"OK, I am going to have my team give all the newborns and toddlers a sedative. We will then put bracelets on each and begin to port them in our orbs which are set up better to handle this. Then we will get the younger children out. I need you to go the nursing mothers' and explain to them the situation and then get them out of here, mother and child as one port in your regular orbs. Add to those the older children. I will request more special orbs as you need them."

"OK Rose, but we need to hurry, I don't know how long we have before a possible counter attack by the LuQuarin."

"Understood." The room slowly grew quieter as the crying infants were sedated and ported out. Two of his men helped with the other children. It took twenty minutes before the room had been emptied. Thyon contacted Matt.

"How are you doing down there, almost done?"

"We're gaining on it Thyon. What's the situation up there."

"The LuQuarin have launched two counter attacks, but we have been able to destroy all incoming ships so far. They now are moving in from east and west with ground assault vehicles and troops behind them. The major has sent down two groups of our fighters and they are engaging them now. How much more time do you need?"

"I don't know Thyon, each new chamber we enter we find more humans of all ages. We are about to enter the next chamber."

"Understood, I have heard the same from the other three assault teams. It is a huge complex. Keep me posted."

"Ten-four."

Matt's team found another doorway and blew it open. Here they discovered a handful of men, chained to the walls. They were quickly unshackled and ported away. He checked with his other teams and received a progress report. The evacuation was going well. He turned on his scanner searching for signs of any more human life forms. His team found a corridor. The scan showed more life forms fifty yards distant. His team ran down the tunnel and positioned themselves outside another chamber door. Once again, they blew it open and proceeded in weapons at the ready. Inside there were approximately forty adult humans both male and female. The difference was they were all obese, from overweight and fat to extremely obese. He walked up to a female probably weighing over 250 lbs.

"What is your name?"

"I am Lydia."

"Well Lydia we are going to get you all out of here and to safety. You are no longer prisoners of the LuQuarin. Just follow our instructions."

"OK." Matt signaled his men to use more transport orbs. He called up to the Major on the command ship and informed him. Once complete they scanned the area for any more survivors. The area was clear. He checked with all the other units. They reported the same, no more human life signs were being picked up. The order came from the Major for all teams to leave. A LuQuarin counter attack was approaching. Matt gave the order and his team vaped and ported back to the command ship.

Thyon had been listening in to all the teams as they reported and watching the progress on the live streaming videos. One by one they left the compound in quick fashion. Thyon was positioned right above the main structure, its' shields down and watched the approaching enemy forces from the east and west. He gave the order for the fighters to return to base aboard their respective ships. Positioning his ship to the west he opened up another control panel. A long protruding weapon emerged from the front of the ship. Lorakit watched as he hit a few switches and then a red one. The ship shook, as a massive coned shaped blast emerged from the gun directly at the oncoming LuQuarin forces. When it hit the whole front line took the impact and was melted down to almost nothing. He turned the ship around to the east and fired again.

Lorakit's eyes opened wide as she witnessed a thousand troops and vehicles melt away. The troops and vehicles behind the first wave stopped and then quickly retreated.

"What the hell is that, Thyon?"

"Oh, just something my sisters and I designed and developed should we ever be greatly outnumbered. Pretty effective eh?"

"No doubt of that."

"Time for us to leave. The rescue has been completed." Thyon maneuvered the ship up and headed out of the atmosphere and was alongside the command ship a minute later orbiting the planet. The Major gave the order and all the ships turned and headed away from what once was a LuQuarin slave encampment. Lorakit saw Thyon smile, seeing the elation of what they had just accomplished on his face. The small fleet of ships was now speeding through the galaxy towards the Admiral's main base of operations.

Chapter Seventeen
Galan

Alett sat at the back table of Triginor's establishment. It was another beautiful day on Galan, the sun shining with blue skies, a light breeze.

It was mid-morning and Alett was working on her portable, setting up the final array of sensors dispersed all over the planet to detect when toxic substances were present and set off the alarms now in place to warn the citizens. They were being programmed directly to what they called sweepers, large crafts that could come in quickly and neutralize the threat, offering additional protection if ever attacked by such means.

Galan was the last installation. Alett and her team completed the seven other planets previously attacked by the LuQuarin over the past 800 years. All that remained was to send out a communication to all the citizens of Galan and then run a test. If the sirens went off they would need to follow instructions and get as quickly as they could to the underground bunkers that had been installed.

Alett sat back and looked out through to the open area of the large tiki hut to the docks and waterways that lay in the distance. She could see a few small sails, fishing craft heading towards the open sea, and a few birds flying. She took a sip of her OBJ. A handful of workers outside set up additional tents and food stands to be used for the festival starting that evening. They would be celebrating a worldwide holiday, the anniversary of their freedom from the LuQuarin. It would be filled with music, food, spirits and fireworks display at all the main villages.

Triginor entered and sat down next to Alett, a tall OBJ already in hand.

"So Alett, are you almost finished?"

"Yes Trig, we will just need to send out a worldwide communication and then test it, so that your citizens will know the sound and what to do should a real event occur."

"Well, it's been fifteen years since we last saw a LuQuarin and all the reports I get from Elior tell me they have moved far away to another galaxy."

"True Trig, but the Council felt it important enough and with their stargate technology, the possibility for them to return does exist. Better to be safe than sorry."

"I guess you're right. How is your mother these days?"

"She is good last I heard. I try and send her messages each month and when I stay long enough in one place I get a message back. She still resides on the Council overseeing all human affairs on the planet, and is part of the defense ministry. It was her idea to set up these new defenses for all our friends since our military has shrunk in size.

Triginor got up and walked over to view the grassy area they used for a few vendors and the citizens of his village during the celebration. There were more workers now setting up additional tents, tables and BBQ stations over the grounds. As he was looking out, he heard the sound of fireworks launching, as they flew up into the air. The projectiles were going up a few hundred feet and then exploding.

"Damn kids." But instead of the beautiful colors fireworks make, the explosion created a massive cloud of yellow and gray dust.

"What the hell is that!" he shouted. Alett ran to his side, the alarm in his voice driving her instincts." When She saw the cloud now dispersing and moving inland due to the trade winds blowing.

"Triginor, we are going to need to run."

"Why?"

Alett dashed back to her portable and hit a few keys activating the sensors.

A Divided Universe

"We are in grave danger, Trig. Everyone needs to get to the shelters at once. Those clouds are biological and chemical agents and will kill anyone on contact."

"I must warn those out there working." Trig ran out into the grass area shouting to the workers. At the far side where the clouds had entered, people were dropping down to the ground like dead flies.

"Trig no! Come back!" Triginor continued to run forward yelling and shouting for everyone to run away from the strange clouds. More fell to the ground.

Alett pulled out her orb and ran after Trig. If she could get to him before the clouds she could save him. She stopped only 50 yards away. Trig had gone too far and now was at the dusty cloud. He grabbed his throat and fell. Alett her herself cry out. "NOOOOO!" The cloud continued to advance, the light breeze pushing it farther inland. No choice, she vaped up into her orb, and positioned it high and away from the advancing deadly agents. When she felt safe she used her portable, connecting it to the control panel in the orb and pulled up the entire array of sensors. She brought her hand to her mouth and gasped. The explosions were happening all over the planet. She linked her unit up to the main satellite in orbit and clicked it to send the alarm out over the entire network. Immediately the sirens started. She hit another link which would dispatch the five sweeper units to the most populated areas. Now looking down on her screen she witnessed the deadly agents spreading, knowing they would kill any life form they came in contact with. She contacted the satellite and had the officer in charge on the line.

"Dispatch our military units immediately. We are under attack worldwide. Look at your screens and you will see what is happening. You have to issue the order to dispatch all rescue units with our fighters. Galanians lives will be dependent on them. Hurry!" She held her hands to her head, tears rolling down. "What else can I do?"

The sweeper unit appeared out of the sky and moved down to the cloud of poisonous gases. It dispersed its' collection arms as it entered the cloud of yellow and gray, now activated it sucked in the death it represented. The large craft was operating at capacity, removing the biologic and chemical toxins and emitting a spray from the belly of the ship which would neutralize any particles below the ship and on the ground. Alett watched the mist fall to the surface, the moisture raining down on the dead Galanians below. She could see hundreds of fallen souls.

Alett contacted the main military base and asked to speak to the Commander. A minute later he was on the line.

"Alett, what is happening?"

"We have been attacked worldwide by toxic chemical and biological agents. I have sounded the sirens and all alarms and initiated the sweepers, of which all five are now trying to remove the gases. Have you dispersed our fighters to seek out whomever caused this?"

"Yes, they are sweeping the planet now, but we have yet to discover an enemy or how this was started."

"Do you have any hazmat teams?"

"We have a few, and I just gave the order for them to prepare and go out in rescue ships. If this is worldwide we won't have nearly enough."

"Do you have a lab there?"

"Yes, it is small but well equipped."

"Good, I am going to take my orb and draw samples from the clouds created by the explosions and am also starting to get data from the sweepers as to what they are collecting. As soon as I have my samples I will port to your lab to see what we are up against."

"OK Alett, I will have the lab ready and some assistants there for you."

A Divided Universe

"I will be there as soon as I can." Alett ended the conversation and moved her orb into the nearest ugly vapor cloud outside of the sweeper. Her orb was specially designed to extract samples from the air, land or oceans. She used her control panel and a tube emerged from the orb into the yellow and gray cloud. The instrument collected the vapors then sealed itself up in a container designed to handle toxic agents. She punched in the coordinates to the base and ported. Now on base outside the lab, she had the container sealed inside a second container as an extra precaution. She grabbed the cylinder and walked into the lab.

There were five attendants waiting for her as she walked in, leading her to the equipment to analyze the deadly agents. She placed the cylinder onto a special table which then covered the device with a clear seal proof top. Now at the control panel she slowly keyed in the instructions to first remove the outer cylinder, and then the second smaller one which held the elements that had caused several deaths. Carefully she extracted the components of the cloud into a tube which then went a detailed diagnostic scan down to the atomic level. The results and the formation of the elements came up on the viewer. She looked at the components, and realized there were three different toxins within the deadly mixture. The first was a chemical agent similar to others she had studied that resulted in almost immediate death to anyone who came in contact with it. Its' only weakness is it could not spread very far and lost the toxic effects to natural elements within a short period of time.

The second discovery was also a chemical weapon, deadly, but did so in a slower manner taking an hour or two before claiming the life of its' victim. It could disperse for a longer period of time and carry farther than the first agent.

The third was biologic, a virus that could remain airborne for days, weeks or even months under the right conditions. It would act slower on anyone it came in contact with, with symptoms that would not emerge for a day or two but would progress then on the body, slowly breaking down major functions and organs that would lead to death if untreated. Although the slowest of the three agents mixed in the deadly cocktail of clouds, this by far was the most dangerous. Unless an antidote could be found and injected into the victim, they too would perish in a slow and painful manner. Alett took her eyes from the screen as the Commander entered the room.

"What do we have Alett?"

"A very dangerous and perilous situation, Commander." She explained to him and the others what they were dealing with. Alett took a disk from her pack and placed it into the control panel.

"What's that?" Asked the Commander.

"It is a library of every known virus, bacteria or disease that we know of from many planets and decades of research. I am going to try and get a match if possible to the virus we have here to see if there is an antidote or vaccine we can provide to save lives. The disk opened up and a side by side viewer emerged on the display trying to match the virus on Galan they had just obtained samples of to a screen on the left which was going through thousands of entries to try and match it up. Time passed, and Alett and the others watched with intensity. In the end it displayed in red on the screen. "NO EXACT MATCH." They all heard Alett say "Shit." She then keyed information into the console.

"Now what?" An assistant asked.

"Now we expand the parameters to see if we can at least get a close match." The monitor again went into a rapid search mode. Another ten minutes passed before the pictures on the left stopped. Alett looked at it closely comparing the information of the virus on the left to the one they were dealing with.

"Damn!" she said. "It appears as if this virus has mutated, either on its' own or by science. She read more of the information now on the display.

"The virus on the left was the deadliest one ever on Earth. It was created in a laboratory but never used and had no known antidote or cure.

A Divided Universe

The one on the right is even more complex and appears it can adapt and mutate on its' own if necessary. At this point I don't know of any way we can stop it from infecting and killing any being that comes in contact with it. The only thing we can do at present is quarantine any area once the symptoms begin to appear which will be in a day or two. Commander, you will need to use your troops to segregate all villages from each other and then separate healthy individuals from any that show symptoms. Unless we can find a way to neutralize or stop it there will be little else we can do. With only five sweeper units operating on the whole planet, containing this could prove to be very difficult. I will begin working on a solution here in your lab and pray I can find one."

The Commander then addressed the whole group.

"I want all of you to assist Alett in any way you can. Use all our resources. I am going to send urgent messages to Elior and all the other planets that have been attacked in the past, and will include our video surveillance from our space station to show just what has happened here and the efforts we have undertaken to try and remove the threat that now plagues this planet. I will also request as much aid as Elior can send as quickly as possible. The entire population of Galan could now be in jeopardy. I must return to the command center but keep me posted on any new developments."

Alett also dispatched a private message to her mother, Olisaria, with what had occurred knowing the Council had grown conservative over the years and was hesitant to take action. Perhaps her mother could influence the Council of the gravity of the situation. She also requested more resources for lab work and testing as what they had on Galan was good but not enough for the work that lay ahead. Time was of the essence as millions of lives were at stake. She ended the note with her love and a prayer to those now suffering on Galan.

A Divided Universe

Chapter Eighteen
A Final Plea

Alex woke up, realizing he had fallen asleep on the deck, an empty bottle and beer cans next to him on the table. The sun was just rising in the distance. It would be another beautiful day on Elior. Feeling groggy after drinking more than he should have, he activated the Medallion to utilize the healing powers to sober up and get prepared for the day. He walked inside and ordered a restoration drink, downing it in a few chugs. No one was up yet, but would be soon. He headed to the shower hoping the Council would call for his presence soon and wanted to be ready at a moment's notice.

The day progressed and Diana and the kids had gone through the morning routine and were gone. Still no word from the Council

"Damn it! Don't they understand the gravity of the situation? How much discussion does it take to come to your senses that Elior is at serious risk?" The waiting was driving him crazy.

Olis returned home as the sun was rising. The Council met and reviewed all the information during the night until Deloria called for a break. They would re-convene at noon so all members could get rest. The Council appeared to be torn between taking serious action and activating all military assets versus maintaining the existing course in a defensive posture. She shook her head. If just half of what Alex had shown them was true, even Elior's advanced technology and defenses could not withstand the possible massive attack that may be coming. There had been a great deal of debate and even arguments over the choices the Council needed to make. The Council was at an impasse and one not likely to be easily resolved.

Two more days passed. Alex received messages from the Council that they were still reviewing all the information he had provided and needed more time to learn the depth and degree their enemies now appeared to possess.

A Divided Universe

Alex tossed the latest message aside, frustrated at the lack of action. It was afternoon and Alex just finished a long run on the beach. Sweating as he walked back up on the deck and looking back to the beach where the waves were gently rolling in, he stared out over the water looking for an answer that wasn't there. He could feel the anger boiling in his blood. Something needed to be done and now. But what? His hands were tied. The house was empty and he realized that Diana and the kids were keeping their distance from him sensing his ever-growing impatience and anger towards the Council.

A message disk appeared. It was from Olis. Alex opened it up and read. She received an urgent message from Alett on Galan. She didn't detail what the message said, but indicated that the contents may persuade the Council into action, and she was taking the information to the Council immediately. He final sentence was for Alex to be ready to meet with them at a moment's notice. He set the note down and wondered what happened on Galan that was more important than what he had presented to the Council. He went into the house to clean up and be ready as Olis had requested.

Another two hours passed as Alex paced back and forth on the deck. He was dressed in his finest uniform, the Medallion displayed on his chest, when the message disk appeared from the Council. He was to appear before them in a half-hour, the coordinates provided. The time seemed to pass at a snail's pace before it was time to go to the meeting. He vaped and ported to the coordinates. He found himself outside the original Council chambers he had been to in the past. The large waiting room led to the entrance where the Council presided. He approached the two guards standing at the entrance. Nodding, they opened the doors, stepped aside and motioned for him to go in. Inside the doors closed behind. It was the old curved head table in front of the room where the nine Council members were seated. He stepped forward and stopped five paces away from the center where Deloria sat.

"Alex, as you know we have been deliberating for over two days with the information you brought us. To be honest the Council is divided as to the correct course of action to take based on your information. However, we were just informed today of some horrific facts that have now swayed this Council to reconsider. Two days ago, Galan was attacked, not by conventional means but by chemical and biological weapons that carry the deadliest of consequences. The perpetrator is unknown but it appears to be of LuQuarin design. Thousands of Galanians are already dead and we fear more will have perished in the time it took to get the message to us. The resources we have there are doing everything within their power to combat the situation as best they can. As the Council has agreed upon, we are immediately going to dispatch aid and technology to Galan to hopefully negate and get under control the hardships they are facing."

"Setting that aside for the moment, we now have the looming question as to what to do with the threat you proposed is on its' way to Elior. At present it seems we have only the Admiral's battlegroup standing between us and the threat. As strong a force as the Admiral has of a million, it would not be able to stop the size of the force you say is gathering to attack us. The sheer numbers you painted and the alliances the LuQuarin have made is quite frightening. We brought in all our Generals yesterday and shared the information with them about the enemies' strength, size and numbers. It was well detailed, with the weaponry they possess, not just the LuQuarin, but the Blisscrell, Thornoks, Flemjots and Secarios. The only possible missing enemy alliance was that of the Lycoats. Lorakit in her briefings said the Lycoats were as dangerous as the LuQuarin, yet we found no real information about them, their size, strength or capabilities, yet she feared them the most. Is there any chance you have more information about the Lycoats?

"Council leader, Deloria. No, I do not. Only the information that Lorakit provided."

"To be honest Alex, this Council is having a hard time, given that all we have to make our decision on is based on one agent's theft of the Secarios systems. Could not this information have been provided to her as a ruse, that they wanted her to have it to bring back to us to create a fear amongst our people and lead this Council into action unnecessary or misdirected? To believe in one thing when the truth is actually another?"

135

"I find that hard to believe Council members. She had been among them for fourteen years, all the while risking her life to obtain information for the Elior cause."

"True, she is a loyal Elior, but the LuQuarin can be deceptive and cunning, so we cannot rule it out as a possibility. If this Council were to remobilize all our troops and fighting equipment, how can we be sure to deploy it in the most effective manner? The answer is we can't be sure. Initiating a complete remobilization would also set off fears and concerns among our population. To do so without further proof of our enemy's intentions would be reckless, and circumvent the governing we provide to our people. Simply put Alex, in order for this Council to come to unanimous agreement we will need to validate and vet the information provided."

"Even after what just happened on Galan? You want more proof?"

"Yes Alex, that is what this Council is asking for." Alex's temper grew and he took a few steps back and forth before answering.

"The risk you are willing to take by waiting to validate this could cost the lives of many Elior and the fate of this planet. Failure to act now, or no decision can be worse than even a wrong decision. You must at least consider mobilizing our military and prepare a better defense than the one in place. The people of Elior have a right to know what they may be facing."

"I am sorry Alex, to do so would create an unnecessary panic."

"Then I have wasted my time and yours, dear Council. Evil will succeed only when good men do nothing. You have opened up the door for evil to come to our homeland and destroy all that has been built over the millenniums."

"That is enough!" Deloria standing, shouting to Alex. They stared at each other, anger in both sets of eyes. Finally, Alex spoke in a calm directed manner.

A Divided Universe

"I thank the Council for at least hearing me out and considering the information provided. I will leave the matters of governing this planet and the people to you, but wish to return back to the Admiral with all haste to let him know your position. As well, we will look for validation and provide it to you once obtained. So, unless you need anything else I will be on my way."

Deloria nodded. Alex bowed and left the room.

Alex ported home and found Diana and the kids had just finished dinner and were sitting out on the deck talking. He walked in and greeted them, kissing Diana on the forehead as he passed by. Retrieving a drink, he returned and sat with them. He caught up with AJ and Xia about the academy before they excused themselves to do homework. It was just the two of them now sitting on the deck and enjoying the starlit sky. Diana knew that Alex was troubled. She came over and sat on his lap.

"What is it Alex?" He remained silent but drew Diana into his arms before speaking.

"I must leave my love and return to the Admiral and his battlegroup."

"Why? You just got here a few days ago."

"The Council has made their decision and I must bring the news to the Admiral."

"Can you tell me what is happening?"

"Not really. Let me say that I do not agree with the Council and leave it at that. I have to depart in a few minutes. My clone will return in my place shortly."

"When will you return?"

"I honestly don't know. Hopefully soon, with the information the Council has requested.

A Divided Universe

Diana knew better than to push him for more information. He was a soldier now transformed from the man that was her husband. She hugged him tight as tears flowed from her eyes. Alex held her, hating the need to leave her to travel back out into space. But the necessity to confront and stop the evil that threatened Elior and his family resided deep in his soul. A message disk appeared. It was from Olisaria. Diana got up so he could read the disk.

"Alex. The vote in the Council was 5 to 4. Deloria has just enough support for the position taken. There are those of us who disagreed and wanted to take a different course of action. I will be meeting with all our military commanders tomorrow to see what else we may do to prepare for the LuQuarin threat. Also, I need to inform you about the make-up of our military. With peace reigning over the past 15 years many of those serving have been replaced by clones when their terms of service were up. Shuttles and transports are regularly run between Elior and the Admiral's fleet replacing equipment, supplies and technology as it improves. Personnel also have been replaced, and with our newest cloning techniques a large number of the Admiral's manpower is now made up of clones. The Council elected to take this approach and make the offer to those serving as they returned to Elior. Based on the information I have, approximately 60% of his forces are now clones. The Council feels that in this way the fleet still maintains the same capabilities, while offering a home life to those that have served Elior. Be safe on your journey." It was signed Olis.

Alex stood and then embraced Diana.

"I must go now, my lovely wife. He kissed her and held her tight for a minute, then broke the embrace. Together they walked in the house so Alex could retrieve his clone and gather a few things. Ten minutes later he said good-bye, vaped and ported to the base where an SSSTS awaited.

Chapter Nineteen
The Fury of Tenekaris

Two days passed since the celebration ended. Tenekaris emerged from his private chambers and sat in a chair in the adjoining room. He took the giant mug that sat on the table next to it and chugged down the rest of his LuQ grog. Laughing he got up and went to the door, opened it to where the two guards were standing.

"Find Eftar for me and bring a stretcher." The guards nodded and left to do his bidding. He walked back into the sitting room drinking more grog. Eftar showed up a few minutes later followed by the guards with a stretcher in hand.

"Yes Master, what is it you wish?"

"Take the Secarios female and get her out of here. Clean the bitch spy up, and prepare her for a long-range auto-pilot shuttle, and put the others in it. Program it for the nearest Elior outpost we know of. Then get chamber maids in here to clean this place up.

"Yes Master. I must inform you that all three of your Queens have returned.

"What, why?"

"They informed me it is a matter of urgency and need to speak with you at once."

"Damn! Get my personal attendants in here then too and tell my Queens' that I will meet with them in an hour."

"Yes Master, as you wish."

Eftar ordered the guards to retrieve the Secarios female and put her on the stretcher. The listless, naked and scarred body was quickly removed from Tenekaris chambers, Eftar in the lead as they walked out. Two

A Divided Universe

LuQuarin female attendants were there a minute later to assist Tenekaris is preparation to meet his Queens. Three chamber maids also entered heading into the private area to clean up after the Master and the tortuous hours spent with the female Secarios.

Forty-five minutes later Tenekaris left his private chambers area, dressed immaculately to meet with his three Queens. They would be in the great hall where his throne and theirs awaited. His two guards followed as he walked down the long hallway, finally reaching the entrance area to the great room where he presided over matters of importance. He walked to the front and sat down on his throne made of gold, his two guards taking up station on both sides and behind him. Within five minutes Eftar entered the room leading a procession of his three Queens and their consorts. They reached the front of the room and stood before Tenekaris. He stood and walked over to them. One by one he gave them each a small embrace after they had bowed to their King and Master. He motioned for them to sit on their thrones, their consorts stepping back and to the side. Eftar took a position to the right side and back from his Master.

"So, my Queens. What is it that brings you here? All three of you should be back and running your encampments after our celebration and restocking our personal encampment here."

The first Queen in the middle of the other two spoke first.

"Master Tenekaris III, all three of us did return to the compounds to attend to our duties. However, when we got there we were shocked and horrified by what we found. All of our guards and workers were either dead or seriously wounded. All of the prisoners were gone, not a trace of even one. We were met by the Commander of the military stationed there. He provided us with a surveillance video of what had occurred, which we have for you. The Elior attacked the compound and all surrounding bases, disabling all of our defenses and military equipment. Somehow, they made it through all the shields, took out all the guards and rescued the humans in quick fashion. It is all on the video my Lord."

A Divided Universe

They could see the anger in his face as he spoke.

"And it is the same for all three encampments?" The three Queens nodded.

"And our military guard there could do nothing?"

"My Lord, when you look at the video you will see that somehow all the fighter craft and equipment was rendered inoperable, all of the defense positions and weapons were taken out. We do not know yet how they even got in, but once they did they reached the control room bringing down the shields as they killed our soldiers and workers. When the Commander mounted a huge counter-attack it was met with a powerful weapon unlike any we have ever seen. It vaporized and melted the entire first assault wave in an instant. You will see the ship that attacked us in the film. They extracted all our slaves in their orbs taking them off-planet to a larger craft in space. The entire operation conducted lasted less than an hour. Our fighters and equipment are still not functioning. The propulsion systems and weapons have been deactivated somehow. That is all we know my Lord, and thus the reason for our hasty return."

Tenekaris III stood up and paced back and forth in front of his throne, taking in what he had just heard. He turned at looked at Eftar.

"Eftar, please take their videos and have our technicians go through them carefully. There must be a clue in them to tell us how they disabled all our equipment and how they got into the compound. Also, send a message to the Commanders of the three planets requesting more information of what occurred and an assessment of their equipment and how they plan to restore it. He turned then to his Queens,

"I want the three of you to provide me in detail as to how many slaves were lost, and how many of our soldiers and workers were killed and wounded. Give it to Eftar when it is completed."
The three queens took this as a signal to stand and leave, bowing to their Master before departing.

"Eftar, one more thing. I need a count on how many slaves we have remaining here and what their condition is, as to whether or not any of them can still breed."

"Yes Master, I will do all required tasks at once." Eftar bowed and left the room.

Tenekaris sat back on his throne, the anger within growing. Thinking. "So, my nemesis is back and strikes the first blow in fifteen years. Their passion for the human pets is admirable and perhaps a weakness to yet be exploited." He stood and left the room, the two guards in tow yet again, and headed to his main command center to see how the other operations were proceeding. The time was growing closer to when he could inflict the final blow to the Elior opening the door to an unstoppable conquest. He walked briskly, a sneer on his face in anticipation of learning how much closer he was to the objective of exterminating the Elior.

He entered the command center, his guards remaining outside. He went directly to the head of operations. The room was filled with equipment which monitored all central activities and to the office of Kentarious who oversaw it. There at his desk Kentarious looked up.

"Master Overlord, you grace us with a personal visit."

"Yes, my younger brother. I wanted to see for myself how we are progressing."

"I am waiting to receive confirmation that our last three convoys have reached their destination and unloaded so that we can bring them back for the final transport we need in place prior to the final attack. We should be receiving it at any time. Our new sub-space low frequency encrypted communications is now the fastest method we have ever had to coordinate all our efforts."

"That is good to hear, Kentarious. When would the final convoys be ready to deploy?"

A Divided Universe

"It will take a week for them to return to gather the remaining equipment, supplies and troops which are being staged now. A couple of days to load, and then a week to get them in place. We are drafting the final plans for once they're in place to make a three-pronged attack on Elior. I noticed you have held back a large portion of our military across from the Lycoats. Is there any special reason, brother?"

"It is just a precaution for now to insure the Elior do not have anything in place which may thwart our major assault. We outnumber them greatly and have advanced our weaponry to be able to break down their defenses, but to underestimate them and commit all our resources at once would be foolish."

"Yes, I agree."

"Now please show me where we are at with the plan."

"Sure, please follow me to the strategic map room which shows just about everything you wish to know."

Tenekaris and Kentarious went through the entire mammoth operation, from supplies, munitions, troops and warships already moved, in transit or would be moved shortly, and how many of each had come from the LuQuarin or her allies. The logistics were massive but well-aligned and timed to lead to the day long awaited for. Tenekaris had shared with his brother what happened to the slave encampments and asked him if he knew of any new Elior weapon like the one used on his military guarding the prisons. His brother shook his head, as this was new to him.

They spent the next three hours going over the plans from beginning to end as Tenekaris questioned several areas, which his brother quickly answered to his satisfaction. Tenekaris smiled. His younger brother had every detail covered and managed the program almost to perfection. They were ready to adjourn for the day when a messenger knocked on the office door. Kentarious looked up at the messenger.

"Yes, what is it?"

"Excuse the interruption, but we have urgent messages from all three convoys."

"Bring them to me." He walked in and handed the messages to Kentarious, then left the room. Kentarious read the first message, then the second. Looking up at his older brother he handed him the first two as he read the third. Two minutes passed before Tenekaris finally spoke.

"This can't be possible. Brother, is there any way we can validate this?"

"These are highly encrypted messages from the Commanders of our fighting ships escorting the convoys. I know all three of these men, they are the best, respected and most successful of our military commanders. They would have only have sent this if it were true. They are also sending us the videos of the incidents, but those take a little longer to transmit. We will have those within an hour."

Tenekaris was trying to withhold his anger, now boiling up deep inside. If what he had just read was true then the plans in front of him could not be executed, or at least within the time frames as they stood.

"What is the status of the ships, little brother and what action have they taken so far?"

"With all the transports immobile they are using some of the destroyers and cruisers, taking them in tow to reach their final destination. At least some of them will get there soon to be unloaded. They also have their engineers working on the problem trying to resolve it and get the propulsion systems back on line."

"Any progress there?"

"Unfortunately, no."

"Do they not have spare parts for repairs?"

"Yes. The messages read they are replacing as many as possible, but a number of the components needed are not readily handy on the ships.

A Divided Universe

Those are kept as cargo in other ships and need to be set up at a space station where the ships can dock and a complete overhaul done if necessary. Work on the space stations was just started last month and they are not yet operational. Unless they can find the source of the problem and identify how to fix it, the ships will remain inoperable."

"Damn! Kentarious. I will return home for now to think all of this over. Send me a copy of the videos when you receive them and keep me informed of any progress. We may need to rethink our plan and devise a new one." Tenekaris left the room, walking quickly, his anger barely controlled, his two guards following him.

Back in his chambers Tenekaris ordered some of his special grog as he paced around the room, his rage evident from the day's events. His plan, the master plan to rid the universe of the Elior had been thwarted, at least for now. It would be necessary to devise an alternate plan if the ships could not be fixed in short order. Eftar knocked and entered the room.

"Master, I have news that Lanatar II has returned from Galan and wishes to report to you directly."

"I pray for his sake he has good news Eftar. Yes, show him in."

Eftar left and a few minutes later returned and led in Lord Lanatar II. He bowed to his leader as Eftar stood to the side but remained in the room.

"Master Overlord Tenekaris III. I am here to report to you directly about the success of our operation on Galan."

"I will be the judge of whether or not it was a success!"

"Yes master."

"Well, report then, I don't have all day."

"Master. We made it to Galan with the ships and weapons as ordered. With our cloaking abilities we planted the weapons at hundreds of villages, and also deployed our new cloaked video surveillance units at the largest villages to record the events once the weapons were detonated."

"Yes, go on."

"It was originally timed to be set off during their celebration when the greatest populations of Galanians would be present in the early evening. However, we needed to move the time frame up as there was an Elior team installing a new defense system to warn the planet if any chemical, biologic or nuclear weapons were used. They were in the final stages of the installation and about ready to test it so that the population could be warned and seek special underground shelters in the event of such an attack. I needed to make the decision whether to wait or deploy the weapons before the system was in place. It was mid to late morning and there were hundreds of workers preparing for the evening's celebration. Wishing to inflict as much damage as possible, I gave the order to set off all the charges, then record the events once all our ships and men had retreated back through the stargate. Master, I hope you will be pleased with the results. Here are some of the videos from their largest tribes and towns. In them you will find that once we set off the weapons and the agents dispersed in and around the villages that the Galanians were falling like flies, dying almost instantly, with the biologics going airborne to infect a wider area. Please see for yourself."

Lanatar held out a video disk which Eftar took and put it into a small unit on a nearby table. A video image appeared looking down at a large village where Galanians were working and walking about. True to form the weapons were set off and a cloud of death appeared, then another, each being recorded all around the village. As the clouds drifting from the wind covered a wider area you could see the inhabitants dropping to the ground, killed in just a matter of seconds. Within a minute there were bodies lying all over the open areas, and streets. Tenekaris and Eftar watched closely observing the instant death it brought to anyone in its' path. The video played for a few minutes longer than stopped. Tenekaris looked at Lanatar.

"So, you say this was done on all their villages?"

A Divided Universe

"Master, we deployed the weapons on as many as we could, perhaps a thousand. There are many smaller outlying villages that have but a few inhabitants. Our focus was to take out as many as we could and get out of there undetected as ordered."

"Will all the videos show the same?"

"For the most part yes. Many Galanians have perished or will so soon once the virus takes hold."

Tenekaris paced back and forth a few steps, chugging down the grog still in hand. He turned back to Eftar and Lanatar, a small evil grin on his face.

"Congratulations, Lanatar. You are the first one today to bring me good news. I understand your decision to launch the weapons earlier than planned, as I would have done the same under the circumstances. I want you to provide me with a summary report based on all the videos, as to how many Galanians have perished and/or will perish in the days ahead. Eftar, take Lanatar to my three Queens and have each of them pick out a suitable mate for Lanatar. I will give you three days of leave to enjoy your new playmates and celebrate with your troops who also will be rewarded. Then return to me on the fourth day as I will have a new assignment for you."

"Yes, Master." Lanatar bowed and departed the room with Eftar.

A Divided Universe

Chapter Twenty
Solaria

Alex exited the SSSTS returning to normal size. The trip back had given him the time to think of the Councils answer and what possible steps could be taken to thwart the imminent threat that loomed. He sent a message to the Admiral announcing his return and if asked he should come to the command center to meet. Looking around the rest of the fleet had returned as the number and size of the warships on the base had multiplied many fold. He pulled out his orb, vaped and ported to the bar he had last been at where Mora worked.

Arriving at the bar, he found it packed with officers and troops of the now returned fleet. He saw one open spot at the end of the bar and made his way there. It took a few minutes before he was able to order a drink, from a fresh new female Elior attendant. Mora was most likely working at her primary job servicing the warships. It all seemed so different in just over the week he had been gone.

The Admiral was sitting at his desk going over the transmissions he received from Thyon, Kira, and Tira when the messenger disk appeared from Alex. He dispatched a return message to Alex to meet with him in two hours. He needed the time to prepare for the return of the three rescue mission groups who apparently had all succeeded. Thyon's group had saved just under 10,000 humans, Kira over 19,000 and Tira well over 21,000. As Thyon had rescued all of them in one sweep, it had taken Kira two and Tira a third sweep with the orbs used for extraction. There had been no casualties with Thyon's group, but with the additional sweeps in Kira and Tira's a few Elior had been killed and wounded. The extra time they needed to rescue the humans had allowed the LuQuarin defenses to launch large counter attacks. Both Kira and Tira used all three of their pulsar blasts to keep the enemy at bay during the final minutes of the rescue. Their three ships would be arriving later in the day, and the Elior fighters and transport ships carrying the humans were two days behind them. There was a brief about the humans rescued, suggesting steps that would be necessary when the transports carrying them arrived. The Admiral set the reports down waiting for the chief medical officer that resided over his entire fleet to arrive whom he had sent a request to earlier. As he stood to walk out of his office he was met by his newly appointed Major Crystal.

"Admiral, the Chief Medical Officer is here as requested."

"Good, show her in please."

A minute later Crystal returned and ushered in Saratan, the Chief Medical Officer. Saratan entered as the Admiral gestured for her to take a seat.

"Saratan. The rescue missions will be returning in a couple of days with approximately 50,000 humans that were enslaved by the LuQuarin for a very long time. I will need your assistance to set up a temporary receiving and housing area for them upon arrival. They range in age from newborns, toddlers, all the way up to 50 or 60-year old adults. There are perhaps 80% females, and some are pregnant. The brief I received did not go into great detail but I expect they have suffered physical wounds, and no doubt emotional and psychological damage. With the fast rescue and now transporting them back through space they will have experienced even more trauma and shock over the events. What will you need to have in place?"

"Admiral, each transport has a medical processing team on board. In anticipation of this we set up a protocol to process them the minute they were received on the ships. Each person rescued will go under a quick medical evaluation. Those needing treatment for any serious physical wounds will be attended to first. With the sheer numbers being larger than we expected, the medical teams will have their hands full. To make the transition easier I had most of the medical team on board each ship take human form. With the transport being done by the orbs, we did not return them to normal size, and they are in a special area on the ship which can accommodate a larger number miniaturized. Each victim will be provided food, water and clothing. A supplement has been added to the water to assist with the space travel to avoid them becoming sick during the journey. They will also go through a series of debriefings to assure them that they are safe and now free of their captors. Sedatives will be given to those that exhibit behavior outside of what is expected. My teams are well-trained Admiral, and I expect when they arrive, we will need to continue their transition and prepare them for the journey to Elior. With three groups returning I will suggest you keep them separate for now. It is what they are used to and seeing familiar faces will aid in the process. From our previous meetings before the missions started we set up three compounds here. Unfortunately, two of them will not be big enough. So, if you could authorize additional resources and personnel to accommodate the larger numbers, we can be prepared for their arrival."

"See Major Crystal and give her the details of what you will need. She can set in motion anything you require in short order.

"Is there anything else Saratan?"

"Yes, Admiral. How long will we have before we need to send them to Elior?"

"With the events that are taking place I would say one week at the max. I know it is a short time frame to transition 50,000 humans that have been enslaved for 15 years or longer, but it will be necessary. Our enemies are on the move and we cannot delay."

"I see, Admiral and understand. A week at most it is then. Now if you will excuse me I must see the Major and get the ball rolling."

"Thank you, Saratan, and if you need anything, please ask and I will make sure you have what you need."

"Thank you, Admiral." Saratan rose, nodded to the Admiral and left his office.

The Admiral got up and paced, then walked out of his office on a balcony overlooking the command center, where hundreds of terminals were being attended to by operators overseeing all the activities of the entire fleet. He saw Crystal and Saratan discussing the human situation with three additional officers. A small smile emerged in his mind. "At least we rescued all those enslaved."

A Divided Universe

He saw Alex walking in the far side and realized two hours had passed. Alex made his way through the command center and then up the flight of stairs to where the Admiral was standing.

"Admiral. Reporting as ordered."

"Yes Alex, please come into my office."

Inside and both seated, Alex began.

"Admiral, unfortunately I do not bring the news from the Council we were hoping for. The vote was 5 to 4 not to activate our military to full capacity unless we can provide further proof and validate our enemies' intentions." He continued detailing what the Council had said, adding the attack on Galan which had occurred, the new technology that had been deployed to thwart or contain attacks on their friends on the eight other planets, finally sharing that most of the Elior military forces were now clones. The Admiral listened until Alex was finished.

"5 to 4 you say? And, they want more proof?"

"Yes, Admiral."

"Then proof they shall have. Alex in your absence much has happened." The Admiral explained the ideas Thyon had provided and then the operations deployed, all which had been recorded, completed, and the return from the mission, which was in progress.

"That is good news, Admiral."

"Yes, it is Alex. The enemy has at least been deterred for the moment, and the rescue of the humans was a great success which should be pleasing to the Council. I will prepare a dispatch for the Council immediately which will give them undeniable proof that the LuQuarin and others intend on attacking Elior and others as well. Do you know how bad Galan was hit?"

"No, Admiral. It seems they were attacked with biological and chemical weapons in all the major population regions. No enemy was detected, but the weapons used for the attack are those within the LuQuarin arsenal. They must have used their stargates with greatly improved stealth and cloaking technology to be able to have achieved this."

"One would think that this attack on Galan would have convinced the Council."

"I was hoping for the same, Admiral. Deloria seems hell bent on not using military resources and thus the request for additional proof."

"Where does Olis stand on all of this?"

"Olis agrees with us and is the one that shared the cloning of our soldiers with me. Seems the Council was keeping that to themselves as well. She is meeting with the Generals of our remaining forces on Elior to try and prepare them for what we fear is coming."

"Good, if anyone can convince our Generals, it is Olis. Thyon, Kira and Tira will be back here in a few hours. I am eager to hear from them what they saw and were able to accomplish. Your son and daughters have been our blessing and without their help the situation could be much worse."

"Yes, Admiral I am looking forward to seeing them."

"Let me get the dispatch prepared for the Council. Here are the reports from the three operations to familiarize yourself with what has occurred while you went to Elior. Would you be willing to carry the dispatch back to them?"

"Admiral, if the information serves as the validation the Council needs, I don't believe it would be necessary for me to hand deliver it. I would rather remain here and contribute to our cause and work with my children and your commanders on the front line."

"True Alex, I will have one of my elite officers deliver it to the Council. By you remaining here only substantiates the urgency of the matter. I would ask that you add a personal note in with the dispatches to the Council and Olis as to why you are remaining here. It will support our plea to a greater extent."

"Will do, Admiral. I will draft it immediately after I read the reports. If I may Admiral, I would like to find a quiet place to read these and draft my dispatch."

"Of course, Alex. Might I suggest our small private resort we have in a dome here on the planet. It is where our scientists and engineers hang out at times, and is usually pretty laid back and quiet. Here are the coordinates."

"Excellent, Admiral. I will return in a couple of hours with my dispatches, and await the arrival of Thyon and the others."

Alex stood up, nodded to the Admiral, pulled out his orb, vaped and ported to the coordinates.

Major Crystal appeared at the Admirals door.

"Yes, Major what is it?'

"Admiral. First, I have assigned three officers and engineers to assist Saratan with all she requires, the construction of the additional facilities and equipment needed is underway. Second, we will have within an hour all of the videos and information you requested for the validation of our enemy's intentions ready to go with your dispatches to the Council. Finally, Admiral, we have just received an interstellar message from space station outpost 18."

"What does it say?"

"Here Admiral, I think you should read this for yourself." She handed him the message.

Outpost 18, Urgent report.

To: Command Central.

A Divided Universe

From: Lt. Domtar.

Today we came in contact with a long-range Secarios shuttle heading directly to our position. Our scanners revealed there was one life form aboard. Once in range, we deployed our tractor beam to gain control of the ship while keeping it at a safe distance. I sent over our technician, and once on board he discovered a female Secarios barely alive and three body bags containing deceased individuals. There was a Blisscrell, a Thornok and a Flemjot in the bags. We sealed the body bags in containment wraps and ported them to our space station. We then ported the female on board and provided what medical attention we could. As she came to, she was able to utter a series of words which made no sense. She repeated them over and over. We entered the words into our system and they came back as a decoded message indicating she was an Elior agent in Secarios form. We validated the message three times. She would say no more. Since we are a retrieving station for our agents we followed protocol to return her quickly. Since the Secarios shuttles log showed that it was programmed directly to our position, it was evident our enemy knew our location. We examined the shuttle one more time and to insure our safety released it back into space and destroyed it. We then put the body bags and the agent into our SSSTS and set a timer to destroy the space station. All information was erased from our systems. Once complete we launched our craft and are heading back to the command center, the space station exploding shortly after our departure. This message is being sent prior to our departure and should be in your hands a few hours before our arrival. Based on the Secarios logs our enemy is no more than 4-5 days travel time away from this space station. We are requesting that you prepare for our hasty return and have a medical team standing by for our agent, she is in bad shape. It was signed by the Lt.

"Damn, Major. What do you make of this?"

"I am not certain sir. But the words she spoke do match up to one of our agents that was sent to the Secarios nine years ago. She was in a special logistics group gathering information. We have not heard from her in a long time."

155

"Prepare for their arrival and have our medical team at the ready. We need to do whatever is necessary to save her life. She may have important information for us."

"Yes, Admiral I will make the preparations immediately."

Alex was sipping on a cup of coffee as he read the last of the three reports. The convoys had been stopped in their tracks after coming out of hyperspace and rendered immobile, at least for the time being. The size and scope of the enemy ships matched the previous information. The rescue missions had also succeeded with only a few casualties. He put the last report down and looked out the dome at the barren planet outside. There were mountains in the distance and a flat wasteland between them where the dome had been erected. He drafted his own dispatches to the Council, Olis, and a final one for his wife. An hour passed before he sealed the one to Diana in the messenger disk, gathered up his materials, vaped and ported back to the command center.

Alex found the Admiral in his office.

"Come in Alex, have a seat. I am just putting the final touch to the dispatches." Alex took a chair across from the Admiral's desk and watched as he sealed them in a messenger disk now encrypted. He set them on the corner along with the information and video of all the operations they completed. Alex handed over his three dispatches and they were added to the pile.

"If this doesn't convince the Council, Alex, I don't know what will. We have a new matter that has come up."

"What is that, Admiral?"

"Here, read this." He handed Alex the report from station 18.

"They arrived a few minutes ago. I hope we can save the agent and learn more of what we are up against. I would like you to go with me so we can assess the situation. Let's get these dispatches sent and then head over to the medical facility." The Admiral stood as did Alex. Grabbing the pile of dispatches, the Admiral sought the Major to get them on their way. They found the Major in the center of the command and control room.

"Major, please get these off to Elior in the SSSTS."

"Yes, sir. I have officer Colonel Garetin at the ready."

"We are heading over to the medical center to see our agent. If anything important comes up, please notify me."

"Yes, Admiral." The Admiral gave Alex the coordinates and the two vaped and ported.

At the medical center reception area, the Admiral inquired about the patient just received. The receptionist told the Admiral that the Doctor would be out in a few minutes to meet with him. They both took a seat and waited. A few minutes later a Physician came through the doorway from behind the reception area and approached the Admiral.

"Admiral, I am Doctor Jenro. Our newly arrived patient is in a bad way I'm afraid and is barely holding onto life. She sustained multiple injuries and even our advanced treatments may not be enough. We cannot risk transforming her back to her Elior form as that procedure would kill her at this time." Alex spoke up.

"If you would allow me, I believe I can help you with this situation." The Admiral chimed in.

"Doctor, Alex has some unique talents which could save her and I am requesting you allow him to see the patient."

"Of course, Admiral, please follow me. The Doctor led them through the doors, down a hallway until they reached the emergency room. Once inside they found four other Physicians attending the female that was stretched out on a hospital gurney. Doctor Jenro led them to a series of displays on the wall showing all of her injuries from the scans performed and went through each one detailing for the Admiral and Alex the situation. Alex spoke.

A Divided Universe

"Doctor, please have your attendants' remove her gown for me."
As they did Alex took his Medallion outside of his military tunic, undid the
top of it and placed the Medallion on his chest. A second later the
Medallion sank into his chest and glowed through his skin. He walked over
and stood above the female lying on the gurney. He took his hands and
gently placed them on her head, his hands glowing a blueish yellow. He
touched her forehead gently the glow transferring into the skull. He could
feel the concussion within. He lowered his hands down the sides of her
face where claw marks existed and then down to her neck, then to her
shoulders. As his hands passed the injuries were now healed. He ran his
hands down her chest where the irregular heartbeat and breathing were
soon restored to normal a few seconds later; down to her ribs of which
seven were broken and the other organs beneath them also laden with
injuries.

The physicians watched in awe as Alex slowly caressed her entire
front side, his hands glowing, the injuries were now gone, repaired to
normal. He then did one shoulder and arm which had been dislocated and
broken, down to her hands and fingers, finding two of those broken. He
did the other shoulder and arm. Finally, he worked over her groin section
and down each leg, healing every inch of her body. A dislocated knee was
soon replaced by a healthy one. The equipment in the room signaled her
vitals had gone from critical, near death, to that of a healthy young woman.
With the help of two attendants they rolled her over onto her stomach.
Alex then did the same down her entire backside, all the way to her feet,
his hands glowing the entire time. Fixing a broken ankle and a few toes he
withdrew his hands for a minute and they rolled her over again on her
back.

"Doctor, please run a scan over her body, to insure I did not miss
any injuries." The Doctor grabbed a long wand and ran it from head to toe,
the screens on the wall displaying her current state.

"Damn Alex, every injury is gone and completely healed. You would
think we were looking at an Olympic athletes' body."

"That is good to hear, Doctor. We now have just one more step.
Please cover her back up." A sheet and blanket were put over her.

A Divided Universe

"What is her name, Doctor?"

"On Secarios she was known as Saratina, but her true Elior name is Solaria."

Alex stood over her again looking down at her eyes which were opening, a beautiful emerald green. He heard her speak.

"Who are you and where am I?"

"I am Alex, and you are safe now back among the Elior in a medical center. You have had a rough go at it."

"What did you do to me?"

"Let's just say you needed a few repairs, which all but one has been taken care of."

"I felt like I was dying about ready to drift into nothingness, my entire body in pain and my mind twisted with horrible scenes. Then there was this light that began to flow over me and through me, a warming sensation enveloping my entire body, the pain leaving as the light passed."

"Good. Now Solaria we have one more step. Close your eyes and try not to think about anything for a minute." She looked up, nodded and closed her eyes.

Alex bent down and his hands glowed again. He placed them on each side of her head, then lowered his mouth to hers. Touching lips, he began to gently suck the breath from within her. His hands grew brighter as Alex withdrew all the horrible memories and events within her mind. The visions he saw as each passed were horrific. He even saw Tenekaris III image repeatedly, inflicting pain on Solaria. He stopped and took a new breath and then continued. Finally, the horrors stopped, replaced with the warmth of Solaria trying to kiss him. The healing was complete and Alex withdrew, his hands removed from her head, the glowing ceased. Solaria opened up her eyes, smiling, a tear coming from one. She whispered,

"Thank you, Alex, with all of my heart I thank you."

159

"You're welcome, Solaria. I want you to rest a while, then they will get you some nice clothing to wear and some food. Doctor, I believe you should now be able to transform her back to Elior form when she is ready to do so." The Doctor nodded, still in awe of what he had just witnessed. The Admiral turned to the Doctor.

"As soon as she is transformed and feeling up to it, we need to talk to her."

"Of course, Admiral. I will keep you informed and messenger you when she is ready."

"Very well. Alex seems our work here is done for now. We need to get back to the command center as I expect Thyon and the others will be returning very soon." A minute later they we both back in the command center.

"Admiral, I need to tell you what I found from withdrawing all of the terrible memories Solaria had within."

"Of course, Alex. Let's go back into my office."

Seated back in the office, Alex began.

"Admiral, there is no need for me to share with you the horrors of her torture. You saw them for yourself. But I found something else in her mind. Between bouts of torture she used her mind reading abilities and read the Master Overlord's thoughts which are quite revealing. I have a vision of Tenekaris III now as if I was standing in the room with him. As we suspected he has infiltrated all of his allies with the Ignots and Ess, their leadership, military, science and logistics. He is controlling their actions, the same as he had done on Earth. The only ones not infected are the Lycoats. For some reason he has been unable to infect them. The Lycoats are a formidable force and come from a galaxy on the other side of where the LuQuarin operate. At this point they have a non-aggression pact between them and are separated by a neutral zone. He does not want to engage in battle with them as the price tag would be too high. He has 200 divisions on his side of the neutral zone to thwart any possible attack the Lycoats may attempt. For now, he will leave them alone.

His true mission is still to destroy Elior and her allies. With the control and assistance of his allies his force as we know is huge and merely delayed at this time by Thyon and his sisters.

Admiral, Solaria should be recognized as a hero and given the highest award for bravery and duty. I have additional details I withdrew from her mind, but I suggest we let her tell us those. I also want to share her memories with Thyon when he returns so he can see first-hand the brutality and evil we face. Admiral, I read some most disturbing thoughts from her that she read from Tenekaris. He is planning an attack on Sereptin which may already be underway. There is more but I want to share with Thyon first to see if he interprets the information the same as I have. If true, Elior is in grave danger."

"How is it Elior is in grave danger?"

"Admiral, let me first share with Thyon. I do not want to be wrong on what I think to be true."

"As you wish, Alex. They should be here soon, and I hope then you will share with me this imminent threat."

"Yes, Admiral."

A Divided Universe

Chapter Twenty-One
Thyons' Return

Thyon opened the viewing window of the spacecraft after coming out of hyperspace. It was a spectacular view of the galaxy and the solar systems ahead leading to the Admirals command center which resided on a large deserted planet a few systems distant. He looked at Lorakit sitting at the console next to his, smiling. They made a good team and had accomplished a lot in just the past week. He had removed the autopilot feature and was letting Lorakit fly the ship manually. He had opened up the joystick feature and she was enjoying maneuvering the large spacecraft to her own wishes making various maneuvers.

"Thyon, this ship handles beautifully."

"Yes. It is a good skill to develop should we ever get into a battle. Better to rely on your instincts and be unpredictable than rely on programs to evade and attack. Once you're done playing, we do have to meet with the Admiral and report in."

"Just a few more please?"

"OK, a few more, then get us to the base." She smiled and took the ship into a wild move to evade an imaginary enemy and then re-align to attack.

"Well done, Lora."

"Thanks. I will get us back to the command center now." Lorakit changed the heading and zoomed forward to where the command center lay in the next solar system. They quickly passed several planets and Lorakit slowed the ship down as they made the final approach. A few minutes later down into the atmosphere she landed the ship in the spot reserved for them. They disembarked and walked into the command center.

A Divided Universe

They found Alex and the Admiral in his office awaiting their return. After exchanging greetings, the Admiral moved them to the conference room.

"Thyon. I read your report and it appears as if you had a great deal of success in both slowing down our enemies and rescuing the humans."

"Yes, Admiral, it all went rather well. The size of the convoy should be more than enough to convince the Council into action. With three of them, an attack on Elior would be an overwhelming event. Father, did you have any success with the Council?"

"I am afraid not, Thyon. But there is new and more disturbing news I need to share with you. Admiral please tell him about Solaria." The Admiral then debriefed Thyon and Lorakit about the agent and also how Alex had saved her life with healing abilities. Alex then spoke.

"Thyon. When I was doing the final stages of healing I withdrew all the horrible memories of what she had suffered. Solaria had also read Tenekaris III mind when she was not being abused and tortured. I need to share all of it with you to see if you see and hear what I have."

"Of course, father." They both stood and joined hands and touched foreheads, Thyon bending over far enough so the tips of their foreheads touched. Alex initiated the process and his hands glowed as did a spot on his head where it met with Thyon's. It started a process of a video and an audio being transferred from one to the other, including all the thoughts Solaria had extracted from Tenekaris mind. It took a few minutes before the transfer was complete, the two disengaging.

"Damn father. The woman suffered a great deal and is lucky to be alive."

"I know son. Now filter through. You should find the same as I did about the control of all his allies. Then the attack on Sereptin. I want you to look at the part after he had violated her and was walking around drinking his grog and the thoughts he was having." Thyon did as he asked.

A Divided Universe

He closed his eyes and was going through the live video of the memories in his mind. Several more minutes passed before he opened his eyes.

"Father, how is this possible?"

"Thyon, what did you see and hear?"

"Father, I went over it three times to make sure. The vision I saw was Tenekaris walking around after he had violated her, drinking his giant mug of grog, mumbling and thinking. He laughed and then in his mind was saying that Eliors' days would soon come to an end. That after 200 years of waiting how his implant into the Council was awakened. The Council would soon perish and Elior would be without any leadership or guidance, that chaos would take hold. He would attack thereafter and rid the universe of the only force that held the power and technology to oppose him. He laughed again saying the time was near. Father if I understand this correctly it means that one of the council members is infected with a LuQuarin and controls their actions."

"Yes, my son. Most likely there is more than one as they usually work in pairs."

"But father, were not all inhabitants on Elior screened for LuQuarin?"

"They were supposed to be. But, the Council is above reproach and may have not been included in the worldwide scanning of all inhabitants."

"But all species are screened if they leave or come back to Elior."

"True, Thyon. But what if a member or members of the Council have never left Elior?"

"Then it is possible they were infected a long time ago with a sleeper agent, which was awakened recently."

"Yes, that is my fear, Thyon. The way Deloria was acting when I met with her and the Council suggests that very possibility."

"What other member do you think is infected?"

"That I can only guess at, Thyon. I can only tell you that Olisaria is not infected, as she has been off world numerous times and been screened each time. Admiral, do we have any records of the Council members history of coming and going from Elior?"

The Admiral had been listening, his jaw down low from hearing this possibility.

"Alex, I will have Major Crystal look into it immediately. But I doubt it. The Council is immune from normal tracking and there may be no records of their movements. Let me see Crystal. I will be back momentarily."

"Thank you, Admiral. Thyon, we need to figure out our best choices to insure the Council is sustained somehow, and free from infection of the LuQuarin hold."

The Admiral returned. "I have Crystal looking into the history but I don't expect much. She also informed me that both your sisters are landing now and will be joining us in ten minutes. Now. If the Council is infected by the LuQuarin we need to take action immediately. If the Council falls apart, Elior will fall into chaos." Thyon chimed in.

"Admiral, both my father, my sisters and I have the ability to see if a being is infected by a LuQuarin. My father does it through the Medallion being active, but we have the innate ability to see the infestation. Admiral, with your permission, I am going to suggest that my father and I return to Elior in my ship immediately. We will get there even before your SSSTS does. My father can demand a meeting with the Council and I will accompany him but do it invisibly. If they saw him activate the Medallion it would raise the alarm to the infected host. We can communicate telepathically and once I discover where the LuQuarin reside within the Council, then decide what is the best course of action. I will also need to bring a copy of all the other evidence we have gathered that the SSSTS carries. When my sisters arrive here I am going to suggest we send Kira and Croulac to Sereptin to meet with Claudicus and the tribunal powers there. Do you have the neural net defense systems capabilities here, Admiral?"

"Yes, Thyon."

"They should take those with them as well and have Claudicus erect them around any known LuQuarin stargate areas. In this manner if the LuQuarin enter the planet to attack they will set off an alarm, even if cloaked, and Claudicus and his forces can thwart the attack before it gets underway. Then, let's have Tira and Stilzen go to Galan and see if they can't help with the virus. My sisters and I also have our mother Kates knowledge of the work she did on eliminating and curing many virus and diseases that were created on Earth that the LuQuarin have and apparently used. Forgive me ,Admiral, for being so forward and taking the lead on this situation. I am only using the powers and intelligence I was gifted with at birth to help save the Elior and all other good species."

"No need for any apology, Thyon. I welcome the help and use of your gifts. We are at critical times and your knowledge and wisdom may yet save us all from annihilation."

"Thank you, Admiral." Kira and Tira walked in followed by Croulac and Stilzen. After greetings were exchanged, the Admiral had them all sit and stood at the head of the conference table.

"Welcome back Kira, Tira. You both had successful missions and we are all thankful you have returned safely. The transport ships and escorts that were with you are two days behind, but much has happened and we will need you both for other missions now." The Admiral summarized all the events to the group. Twenty minutes later everyone was caught up on the situation and provided with Thyon's suggestions. Kira spoke first.

"Admiral. How soon could you have the neural net equipment loaded on my ship?'

"It shouldn't take more than a couple of hours."

"Good. We can depart immediately and be on Sereptin within two days' time. Tira how long would it take you to get to Galan?"

"Galan is in the adjacent galaxy, so we should be able to get there in a day and a half." Alex spoke.

"Thyon, with your ship, how fast can we get to Elior? The SSSTS took better than a day, almost two."

"We could be there in 23 hours, father, as my ship is very fast. Admiral, if we are all in agreement, we should get started immediately to depart. Time is of the essence."

"Yes Thyon, I agree. While you are away I am going to prepare for all the humans we saved and also set up a multiple defense perimeter around our forces here in case our enemy decides to attack, since it is apparent they know we are here. The three of you need to get the passwords to enter the space of those three planets. See Major Crystal to get them, otherwise you might be attacked by Elior fighters when you enter their space. Good luck to all of you. A little luck would be welcome and may save us all if our courage and tenacity hold."

They all stood up, nodded to the Admiral and departed the room, their missions defined.

Chapter Twenty-Two
A Truth Discovered

Thyon sat back in his command chair as Lorakit piloted the ship. His father was in the other pilot chair watching Lorakit man the controls. They decided when they entered the area of Elior territory that Thyon would shrink himself into a pea sized orb and become invisible. In this manner he would not be detected by the Elior sensors, only Lorakit and his father would appear to be on the ship. It had been a fast journey and they were about to come out of hyperspace and close in on Elior territory.

Alex looked back at his son who was deep in thought. In the hours of the flight they discussed and come up with a plan to meet with the Council as soon as possible. Knowing the Council would be slow to respond, once on Elior Alex would seek Olisaria and also try and arrange a meeting with Ezmull, the previous head of the Council, now retired for over 15 years.

"Thyon, it's almost time."

"Yes, father."

"Are you going to be ok in the orb? You may be in there a while."

"Yes. We need to keep my presence hidden until we can discover the truth. You and Lorakit will have to be convincing. We can communicate telepathically as we discover what is what."

Lorakit began the process of slowing the ship down, coming out of hyperspace in the solar system beyond the one Elior resided. Thyon stood up and pulled out his tiny pea sized orb. He came over and kissed Lorakit on the head and shook his father's hand, then vaped into the orb. Alex took the floating orb and put it in the pocket of his tunic. The shipped slowed, coming out of hyperspace and Lora opened up the viewing window, the sight an amazing array of colors. It was a beautiful galaxy containing hundreds of solar systems, many with planets that sustained

169

life. As they closed in they were hailed by an Elior fighter which had uncloaked and was flying to their right side.

"Unidentified ship. You have entered Elior territory. State the nature of your business." Alex answered.

"This is Alex, Earth bearer of the Medallion and we have traveled here with urgent news from the Admiral's command center for the Council."

"Then please transmit the proper codes immediately." Lorakit punched in the encrypted code and sent it to the fighter.

"One minute please as we need to confirm your code." Lorakit continued to fly the ship in a steady manner. Their shields were down and no defense systems or weapons had been activated demonstrating their peaceful nature. The fighter responded.

"Proceed to the space station outside of the first moon of Elior where you will receive docking instructions." Alex looked on the radar screen and noticed there were now five Elior fighters, one just ahead and then four behind them. It was good to see the Elior defense systems were taking no chances with an unknown ship. Lorakit flew towards the space station, now coming into view. A new voice came on.

"This is Elior space station K-1. Please take your ship to dock number two since your ship is so large. There prepare to be scanned and boarded for inspection. Alex responded.

"Thank you K-1. We will do as instructed." Lorakit slowed the ship down preparing to dock with the space station and slowly maneuvered the ship into a perfect position where a set of arms extended from the station and attached to the ship. Once locked Lora turned off all the systems and awaited boarding. She unlocked the side door hatch. A space docking bridge extended and attached to the door. A compression sound echoed signaling the lock was complete and pressurized. Alex went over to the side door and opened it, then stepped back and stood next to Lora awaiting the boarding party. A few seconds passed and an armed officer entered the ship followed by two armed guards. Alex had taken out his Medallion and it was on full display of the front of his military uniform. The officer approached and stopped ten feet in front of Alex.

"I am Sargent Nopril, here to escort you inside while we inspect your ship. Are you carrying any weapons?" Alex answered.

"No Sargent. We are here on an important mission from the Admiral and need to see the Council as quickly as possible."

"Who is she?" Lorakit answered.

"I am Lorakit, special agent of the Elior under Commander Stilzen and have recently returned after 14 years of undercover service with the Secarios with important information for the Council. Since I outrank you Sargent, a little more respect in your tone would be appreciated or I will speak to my superiors about your manners and we will see where that gets you."

"My apology, Lorakit. It is my duty to properly screen any travelers that enter Elior space. This ship is of unknown design, can you explain that?" Alex retorted, growing angry at this petty delay.

"This ship is of a new design and created for Elior use in the ongoing battle with our enemy. I am confident your inspection will provide the details you seek. Now if you could please take us to your commanding officer as we do not wish to delay getting the information the Council needs."

"Very well. My men will escort you, as I need to remain here to supervise the inspection team." He motioned to the two guards, one taking the lead. Lorakit and Alex followed him, the other guard taking up station behind Alex. They walked through the space station until they reached the command center. There Alex was surprisingly greeted by Solarin.

"Alex. Welcome. It has been a long time."

"Solarin, it is good to see you. I thought you retired from service?"

"I was recently re-commissioned by request of General Ankwik of the second battle group along with the rank of Major. Seems our forces have become a little lax over the years and the General asked me to get things back into proper order."

"I understand, Solarin. It explains the protocol we had to endure just to get to see you."

"Likewise, Alex. Sevarin is also back now as a Colonel. You will see him when we transport you to the command center of operations on Elior. What brings you back with such haste Alex?"

"Solarin, may I speak to you in private please?"

"Of course, Alex, let's go into my office." Alex and Lorakit followed Solarin into his office. Now seated Alex continued.

"Solarin. We need to get in front of the Council as soon as possible. New information has come to light which increases the threat Elior is under. There is an SSSTS that was dispatched before the news came to light and thus the reason we took a faster ship to get here sooner. The SSSTS is about 16 hours behind us."

"Damn, Alex, your ship is that much faster?"

"Yes. Thus, you understand the urgency."

"What is it, Alex?"

"Solarin, I wish I could tell you but this is for the Council's ears only at present under strict orders from the Admiral."

"Understood. We will need to transport you to Elior first. We are not allowed to contact the Council from here directly for security reasons. Lorakit, I pulled up your record when you identified yourself. Welcome home."

"Thank you, Solarin. I have not seen Elior in 14 years."

"Let me get an encrypted message to Sevarin that you will be on your way. We have to use a shuttle from here, but it is only a 30-minute journey."

"Thank you, Solarin." They all stood up and Solarin led them out giving orders to a staff Sargent to prepare the shuttle for immediate take off. He shook Alex's hand.

"Good luck with the Council Alex. If there is anything you need let Sevarin know and I am sure he can accommodate any request you have. I have not forgotten the days when we fought our enemy side by side and how you led us to victory more than once. We are fortunate to have you back."

"Thank you, Solarin. I pray those days are over, but fear we both may soon be in battle yet again." The staff Sargent led them to the shuttle.

Thirty minutes later Alex and Lorakit departed the shuttle craft at the main command center on Elior. They were greeted by a Captain who led them in the complex. At the command center Alex spotted Sevarin who looked up as they approached. A warm handshake followed as Sevarin and Alex looked in silence at each other. It had been quite a few years since they last met.

"Sevarin, I thought you were enjoying retirement life with your family?"

"I was Alex, but the kids are grown up now and the General asked me to come back a week ago and get this place back into top order. Seems you had a visit recently with the Council and then Olisaria. Olis then had a meeting with all the Generals and asked if they might be able to prepare Elior for some possible trouble. So, the Generals have quietly reinstated a number of us in various positions around the planet, those that have been in combat and faced the enemy and understand their capabilities. Elior has grown soft over the past 15 years and a few boots in the ass were needed. More veterans are returning each day, especially those with advanced technical and tactical knowledge. It is all being done quietly as it was not approved by the Council. They could disbar Olisaria for her actions. So, Alex what brings you back with such haste?"

"Sevarin, if we may have a word in private. By the way this is Lorakit, a decorated agent that has spent 14 years of her life to bring to light much of what we know now. If not for her bravery we would be blind to what we feel is coming."

"Hello Lorakit. Alex's words are enough for me. For him to hold you in high order speaks volumes. Please follow me to my office where we can discuss this further." They walked up a short set of stairs and down an aisle to Sevarin's office. Once inside and the door closed Sevarin asked."

"What troubles you so, Alex?"

"Sevarin, you are one of only a few I truly trust. Elior and our other friends are in grave danger. The LuQuarin have made a number of allies and their forces are far beyond anything we could imagine. They are assembling now only a galaxy and a half or so away with mass military and armaments. At present we would be outnumbered over 200 to 1. More disturbing, my friend, is that we have come to believe that the Council is infected by LuQuarin agents. I will tell you more when we have time but I need to get a message to the Council to meet with me as soon as possible and also to Olis outside of the Council's knowledge. If they have infected us at the highest level the entire Council is in danger and the fate of Elior lying in the balance."

"Damn, Alex, are you kidding me? The Council infected?"

"Possibly, no most likely, Sevarin. It explains the isolationism of the past 15 years giving Tenekaris the time he needed to form new alliances and amass such a force to destroy us all."

"What's the plan then, my brother in arms?"

"I must send a message to the Council forthwith, although I am sure they will take their time responding. Then a private message to Olisaria to meet me somewhere discreet and away from the eyes of the rest of the Council."

"As you wish, Alex. Here are two message disks. Put on them what you wish and I will carry out your request."

"Thank you, Sevarin." In his mind Alex telepathed Thyon. "How are we doing my son?"

"Good, father. The plan is forming as we had hoped, and with Sevarin even better than expected. I will remain silent unless you need me."

"OK, my son."

Alex wrote the two messages and Sevarin had them encrypted and sent. It was now a waiting game for the responses.

"Alex, you and Lorakit I am sure had a fast and hard journey. Are you hungry old friend?"

"Yes, we could use a little food and a beverage or two."

"OK let me leave a few commands and then I will take you to a place you will enjoy." Sevarin walked out of the office and handed the messenger disks to a Captain and then gave a few more orders to others at the command center. Returning he asked,

A Divided Universe

"Let's all go in my orb." He handed them the bracelets and a moment later the three vaped and orbed away. Ten seconds later the orb was inside a huge cavern well-lit with numerous lights on the ceiling. They vaped out and Sevarin led them down a path to a doorway that opened up into tavern and restaurant where several patrons, all military, were eating and drinking. Sevarin walked further in and took a seat at a large table near the end of the bar. A hostess greeted them handing out menus and took their drink orders. Alex spoke.

"A unique place Sevarin, but why are we inside a mountain?"

"Alex. This is one of a few places we built here on Elior that is away from the eyes and ears of the Council. They recently commissioned to have cloaked orbs containing artificial intelligence to obtain audio and video of anywhere they are sent. We believe they have thousands of them now operating around the planet. The Council approved the measure by 5 to 4. Once we found out Olisaria and the Generals elected to secretly build these establishments where we would be safe from the AI orbs."

"Why would they do this? It is a violation of basic rights."

"I agree Alex and so do all the Generals and Olis. It makes sense if what you say about the Council being infected. They could use all the information they are gathering and have a complete picture to give the enemy for an invasion. They would know exactly where all of our military forces, equipment and defenses are. Only the Council and the military know the six selected pathways through the neural net where we regulate all ships coming and going to Elior. If our enemy has those and all our defenses they would have a huge advantage to attack and invade."

"Yes, that is why we must first face the Council and learn the truth and regain control of the planet. I doubt the Council will grant my request for a meeting right away, so we must use that time to form a plan to make changes quickly if needed."

A messenger disk appeared for Alex. It was from Olisaria.

A Divided Universe

He read it and there were coordinates included where to meet her in twenty minutes. He handed the message to Sevarin to read.

"Sevarin, I want you to join me and Lorakit to meet with Olis."

"My pleasure, Alex. The coordinates she gave you is for her safehouse where we meet with the Generals. It too is outside the eyes and ears of the Council. Let's get a quick bite to eat and then go." Sevarin ordered some mini sandwiches which were brought quickly. They ate and downed their drinks. They stood and vaped into Sevarin's orb and ported to the coordinates.

The orb was now in a cavern, perhaps only 20 by 30 meters and 10 meters in height. They vaped out and stood in front of a conference table. Olisaria was on the other side sitting and watching as they came into form. She stood, came over to Alex and gave him a hug. Alex smiled and chuckled as Olisaria was over a foot taller. Alex introduced Lorakit. They shook hands and then Olis shook Sevarin's hand.

"Where are we?" Alex asked.

"Actually, we are below the island we live on, underneath the sea. Please have a seat." Alex started the conversation.

"Olis, I fear the Council is infected and has paved the way for the LuQuarin to attack Elior. How they accomplished this is a bit of a mystery but the enemy no doubt planted their agents within some Elior a long time ago and then activated them. My first question is, where is Ezmull these days?"

"Ezmull has a couple of places, but at this time of year he is most likely at his ranch where he raises pimlors."

"I would like to go see him if you could arrange it."

I visit him a few times of year there and. Alex, he is over 900 years old now and as you know retired 15 years ago. You think he is infected?"

177

"Yes, as well as others."

"I will send him a message saying I am going to drop in and see him within an hour. He is used to my last-minute decisions to visit and has always welcomed me seeing I am his granddaughter. I hope what you fear is not true."

"Think about it, Olis. In his final speech worldwide he announced a major shift in position, from Elior fighting the enemy to one of withdrawal and isolationism. If memory serves me correct he had been in the military prior to being appointed to the Council and fought in many battles and obtained the rank of General. He was a fighting man, Olis, determined to rid the galaxies of the LuQuarin evil. We should have paid more attention to this shift."

"Yes, Alex, but the Elior had been fighting them for a very long time. The Elior people were tired of war and many died over the centuries protecting freedom. The LuQuarin vanished until just recently so his position was warranted. It is hard for me to believe his decision was not his own but a ruse originating from a LuQuarin parasite within him."

"Remember how they infected Earth and all of humanity? They controlled every aspect of life on Earth to its' ultimate destruction. With Elior governed by only the Council the enemy could influence a great deal if they were hosted by the key leaders."

"Who else do you feel is infected?"

"Deloria and at least one other member of the board. You are the only one I know for certain that is not infected." Olisaria paced back and forth absorbing Alex's words. The actions of the Council over the past 15 years and even more recent gave credence to the theory.

"How do you plan on dealing with this if it is true Alex?"

"We have a plan, Olis, you will need to just trust me for now."

"You know I trust you, Alex. If not for you I would have perished that day when Vivacious almost took my life." A return message appeared from Ezmull. It read that he was looking forward to seeing her.

"We can go whenever you are ready, Alex. He may be a bit surprised when you show up with me."

"Lorakit, you and Sevarin remain here, but if you can prepare to receive a prisoner or two." Olis pulled out her orb and gave Alex a bracelet. The two vaped and were gone a moment later.

The orb appeared above a large ranch set at the base of a small mountain range. It was late afternoon, the sun setting in the distant sky to the west. The two vaped out near the front door. Looking out there were large corrals with hundreds of pimlors herded, a few bellowing the strange sound they made. The pimlors reminded Alex of something between a cow and a large pig, but their skin was a mixture of browns and greens in almost a camo pattern. Alex saw a Galanian caretaker locking up the gate to the corral. He looked over and nodded to Olis and the headed to a large barn. Olis told Alex that the Galanian was Fredorio or just Fred for short. He was Ezmulls right hand man on the ranch and had been with him for a long time. Olis walked to the front door of the large ranch style home. As they approached the door opened and there was Ezmull. Olis walked up to Ezmull and gave him a hug.

"I brought a visitor today, grandfather. He just returned to Elior again and I thought it would be a nice to let him see your ranch."

"Alex, nice to see you again. You are looking well." They shook hands and Ezmull led them inside.

"How are you, grandfather?"

"I am good. We just finished bringing in the herd and will prepare them for market in the next two days. We have over 1,000 this year and as you know the pimlors are now considered quite a delicacy. So, Alex, where have you returned from?"

"I was assisting the Admiral again since my last visit here recently."

"Ah, yes the Admiral and his never-ending quest to hunt down the LuQuarin. How goes that?" Alex felt the orb inside his pocket move slowly, Thyon seeking to get out and join the group but invisible to all.

"The same, Ezmull. Nothing has really changed; the cat and mouse game between old rivals."

"How are your wife and children?"

"Diana and the twins are good, almost grown up now. They start at the University this year."

"Damn, seems like yesterday they were just toddlers. Please have a seat. Can I get you both a drink? It's happy hour time."

"Yes, that would be nice, Ezmull. Do you have beer and southern?

"How about you, Olis?"

"I will have an OBJ, grandfather."

"Very good, I will be right back." As Ezmull left the room Thyon's orb popped out of his pocket became invisible and disappeared before Olis could notice. A moment later Thyon telepathed to Alex.

"Father, Ezmull is infected. He is nervous that you are here and knows this is not a social call. He has armed himself with a small but powerful laser pistol. It is in his right pocket. Fred is just outside the back door on the deck. He too is infected and is armed with both pistol and a shotgun laser. I am going to neutralize Fred and will be back in the room with the rest of you in a minute. Be prepared for anything. I am going to telepath Olis the same."

A Divided Universe

Alex acknowledged Thyon telepathically. A minute later Ezmull returned with a tray of drinks and handed them out. He sat across from them in a big chair as Alex and Olis sat on two different couches.

"So, Alex, you did not come back so soon and all this way to just say hi to an old man. Why are you here?"

"Ezmull. I have always held you in the highest regard, but for a long time now I have been wondering after such a distinguished military career and then your leadership in the Council fighting the LuQuarin, why you made such a major shift in position and basically abandoned the fight against our enemy and the evil it terrorizes the galaxies with?"

"A fair question, Alex. We had been fighting them for almost 1,000 years and to what avail. Many an Elior died as did thousands of our friends on other planets. When the LuQuarin disappeared, I saw no point in pursuing them. Our galaxy was clear as well as those where our friends and allies reside. It was time to stop policing the universe and let our people just live. There was no threat and we erected the neural net around the entire planet to protect it. Maybe it was my age as well. I was tired of fighting, as were our people. And look, have we not enjoyed a good life and prosperity since?"

"Yes, Ezmull. Life on Elior and other worlds has been good. But the threat is back now and greater than ever."

"Yes, so you told us on your recent visit Alex." Alex heard Thyon's voice letting him know he was back in the room.

"Well, Ezmull, our enemy has made a number of allies and amassed huge forces which are heading this way. Their technology and weaponry has greatly improved along with the speed they can now travel with such forces. They also just attacked Galan and unleashed massive amounts of chemical and biological weapons. Many a Galanian have perished and more yet may follow with a virus we cannot figure out. The threat to Elior and others has never been greater."

A Divided Universe

"I see. That is most unfortunate. But what can an old man now retired like me possibly do to help at this point?" Ezmull shifted in his seat his right hand lowered down near his pocket.

"Ezmull. I sense the Council has been infected and is aiding our enemy. If true they must be stopped and we must prepare to defend ourselves from an invasion." Ezmull stood up and paced a few steps away from Alex and Olis. He reached into his pocket and pulled out the laser pistol.

"That, I cannot allow, Alex." As he pointed the gun directly at him.

"What are you doing, grandfather?"

He looked at Olis. "I am paving the way for a new order in all the universe where the LuQuarin will reign over all."

"No, grandfather. That is not the way. You would open the doors for all of Elior to be destroyed."

"I am sorry, Olis, but it must be done." The gun in Ezmull's hand was ripped away from him by an invisible force and flew 20 feet and stopped suspended in midair. Thyon became visible, the gun in his hand. Ezmull had a look of shock on his face.

"Hello, Ezmull. Maybe you remember me, maybe not."

Ezmull looked closely at Thyon. "It can't be."

"Yes, Ezmull it is I, Thyon, son of Alex and a Humedlior. The time for the LuQuarin to rule Elior I cannot allow."

Ezmull charged at Thyon but was stopped in his tracks and suspended up a foot into the air. A gel emerged from a bracelet on Thyon's wrist and enveloped Ezmull in a clear cocoon of material. Ezmull was trapped inside, barely able to move and struggled to get out.

A Divided Universe

"Relax, Ezmull, there is no escape. You are a LuQuarin agent and must be restrained until we can extract the parasite from you. Oh, and your friend, Fred. I have imprisoned him as well, so don't expect any help because none will be forthcoming."

Alex and Olis stood up. Thyon attached a small disk to the encasing Ezmull was in.

"Olis, this will act the same as a bracelet with your orb. We need to take him and Fred back to your hideaway and then get a meeting with the Council as quickly as we can. I discovered a communications device here as well. It sends encrypted subspace messages in the LuQuarin language. Apparently Ezmull has been feeding information to our enemy for some time now.

They all ported back to Olisaria's hideaway where Sevarin and Lorakit were waiting. Sevarin had retrieved the materials necessary and built two cells to house any prisoners. Thyon levitated the two prisoners contained within the gel and placed them inside the cells, then sealed it with an electronic field. There would be no chance for escape. Olis suggested that Sevarin return to his command position to avoid any suspicion. He nodded and headed out in his orb. Olis turned to Thyon.

"I have not seen you since you were just a child. That was quite impressive what you just did. Apparently, you have a number of powers which are quite useful."

"Yes, Olis. I have many gifts as do my sisters. We have all returned to our heritage to stop the evil which now permeates the galaxies. How can we get a meeting with the Council quickly?"

"I will go to the Council chambers and invoke the emergency demand for a meeting which is in our by-laws. It states. "If any member of the Council of Elior feels that our code of laws and morals is threatened by forces from within or outside, said Council will meet to preserve, protect and defend those ideals by taking a proactive set of steps to insure the integrity of freedom of the people and planet are sustained." I expect

183

some resistance but all members of the Council took an oath and will only have two hours to respond to the request and formulate a time and place to meet."

"Excellent, Olis. You need to ensure that my father attends the meeting."

"That will be easy, Thyon. He has the information which clearly demonstrates and proves the threat. I will also bring Lora to the meeting. I will send you all a message when I have the time and place. I wouldn't expect the meeting for about four hours at best. It is late in the day and, if anything, they will push the meeting to tomorrow morning."

"I will remain here, Olis, as I want to remain invisible to the Council, but will be there when the time comes as I was today in order to identify if they are infected and protect all others from possible harm. Father, you and Lorakit should go about normal activities like you usually do when you are here on Elior to avoid suspicion while we await the Council. We already have our plan when the time comes."

"Very well Thyon. I think I will go visit an old friend with Lora until it is time."

Olisaria nodded to all of them and then vaped away. Alex waited while Lorakit kissed Thyon good-bye and then the two of them vaped and ported in Alex's orb. Thyon turned and looked at the prisoners both of which were staring back at him with an evil look.

"Now that they are gone it is time for me to extract from you all that you know and have told the enemy." Their faces changed from one of evil to that of fear, as Thyon walked up to the barrier with a devilish grin.

Alex and Lora had reached their destination. It was a human colony. They vaped out and stood in front of a bar, the same one Alex hoped to find his old friend Derek. Walking in, Alex smiled. At the end of the bar Derek sat sipping on a beer. He walked up to Derek, Lora right behind. Derek looked up, smiled and stood, his hand shaking Alex's.

"Damn, Alex, it is good to see you. What brings you back so soon?"

"Thought I would come and check up on you, make sure your behaving." They both laughed. Alex introduced Lorakit and the three made their way to a small table and sat. Derek ordered Alex a beer and a shot and Lora asked for the same.

"So how goes it for the bearer of the Medallion?"

"Just trying to earn my keep, Derek. They have kept me busy chasing down our enemy. The LuQuarin have been quite active these past many years but out of our sight most of the time. I do bring you good news. We successfully raided and freed over 50,000 humans from their slave camps. They are all now on their way back to Elior, so soon you will have new human friends to watch over. They have had a rough go at it and will need your help settling in."

"It would be an honor, Alex. As you know Olis appointed me to watch over all human colonies which are doing quite well. We will do our best to welcome them with open arms."

"Thank you, Derek. I knew we could count on you."

The conversation continued as they caught up on various subjects. Lorakit told Derek of some of her exploits and time as a Secarios. They ordered dinner and the time flew by. Derek finally asked Lora a question.

"Lora, you have chosen to have beautiful long maroon hair. I have noticed that many female Elior now have hair and in a variety of colors and that human females now dress more in the Elior style of tight fitting body suits. Why is that?"

"I am not sure, Derek, as I just got back to Elior, but personally I think having hair is rather elegant. The body suits have a lot to do with the materials available and the comfort level they offer as well as being attractive."

"True, Lora. If not for the height difference telling human from Elior would be more difficult. I also believe the food and life here has made humans get into better shape and take better care of themselves. The integration of our species has worked well. I don't see the heated competition of humans like it was on Earth, but more a greater cooperation of helping each other in all facets of life. Alex, I have a question for you."

"Sure, Derek, what is it?" Derek paused his face taking a more serious tone.

"Alex, my instincts in the past few days tell me trouble is brewing."

"How so?"

"When I met with Olis a couple of days ago she wasn't herself. It was like she had the weight of the world on her shoulders, but would reveal nothing to me."

Alex looked at Derek, their eyes meeting. His instincts were good and Alex thought before he spoke.

"My friend, your instincts serve you well. Our enemy has been most active and a new threat has emerged which we are taking seriously and steps to alleviate. I won't go into it now my old friend as it would be premature, but do keep your eyes and ears open. Hopefully within a short time the discord you are feeling will dissipate and life here on Elior will continue as it has."

"Ok, Alex, you know I trust you. But if there is anything I can do, please let me know. I would gladly put my life on the line to protect this beautiful world."

"I know my friend, but let us pray it does not come to such a thing." A message disk appeared next to Alex. It was from Olis and a meeting had been set in two hours' time, the coordinates included. It also asked him and Lorakit to join her at her home to talk before the meeting. Alex finished reading the message.

"Well, Derek, it seems duty calls. We must depart now." Alex stood up as they all did. He shook Derek's hand wishing him well and that he hoped to see him soon. The two then vaped and ported to Olis home.

Olis was standing on her deck overlooking the ocean in the distance the sun having set and a full moon rising, the stars lighting the sky as the waves gently rolled up onto the beach in the distance. Alex and Lora vaped down near her and the three took seats at a table with two candles lit. Olis had a tray of drinks waiting as they exchanged greetings. Olis started.

"Alex, what is the plan when we are in front of the Council?"

"Thyon will be present but invisible as he was when we met Ezmull. He can identify if they are infected and will telepath us what he finds out. A lot will depend on Deloria and others, how they react when we plead our case that Elior is in grave danger. Olis I want you to bring your staff but keep it well hidden under your robe. My instincts are running wild as if we may be walking into a trap. Tenekaris would like nothing more than for the Council to be destroyed and put Elior into a state of chaos before he attacks."

"I have a shorter staff which is easily concealed Alex. What about you and the Medallion?"

"I will have it active and within me, but not the gauntlets as that would be too obvious. Lorakit will remain close to me so if necessary I can shield her." Her heard Lorakit laugh.

"What is it, Lorakit?"

"Alex, there will be no need for you to protect me, as agents we have a number of things we use to insure our safety. I know that weapons are not allowed in Council chambers, but my boots are special and contain a strong shield that activates if I simply click my heals together. And my beautiful maroon hair can transpose into a sword harder than steel that has laser capabilities if I so choose to use them."

"Damn, Lora. Remind me later never to get on your bad side." The three laughed and toasted to that. Thyon's orb appeared but instead of vaping out, the pea-sized orb made its' way to the right pocket of Alex's tunic. Olis stood up.

"It is time for me to go as a Council member and meet with my peers before your arrival. I have no idea how this is going to play out, so please all of you be careful." Alex answered.

"We will, Olis, but we must be prepared for anything." Olis nodded, vaped and ported away.

"Thyon, any last instructions you want to give to me and Lora?"

"No, father. Until we know what we are facing we will just have to adapt to whatever situation comes to us." Alex stood and walked out onto the deck and looked up into the starlit sky. The fate of Elior was at stake and this meeting would lead to what direction the people and planet would take. The sounds of the surf were in the distance, a peaceful distraction for a moment as Alex cleared his mind preparing for the unknown he was about to face. Lorakit joined him on the deck and looked up into the night sky observing the beauty of the stars. She turned and looked at Alex.

"It is time Alex." He looked back at her and saw she had tied her long hair into a braided ponytail, an ornamental clip at the base of her neck and then a smaller one near the end for decoration. Alex smiled at her.

"Let's hope you won't need to use that."

Chapter Twenty-Three
Confronting the Council

Alex and Lorakit vaped out into the reception area to the Council's chambers. Two guards stood outside the entrance doors, a familiar sight to Alex, but new to Lorakit. The room was an impressive array of marble walls and floor with simulated torch lights along each side of the pathway leading to the main doors. The guards were at attention but aware of their presence and were waiting for them to approach. He felt Thyon's tiny orb slip out of his pocket. He looked at Lora.

"Ready?"

"As ready as I'll ever be. Let's get this over with."

Alex and Lora walked up to the two guards who nodded, then opened the doors to the chambers and led them inside. They brought them to a small table with two chairs and motioned for them to sit. Once seated the guards turned and walked out of the room. The semi-circular table where the nine Council members would sit was empty. They had yet to enter. Lorakit looked up at the long table where the council members would sit. Nine chairs, the center one red, the others black. A minute later two large doors from behind the table opened and the Council members began to enter. Olis was the first member on the right of the two columns of four members who proceeded in; the others proceeding left. They reached their chairs and stood behind them as Deloria entered making her way to the center chair. Behind her were two more guards that walked around each side of the long table, down a few steps and took a position behind Alex and Lora in their blind spot. Alex turned his head to the left to see the guard standing at attention, then to the right seeing the one behind Lora. Facing forward Deloria was now standing behind her chair draped in a long robe of red, laced in gold. She motioned for the Council members to sit. She looked down at Alex and spoke.

"So, Alex, you have returned to us in quick fashion from our last meeting. No doubt you bring news and evidence to convince this Council into taking action. I first have a question for you. Where did you obtain the ship you traveled in so fast to get here?"

"It is a new design that my son and daughters built for me."

"Ah, yes. The three newborns from years ago that we classified as a new species, the Humedlior. Where are they now?"

"They are traveling the universe as explorers and scientists but visit me once in a while and brought me this ship as a present when I was stationed at the Admiral's command center a few days ago."

"I see. Before you present to this Council whatever new information you have we need to address one matter."

"What is that, Deloria?"

"I have signed an executive order which is within my powers as head of this Council. Lorakit, I understand you have served for a long time as an agent for the Elior as another species and are responsible for bringing a lot of the information this Council heard recently."

"Yes, that is true."

"Unfortunate for you, Lorakit. You were part of a group that the Admiral commissioned without authorization from this Council and as such is considered an act of insurrection. I have ordered your arrest and you will be taken from these chambers immediately and imprisoned until a trial can be set for your acts of treason against the ruling Council and Elior." The two guards were behind Lora, grabbing her shoulders, forcing her to stand."

Alex stood up raising his voice to Deloria.

"How dare you arrest her! She should be treated like a decorated hero, not a prisoner."

"Do you wish to join her, Alex, in contempt of this Council?" Lorakit spoke.

"It's OK, Alex. I will be fine." Thyon telepathed Alex, Lora and Olis.

"These two guards are infected and LuQuarin agents. Deloria is infected as well as the Council member on the far left. What is his name?" Alex replied.

"That is Clendistin. He is the other junior member on the board." The guards began to lead Lora out of the room. Thyon again spoke to the three.

Deloria and Clendistin have bombs strapped to their chests. The meeting today was for them to kill off the entire Council and have no intention of listening to your plea, father. Alex looked straight at Deloria.

"Deloria. The only insurrection I see here today is yours. You refuse to listen to reason or proof that our enemy is going to attack Elior. I will not stand by and see all that I have come to know and love be wiped out by weak leadership." Alex telepathed to Olis, Thyon and Lora.

"Silence! Deloria shouted while standing.

"Who are you to defy the actions of this Council and the thousands of years of leadership?"

There was a bright flash of light which came from the right side of the Council table. Olisaria had pulled out her staff and slammed it to the ground freezing time. Everyone was still in the room except for Thyon, Alex and Olis. Thyon appeared in full visible form and took his sword and beheaded the two guards escorting Lora. Alex had jumped to the left side to Clendistin grabbing his head and snapped it, breaking his neck. Olis had moved around a behind Deloria and took the opposite end of her short staff where a blade protruded and thrust it into the back of Deloria's head. She then stopped the time freeze. The Council and Lora came back to life, Lora noticing blue blood all over her face and uniform, the heads of the two guards nearby on the floor. Thyon stood in front at the center of the Council's table, and spoke.

"Council members. Do not be afraid, you are safe now. I am Thyon, son of Alex. Deloria was infected with a LuQuarin agent, as was Clendistin and the two guards. They were carrying explosives and were about to blow up this entire room eliminating the Council in hopes of throwing all of Elior into chaos."

The two outside guards rushed through the doors, their weapons drawn. Olisaria yelled to them.

"Lower your weapons, the threat is over." The two guards held fast, weapons still at the ready. Olis spoke again.

"Who is your commanding officer?" One guard spoke.

"General Uraguard."

"Then send word for him to come here immediately." Olis slowly walked around the table and towards the two guards.

"I said lower your weapons. Look at the two guards on the floor at the base of their necks. That is what is left of the LuQuarin parasite that was inside of each of them. The same is true for Council member Clendistin and Deloria." Thyon chimed in.

"I will show you as I have the ability to see within others and project the image through my eyes." Thyon looked first at Clendistin and projected the Ess agent attached to his neck and skull. He then did the same with the now deceased Deloria. The guards and everyone in the room could clearly see the LuQuarin infestation in each. The guards finally lowered their weapons. Thyon went over to the dead council member, opened his robe exposing the bomb. He found the detonator and disarmed it. He then walked over to Deloria's lifeless body and did the same. The room was now safe. Olis spoke to the guards again.

A Divided Universe

"Now go get the General, and if you need more proof bring one of the portable scanners we have that detect LuQuarin infestation. It will confirm all that we have said and shown here." The two guards walked out quickly to attend to the requests. The six other Council members remained seated, still in shock of what lay before them. Olis turned and faced them.

"Council members, there are seven of us remaining and we must listen and hear the information Alex has brought us. Elior is in grave danger. Deloria and others have been feeding our enemy information and we suspect for a very long time. The decision for isolationism did not originate with this Council. It was a long-term ploy by our enemy to weaken us to the point where they could attack and overwhelm all of Elior." An older Council member Levilor spoke.

"Olisaria. I think it best if we all take a short break from here and return in an hour. The room can be cleaned up and give us time to absorb what has just occurred here. We will all return then and listen to everything Alex or you can tell us."

"That is a good idea, Levilor. Feel free to leave but return back in an hour." The other Council members all stood and left the room. Thyon went up to Lorakit and put his hand gently on her cheek. Alex watched, realizing his son was in love with her, smiled and moved around and stood next to Olis.

"Nice work, my friend. You still have the touch with the time freeze."

"I never thought I would have to use it again." The two guards returned, leading the General into the room. He surveyed the situation before speaking.

"So, our enemy infected us at the highest level. It explains a lot of the actions over the past 15 years. Maybe now we can get Elior back in good order." Olis replied.

A Divided Universe

"Yes, General. The time of half measures and isolationism is over. We have much to do. First, if you could have this room cleaned up and prepared for the Council to meet here in an hour it would be greatly appreciated. The four of us will be back then. Also get ahold of all the Generals and senior military personnel. We will meet with them in the morning after the Council's meeting to take any necessary action."

"Consider it done, Olis. Use the time to change and clean up. Blood on your uniforms would not be fitting attire for your meeting." Olis smiled.

"Thank you General." Olis motioned for Thyon, Lora and Alex to join her. A moment later the four had vaped and ported away.

They arrived inside Olis' home where she led Lora into a master sweet to shower and change. A clothing and make up unit was in the room. She left and took Alex and Thyon into another suite where they could clean up. She then went to her own room. Looking in the mirror she saw a lot of Deloria's blue blood all over her clothes. She shook her head slowly realizing she had taken the life of another who once was a great Elior before being infected. It had been necessary and was part of her many years of training. War was coming and many more would die before it was over. Her face changed to one of anger, the hate for the evil in the universe that never seemed to end. Evil had grown larger and more powerful, but the time to face that evil and stop it had begun with the day's events.

The four met up in Olis' living room and sat on the plush couches. It was the middle of the night. Olis brought each a mug of warm OBJ tea with restoration honey added. They sat in silence for a minute just sipping on the warm liquid all dressed in clean uniforms. Thyon set his cup down and spoke.

"We have a long night and day ahead of us. If it's Ok, I will speak first to the Council and show them the video I took of the enemy forces and ships so they can grasp how large a force is being massed against us." Olis replied.

A Divided Universe

"Yes, Thyon I agree, you start with the video and then have Lora explain what she captured from their systems and then Alex can add any additional information if needed. We have only ten minutes before we need to return to the Council. I am going to have another cup of tea. Would anyone else like another?"

All three nodded and Olis retrieved fresh cups and handed them out. The minutes passed quickly; the four stood, vaped and ported in one orb. Arriving at the Council room entrance they were greeted by the General and four guards now at the doors. The guards opened the doors and the General led them in, the doors closing behind. The room had been cleaned and there was no sign of the events of earlier that night. The six other Council members were just shuffling into the room as Olis joined them at the Council's table now modified with only seven chairs. Levilor, now the most senior member of the Council, took the middle chair. Alex, Thyon, Lora and the General all took seats at a table down and across from the Council. Levilor started the meeting.

"I believe I can speak for what remains of this Council. You all have our heartfelt thanks for your abilities, actions and courage earlier this night. Had you not taken such action none of us would still be alive. You now have the open ears and clear minds of this Council." Thyon stood up.

"I would like to show the Council the video I took from my ship when our enemy exited hyperspace in an area just a galaxy and a half away from here." Thyon started the projection from his handheld unit forming a large 3D display in front of the Council members. First at normal speed, then he sped the video up revealing the hundreds and hundreds of warships and transports as they exited hyperspace. After 10 minutes he stopped the projection.

"Council members. This video goes on for nine hours and there were thousands of ships laden with the weapons of war, supplies and personnel. This is only one of three such convoys that are now assembling within just three weeks' time of attacking Elior once they are ready." He turned the video back on and forwarded it to the end where all the transport ships suddenly stopped dead in their paths.

195

"We were able to slow down their progress with a special device invented to disable all the propulsion, weaponry and other systems except for life support. It could only be used on any ship that did not have its' shields active, thus many of their fighting ships were not affected. Eventually they will figure out what happened and make the necessary repairs, but none-the less we were able to delay their plans to attack Elior or others."

Thyon sat down and Lorakit began her passing of the intelligence of the LuQuarin network, the alliances, the species involved and the role they were playing under the leadership of the LuQuarin. The Council interjected and asked several questions which she and/or Alex answered. The meeting went on and the details of the human encampments and subsequent rescue were also brought to light. Alex also debriefed the Council on the agency network and the return of Solaria and how they had obtained the information of the LuQuarin infestation of the Council. Alex concluded with the events and capture of Ezmull and Fred. It was now four in the morning when Levilor addressed the group.

"There is no doubt in my mind or that of any Council member that Elior is in grave danger. The attack on Galan is further evidence, and your information that Sereptin may be under attack leaves no doubt of the dangers we now face. It is late and has been a trying night. I would like to halt the meeting here and then have the seven Council members meet later at 8 am, so that we may come into agreement as to the best course of action. Then at 10 am if the rest of you could return we can form a plan of action. Fear not, we will not delay, but a few hours of rest would do us all some good." Levilor stood and bowed to the four seated across from him.

"Thank you once again. You saved our lives and we are most grateful for your actions." He turned and walked out the back entrance, the others following him except for Olisaria.

Olis walked down to the others.

A Divided Universe

"Levilor is right. We could all use a few hours before we meet with all the Generals and military leaders. General do you have the coordinates of where we are meeting at 10?"

"Yes." He handed each one the coordinates for the meeting.

"Very good, General. Now if you will excuse me I am going to get a hot shower and a nap in before the Council meeting." They all bade Olis good-bye. She vaped and ported away. Thyon then addressed the General.

"General could you have my ship released from the dock at the space station? I would like to bring it down here to the surface so Lorakit and I can use it to rest for a bit."

"It has already been released. You need to merely port there and bring it down to the surface. I chose a small private island for you to use. Here are the coordinates."

"Thank you, General. We will be on our way then and see you in a few hours." Thyon and Lora used Thyon's orb and were gone a moment later leaving only the General and Alex.

"What about you, Alex?"

"I was toying with the idea of going home, but it is the middle of the night and I do not want to wake my wife or children nor do I have the time to get updated from my clone. I think I will just head to New Ventura and get a room for a few hours. I will reunite with my family after the meeting."

"All right, Alex. I will see you at 10. Get some rest."

"Thank you, General. You too."

A Divided Universe

Chapter Twenty-Four
Aid for Galan

Tira's ship approached Galan having given the password to the Elior fighter craft that intercepted her when she came out of hyperspace. After a brief communication with the sentry ship she was given the coordinates to land at the compound where Alett was working. The ship entered the atmosphere and a few minutes later landed in a designated area. Tira and Stilzen left the craft and walked up to the doors of the building encased in a protective dome that contained the lab. A guard let them in and pointed to the hallway which would lead them to Alett and the others working on a cure.

They walked into the lab where several people were busy at their monitors and lab equipment. They inquired where Alett was and the technician pointed to a tall Elior female bent over and looking through a microscope and then at the display next to it where all the images were enlarged for easy viewing. Alett looked up as Tira and Stilzen approached.

"Hello, Alett. I am Tira, daughter of Alex, and this is Stilzen. We have just come from Elior and brought additional equipment for you and your staff. I also have three leading microbiologist medical physicians on board to assist wherever you feel they would best utilized."

"Welcome Tira, Stilzen. I will have one of my technicians take them to three of our quarantined stations where many Galanians are quite ill." She summoned one of her technicians and gave the order.

"I understand you worked with my mother Kate back on Elior."

"Yes. I learned a great deal from her and to this day still miss her guidance."

"I never really knew my mother, but have within me all the knowledge she acquired before her death. I hope I can be of assistance. What is the situation, Alett?"

A Divided Universe

"Our enemy unleashed a few different weapons. There were a few chemical agents unleashed over numerous highly populated villages which killed many almost immediately. With the aid of the sweepers the chemical agents have been removed or dissipated to where they no longer have a deadly impact. Our biggest problem is a biological agent they released that contains a slow acting but quite deadly virus. Although we have the sweepers going to try and eliminate it, containing it is almost impossible as it can float in the wind currents or waterways unimpeded and has spread over much of the planet. I have been trying to develop an antidote ever since."

"May I take a look at it?"

"Be my guest, I have it under the scope now and on the screen enlarged."

Tira looked down into the microscope and then at the screen which had enlarged the virus a thousand-fold. Alett took a dropper next to a petri dish and with a gloved arm added the drops to the specimen contained in a glass isolation chamber.

"Watch what the virus does when I add healthy living tissue cells." Tira and Stilzen watched the monitor. As soon as the healthy cells were close to the virus it latched on to them, consuming the healthy cells, growing in size with each cell it consumed. Then is stopped and split into two virus cells each now seeking more healthy ones.

"Damn. That is one nasty virus," said Tira.

"I have tried hundreds of combinations against it, but not one has survived the attack, yet alone even neutralize it. Those that came into first contact with it are now on their last breaths. It slowly consumes the living tissue from within the victim making for quite a painful experience and ultimate death. All we can do so far is make those inflicted as comfortable as possible with pain killers so that they do not suffer. I am at a loss at this point as to what to try next."

A Divided Universe

Tira and Stilzen continued to watch the monitor as the virus cells continued to consume all the healthy cells remaining in the dish. She went through the list of trials that Alett had tried. Alett was a genius with microbiology and had tried every known method ever discovered and used throughout the galaxies.

Tira raced through her mind seeking any information from her or her mother's memories that might aid in the fight with this virus. Stilzen knew the look she had on her face. It was like watching a living computer vacillate a million lines of code searching for an answer. He waited knowing not to disturb her as she thought. She shook her head and came back to reality not having found a viable solution. Stilzen spoke.

"Welcome back, Tira." She smiled, then looked at Alett.

"Alett, we may need to try a different approach."

"What do you suggest?"

"I have something on my ship I need to retrieve and bring here to show you. I will be right back." Tira quickly walked out of the room. Alett looked at Stilzen.

"Any idea what she is up to?"

"Not a clue, Alett." Alett walked over to the corner where there was a dispensing unit. She ordered an OBJ and sat down to take a short break. Stilzen joined her awaiting Tira's return. Five minutes later Tira returned carrying an odd-looking box type instrument. She walked over to the table and set it down.

"What is that?" asked Alett

When my brother, sister and I were last on Kinora, their scientists gave me this. They reached a new level of miniaturization a few years back and this device can miniaturize almost anything down to the cellular level. They showed me how to take a nanobot and shrink it down to the size of a single cell organism and completely programmable. If we could find some kind of antidote we could shrink it down as well and introduce it to our most unfriendly virus. I thought that perhaps one property in the plants that OBJ is made from may offer a solution."

"Eureka!" cried out Alett. She stood up and yelled out into the room.

"Someone here please go and find Halizan immediately and bring him here."

"Halizan was not in the village at the time of the attack. He was out gathering plants for his OBJ, since he is one of the best makers of it on all the planet. When he returned the village was encased in a dome and sealed off, quarantined to contain the virus from spreading further. He was carrying a number of the Olberganja plants but was redirected away from his home due to the quarantine. He is one of only a few that has not yet been affected by the virus. In fact, when the sweepers have passed over the areas where they grow, there is no sign of the virus at all. We first just played that off as if the wind and water had taken it in other directions. But it makes sense now. There is something in those plants perhaps that the virus wants to avoid. We need to find Halizan and those plants." An attendant walked up to Alett.

"We found Halizan, he is at the center where Trig's wife Tilly is hospitalized with the virus. We have someone bringing him here now. A minute later Halizan was being escorted into the lab and brought to Alett.

"Halizan, how are you feeling?"

"I feel just fine. I have been lucky so far as to not get the virus. But Till is not looking so good and my friend Triginor is dead."

"What do you have in the pouch you are carrying?"

"About a dozen Olberganja plants. Why?"

A Divided Universe

"Can I see one please?" Halizan opened the pouch and took out one full plant and set it on the table.

"Tira, let's take a small part of the plant and put it with a nanobot and shrink it down to the cellular level, and then introduce it to the virus. The nanobot can act as the delivery agent."

They all stood up and went over to a large lab table with open space. Tira set up the unit, and then placed a nanobot from a small vial into the unit. Alett tore off a small piece of the plant and put it into the unit next to the bot. Tira closed the door and activated the unit. When complete the two items would be dispersed out a small slot in the front of the unit and into a hypodermic needle chamber that contained plasma. It only took a few seconds and the machine signaled the completion. The two items were now at a cellular level and contained within the syringe. Alett took it and walked over to the containment unit where the virus was still active. She passed it through the outer chamber inside where she could then use the arm gloves to inject it into the petri dish. All eyes were on the monitor as Alett dispersed the liquid into the dish.

The plasma simply made the dish fuller, but the bot and plant were now visible across from the virus. The nanobot program was activated and it moved towards the virus, the microscopic plant riding on its' back. The virus tried to move away from it but there was nowhere to run. The bot closed in on the virus and then in a flash injected the plant into it. The virus became violent squirming around trying to shake off the plant, but the bot had gripped the virus and held it in place. The virus changed color, its movements slowing down. A few seconds later it stopped and turned black. The nanobot released it and backed away. Turning the bot sought out another virus in the dish. The same sequence of events ensued. One by one the bot chased down each virus in the dish until they all were still and black.

"Tira, how many nanobots do you have?"

"Thousands Alett, they don't take up very much space on my ship."

203

"Excellent, we are going to need them. I am going to run a couple more tests on the virus to make sure we get the same results. Then we will need to test it out on one of our sickest Galanians to see if it will work." Halizan chimed in.

"Alett, try using the root of the plant versus the leaf. The root has more potent properties and may work even faster."

"I will take your advice, Halizan. Let's get another bot and try it out on a few more of these bastard viruses we have here."

Tira and Stilzen left to retrieve all the nanobots they had on board. Alett looked at Halizan again.

"Halizan, you must be doing something different than all the other Galanians in the village as you are only one of a few not infected. Tell me Halizan, anything you do that might be different than your fellow Galanians?"

Halizan pondered for a moment, then spoke.

"Well, Alett, the only thing I can think of is what I and some of the other OBJ masters do."

"What is that, Halizan?"

"To make the best OBJ a few of us taste the roots of each plant before we use it. Not all are the same and we seek a certain taste. To most people it tastes terrible but for those of us in the trade we have become used to it. I must taste several roots almost every day."

"This specific taste in the roots. Is there any way you could extract it and make it into a liquid form?"

"Why yes Alett, that is simple. I just need a standard plant extraction unit. But mine is locked up back at my establishment which is within the quarantine area."

"That's not a problem, Halizan. I will have one of the hazmat teams go and get it. We are going to need more of those units if my hunch is right. Where can we get more units, Halizan?"

"There is only one place. The builder of the units makes them in a village not far from here. We all get our units from him."

"Ok, can you do me a favor and go and see him, explain our situation and see if he will lend us as many units as possible?"

"I am sure he would be glad to help, that is, if he is still alive."

"I will contact the Commander in charge and have a unit of his men accompany you." Alett ran over to her desk and contacted the commander. After explaining the situation, the Commander issued the order and an orb with his men would be there in a moment to take Halizan to his friend's shop. He issued a second order to a hazmat team to retrieve Halizan's extraction unit. With the orders now issued she went back to the table waiting for Tira to return. She took a part of the root and handed it to Halizan.

"Taste it please and if it is the right kind I will taste it as well so we know which roots to use." Halizan tasted it, then he tried another from his pouch, handing it to Alett.

"This is the taste you want, Alett. But I warn you it is a taste you will not like."

Alett tasted the root. True to form it tasted horrible and she fought off the urge to vomit. A small price to pay she said to herself. She yelled at a few technicians to come over. She handed them the root.

"I want all of you to taste this root, then go out into the Olberganja fields and find as many plants that taste the same and bring them back here. Recruit as many helpers as you can and bring the plants back quickly.

We will need to set up a production area to extract from the roots and make it into liquid form. Do you understand?"

They all nodded and quickly made their way out, grabbing other team members to assist as they left. Tira and Stilzen returned and each had a case of nanobots under their arms. Alett moved over to the miniaturization unit and pulled off a small portion of a root. Tira added a bot, closed the door and activated the unit. A few seconds later their second test was ready. Alett took the syringe and brought it over to where another petri dish with the virus awaited inside its enclosure. She followed the careful process and ejected the syringe into the dish and looked at the monitor. There were almost a hundred of the virus floating around seeking a new victim. The bot landed with the root on its back. It quickly engaged a virus clamping onto it and injecting the root. The virus perished in just seconds. The bot continued and every few seconds another of the deadly virus perished. Within a couple of minutes, the bot and root had done the job and no living virus remained. They did a few more tests, each one successful. Alett turned to Tira.

"I have seen enough. We need to test this on a very sick patient. I have one question for you Tira."

"Go ahead."

"If the bot and roots work and eliminate the virus from the patient, how do we get the bot out when all is done?"

"That's easy, Alett. The Kinorian scientists have thought of everything. Once the virus is completely gone a small homing device is placed on the lip of the victim. The bot or bots get the signal and make their way out to the receiver on the victim's lip."

"Very clever they are indeed, Tira. How many bots do you think we could inject into a patient? Those that are near death will need quite a few before it is too late and all their organs start to shut down."

A Divided Universe

"Based on the Galanian physiology, we should inject some into the chest, the abdomen and then at the top of each leg and arm. I would put three or four bots into the chest and abdomen, then one each in the other areas. As fast as they work we should see results within a matter of minutes."

"I agree, let's get a batch ready and over to the hospital."

Within a few minutes Alett had six syringes, 2 bots with 3 roots, the other four one each.

"Keep making more Tira. If this works we may yet save many lives. I am going to the med center and will let you know the results."

"Good luck, Alett."

Alett ported to the med center and quickly found the head physician just outside the critical care room where ten Galanians were inside. She told him what they had discovered and tested.

"Wait here, Alett, you can watch through the window and the monitors above the patient. I will go and inject them myself as I already have the hazmat suit on. The Doctor went through the first set of doors. Once sealed he went through the second set and into the room. The patient in front of him was barely alive, vital signs on the brink. He removed the blanket covering the patient and injected the first one into the chest. Then the other five syringes. He stepped back and watched the monitors. Alett stared at the patient and the monitors looking for any sign that the procedure was working. Five minutes passed and there was no change. She spoke out loud to herself.

"Come on bots, do your job. I know you can do it." A few more minutes passed. The monitor for breathing changed from red to orange. Breathing was improving. Then more monitor lights changed. The doctor used a scanner and passed it over the patient's entire body, then looked at the results. He turned and looked at Alett and gave a thumbs up. It was working. Alett continued to watch. The bots were chewing up the virus quickly. Ten more minutes passed and most of the monitor lights had turned to green. The patient opened his eyes, smiled, a tear rolling down from his eye. The Doctor ran the scanner over his body again, spoke to the patient and then exited the room going through the two sets of doors to insure the virus did not escape. Outside he took off the helmet portion and spoke to Alett.

"I hope you have a lot of these, as we have a lot of patients in serious condition."

"Yes, Doctor we do. We are making them up now as fast as we can. I will have one of my technicians start to bring them over. Work on the most critical first, then the others. I will also be sending you a rather nasty tasting liquid. It will prevent others from getting the virus and we hope to make enough to inoculate the entire planet."

"Thank you, Alett. You have just made a miracle happen."

"Doctor, there were a number of us that worked together to make this possible. But thank you, that had a nice sound to it. I must get back to the lab. We have much to do." Alett shook his gloved hand and left the facility.

Three days passed. Alett was at the command center meeting with the Commander, reviewing all the events and actions taken. Galan was on the mend; the death toll had ceased. The military had set up additional purification centers for air and water. Two additional sweepers had just arrived from Elior and were put into operation. The military had located the LuQuarin areas for the star portals and set up a defense system around each one. The population were being given the nasty tasting root extract and more was being sent now to the outlying areas. The commander looked at Alett.

"You need some sleep young lady. You have been at it for many days. We have the situation now under control. I understand you have a nice quaint small home here that the Galanians built for you. I had it completely inspected. It is free from any harmful agents and has the freshest air and water. Now go. That is an order."

"Thank you, Commander. Yes, I am very tired. Alett stood up from the conference table and pulled out her orb. She looked at the commander.

"Tira and Stilzen should be arriving back on Elior about now. Without their help things might not have gone so well."

"Yes, Alett, that is true. Now get out of here and get some sleep." Alett nodded, vaped and ported to her Galanian home.

A Divided Universe

Chapter Twenty-Five
Sereptin

Kira made the final approach and then landed on Sereptin just outside the capitol city of Aqualite. She and Croulac departed the ship and were met by a welcoming party led by Claudicus.

"Welcome, Kira. It is good to see you once again Croulac. That's one hell of ship you have there." Kira responded.

"Thank you Claudicus. It is the design of my brother, sister and I. We are here as Sereptin is in danger of being attacked by the LuQuarin. We have brought you some equipment you might find most useful."

"So, the LuQuarin scum will be returning, eh? I think they might be in for a few surprises we have in mind for them this time. I understand you have brought us the new neural nets."

"Yes. We need to get them off the ship and put up around three of the five known star gate areas the LuQuarin have used in the past. I wish we had more. The question is, which three?"

"My men will get them unloaded and transported to the areas. We have chosen the three that are closet to all our inhabited areas. The other two are quite distant, so if they use those we will have more time to react. It's our best choice at the moment. I am having additional armaments and personnel sent to the other two to try and detect our enemy should they use either one of those. Now come and have some food and drink. You must be tired from your journey."

Claudicus barked out a few orders in his native tongue and then led Kira and Croulac inside a reception building. He led them to an open-air restaurant that looked over the city built along the shoreline. It was an impressive sight with unique structures and buildings with an aquatic theme to them. There was a small harbor where a few vessels were docked and two more were making their way towards the open sea. The sun was bright with a few stray clouds drifting with the wind. Claudicus ordered some food and drinks as they sat and discussed what needed to be done. The food arrived, a large platter of fish, shellfish and other delights from the sea. Tira and Croulac tried each one, the taste and texture as fine as anything they had ever had. The drinks were the Sereptin equivalent of OBJ and refreshing.

With the meal finished Claudicus led them to another building, his local command center for operations. Tira asked if she could view a map of the planet and where the stargates were. Claudicus had a giant projection of the entire planet in 3D brought to view in front in the center of the room. The stargates were clearly marked. He zoomed in to each one showing the relative position to the cities and other structures. Tira and Croulac explained how the neuro nets should be set up, basically invisible dome ten kilometers wide and a kilometer high that would be placed over the known positions. They would be connected to several consoles, the primary one in his command center, another on Tira's ship and then a few portable units to be used in the field by his officers.

All could detect whether anything passed through the net. If an enemy ship was cloaked, the neural net could detect motion and should such a craft go through the net, it would emit a spray covering the moving object to make it visible. It also would attach an emitter that would give its' exact coordinates. A weapon then could be fired and destroy the intruder. She suggested that Claudicus position his powerful anti-aircraft cannons around the entire perimeter of the net and additional ones at the outer edge of the cities which were most likely the targets. The only weakness in the defense were the two stargates that would not have a neural net. Tira indicated that she would position her craft up in space overlooking those two and have all her weapons at the ready directed at them. She would activate advanced sensors that would detect any heat signatures which every craft emitted and even if cloaked she could identify their position and take them out. Tira then asked,

"What about your cities and citizens Claudicus?"

"The land cities are being evacuated as we speak, and moved to their mirror imaged underwater counterpart. Only military personnel will remain on shore. It is the one great advantage our species has, being able to live underwater and at great depths. The underwater cities will then have all women and children and our elderly moved even deeper in the ocean to safe haven structures we have constructed. Only defense and military will remain in the primary underwater cities. We expect the LuQuarin to attack those if given the chance and have set up additional defenses there. We learned a great deal the last time we fought them and are better prepared now than ever before. If/when they attack we will make them pay dearly."

"Excellent, Claudicus. You should be able to have the neural nets up and operational within a few hours. Once they are in place, tested and operational, Croulac and I will head up into space and cloak the ship to protect you from the two open stargates."

The day passed into night. All the preparations for an attack were made and every Sereptin at the ready. Kira and Croulac were orbiting the planet in the northern hemisphere where to two stargates that were without neural nets lay. Kira looked at all her monitors and systems again for the umpteenth time. It was past midnight and no sign of an attack. Croulac had dozed off at his station next to hers. She looked at him sleeping in his chair quietly. Her feelings for him had grown strong since the day they met. She checked in with Claudicus down on the planet at his command center. He too had nothing to report, all was quiet.

Two more hours passed and Kira nodded off, tired from the many days without real sleep. A little beep and a light went off on her monitor. It beeped again, this time waking up both Kira and Croulac. They both quickly came to their senses and looked at all the displays. First it was just one of the three stargate areas near the cities which had detected a reading, then the other two, signaling a stargate was being activated and opened up. She contacted Claudicus. He simply replied,

"It has begun. We are ready here. Good luck, Kira. Let's take these bastards down."

A Divided Universe

She watched as the neural net became active and a cloaked enemy craft flew through it, instantly being marked and targeted. Then another. Soon all three stargates showed dozens of LuQuarin craft breeching the invisible barrier. She heard Claudicus give the order. A barrage of anti-aircraft weapons fired their missiles and lasers each finding their mark and destroying the crafts. Kira witnessed the explosions from above. More craft flew into and through the neural nets, the volume of enemy crafts increasing. A few broke through the defenses and headed to the cities firing their missiles as they approached. Most missiles were intercepted by defense fire from the cities perimeter, but two got through and a tremendous explosion occurred. They were using nuclear warheads. Kira noticed the two northern stargates becoming active and with her sensors could detect the heat signals as the cloaked enemy crafts emerged through. She yelled at Croulac to take the left one, she would focus on the right. They engaged the ship's weapons and fired from above down on each heat signature identified. They were coming too fast. They both targeted and kept firing taking them out one by one. She could see a few had escaped their fire and were making their way quickly towards other cities. She honed in on each one and fired, taking out five more of them before they could release their missiles. There was one more left racing towards the capital. She fired again.

"Shit, I missed." Firing again and again she hit it causing the ship to disintegrate just before it released its' nuke. She looked at the remaining ships exiting the portals, fewer now in number.

"Croulac, keep firing. I am going to take the ship down between the two stargates. I don't want even one of those to get through."

All the monitors were displays of ships and gunfire from both sides. The two cities hit were in flames amid the fallout of explosions. As she went down into the atmosphere, Croulac kept firing, hitting the enemy ships hard and fast. She positioned the ship between the gates and switched the position of her weapons at the stargate on the right. Croulac was still firing as she opened fire again taking out the last three that had emerged from the gate. Croulac stopped and told her no more enemy ships were coming through the gates. Kira looked at her monitors to see how the other defenses were holding up. Claudicus contacted her as the sounds of weapons and explosions rescinded. A thousand burning flames from enemy ships covered the ground.

"Only two got through, Kira, and both cities were empty except for our outer defenses. Casualty reports appear to be minimal."

"Claudicus. I am going to see if I can capture one of the northern stargates." She maneuvered the ship and pointed it and sped towards the gate. She could see one downed ship just through the gate, and a survivor crawling away from his burning vessel trying to make it back through. She saw more explosions on her monitors. The LuQuarin were blowing up the other gates so they would not be captured. Kira was only two hundred meters away watching the LuQuarin soldier reach the gate. She fired a freezing stream of liquid at the gate, trying to stop the lone soldier and keep him from exploding it. He slid through just as the freeze hit the gate and froze it completely. The soldier was gone but the gate preserved. They would not be able to blow this one up, and perhaps finally the Elior could learn how they operated.

She heard the sounds of other Sereptin fighters in the sky above her ship. They surrounded the entire area insuring that no one could attempt to explode it. Claudicus came on the line.

"The other four gates are gone. I hope the one you froze will remain intact. I am sending out a team of our scientists to inspect it."

"Excellent. I am running my scanners on it now to see what they may reveal. It would be to our advantage if we can finally learn how they are used."

"Be careful, Kira, the LuQuarin are known for setting traps."

A Divided Universe

Chapter Twenty-Six
Lanatars' Return

Eftar ran through the halls of the great home of Tenekaris III looking for the Master Overlord. The news he was bringing would not be received well. He was not in the great hall and throne room which usually meant he was being entertained in his private quarters.

"Damn." Eftar hated to disturb him at such a time, knowing any such interruption in his drinking and sexual exploits was met with anger. Not the way to start a new day with the most powerful LuQuarin. He approached the outside of Tenekaris personal chambers where two guards stood at the door. One guard looked at Eftar and shook his head with a no. Eftar acknowledged with a nod and slowly walked away. As important as this was it would have to wait until his Master was done with his exploits. He would wait in the great hall.

Tenekaris woke up on his huge bed, opening his eyes to a pounding in his head, a by-product of all the grog he had consumed through the night. Sitting up he discovered a naked chamber maid next to him, passed out or dead, he wasn't sure. Another chamber maid was sprawled out on the floor next to the bed. He laughed to himself.

"Guess I had a good night with these two. He got up and found another pitcher of grog and chugged it down. He needed the pain in his head to go away and from experience knew this would help. He staggered to the doors and opened them where the two guards quickly came to attention.

"Fetch me new chamber maids and attendants as it seems the ones I have in here are not up to the task of serving their Master anymore."

One guard ran to meet the Master's request. To the other guard he spoke.

"Take these two out of here, they are no longer any use to me."

A Divided Universe

The guard entered the room and carried them out one by one laying them next to a wall. He then walked away seeking a cart where he could transport them from the Masters' chambers. The other guard returned with two new chamber maids and three attendants, there to bath and clean up the Master and the room. They entered as the guard closed the door behind them. This was not a new event; the guard was used to the great Overlord's incessant behavior. An hour later Tenekaris emerged from his chambers asking the guard.

"Where is Eftar?"

"He waits for you in the great hall, Master."

Tenekaris nodded and walked towards the hall. He found Eftar sitting on a side bench near his throne. Eftar raised his head as the Master entered, and stood up to great him.

"Master Tenekaris. Good morning, sir. I take it you had a fine evening?"

Tenekaris just grumbled and took a seat on his throne, now dressed in his immaculate style of black and gold light armor and a silver cape.

"Eftar, is there any word of the mission to see the Lycoats and preserve our non-aggression pact?"

"Master we sent your least favorite Overlord and his contingent with two large Secarios transports filled with precious metals, gems and the other items you wanted as a gift for them. They should have arrived two days ago. As you requested, as another sign of peace we are withdrawing all 200,000 of our troops and weapons and leaving only an outpost there. They should be on the return journey and should be here within 3-4 days."

"Very good. How are the repairs of our three convoys doing?"

A Divided Universe

"My last report showed we are at 80% completion and have the other supplies being transported there now to complete all repairs. We should be completely operational within a week."

"Excellent, Eftar. And what of Lord Lanatar II and his mission?"

"That is what I need to speak to you about, Master. He returned here just a few hours ago, and it is with regret that I must tell you things did not go well for him. He was seriously injured in the attack and is being attended to by our finest physicians a short distance from here."

"What?" He yelled out.

"Master, he suffered great wounds during the attack, which from what little I know was a complete failure. He has rejected taking any pain meds for his wounds until he can speak with you himself. I have a shuttle standing by to take you, Master."

Tenekaris stood up.

"Let's go, this I need to hear for myself."

After a short shuttle ride Eftar and Tenekaris III arrived at the medical center where Lanatar was being attended to. The lead physician met them outside the critical care area.

"Master Overlord Tenekaris. Thank you for coming. Lord Lanatar has been asking to speak to you. He is in a bad way I am afraid and we are not sure how much longer he has. His wounds are unlike anything we have ever seen." Tenekaris asked,

"How are these wounds different?"

"His left side from his head, down his shoulder, body, hip and leg are coated with some type of gel that is frozen onto him and his body armor. We can't get it off of him no matter what we try. We scanned it and were able to get just a tiny sample to put under the microscope. We

219

have no idea what it is made of or how it stays frozen. It has begun to affect his circulation on that side and some organs. Even if we find a way to save his life he will lose his arm and leg. He knows he is dying and demanded to speak to you."

"Very well. I will see him now." They entered the room and saw Lanatar lying on a gurney with a blanket thrown over his body except for his head. Two other physicians were in the room looking at the monitors displaying his vital signs from the perpetual scanner above. He opened his eyes at the sound of the three entering.

"Master. I must tell you what happened. My time is short."

Tenekaris motioned for the physicians to leave the room, leaving only Eftar with him. Lanatar took a breath and started.

"Master. I executed the plan perfectly. I brought my command ship through the northeast portal very slowly in stealth mode so as not to be detected. I ran a scan on the planet and cities. Only a few lights were visible on each. I gave the order for all our attack ships not to rely on visual but use the coordinates of the cities when attacking in case the Sereptins went into a blackout mode. I also told them to record their attack in normal and with night vision. Once acknowledged by all five groups I gave the order to attack. The first waves came from the three central portals near all the major cities. I had two hundred fighters in each group, each carrying a nuclear missile. They began to go through the portals, cloaked. At first all seemed well, they made it perhaps five kilometers and then all hell started.

As I viewed my video monitors of the lead ships at a certain point their cloaking ceased and each ship turned a neon green for no reason. They sped up each one heading for a designated target. Then boom! One by one they were shot down, exploding to the ground. A barrage of weapons was unleashed against us. I gave the order for full out attack, full speed. Our fighters were rushing through the portals as fast as they could, each one being tagged, uncloaked and destroyed as it passed that same invisible point. The two northern gates were opened and started their attacks. They were uninhibited and remained cloaked and headed for their targets. Then from space above they too were met with powerful weapons blasting them out of the air.

   I saw two get through from one portal on my screens and unleash the warheads which found their targets. They then disappeared from my screen. I watched as all our 1000 ships were destroyed, my command ship the only one remaining. I gave the order for my pilot to back us out of there into the portal and put all our shield power forward. This huge strange ship came down on us from above and fired. We were hit twice our shields weakened but holding. We were almost back to the gate when we were hit again. It disabled the ship and we went down and crashed very close to the gate. My pilot and crew were all dead.

   I managed to pop the hatch and crawl out onto the ground. I ran to the portal, reached it and began to crawl through when I was hit with this weird freezing gel that came from the huge ship which had followed us down to the gate. As I went through I tried to hit the switch for the gate to explode so no one could follow us or learn of our technology. The whole gate was enveloped with the gel and the destroy switch frozen. My whole left side was writhing in pain as I made it the last few feet to the activated worm hole. I must have passed out, my Lord, as next thing I knew I was in here, my entire left side in pins and needles from the freezing pain. Master, it was if they knew we were coming, how and when. My troops and ships were crushed, all of them lost. I am sorry, Master, I have failed you." Lanatar reached under the blanket into his uniform with his right hand and pulled out a small disk and handed it to Tenekaris.

   "I was able to retrieve the disk which recorded the entire battle before I left my ship. I hope it can reveal to you more than I have been able to tell."

   Tenekaris took the disk and handed it to Eftar.

   "No, Lanatar, you did not fail me. You did exactly what I requested. Your survival and what you have told me this day are invaluable and will help us destroy the Sereptin and the Elior one day soon. Now get some rest and let our Doctors get you fixed up."

"No, Master. My death is near. I can feel it approaching quickly. I ask only one last favor."

"What is it, Lanatar?"

"The three maidens you provided me with. If any of them were to be with child, my heir, I ask that they be looked after to carry on the name of my father and myself."

"Yes, of course, Lanatar."

"Then may I have your short blade please, as I do not wish to die from some foreign gel, but a soldier's death. I beg of you while I still have the strength."

Tenekaris looked down at Lanatar's pleading face. He withdrew his knife from the scabbard on his hip and handed it to him, nodding. He turned, Eftar following him out of the room closing the doors behind. The three physicians were ready to go back in but he stopped them.

"Let him die in peace now. You will know when it is time to go back in. Then, make sure his body is taken and prepared for a soldier's memorial. Do you understand me?"

The three physicians all nodded knowing they could not defy any order given. He and Eftar left the building and headed back to the main command center.

Reaching the command center, they made their way to Kentarious, who was in his office. Tenekaris entered, greeted his brother and handed him the disk provided by Lanatar.

A Divided Universe

"The attack on Sereptin seems to have been a huge failure. Look at the videos and see if you can figure out how they destroyed our forces so easily."

"Yes, Master, at once. But I do bring you some good news. The operation on Cryplas goes well. Seldon has been able to establish two mine fields and is already sending back Plastacious. It appears the Cryplasians have their forces nearby, but since we did not use any force, seem content to let us mine, at least for now."

"Good to hear, brother. Now I must examine our large map of the galaxies and think through our next steps."

"Of course. I will have our massive 3D display down below in the center of the room for you so that you can walk through all the operations." He hit a button on his desk and outside the office the entire center of the command structure receded in all four directions, followed by a set of columns raising up a platform above the other workers. The platform was 50 meters square with a pathway ramp emerging that led to the level of his office. He hit another switch and the 3D map of three galaxies appeared. Tenekaris walked down the ramp and stood at one end showing the entire picture of stars, solar systems and planets. He was on the edge of the farthest galaxy to the right of the other two where the neutral zone was separating the Lycoats from his remaining outpost, the delivery of the gifts completed and his troops now on the return journey back to this main center. He walked a few feet within the display and with his hand waved and enlarged an area. He found the relative position of the 200,000 returning, estimating it would be four days before they would arrive. He walked further along until he reached the planet where he was now, the left edge of this galaxy. He walked farther into the center of the three and sought the three locations where the convoys had been deployed with the combined forces to be used on the final assault on Elior.

A Divided Universe

Each group would have 200 million military personnel in total once the final convoys reached their destinations with all the equipment and weapons to prepare for the final journey. He walked farther left, this galaxy larger than the rest, and found where they had plotted the Elior Admiral's position and troops estimated at merely a million, the only troops they had standing between his and Elior. He smiled. Taking out the Admiral would be easy and reduce the defenses Elior had. He trekked through the rest of the center galaxy, stopping and enlarging certain areas. He proceeded then into the third galaxy where Elior lay, halfway between its' center and the farthermost left edge. The Admiral's troops were a five-day journey to engage once the order was given. Figuring a day to take them out, it would be a two-week journey for his forces to be just outside Elior space. He stopped at Elior and enlarged the planet. It showed their outermost forces on three nearby planets and their moons, then the neural net that the Elior's had constructed. A new addition was now displayed showing the six paths the Elior used to shuttle craft through the neural net and the planet; the information gained from his Ess agents within the Council. These six pathways were the ideal breaching points. If they could penetrate them, it would open up holes large enough for his fighters and troops to enter the atmosphere, making the final assault and destruction of his nemesis. He turned to Eftar.

"What is the estimated strength of the Elior defenses and military?"

"My Lord. Our latest count shows their military is down to five million, perhaps even less when you count how many troops they have dispersed to protect their friends."

"Hmm. Five million, and with the Admiral makes only six in total. How many reserve troops do we have, including our allies?"

"We now have 600 million deployed as you know. We have 150 million LuQuarin reserves, all near or on this planet. Our allies have anywhere from 60-80 million each in reserve. Our combined total forces are now at a billion, Master."

A Divided Universe

Tenekaris walked around Elior again noting where each of his three convoys would be attacking once the Admiral had been vanquished. He turned again to Eftar.

"Have the leading commander residing here of each of our allies summoned and the remaining Overlords and Lords that are here as well. See if you can have them assembled in the planning room later today. We may just be adding some additional firepower to the final attack."

"Yes, Master, I will see to it at once."

"Good, let me know the time when you have it. I am going to return to my quarters after I talk with my brother to see what he learned from Lanatar's disk and the failed attack."

"Very well Master, I will send you a message once I have confirmation from those that will attend." Eftar left to attend to the requests. Tenekaris walked back to his brother's office.

"Kentarious, have you learned anything from Lanatar's video?"

"Not much, brother. It shows exactly what he stated. The three of the five stargates had some kind of neural net dome shaped over each, with a radius of five kilometers. The lead ships video had little as they were destroyed almost immediately at that distance from the stargate. The ships following did record the ships being coated at that point with a neon green colored spray making them visible. As soon as they were visible they were destroyed. The video is like a replay of the same event over and over with every ship being coated, then subsequently blasted out of the sky. There were two of our ships that made it through and deployed the warheads nuking the cities targeted but were taken out a moment later. Lanatar's command ship was recording the action from all five of the gates, each showing the same results. The last part of his video was his command ship being hit and downed just before he made it out. All 1000 of our fighters were destroyed, and with no ground established, our land forces never even had a chance to deploy before the gates were shut down. If anything, the quick decision by Lanatar to close them saved those troops from certain annihilation. He saved the 100,000 we had at the ready at each gate and they have all returned here awaiting future orders. The battle, if you want to call it that lasted only 28 minutes with only two cities nuked with unknown results.

Lanatar's ship did record this large ship that attacked his, coming out of space taking out what few fighters that remained before targeting him. It has a design I have never seen, but matches the three ships that attacked our slave compounds. It has similarities to some Elior designs but is unique in many other ways. The question is, how many ships like this do they have, and what can we put up against them to take them out?"

"A fair question, brother, and one we need to consider before we attack Elior. I am going to take a break for a while. I am having Eftar assemble all of the commanders for a meeting later and would like you to attend as well so we can formulate a revised plan."

"Very well,

Tenekaris. I will be there." Tenekaris nodded to his brother and left the compound.

Chapter Twenty-Seven
A Council Revived

Alex was wide awake after only an hour of sleep. Thankful for the Medallion and restoration drinks, he was alert and eager to see what the Council would say and the new plan to defend Elior. It was already 9:30 and the Council was in session. In a half hour, decisions would begin which would impact millions of lives. Grabbing a cup of coffee, he sat on the terrace of the suite overlooking the bay below Ventura, the sun high in the sky with a light breeze flowing, pondering where the fate of this beautiful planet may yet wind up. At 9:55 he sat up, vaped and ported to the meeting place.

In the lobby Alex took a seat. A moment later Thyon and Lorakit vaped in, followed by General Uraguard. They exchanged greetings. Standing outside the chamber doors were two guards who stood awaiting orders to usher them in. Promptly at 10, the guards motioned to the four and opened the doors. Walking in, they took their seats at the table across from the now seven remaining Council members. Levilor spoke first.

"Welcome back. I hope you were all able to get a little rest. We have much to discuss this day as the fate of Elior and others rests in our hands. The Council members and I have come to agreement on a number of items. First, we are going to send an SSSTS to the Admiral to have him return with all of his forces back here to Elior. If he were to remain where he is he would be overwhelmed by the sheer number of the enemies' forces. By returning here it will add to our defenses and improve our chances of survival." The General raised his hand as if to interject.

"Yes General, what is it?"

"Levilor. We have a new technology recently developed and tested which would provide some benefits while the Admiral's forces return here."

"Go on General."

A Divided Universe

"We now have the capability of projecting a realistic hologram depicting an army of forces, quite large, which in essence would provide the appearance that the Admiral's forces were still there and ready to fight and defend their territory. Even scanners from a distance would still depict the apparent reality of said forces luring the enemy in to attack. Not until they have actually breached the space where the hologram exists would they be able to tell that it was not real. The hologram then disappears and underneath it we would have thousands of missiles that would launch up into the enemy and destroy those within the distance of the missiles' capabilities. This is accomplished by filming the actual forces as if they were ready for battle and the associated movements. The Admiral could start sending his forces back, but at the same time stage the film as if they were about to be attacked. This would only take him a few hours to accomplish and put in place, at which time the remaining forces could return to Elior. This also would give our enemy pause to think before they attack any installation here or nearby Elior. They will not be able to tell what is real from that of a hologram. This would be a nice tactical advantage for us when they approach Elior. Only we will know what is real and what isn't and can deploy our forces for quick counter attacks and measures."

"How big a hologram can you produce, General?"

"Each hologram would be large enough to depict a fighting force of 200,000 or so. We would need to send the Admiral five of the units. The good news is they would fit in the SSSTS you are sending. I need only add my senior technician to go with the pilot."

"Very good, General. I will send word to the SSSTS to await their arrival. This could prove to be quite valuable in our defense."

"I will send a message to my technician immediately." Levilor then continued.

"The Council has also come into agreement to begin adding our strongest shields underneath the neural network that surrounds Elior. If the net were breached the shields would provide an extra layer of defense.

A Divided Universe

We will not be able to build a shield around the entire planet but will get in place as much as possible in the time we have. Next, we will reach out to our architectural engineers for construction of underground safe havens for our citizens to be built to withstand an attack of any kind be it nuclear, chemical or biological. This will insure our people survive if they make it through the net and shields and our defending forces. We are responsible for over 4 billion inhabitants on this planet not including all the wildlife. The preservation of our species is at stake here. We will also use our miniaturization abilities in order that the complexes can be smaller than normal, yet house many inhabitants. We will request that medical facilities be built to handle our wounded when the time occurs." Levilor took a sip, then continued.

"Tonight, we will make a worldwide live broadcast to inform all those here on Elior or nearby planets of the events that have taken place and prepare them for what we expect to occur. We do not wish to panic our people, but they have a right to know. In the broadcast we will request that all non-active or retired military personnel return to the previous command posts for reassignment. Since many of our existing forces are clones they will be dispersed in our first line of defenses so that any possible casualties incurred would be the clones first. This will more than double our forces to defend Elior. Would you concur with this, General?"

"Yes, Levilor, and might I also suggest we send SSSTS to our other 8 friends and allies and ask if they could send some of our troops back. If Elior were to fall, their fate would soon follow, and I feel it best if we could face the enemy with as many forces as we can muster sir. I would also suggest we take as many of our advanced cloning units and match them up with our best soldiers in all categories to further increase the size of our fighting force and the munitions and equipment we need to make." Levilor looked at the other Council members to see if they agreed with the Generals idea. Each one nodded.

"Agreed, General by all members here. We will dispatch the SSSTS to the 8 planets. I will send word to our leading clone scientist to assemble all units for your use." Uraguard spoke again.

A Divided Universe

"Council, I suggest we change the six pathways we currently have from the neural net to the planet. I have no doubt that the existing paths were given to our enemy and would be a weaker point for them to breach, thus they should be sealed completely and new paths created." Levilor again looked at all the Council members for agreement.

"Yes, General, make it so." Thyon then added,

"With the Council's permission I would like to provide the General and the Elior military the plans to build the pulsar cannons, like the ones that reside within our ship. You won't have the time to incorporate them into your spacecraft, as that is a much longer and more difficult process, but you will be able to build base cannons and position them around the globe. You have all the necessary components and energy here on Elior. This is a very powerful weapon which we designed for our defense and protection when we traveled the universe. It was never intended to be used as an offensive weapon. Thus, we ask that the secrets contained in its' construction be held in the strictest confidence."

"You have the word of this Council, Thyon, and only those that need to know will harbor its' secrets."

"Very well Levilor." He handed an information disk to the General.

"Uraguard, when you begin to make the pulsar charges used as ammunition for the cannon, I would like to request that you restock our three ships first. Each ship can carry a maximum of 100 charges, and with our speed and maneuverability we will be able to inflict serious damage to the LuQuarin and others. Then I suggest you place the newly produced cannons around the six pathways you are closing, as the enemy will try and breech those first and run into a fireball from hell when they try." The General nodded in agreement. Levilor continued.

"When we speak to our people tonight, we will also inform them that many of our production facilities will be converted to producing military equipment and munitions, will run non-stop and request volunteers from our society to help us man them, assisting and speeding up the operations. Since our production facilities are primarily robotics, it will not require that many volunteers. We have many semi-retired scientists and engineers and production experts that these positions would quickly be filled. Now in order to expedite all the matters that face this Council and our people we have drafted up a list for each Council member to begin carrying out once this meeting is concluded.

The general will meet with all top military personnel and draft a detailed plan how we will defend Elior. Thyon, when your sisters return please coordinate with the General and his staff to integrate your ships into the defense plans. Alex, you are a great warrior and a hero to our people. I would like you to be present when we broadcast tonight to our people. In the meantime, you are free to decide where you may be best-suited to assist us in defeating the evil that approaches. Now if there is nothing else I suggest we all begin the tasks we have at hand." Thyon spoke up.

"Levilor. If I may ask, can we send Ezmull and Fred to the Kinorians so they can extract the LuQuarin and return them to their normal selves. I chose not to kill them as both served the Elior well in their lives for hundreds of years and deserve the opportunity to regain their dignity and honor with the Elior. You merely need to dispatch a small ship with an emissary as I have the coordinates and passwords they will need to meet with them. As you know, the Kinorians live in secure underground facilities and in the eyes of our enemy no longer exist. The Kinorians were the ones that provided the LuQuarins with the technology over 1000 years ago while being held hostage to their wills. If anyone can extract and return Ezmull and Fred to normal it would be them."

"Yes, Thyon, you have our permission to commission a ship."

"Thank you."

"This meeting is officially adjourned. I will see you all tonight a half hour before we broadcast to the entire planet."

A Divided Universe

Levilor rose as did the other Council members and exited out the rear of the room. The General nodded to Thyon, Alex and Lora and headed out to gather the top military leaders. Thyon and Lora bade good-bye to Alex and were heading back to his ship. Alex walked out of the great hall and stood outside, the bright blue sky and a light breeze greeted him as he exited the building. He vaped and ported home.

Alex summoned his clone. After meeting and getting updated he put the clone back into hibernation. He caught up with Diana at their home. She was sunbathing by the pool and reading. As he walked onto the deck she looked up, a smile on her face, knowing that her real Alex had returned. She stood, walked over, hugged and kissed him. Their embrace lasted as he hugged her tight. She could sense there was more here than just a kiss, like an embrace of a soldier returning from war. They sat down together at the patio table. Diana first stopping at the dispenser unit getting them each a cup of OBJ tea.

"Welcome home, my soldier. I have missed you."

"As I have missed you as well, my dear wife."

"So how long do I have you this time before you have to leave again?"

"I will be on Elior now for a while. Much has happened, my love, and I can tell you some of it."

"You seem troubled, Alex, what is it?"

"Elior is in danger. We may soon be attacked here by the LuQuarin and others."

"Here on Elior? No way, Hon. We have always kicked their ass in any battle from what I know. Our technology and military are greater than theirs."

A Divided Universe

"Yes darling, in the past we have proven victorious. But this time it is different." Alex went on to explain many of the events that had happened, watching Diana's face slowly turn to one of fear. Alex pulled her into his lap and cradled his wife.

"It will be OK, Diana. We are in the process of preparing for the attack and have many advantages over our enemy except for sheer numbers. Tonight, Levilor and the Council will be making a worldwide broadcast and explain many things. You need to gather the family and watch. I will be with the Council during the broadcast. Afterwards, I want you to have ready a nice BBQ on the beach for everyone. It may be the last time we can all dine together for quite a while."

"OK, I will call my sister in a while and get everything ready for tonight. But now my dear husband I want you to take me to the bedroom so I can ravish you with my love."

The day passed quickly. Alex and Diana head spent a few hours of intimacy before emerging in mid-late afternoon. Diana called her sister and Alex sat on the patio having a beer and a shot, simply enjoying the pleasures of his home. It was quiet, peaceful, the waves beyond rolling up onto the sand, the sky bright with a few scattered clouds and a gentle breeze. He cherished these moments as they were too few and far between. Diana walked out, sitting next to Alex.

"Diana, I want you to attend the meeting with me tonight. Your sister can handle all the dinner preparations and the kids can help as well."

"But Alex, I have nothing to wear, and, well, I have never been to such a meeting. Do you really want me to go?"

"Yes, my beautiful wife. It is about time the planet met the woman who discovered the Medallion with me and has been my greatest supporter through the entire journey which has led us to this day."

"Ok, baby. I need to get ready and find something suitable for such an event." Diana got up, kissed Alex on the head and went into the house, bubbling with excitement to be included in such an important event.

Alex heard footsteps, turned and saw AJ and Xia walk out.

"Hello, father," from AJ. Xia came over and gave her dad a kiss on the forehead.

"Sit my children." They both took a chair at the table across from Alex.

"Tonight, your mother and I must attend a very important meeting which will be broadcast worldwide. After which, we are going to have a nice BBQ dinner out on the beach. I want the two of you to help your Aunt with all the preparations. You may ask some of your friends to join us if you wish." Xia spoke up.

"Father, a worldwide broadcast? I can't remember ever seeing one of those. What is so important that the entire planet must hear?"

"You were just toddlers when the last broadcast was made. It was an important day for Elior then, and an even more important one now. Just listen to the broadcast and you will understand." They both nodded.

"Now, find your Aunt and see what she needs help with. I have to get dressed and ready to leave." The two got up and headed to the home next door where their Aunt lived. Alex went into the house. It was time to get ready for the meeting.

Almost two hours passed when Alex walked out into the family room clad in his finest uniform with the Medallion around his neck, displayed on his chest. It was olive green, trimmed in gold and black, with black boots. Diana came out a minute later, dressed in a long teal dress with a silver lining. Her hair was tied up in an elite fashionable manner, exposing her ears and neck, clad with silver earrings and two necklaces. The dress had a slit down one side from just above her knee down to the bottom which was mid-calf. Matching heals completed the outfit. Alex looked at his radiant wife a huge smile on his face. She looked like a princess out of a fairy tale. He walked over and hugged her and gave her a small kiss.

"Ready, my queen?" She nodded as Alex took out his orb and gave Diana a bracelet. A moment later the two were gone, having vaped and orbed to the great hall of Ventura where the broadcast would take place.

A Divided Universe

Chapter Twenty-Eight
Elior Prepares

The entrance to the great hall was crowded as those attending were arriving quickly. Alex and Diana looked around and saw Thyon, Kira, Tira, Stilzen and Croulac all in a small circle. Kira and Tira must have just returned. He also saw Alett and a few others he recognized. He walked with Diana over to the group. After shaking Thyon's hand and kissing Kira and Tira, he greeted the rest and introduced Diana. It was time. Alex led the group into the great hall to take their places.

At the front of the were seven large elegant chairs of silver with maroon padding. To the right and down were numerous chairs in rows where all the Generals and the military were taking their seats. Alex led them to the left where they were to take their place near the Council at the front of the room. The main body of the room had three sections with many rows. The center section was filled with the governors of all the major cities on the planet. The left section filled with the heads of all the science and engineering groups. The right side filled with the leaders of construction, building, production and trade. All in all, more than two thousand were now gathered for the broadcast. The noise from many conversations could be heard over the quiet classical background music being played.

Alex sensed some tension in the room as everyone had noticed only seven Council chairs versus the nine of the past. Quiet rumblings stirred through the crowd. A chime sounded, the music stopped and the room quieted down. From behind where the Council sat, two wide doors opened and the Council members led by two guards entered the room. The guards dispersed left and right and Levilor led the procession of seven. Once standing in front of their elegant chairs all seven took a seat. Levilor then stood back up and went to the podium on the stage in front of the crowd. He held his right hand up to ask for silence. The videos were recording everything and broadcasting to the entire planet.

"Welcome my fellow Eliors, humans and all in attendance. I come before you with the other Council members with a sad heart. Yesterday we lost two of our Council members, Deloria and Clendistin. They were infected from our enemy the LuQuarin, and were about to set off explosives which would have killed this entire Council and many others present at the time. To my right sits Alex, the Earth bearer of the Medallion and his son Thyon and his two daughters Kiramea, and Tiramea, all three born of Kate whom we lost 15 years ago when the LuQuarin attacked our planet. If not for their abilities to be able to see the LuQuarin infection held within others, I would not be speaking with you this night, Our planet and species would have been thrown into chaos."

"Fifteen years ago, after the attack here on Elior, our leader Ezmull and other Council members set us on a course of isolationism after almost 1000 years of being at war with the LuQuarin. That decision was also influenced by our enemy who seemingly disappeared. I am here now to tell you that our enemy has not disappeared, but rather has used the time while we lived in peace to build an army, the likes and size of which has never been seen in the universe. They have infected other species and made them allies and increased their numbers and abilities even more, while we stood down and reduced our military, replacing much of it with clones and technology. Only our Admiral and one-eighth of our force has continued to scour the universe for their whereabouts and to insure the protection of Elior and our friends. His work and efforts have provided us now with valuable information, without which would have led us to being completely vulnerable to a LuQuarin attack. The LuQuarin have already attacked our friends on Galan and many have died. They also have attacked Sereptin but with our advanced intelligence we were able to meet and defeat them in battle and Sereptin suffered only very minor losses." He paused and took a sip from a glass before continuing.

"In just the past two days we have learned of a massive enemy force building up and getting ready to make their way into our system and attack us. Our time grows short. Thus, this Council now has to call on all of Elior to unite and prepare to defend our planet and way of life, and the reason many of you were invited here. You represent the leadership of Elior in all our major facets and we call upon you to work with us in order to meet this threat and preserve our way of life. The Council is in complete agreement of what steps we need to take now with all haste while we still have the time. The following is a basic outline of these steps, with more details to be filtered down to each group, be it our military, science, technology or construction."

"First, I am asking that all non-active duty military personnel, or those that retired early report back tomorrow for duty and re-assignment."

"Second, I am asking our scientists, engineers and technicians to begin to reinforce our neural network, with advanced shields to be built and put in place as quickly as possible."

"Third, We submit to our buildings and facilities team plans to begin constructing underground cities for our citizens to give them safe harbor and protection in the event our enemy breaches our defenses."

"Fourth. We submit to all production facilities of non-essential items to quickly convert over to the manufacture of weapons and munitions which we will need to furnish our military in our defense."

"Fifth. We have ordered the Admiral to return to Elior with his entire army to help us defend upon the threat that is approaching us."

"Sixth. I am asking the Governors of all our major cities and population areas to coordinate with the other groups to insure we can maximize our defenses and have in place the protective sanctuaries under the surface. I and the Council will be meeting with the Governors tomorrow morning, as well as our military and other groups."

"Seventh and final for now. We are requesting volunteers from our population to help man the facilities and assist in providing the resources we will need in order to make Elior a planet where our enemy will learn to regret they ever attacked."

Levilor looked out over the audience, the silence deafening and the looks on many of fear and distraught.

"My fellow Eliors, and humans. I do bring to you this night some good news. Our Admiral along with help from Alex, Thyon, Kira, Tira and many others helped to free all the humans the LuQuarin had in three slave camps. Over 50,000 humans were rescued and are now on their way back to Elior. We ask that you help us welcome them home from a brutal captivity and take them in to the life all of us enjoy here on Elior."

He paused and took another sip of his drink. Setting it down he looked out over the audience from left to right.

"Many of you may be afraid and despondent now of the hopes for our future. Fear not. The Elior have always risen to the challenge, and for 1,000 years have turned back the enemy and provided a way of life for ourselves and others that represents all that is good and can be accomplished with the proper morals, ethics and work standards. The days of sitting back are no more. The Elior will now rise again. We will not surrender to any enemy. We will fight to drive the enemy back and defeat all the evil that permeates the galaxies. We will restore peace and put in motion the necessary ingredients to insure the preservation of all good species and never allow the forces of evil to grow and threaten us or any others ever again. An old saying goes. "Evil grows and wins only when good people do nothing." It is time for evil to face the wrath of the Elior. Tomorrow begins a new chapter in our history. The first few pages will be filled with hardship, sacrifice and even loss. But we will prevail whatever the cost."

"Now go in peace and enjoy this night with family, friends and others. There will be numerous announcements in the morning, both worldwide and regional to provide answers to what I am sure are many questions. We have assembled a large staff to answer your questions as well as coordinate all the efforts needed for our preservation. Yes, we will prevail and set a new path for greater order and peace throughout the galaxies and the universe. Thank you." Levilor turned from the podium and walked back and then out of the room, the other Council members following.

Alex looked around at the crowd and saw faces in shock, stunned by what they just heard. Some got up and began to walk out, while others talked in small groups. The Generals all stood up and led their military personnel out. They would begin to make their plans and no doubt have a long night. Alex stood, followed by Diana, and walked up to Thyon, Tira and Kira.

A Divided Universe

"I would like you and your sisters to join us for dinner out on the beach tonight. It is time you met you half brother and sister and enjoy good food and spirits. Croulac, Stilzen, Lorakit, please join us as well. It may be the last night we can gather and enjoy that which we have for a while." Thyon stood.

"That sounds like a wonderful idea father." They all walked out of the great hall, vaped and ported to Alex and Diana's home.

A Divided Universe

Chapter Twenty-Nine
Preparation & a New Power

A week had passed since the Council's broadcast and Elior was in a state of tremendous activity as the plans set forth were being carried out. The Admiral's fleet began to return, and the transports carrying the rescued humans had arrived. They were processed and getting settled into three new towns specially built to accommodate their needs. Construction of hidden underground sanctuary cities was well underway. Production plants had been converted and geared up and were turning out new weapons and munitions. All available military personnel had returned and been reassigned with new battle groups formed to be put in place for the defense of the planet. New shields were being put in place behind the neural net surrounding the planet. The six existing pathways to travel in and out of Elior had been closed and new routes established which were controlled by the military. Nothing could get in or out of Elior without their approval.

Thousands of civilians volunteered from all disciplines and been deployed wherever needed. Even Derek had come to Alex and submitted that he and many veterans were ready to serve in the defense of Elior. Alex guided Derek to the General and if they could prove they were healthy enough and willing, would be indoctrinated into the Elior military. The General had sent Alex a message notifying him that over 50,000 humans that had served in Vietnam and the Gulf wars were now being formed into a militia to become part of the defense plan. Many of the veterans were pilots and were now being trained as Elior fighters.

Alex had just left the morning meeting with the General and his staff as details for the defense of Elior were being implemented. He also learned that the pulsar cannons were coming out of production and going through final testing under Thyon's guidance. The munitions for the weapons were in full production and Thyons', Kiras' and Tiras' ship had been reloaded and ready for combat. It was coming together faster than Alex expected. The Elior were working as one giant team with exceptional coordination. He had never witnessed or even heard of anything like the activities which enveloped the planet. He ported home to have lunch with Diana.

As he walked in the house he saw Diana preparing their lunch in the kitchen. After a brief kiss she led him out onto the patio where they sat, ate and discussed the day's activities. Diana told Alex that Olisaria had offered her underground bunker to them, her sister, parents and others on the island when the time came to go underground. She had expanded the facility to house and protect all of those on the island. Alex smiled, knowing Olis had taken the measures to insure his family and others would be out of harm's way when the attack came. After his lunch with Diana he kissed her good-bye and returned to the military ops center to see where he could be of assistance.

He walked into the center and made his way to a small office they installed for his use. After checking the progress and status on the defense and weapons systems, he sat back in his chair and looked out the window. It was another beautiful day on Elior and the thoughts of the skies turning dark from gunfire and battle were disturbing. He had yet to decide where he would fit in best when the battle began. In spite of all his abilities he felt the need to do more. What that was, still continued to elude him. He didn't notice that Thyon had walked into his office, just watching his father in deep thought. Alex saw the reflection of Thyon in the window and turned around in his chair.

"Hello, son."

"Hello, father. Deep in thought?"

"Yes, I guess you could say that."

"Still haven't decided where you want to be when the shit hits the fan?"

"Not really."

"Well father, I have an idea for you if you're up for it?"

"Sure, Thyon. Always open to ideas."

244

A Divided Universe

"Father, I get the strong feeling that Tenekaris will be here when the attack begins. He has waited for this moment his entire life and relishes in the thoughts of glory in destroying us to rule the universe. It may give us the opportunity to actually take him out, along with his Overlords and Lords."

"Damn Thyon, you know even if he shows up he will be so well protected, we would never even get close to him. I know you are powerful my son, but it sounds like a suicide mission."

"Not at all father. Granted a lot depends on how the battle shapes up, but we have an opportunity to use your powers along with mine, Kira's' and Tira's. If we were able to get to him, it could very well shorten the battle and spare many lives from the carnage that we expect to take place."

"True Thyon, but how in the hell are we going to get close to the bastard?"

"Father, you have yet to learn all of your powers, and one in particular that I would like to show you."

"Which power is that, Thyon?"

"You have the ability to fly, and not just fly but at a tremendous speed. You just haven't tapped into your Medallion's power to do so yet."

"You're kidding me, right?"

"No father, please stand and activate your Medallion." Alex stood up and activated it.

"Now father, grab my hands and close your eyes for a minute." The two clenched hands and Alex closed his eyes. Thyon telepathed to his father and led him through the Medallions powers held within to an area Alex never knew even existed. As Thyon's thoughts led Alex to the power of flight, controlling it and speed all came into view. Thyon continued, their hands tightly clenched until his father accumulated the knowledge to use this power. He released his grip on Alex. Opening his eyes to this new discovery he smiled at his son.

"Now father we just need for you to practice. How about we go outside and take a fast flight to one of the moons?" Alex nodded and they walked outside and away from the command center.

"Wait, Thyon we better clear this with central control of they might start shooting at us unknown unauthorized flights."

"No need to, father. First, we will just fly around outside here at a low level below any radar or scanners. Then we cloak. Since we have the flight paths to the new military-controlled routes we can zoom through them and no one will even notice."

Alex laughed. His son had already thought it all through.

"Lead the way, my son."

Thyon lifted off the ground and up about 30 feet then stopped and waited. Alex did the same. It felt a little strange but he was used to that, having developed other powers one step at a time. Thyon flew around in a circle and then back. Again, Alex followed suit. it wasn't long before they were both zooming around at low levels with different maneuvers. After a half hour Thyon stopped in mid-air.

"OK father, time to cloak, and I will lead you up and out of the atmosphere. Once we are clear of the neural net, I am going to increase speed so you can get a feel of how fast you can go." Alex nodded and Thyon led the way up and through the atmosphere. Once past the neural net Thyon zoomed ahead at an incredible speed. Alex followed, trying to catch up to his son. Before he realized it, they were already approaching the smaller of the two Elior moons. He followed Thyon down to the surface. On the surface Alex looked at his son.

"Damn Thyon, that was a rush."

"Yes, the first few times are quite an experience and we don't even need air to breath, at least for a short period of time. But I would recommend that you incorporate your shield space suit if you plan on spending much time in space. Let's get back, we have a lot of other things that need attention, but if you have the time, try and practice each day." Alex smiled at his son and the two headed back to Elior.

Back in the command center Alex and Thyon caught up with General Uraguard to go over the deployment of the new pulsar cannons. The general showed them an improvement they made. Since there wasn't enough time to incorporate into their fleet of ships, they designed a platform that the cannons could be mounted on that was mobile, a single cannon or as many as five on one platform that could be maneuvered either within the atmosphere or outside of it in space. Each platform had a mini control station where an operator could control the position of the platform. A second soldier would be in charge of the firing solutions, plotting in the coordinates to launch the massive projectile, and others there for reloading. The platform could house up to 200 charges before needing to be resupplied. Thyon reviewed the design, making a few minor changes to balance the weight and impact firing would have on the platform. The changes would be incorporated and a test would be performed within a day. Satisfied with the changes Thyon and Alex departed the command center. It was already evening when they walked back outside. Parting ways for the night, Thyon headed to his ship with Lorakit and Alex vaped and ported home.

Two days passed as more preparations continued. The Admiral and the balance of his fleet had returned. The Elior military was coming together and with all the clones that had been made over the past years and those returning to duty, now stood at over 15 million, the largest it had ever been. Reforming each battle group consisted of a million and a half strong in ten major groups, with subdivisions in each that specialized in various types of operations. The planet had been divided into eight primary sections with one battlegroup in each. The other two battle groups consisted primarily of fighting craft that would be off world, either in a defensive position in space or hidden in nearby solar systems. With the size and scope of the enemy they were expecting them to surround the planet and having mobile forces to attack them from the rear or flanks was paramount.

A Divided Universe

Alex practiced his new-found power each day, adding his shield suit for extended travel in space. On one exercise he traveled as far as the next planet in the solar system which took only a matter of minutes. Adding the gauntlets, he practiced firing his different weapons on a few asteroids and floating space debris. After blowing up a small asteroid he stopped, and just floated in space looking around, experiencing a new wonder. The stars, the planets and Elior were in the distance along with her two moons. Alex marveled at the realization of how powerful he, his son and two daughters had become. Thyon's idea of going after Tenekaris and the Overlords became a real possibility. He headed back to Elior, testing his speed to the max.

Back in the central command center the Admiral was gathered with the ten generals in charge of all the main battlegroups. They were reviewing the impending LuQuarin attack and building contingency plans for when the attack began and how the LuQuarin and their allies would beseech themselves for the conquest of Elior. With the sheer volume of how many they would face, reducing the odds early would be critical

if they were to survive. Time was growing short. The attack could be soon, very soon. Once the long-range sensors went off, they would have just three days' time before the LuQuarin would be on Eliors' doorstep. The Admiral knew he could not play a game of attrition, in spite of advanced weaponry, speed, miniaturization and the new pulsar cannons. This would be a bloody battle.

248

Chapter Thirty
The LuQuarin Deploy

Tenekaris paced around the central command room staring at the large 3D map in the center. Another two weeks had passed and most of his troops were now in place and the repairs to the damaged ships complete. Eftar entered the room and came up to the Master Overlord.

"Master, I bring you a message from Elior." He handed Tenekaris the message. Tenekaris read it and put it in his pocket. It was from Deloria and Clendistin, dated over a week earlier. In it she revealed that Alex had returned with evidence that would convince the Council into action. It would be her last message as on the morrow she would take out the entire Council with explosives during the meeting and take Alex out as well.

Tenekaris smiled. It was time to deploy. Elior would be in Chaos and ripe for the attack and invasion. First, he would make quick work of the Admiral and his mere million battlegroup. Then on to Elior and rid himself of a life-long nemesis. From there the universe would be his for the taking. Tenekaris walked to his brother's office and entered.

"Kentarious. It is time. Send word to all the Overlords and leaders of our allies. I will be departing here with our remaining forces today and be heading to meet up with them with our second transport group. They need to be ready to deploy upon my arrival as we will be heading to the last know position of the Elior Admiral. Have the other two groups assemble and begin their journey towards Elior. Have them split up under our revised plan and take position three solar systems away from where Elior lies and wait for my arrival. They are not to engage the Elior in any way until my arrival. I will make quick work of the Elior Admiral and join them shortly thereafter. Now I must assemble my personal things for this journey. The Secarios built me a fine command ship." He turned to Eftar.

"Prepare my ship and the elite guard that will accompany me."

"Yes, Master at once." Eftar ran out to carry out his Master's wishes.

A Divided Universe

"Kentarious, brother. I would like you to join me and bring your staff. The ship is big enough and we can coordinate any changes along the way if necessary."

"Older brother and Master. With the size and scope of our military I must request that you allow me to be on my operations and logistics ship. When you start the bombardment of Elior I will see the attack as it unfolds and will need to ensure that you have a continuous flow of ammunition and stage them accordingly. I have equipped your ship with special consoles and technicians so you can see all troop and ship movements, the same as I do. You will be near the front of the attack groups and I will be staged a little behind you to cover the rear and flanks should the Elior try something we don't expect. Once you have control of the planet and they have fallen I will join you at the time of victory."

"Yes, Kentarious, you are correct and wise. It is why I chose you for this position. Very well then, we will join when Elior has fallen and ride into their atmosphere and plant the flag of the LuQuarin. I will see you on the battlefield, brother." Tenekaris bade his brother good-bye and walked out heading for his new command ship.

Once aboard Tenekaris summoned Eftar.

"Did you load the ship with my grog and enough playmates for the trip?"

"Yes, Master. I have an ample supply of grog and twelve playmates for you. Might I suggest you go a bit easier on them as it may be a long journey and we have not the room for any more than the twelve." Tenekaris laughed.

"OK, Eftar, I will try and not be too harsh on them. But once Elior is conquered I expect to have many to choose from including some fine Elior females." He laughed again relishing in the thoughts.

"I will go to the bridge now. It is time to launch this beautiful ship and get on our way. Send word to all commanders to lift off and head to the coordinates where the Admiral awaits his fate."

"Yes, my Lord."

Tenekaris' ship took off, followed by a large contingent of fighting ships. His ensemble had only 10 million as a fighting force, but soon he would be joined by the second transport group consisting of 300 million ready for battle. He would make quick work of the Admiral and then lead his troops to the outskirts of the galaxy where Elior lay and prepare for the final assault with a billion at his disposal for their ultimate destruction.

A Divided Universe

Chapter Thirty-One
The Hologram Deception

Alex was in the command center in the Admirals office reviewing all the preparations that had been completed in the past three weeks. Eliors' defenses were shoring up and the additional manpower added increased hope of surviving that which was to come. The Admiral started the conversation.

"Alex. When our enemy hits the planet that they believe me to be on, we will only have a week before they reach our system. The space station cloaked there with the two remaining Eliors will wait until the last minute before disengaging the holograms to try and draw in as many of their ships as possible to destroy. Underneath it is a shield we have staged with 10,000 or more projectiles ready to be launched into the enemy, which we can only hope will destroy or damage many. They will then make haste to leave in the SSSTS and return here which will take 2 days. Upon their return we will only have five days until the LuQuarin and others are on our doorsteps. They will film how the LuQuarin approach and their attack formation which hopefully can give us a guide as to how they may approach Elior when the time comes."

"Admiral. With the number of forces we estimated they have, they pretty much can surround the entire planet."

"Yes, Alex, that creates a bit of a challenge for us. With eight groups here and only two battlegroups not on Elior to try and flank them is not adequate. But we have really no other alternatives that the Generals and I can see. The pulsar cannons are going to help, but the numbers still outweigh us. We need to find additional resources or come up with a way to improve our chances. If we are encircled, history shows us that it will not end well or we will be under siege for an undetermined amount of time. Granted our resources and supplies can carry us for a very long time, we non-the-less would still be trapped. We need to maintain an open alley or alleys at all times in order to be able to employ offensive tactics. Although they may bring a billion in manpower and fighting equipment, Elior is four times the size of Earth. For them to control the entire area outside the planet in space will present areas of opportunities we will need to exploit. That is where our two space born battlegroups will come into play, and will need to disrupt their attacks, flank them or get behind them and inflict a lot of damage. It will be a test to overcome great odds in order to survive." The Admiral paused and looked up in the doorway. There stood Olisaria in her full military uniform. The Admiral asked,

"So, what brings you here and in such fashion? I did not know Council members dressed in military garb." Olis laughed.

"Admiral, I have resigned from the Council and asked them to appoint the Director of our science and technology group to take my position. I thought it was about time a female military leader joined all you men. Can't let you have all the fun killing off our enemy." All three laughed.

"Welcome back, Olis. I didn't think Council life suited you all that well anyway."

"If I may Admiral, ask that you have Sevarin reappointed back to me along with all his subordinates. We have worked well together in the past."

"Of course, Olis. I will send word to him immediately, and you will be in charge of the five divisions of the 7th battlegroup. I think having 500,000 troops under your guidance should be enough to keep you busy." All three laughed again. Olis continued.

"Alex, you are more than welcome to join us."

"Olis as good as that sounds, I must gracefully decline. I will be working with Thyon, Kira and Tira in a special ops group."

"Well I will have your back then if needed, and I hope you mine as well."

A Divided Universe

"Yes, Olis you can count on that." Alex looked out of the Admiral's office and saw Thyon gathered with the Generals at the large 3D map in the center of the ops room. He was raising his arms and pointing to various defenses around Elior. Alex turned to the Admiral.

"Perhaps we should join Thyon and the Generals and see what is going on." The Admiral looked out, stood up and walked with Alex and Olis behind to where they all stood. Thyon was still speaking.

"Generals, I ask you again to take two more battlegroups off world and hide them a few solar systems to our west. If the LuQuarin envelop the planet we will need more troops and craft to be able to break apart a pincer move." The Admiral chimed in.

"Thyon, we already have two off-world and have eight here to defend the planet. That would weaken our defenses here."

"Admiral, we all have studied military history and this battle needs to be won in space first, not within the confines of our atmosphere. We need to beat them out in space. The more ships and power we have out there, the better. Tenekaris has staged all three of his main body forces in the galaxy to the east and will most likely put his main body there with the two others to the north and south. That leaves the west open but not for very long. He will move them in and behind us to the west. We simply cannot allow him to completely encircle the planet." The Admiral rubbed his chin as he walked around the map. He turned to General Uraguard.

"How many pulsar cannons do we have now in place?"

"Last count I had Admiral was over 5,000 now. We are producing 500 a day and then one additional day to mount on the movable platforms and deploy. Munitions supply is good and we are adding re-supply chambers at various points around the planet to draw from as needed. We will be adding those to this map later today so we have full view of our defense capabilities."

"Very well, General. Thyon, we will consider your proposal, but before we commit to reducing our strength here, I want to see all our defenses. I agree, Thyon, we need more strength out in space, but the question is, at what expense." Thyon continued.

"Admiral, Generals. I propose that my sisters and I deploy out in space and await our enemy. I will head to the east where we expect the main body to come out of hyperspace. My sisters can take the north and the south. If we can meet them as they come out and blast them with our pulsar cannons we may be able to stack them up a bit and make it difficult for them to get in position. With our ships' speed we could inflict a lot of damage and be gone before they regrouped. My father will be joining me for this task."

"How will you re-supply once you have exhausted the 100 pulsar shells you carry?"

"Our ships are fast enough that we could be back here on Elior and re-supply quickly before the enemy is in place. Based on how they deploy we will head back out and become a constant nuisance to their plans. I have attached a small subspace emitter to our three ships whereby you can see our position and efforts which is a signal they cannot detect. I also plan on seeking out their command ships and if possible, take them out. If we can disrupt their command structure, they will have even more difficulty executing orders. That is when your battlegroups in space can be used to attack and confuse them to an even greater extent."

"Let me think on that, Thyon. Let us rejoin this afternoon and get the specifics in place. You all may return to your duties now." The Admiral departed and went back into his office.

Tenekaris III felt his ship coming out of hyperspace, signaling they were getting close to the Admirals fleet. He finished dressing into his elite battle attire and headed to the bridge of his ship. He wore an evil grin as he stepped onto the bridge and looked out the front to the space and stars now visible. He watched as his battle cruisers and destroyers took up positions ahead and to the sides of his command ship, knowing that soon his whole fleet would be emerged from hyperspace and closing in on their target. Kentarious command battleship emerged and took a position ahead of Tenekaris ship. He would control the attack as they had planned it together. Tenekaris would have a front row seat with the enhanced images being sent from his brother's ship.

All the ships passed through the solar system they had emerged from and approached the one where the Admirals fleet sat on the 4th planet from the sun. Tenekaris marveled as hundreds of his ships passed by getting into position to surround the planet and lay siege. Passing by the outermost planets it would be only minutes now before Kentarious could begin his attack. The video monitor appeared with his brother speaking.

"Well my Lord, the time has come. I am going to deploy our recon fighters in stealth mode to get a closer look. From what we can see here, the Admiral awaits us. There are five compounds active and preparing for our assault. We don't see but a few of his fleet and suspect they are in hiding nearby to try and flank us with a counter-attack. Our secondary group is in place behind us and to both sides should they try such a maneuver, they will be greeted with overwhelming firepower."

"Very Good, Ken. Begin the attack." Tenekaris observed the back of the mighty battleship open up its bay doors and surmised the stealth fighters were launching out the back and heading to the planet. A few minutes later he heard.

"This is recon stealth fighter group one. The Elior is in a defensive position and look to be preparing to fire." Tenekaris heard his brother.

"Take position for the initial bombardment. The cruisers are now in place and will commence fire once you are in position." A minute later Tenekaris heard.

"Open fire! Fire at will!" The cruisers and the fighters now uncloaked so they could fire, sending a barrage of missiles into the compounds. Thousands rained down on the compounds with massive explosives coming from the surface. For five minutes they continued to fire. Ken shouted.

"Cease fire, cease fire!" The clouds from the surface explosions covered the area and they had to wait until the wind blew some of it away. A few minutes later the picture emerged. The compounds were still intact and seemingly undamaged. Tenekaris looked at the monitor which had zoomed in to see what, if any destruction had been caused. He yelled at his brother.

"Fire again, but this time use the nukes as they will explode well on the surface." The order was given and a minute later the cruisers unleashed 50 nuclear missiles at the compounds. When they hit the explosions were massive and mushroom clouds enveloped the entire surface area where the compounds lay. They would have to wait for the clouds to dissipate. Twenty minutes passed before anything became visible and what little that was exposed did not reveal anything. The clouds were still too thick and widespread.

The Elior cloaked space station above the northern ice cap of the planet in space had been observing the attack and insuring the holograms were still in effect. Satisfied, they released the switch which brought the 5,000 missiles from bunkers below the surface up and in the ready position. They would be hidden under the hologram until the very last second. The nuclear clouds were dissipating but the holograms looked normal as if the Admirals forces had suffered no damage. The one officer told the other,

"Get the SSSTS ready. I am going to set the timer for the hologram and to blow the space station up shortly after all the missiles are fired."

The other officer ran to the SSSTS as the idea of getting out of here as fast as possible raced through his mind. The first officer saw it was time to leave. He set the timer on the hologram and the missiles one second behind it, and then the timer to blow up the cloaked space station for five minutes after. He ran to the SSSTS to join his partner after one last view on the monitor which showed the enemies ships closing in to start a third wave assault.

"Let's get the hell out of here." The cloaked SSTS undocked and began to speed away from the fight. They maneuvered away in the opening behind the three sides of the planet that the LuQuarin had surrounded. Once clear the SSSTS engaged at full speed heading back to Elior.

The clouds had dissipated enough that Kentarious could get a full view. The compounds still seemed to be intact. Tenekaris heard him through the monitor.

"What the hell is going on? Their shields can't be that strong." Tenekaris yelled to his brother. Move the cruisers and destroyers in, their shields have to be down to nothing and launch a full assault, all the fighters too. Wipe that son-of-a-bitch out!"

Tenekaris watched as a thousand ships moved closer to the planet just outside the atmosphere now. Suddenly the images of the command centers all disappeared, and thousands of missiles launched off the planet heading right towards the attacking forces. The missiles began to hit his ships, the smaller fighters getting blown out of the air, the destroyers and cruisers taking hit after hit, their shields beginning to break down. Some returned fire after the shock had worn off, and Tenekaris could hear the shouts of many commanders yelling to destroy the incoming missiles and return fire. A LuQuarin destroyer blew up, then another and another. He saw one of his cruisers split in two and then explode. Hundreds of his ships were now damaged or gone. He heard Kentarious.

"Pull back, repeat pull back out of firing range." More ships were hit as they began their retreat. The remaining ships retreated to a safe distance where they were ordered to take up a defensive position and be prepared for an attack from any direction. Two hours passed with no occurrence. Kentarious ordered the fleet to hold their position and sent out video probes with scanners back to the planet they had attacked. The video and scanners revealed nothing. The planet was empty of any Elior or life. There were some signs that they had been there and recently departed. Kentarious moved and docked with Tenekaris ship. It was time to discuss the events. He boarded Tenekaris ship and was ushered to his private conference room. Tenekaris greeted his brother as the two sat across from each other.

"What in the hell happened, my younger brother?"

"It seems the Elior have developed a rather unique deception device. My best guess is that was a very sophisticated hologram, maybe more than one and everything we saw was just a projection. They would need to have a cloaked ship nearby to control the image and to set off the weapons fired upon us. From the surveillance the missiles were hidden underground during our first two attacks, then brought to the surface. This was carefully orchestrated Tene and also suggests they knew we were coming."

"What were our casualties, little brother?"

"We lost 924 starfighters, 14 destroyers and 5 cruisers. One battleship is damaged as it took 14 direct hits, but its' shields held up for the most part. These were powerful missiles. All we succeeded in doing was putting a lot of holes on the planet's surface and a wide-range of radiation on a planet devoid of life. Not quite the victory we were hoping for. So, Master, do we head to Elior now?"

"Yes. I see no need to delay. Our other forces are already on their way and we need to rendezvous with them in a week's time. We learned a valuable lesson today, not to under-estimate our enemy and I don't want to give them more time to prepare for our attack. We know what this new threat is and we will adapt our battle plan accordingly as to not fall prey to such deception again. Prepare our fleet to depart. With our combined forces we have a great advantage over the Elior scum. Prepare a report on the incidents here and provide it to all commanders with an approach as how to seek it out and identify it before launching an attack."

"Very well Tenekaris, I will make it so. The fleet will leave within the hour." Kentarious stood up, saluted his brother and departed. True to form the fleet assembled and started the journey towards Elior.

Chapter Thirty-Two
The Battle of Elior

The SSSTS from the LuQuarin attack on the hologram forces had returned to Elior. That left only five days before the LuQuarin and enemy forces would arrive in the system. The underground facilities were in the final stages of completion and the citizens of Elior were in the process of moving from the surface to the safe haven facilities below ground, hidden in mountain ranges and others well below the surface of the ocean floor. It had been a massive effort by the Elior nation where all had helped in preparation for the battle that would soon begin.

A new fleet arrived from Sereptin, with Claudicus and the Elior commander stationed there. One million Sereptins with their underwater fighting craft along with a million Elior soldiers, many cloned, had returned. The Sereptins were dispersed around the waters of major cities and would lay in hiding if the LuQuarin breeched the outer defenses. The Elior fleet was dispersed three solar systems to the west with three battle cruisers, fifteen destroyers, and 500 small fighters, their land forces placed in other strategic locations on Elior.

Another day passed, the flurry of activity on Elior continued as more defenses were put in place with new pulsar cannons deployed as fast as they came out of production. The Admiral and Generals continued to coordinate and position troops and resources to insure supply lines could be maintained once the conflict began. The Admiral received a new message. The call for help had been answered.

The Mergonolites had assembled their forces along with the Elior forces stationed on their planet and had traveled and were awaiting orders just three solar systems to the west. It had been over 500 years since the LuQuarin had attacked their planet but had been driven away with the help of the Elior. The Admiral sent dispatches to their commander and the Elior commander to hide in the system they were in until given further orders.

The following day the Cryplasians and the Elior forces from their planet arrived. They were ferocious warriors and had good technology.

A Divided Universe

The Admiral positioned them to the northwest in hiding. More Elior cloned battlegroups returned from Elastin adding another 500,000 to the Elior forces and were positioned to the west and south.

The combined Elior forces and her allies now exceeded 20 million. Still they would be greatly outnumbered but the odds for survival were improving. Additional storage of pulsar charges were put in place for Thyon, Kira and Tiras' ships on nearby planets and their moons, well hidden in caches so they could reload quickly if necessary. Thyon had requested four additional crew members for each ship to man the other turret gun weapons systems.

As the fourth day began all remaining citizens headed for the underground facilities and the final positioning of forces, weapons and ammunition were put in place. The Generals dispersed to their command sections on and off the planet and final testing of all communications were run. Central command on Elior now had eyes and ears covering eight solar systems with forces and weapons in four of them primarily to the west, northwest and southwest. Long range sensors were active in the east, north and south where they expected the main bodies of the enemy to emerge. Thyon and his sisters, Alex and Olis met with the Admiral the evening of the fourth day. Lorakit, Croulac, Stilzen and the new crew members were also present. The Admiral arranged a dinner for the group. The information that Lorakit had stolen from the Secarios database was proving to be invaluable. Every enemy ship contained in the database and their cargo had been cataloged and given to all the Generals. Every ship in the database could be quickly identified as to its abilities and cargo giving the Elior a tactical advantage. Neither side had inexhaustible resources and if the Elior could interrupt or destroy the supply chain of weapons and ammunition it may change the course of the battle.

Thyon convinced the Admiral to let him and his sisters go on the offensive when the LuQuarin appeared and attack first before they could get into position and try and surround Elior. Thyon and Alex would head east where they expected the main body to emerge. Kira and Tira would take positions north and south. As soon as the enemy emerged they would use their pulsar cannons and try and stack them up before they could assemble. It was a bold plan and all three would be at risk.

They enjoyed their dinner, Croulac breaking up the serious mood with his sense of humor as the time approached to depart and take up their positions. The Admiral stood up and made a toast. They all stood up and toasted with the Admiral.

"May the forces of good prevail over the evil that descends upon us."

Alex smiled as he set his glass down as did the others. It was a simple toast but the depth behind spoke volumes. The rights and freedoms of all planets and species were at stake and were now prepared to fight and die for that freedom. For if they failed, then the universe would be at the mercy of a force that was unmerciful and darkness would fall on all those in its' path. They shook hands and bade their farewells. Thyon, Alex, Lorakit and the four new crew members headed for Thyon's ship.

The morning of the fifth day since the SSSTS had returned found Thyon in his command chair well east of Elior. His shipped cloaked and scanners all active, they waited. His ship's communications linked with his sisters' and the Admiral's command center had yet to reveal the enemy. As mid-day approached the first sign came from Kira's' ship in the north. Two groups of enemy ships were emerging from hyperspace, one each to the right and left of her position. Kira did not hesitate and relayed she would attack the one on the left first which was closer to Elior and represented a possible pincer mover to envelope the planet. Thyon listened as his sister moved in fast, her ship still cloaked until the last minute when she would need to uncloak to fire the pulsar cannon.

Thyon pulled up his monitor that was linked to her ship so he could observe the action. Kira had moved in and he could see that numerous enemy fighter, destroyers and cruiser had already assembled and were moving to the west, followed by a large battleship. More ships emerged and the force was growing as her ship uncloaked and fired the first pulsar charge at the battle ship hitting it hard. She maneuvered quickly and fired one after another charge at the cruisers, destroyers and then the smaller ships. The fighters were destroyed and two destroyers badly damaged as they began to return fire. Her ship was too fast and her maneuvers unpredictable as she fired again and again and the four turrets were also firing as enemy fighters tried to counter attack. It was a melee of fire and explosions. She fired another round at the battleship, its shields weakening with each hit. She fired at a destroyer, and Thyon watched as it blew up. She continued to unleash pulsar after pulsar, zooming in and out and through the enemy ships.

A few enemy fighters converged on her position, firing madly before the turrets took them out. A few small blasts had hit the mighty ship but her shields deflected them easily. Three cruisers approached firing laser blasts and missiles but Kira sped up and away from the barrage before they could find their target. Up, above and behind the cruisers now Kira unleashed three more pulsars hitting each one, then she fired again. One cruiser blew up, and the other two began to retreat already badly damaged. She quickly repositioned her ship again and fired on the two damaged cruisers, she was not going to let them escape. The screen lit up as both exploded. She was burning through her pulsar charges. Fifty fighters approached from underneath her position. She spun the ship and unleashed five consecutive pulsar charges at the advancing enemy ships as they fired. The pulsar charges expanded their width and blew up all the lead ships. She spun again and flew away quickly, the remaining fighters retreating. Her wild maneuvers continued and more pulsar charges were fired at any enemy ship foolish enough to be in her path. Five minutes passed when Thyon heard Kira's voice.

"Well, brother I am tapped out of charges, time to go and reload." She cloaked her ship and sped away from the battle and was gone in a flash.

Alex and the others on board had been watching the monitor which was now off. Alex looked at Thyon.

A Divided Universe

"Damn, your sister was unbelievable. That was pretty intense but I am glad to see she is now safe and out of harm's way at least for the moment."

"Father, it will take her an hour to reach her cache of pulsar charges, reload and then re-engage. By then the enemy will have thousands of ships in place. It will be a difficult task when she returns."

Sensors went off in Thyon's ship. To the east three groups of enemy forces were emerging from hyperspace. Tira's sensors had gone off to the south and two more groups of enemy ships were emerging near her position. Thyon took control of the ship and the crew manned the turrets. Lorakit was beside Thyon at her control panel and would be firing lasers and missiles while Thyon steered the ship and would fire the pulsar cannon. Alex was to keep the turrets supplied with ammunition as Thyon headed the cloaked ship at the center of the three emerging groups.

The Admiral watched as Thyon's ship headed to meet the enemy and, on another monitor, Tira's ship was about to engage in the south. He ordered two battlegroups of ships from two solar systems from the west to take flanking positions, one each on the north and one on the southern enemy forces which were quickly growing in size. It would take them an hour to be in position to attack. His best cloned fighting men would be at the helms of their craft.

The Admiral watched as Thyon's cloaked ship headed toward the center of the three groups coming out of hyperspace. He sped up and over the emerging ships and took up a position behind where they were entering. More and more ships poured through but Thyon had yet to uncloak and fire. The Admiral wondered what he was doing. More ships and still he hadn't unleashed his arsenal. Finally, he saw a huge enemy battle ship emerge with hundreds of warships in front of it. Thyon uncloaked and fired five consecutive pulsar blasts into the battleship. It shook, shields broken as the sixth blast hit it creating a massive explosion. Cruisers and destroyers had turned and began firing at the intruder that had taken out the lead command ship. Thyon had already begun maneuvering as his sister had done, firing, moving, firing all the while. The

A Divided Universe

Admiral watched as one after another enemy ship exploded, the pulsar blasts reigning terror and all turrets firing. It only took a few minutes before Thyon had exhausted his pulsar ammo so he cloaked and sped away to reload.

In the south Kira had wreaked havoc on the right-side convoy taking out many enemy ships. A few minutes later she too cloaked and sped away. The initial engagement was over and it would be a half hour before Kira would make her second assault. Long range scans showed the Admiral that hundreds upon hundreds of enemy ships were coming out of hyperspace and getting into formation to head towards Elior. They would be entering his solar system within a matter of hours. He checked in with all of the Generals both on Elior and those dispersed in space. Everyone was ready and in position.

Kentarious' ship exited hyperspace, thousands of ships ahead of his command vessel. He was immediately bombarded with incoming communications. His north and south units had been attacked and the lead ships hammered, many destroyed; the lead elements needed to create the pincer move around Elior. The center section leading his group had also been attacked and the Lord's lead command battleship destroyed. The deployment had continued but at a slower pace after the attack and were awaiting orders. He went to his large command map which now showed the status and positions of the entire attack group. Casualty reports came in. A lot of ships had been destroyed quickly by three unique craft, the same three craft he had seen in the videos of the attacks on the slave compounds. The pulsar blasts had been very effective against his lead elements but disappeared. He ordered all battlegroups to move forward towards Elior. If it was a game of attrition the Elior wanted to play, so be it. He would have enough forces in place soon enough that a few losses going in were quite acceptable. He knew Tenekaris would have it no other way. They were a mere few hours from being able to make their first assault on Elior.

With his space force of 600 million in total he would have two million fighting ships to attack Elior in the first wave alone. He would keep his resupply ships back far enough and well-guarded from possible attacks.

A Divided Universe

Once all the ships were out of hyperspace he would establish a rear guard. There were a number of planets and moons available in the next two solar systems to position his ammunition and later the ground troops which for now had been held back. He moved his ship forward so as to be able to set up a central command position closer to Elior where he could monitor and view any engagements taking place. Tenekaris would soon exit hyperspace and be requesting an update. He had convinced his older brother to stay back far enough until he had a firm grip on Elior, at which time he would let him come forward for the final assault and victory.

Kira was rearmed and racing back to the northern enemy forces. Her scanners showed thousands of enemy ships not far away. This was going to be dicey she thought. Time to go after any command ships first and not waste her firepower on the smaller ships. Remaining cloaked she came from below this time and deeper into the line of enemy ships now all around. Using the logistics information, she sought out and soon found a large command battleship, where hopefully a Lord or even an Overlord was in charge. Taking a final look at the enemy ships and positions, she gave the order to uncloak and engage. She managed three pulsar blasts into the battleship before having to quickly maneuver and avoid being hit by enemy fire.

She was almost surrounded by Blisscrell and LuQuarin firing and blasting a hole through them, making quick turns, spins and sideways before zooming away, only to return a minute later back at the battleship this time from above and behind. Two more blasts and she saw the defense shields had been broken. She had to cloak and zoom away again. Thirty seconds later she reappeared now directly underneath the battleship and shot a final blow into its' underbelly. The huge battleship exploded. Cloaking, she zoomed back out and towards the lead elements now. Flying past them she continued until far enough ahead, turned and watched them approach. Fighters, cruisers and destroyers came towards her. She uncloaked and launched a barrage of pulsar blasts into them and before they could respond cloaked and zoomed up and to their left. Twenty minutes later after employing the cloak, uncloak, fire and then cloak she was out of pulsar blasts again and headed back to rearm.

A Divided Universe

The Admiral continued to watch as the three ships attacked the enemy over and over again destroying as many as possible, then disappear and zoom to resupply. Another hour passed and another set of attacks had been made. As many ships as they destroyed, they had barely put a dent in the forces now heading for Elior. His two flanking fleets were in position hiding behind a planet in each zone. The enemy was approaching Elior and gave the order to flank, hit hard and then disperse back into hiding. He watched as the attacks unfolded. It soon became a display of ships fighting from both sides, colliding in battle, massive fire coming from both sides. The flanking maneuver seemed to have a positive effect and the enemy halted their advance to take up a defensive posture against the assault. The engagement lasted only 30 minutes and his Elior ships then retreated as ordered having damaged the elements that were trying to get in position to encircle Elior.

Thyon contacted the Admiral and his two sisters. He wanted to take all three ships and attack the massive enemy fleet to the north and wanted the Admiral to order another counter attack from behind them at the same time. It wasn't long before Kira and Tira had joined up with Thyon, all three ships now reloaded. They would use a three-pronged attack from the front drawing the enemy towards them to give the Elior fleet the time they needed to come in from behind. The LuQuarin, Blisscrell, Thornoks and Flemjots were getting closer to Elior. They took up their positions and Thyon led the way uncloaking first and firing the pulsar blasts into the oncoming ships like a madman, all turrets firing as he made his way in and among the enemy ships. His sisters engaged them from the sides. The rain of fire was intense and all three converged on a LuQuarin command ship, firing at the same time. The mighty enemy ship blew apart, the three dispersing quickly, cloaking and uncloaking. Enemy ships fell into confusion and were no longer flying in formation. The Elior fleet uncloaked from behind and launched an entire salvo from a thousand fighting ships into the enemy's rear. A second round, then a third taking out hundreds with each round. They were ordered to withdraw before a counter attack could be made. The remaining enemy ships stopped, formed a defensive position and communicated back to Kentarious. They had sustained huge losses.

A Divided Universe

Thyon and his sisters went to a small moon on a planet nearby to reload. They disembarked their ships while the reloading took place and met in a small command center deep in the mountains. Taking a seat at a few tables they ordered a fast round of restoration drinks. Alex looked at his three children and the others. They all displayed the fever of battle and the intensity of the action. Adrenaline was at a high. The battle had already gone on for four hours. Thyon spoke to the group.

"As soon as we are reloaded we need to attack the southern group the same way and have the Admiral try and flank them from the rear with his other fleet. We need to slow down their assault and movement towards Elior. If we take out enough of them, it may give them pause to stop and think."

Thyon coordinated with the Admiral the next attack which they executed as they had done in the north. The LuQuarin continued to advance and each attack they made became more difficult. As many enemy ships as they had destroyed, it represented only a small portion of what was now in the theater. Reloading again back in the mountain of the small moon, Alex approached his son.

"Thyon, we need to slow them down even more somehow."

"I know, father. We have taken out their lead command ships in both the north and south. Perhaps we need to seek out the main command ship which is directing their entire fleet. At the speed they are coming in they will be outside Elior in just a matter of a few hours. Let's talk with the Admiral." Thyon went over to the display that had a direct link to the Admiral. A minute later the Admiral's face appeared on the screen.

"Admiral, we are almost finished reloading, but our attacks aren't even really slowing down their advance. We need more firepower quickly if we hope to reduce the time before they get to Elior."

"Yes, Thyon, I am working on that. You and your sisters have done a marvelous job, but I agree we need to bring more into the action. I still have the fleets behind the north and south ready to deploy again and thus far we have yet to suffer any losses. The cloak and quick strikes have been effective. I am bringing up two more fleets from the solar system to the west along with Olisaria's fighters. With five groups we can attack both columns they are bringing in from those two directions. They will be in position in about an hour."

"Very well, Admiral, we will make one more attack, reload and then coordinate a larger attack. This will be quick, as we exhaust our 100 pulsar charges quickly with so many targets. We will also need to know when they have all of their ships out of hyperspace for the impending attack on Elior. We may be able to get behind them at that point."

"Thyon, we are measuring and counting how many enemy ships have arrived so far and comparing that to the manifests of stolen data. They still have quite a few more that will be coming in."

"OK Admiral, we are almost reloaded. Time to inflict a little more damage and upon our return we will formulate the next attack."

"Good luck, Thyon."

Kentarious walked around the large display map in his command ship. The three unique Elior ships had attacked various positions of his lead elements to the north and south. All attacks had been quick and precise, the weapon they used quite effective in taking out many of his ships. Two Elior battle groups had also appeared, uncloaking, firing quickly and then disappearing. He thought.

"So, the Elior have battlegroups out in space, eh. They have to be coming from west of the planet." He reviewed where all his ships were positioned with more still coming in behind from hyperspace. Tenekaris ship would soon emerge and his Master and brother would want a full report. The approach was simple but quite deadly. A bull's head was the main body and the horns were positioning out to encircle Elior within hours. He was reinforcing the horns after each Elior attack in order to extend them when they reached the planet. In spite of the losses, they represented but a mere fraction of the forces available. He reviewed each

270

of the Elior attack points and tactics employed. They all varied not lending to predictability but suggested the Elior forces were small in size and were avoiding a major head-on battle. He summoned three of his tactical officers.

"I want you to assemble from our main body three groups of 10,000 of our small fighters that have the ability to cloak. Send one group above our northern lead group, one to the south. Take the third group and fly them around to the west side of Elior behind their second moon. Have them remain cloaked and silent unless an Elior force appears. If the Elior attack either the north or south lead elements, I want the fighters to sweep in behind them and launch a strong counter attack. They will only have a brief window to inflict damage as so far the Elior come in cloaked, attack for a few rounds and then disappear."

The three nodded and headed off to do his bidding. He looked again at the map. It would take another three hours before they would be in position outside of Elior and their neural net. He felt confident that Tenekaris would be pleased with what he had achieved so far. An attendant showed up with a message from his brother. He was out of hyperspace and would speed up and dock his ship within an hour to Kentarious command ship. Another report came in. The three unique Elior ships just made another assault taking out more LuQuarin ships. He had even lost a battleship and two cruisers this time along with hundreds of fighters.

"They are like pesky flies, but soon will have no planet to harbor them." He yelled to another commander. "Replace what we just lost, no double what we just lost from the main body. Add some of our allies' ships in too, as they have different capabilities than ours and they need to taste the blood as we have to fire them up."

"Yes, sir."

Thyon and his sisters returned after another quick attack on the south. As reloading began he contacted the Admiral and the two Generals that would be part of the next larger attack. They would all head back to

271

the south to try and break the massive lines of enemy ships apart. He requested for Olisaria's attack group to join in. With the three special ships, two main body attack groups and Olisaria's battle group they would have substantial numbers to launch the largest attack on the LuQuarin thus far. The idea was to cut a big hole through the line of advancing enemy ships like chopping a forearm and hand off before it could begin to envelop Elior. Thyon, Kira and Tira would blast the initial hole thru the line, followed by Olis and her 1000 best warships making the breech wider. The generals with 2000 ships each would attack the separated front from head-on and from below simultaneously. While Olis was engaged in the middle, Thyon and his sisters would do a fast reload and return as quickly as possible to continue the attack. This would be a longer engagement and Elior clones and ships would be lost. They would have to move quickly as the advance would be within two hours of Elior by the time this battle was being waged. The Admiral approved the plan. Alex would be firing the pulsar charges from Thyon's ship as he would need to focus solely on flying through the massive numbers of enemy ships they were taking on.

Twenty minutes later and they were airborne, the three leading the charge. Thyon reached his position first, and while cloaked began to scan the area around their launch point.

"Lora, run a heat signature scan. Something doesn't seem right. Their column of ships are moving towards Elior and not in a defensive posture." Lorakit ran the scan.

"Thyon, look at this. It is faint, but there is a long LuQuarin heat trail from here to here but there are no visible ships."

"Open a communication link with Olis, the generals, the Admiral and my sisters through the private sub space channel we are on."

Once all were connected Thyon addressed them.

"It seems our enemy has added a new dimension to their battle scheme. I suspect a large group of cloaked LuQuarin fighters at these coordinates." After giving the coordinates to the others,

A Divided Universe

"We will need to alter our plan a bit. Let's maintain the frontal assault, but take the second battlegroup and instead of attacking from above, reposition your ships below the large heat signature. Olis remain cloaked and below our position and wait until they show themselves. We won't be able to punch as large a hole in their main column but we will be able to take out their fighters in hiding." The Admiral chimed in.

"Olis, split your battlegroup into two elements, have one follow Thyon, Tira, and Kira through the attack on the column. Keep the other half cloaked to cover their flank from the hidden enemy fighters. Thyon, when your pulsar charges are exhausted remain in theater and use your four turrets and missiles to support Olis. We can still punch a pretty large hole through their column and hopefully take out the fighters from our southern forces. Once the hole is punched through, reverse course on all ships and head back through the path you created to take out more and head into the attacking fighters which should have all emerged. With our fire power and faster ships, we could win this battle, then withdraw back to the original starting points and prepare another assault." Everyone agreed and began to reposition.

Now in position the Admiral gave the order to begin the attack. Thyon uncloaked first and within seconds had sped his ship into the moving column, Alex blasting the enemy ships with pulsars one after another. Kira appeared to his left and Tira to his right doing the same. Each pulsar that found its' target blew apart the enemy vessel. They went deeper into the column, the enemy returning fire. Olis led her 500 ships from the split into the battle behind and on the three leading ships' flanks, her own ship in the lead, the head of a wedge of ships firing continuously into enemy craft. The space was an intense display of thousands of weapons being fired, ships exploding, with debris cascading throughout the battle zone. The LuQuarin fighters appeared, uncloaked and came at Olis from underneath and behind. There were thousands of LuQuarin fighters heading at Olis on an intercept course. Her second group of 500 ships uncloaked and hit them from the right side and the Generals' shipped uncloaked behind and below the LuQuarin fighters firing into the rear of their ships. It was a melee.

A Divided Universe

Thyon had blown his way through the entire column as Alex exhausted the last of his pulsar charges taking out two enemy ships with one blast. Thyon raced ahead and did a quick U-turn, his sisters doing the same and they returned to the sides of Olis' lead ship heading back into the enemy all four turrets blasting away, while Alex launched missiles and proton projectiles. They continued past all of Olis' ships and headed into the LuQuarin fighters behind them. The Generals forces were pounding the LuQuarin fighters from behind as they scrambled to turn and face the oncoming threat from the rear. Olis' lead group turned around and followed Thyon and the sisters; her second group pounded the LuQuarin fighters from the side. They had the fighters surrounded now on three sides. Ships were exploding everywhere, mostly LuQuarin fighters. Thyon felt his ship being hit but the shields were holding up well. The numbers of LuQuarin fighters had grown smaller under the attack and the odds evened up. What was once 10,000 LuQuarin fighters had been reduced by 80%, the remaining fighters struggling to survive or find a way out before they would be destroyed. An order must have come in and the fighters made a desperate move to fly straight up and out of the area. The Elior ships fired into the attempt to retreat. It was too late for the LuQuarin ships, and the last few hundred were blown away before they could escape.

The Admiral gave the order to regroup, reform and attack the separated column from behind and above as the lead group was already engaged head on with them. The fighting continued and Elior and enemy ships were exploding as the exchange of fire was non-stop. Thyon recognized some Blisscrell and Thornok destroyers and headed at them. Ships were flying in many directions as dogfights emerged. The communications lines were filled with chatter from a number of Elior ships duking it out with LuQuarin, Blisscrell, and Thornoks. Another half-hour passed, the casualties being felt on both sides. The Admiral gave the order for all to withdraw. They had done a great deal of damage but he saw a large group of LuQuarin reinforcements heading their way. The Elior all cloaked and quickly left the battle zone, each group heading back to a designated safe area, far enough away from the battle and additional Elior forces ready if needed to cover their withdrawal.

A Divided Universe

Tenekaris' ship docked with Kentarious' command ship and a few minutes later he had joined his younger brother overlooking the large display map showing all their forces and the approach to Elior.

"Welcome, Master Overlord." Kentarious debriefed Tenekaris of all the operations, their progress and the attacks the Elior forces had launched thus far, including the casualties suffered up to that point. Tenekaris smiled, a nod of approval. His younger brother had done well and pressed on in spite of the meager Elior attempts to thwart their progress. The casualties were acceptable losses and the LuQuarin held a huge advantage in a numbers game of attrition. They would soon be enveloping Elior, the horns of the bull closing in on the planet, the main body behind his position and almost completely out of hyperspace. A LuQuarin commander approach the two.

"Excuse me, Master Overlord, but a battle has begun in the southern region." Kentarious switched the map to zoom in on the area showing greater detail of all his fighting ships and those of the Elior. The battle was being displayed in real time and they saw the three unique ships blasting through the column, then an Elior attack group following in behind. The 10,000 LuQuarin fighters appeared uncloaked and they watched as thousands of little ships being displayed were engaged in a major confrontation. Two more Elior battle groups emerged one in front of the column attacking it head on, then another behind his fighters, with a third smaller Elior force hitting it from the side. It was an amazing spectacle to watch the battle being waged in front of them on the 3D map. Kentarious recognized a problem; his fighters would soon be getting hit from three sides. He ordered a large reserve to be pulled from the main body and to head into the battle zone as quickly as possible. Tenekaris' smile disappeared as he watched his ships being blown away by the faster and more powerful Elior ships. The attack concluded with the last of the 10,000 fighters erased from the map along with hundreds of his ships from the advancing column. The Elior ships disappeared, no doubt cloaking and retreating. He had witnessed a number of Elior ships exploding and disappearing from the scene during the battle. His smile returned, the enemy had been weakened by their attack. He looked at Kentarious.

A Divided Universe

"What are our casualties so far in the campaign?"

"Well, we just lost 10,000 fighters, and I do not have a count on how many were lost from the advancing column. As soon as I have those I will let you know brother. My best guess is after that last attack we may be around 100,000 ships lost total out of the two million we have available. I will also try and get an estimate on how many Elior ships we have destroyed thus far."

"Very good. How soon will the lead columns begin to encircle Elior?"

"Within two hours they should begin to surround the planet. Once they are in place you need to simply give the order and the barrage will commence."

"Excellent. I am going to return to my ship and private quarters for an hour or so and will return here to the bridge by the time we are ready to commence operations." Tenekaris nodded to his brother and left.

Alex stood over the map in the small command center in the mountains where the three ships were reloading more pulsar charges. They received word that the other Elior battlegroups made it back safely to their hiding places and were also rearming. The Admiral called for a video conference of all battlegroups to take place in 30 minutes. Alex headed to the canteen to get a restoration drink. The battle was now 22 hours old, not even a full day yet.

The group assembled in the small command center tucked deep in the mountains. Thyon, Kira, Tira were joined by Croulac, Stilzen, Lorakit and the local commander in preparation for the Admiral's video conference. Alex walked in and joined the group as the video came to life, the Admiral now in view on the monitor.

All of the Elior battlegroups and her allies were part of the conference. In all, over 20 million forces had been assembled to defend the planet. The Admiral began.

A Divided Universe

"We have done well up to now considering the odds and have put a dent in the LuQuarin lead forces. However, they are now within a short distance of Elior and will soon deploy their ships to surround the planet. This we cannot allow. We have also detected two other large groups of their cloaked fighters, one in the north and another making its' way around to the west of the planet, which as we know will be the only open path if the LuQuarin succeed in trying to surround Elior. First, we must expose the fighters that are taking up position west of the planet and take them out. They have reinforced both the north and south, their northern position stronger of the two. East, well there are so many coming in that way that for the moment there is little we can do against their main body. If we can take out the new hidden threat to the west, I am proposing that we then hit their southern forces hard. Olisaria will be the bait to the west with half of her forces and Thyon and the two other pulsar ships will be cloaked and waiting for them to uncloak. Once engaged, Olis will bring her other half in cloaked farther west. The Elior forces from Elastin will join her and attack from the south. After that threat has been removed, Olis will recombine her forces along with the Elastin troops and wait in reserve in the west. Thyon's ships will reload and be ready to join the southern attack.

"If we can drive them out of the south, only half of Elior will be exposed to attack and in a better position to defend the homeland. We have four Elior battlegroups and our allies have four battlegroups all here in the western region and Olisaria's smaller cavalry-type group for swift action. We add in Thyon's three pulsar ships; then have the capability to face off with their southern force with greater speed, technology and weapons. The four Elior battlegroups mostly consisting of clones will be the major assault force, three to the south and one to the north to thwart the advance of their northern forces. I will keep our other allied troops in reserve at the ready as the battle unfolds. If we can defeat them in the south and hold it, I will shift a number of our pulsar cannons on planet to shore up the north and east. Based on the manifests we have, our enemy was bringing into theater two million fighting ships, of which we have destroyed only 5% of thus far. We will be greatly outnumbered, but that is nothing new for us. Also, if we can hold the south and west, I will release another battlegroup from the surface to join the fight in space and send them to the north. I have reviewed this plan with all our Generals and commanders. Unless someone has anything significant to add we will launch the attack in one hour before the LuQuarin can begin to envelop Elior. Any questions?" No one spoke up. The plan was as solid as could be and the results yet to be known as anything could happen in the next few hours depending on how the enemy reacted.

"Good luck to all of you." The video conference was over.

Chapter Thirty-Three
The Battle Day Two

Tenekaris returned to the command center of his brother's ship. Looking at the huge center 3D map he could see his forces were at the beginning of the phase to envelop Elior. His forces to the north were farther along than those of the south. The entire army was now out of hyperspace and deploying to strategic positions for the major assault on the planet. Kentarious joined him at the map.

"All is going well, Tene. We are still reinforcing the south from the previous engagement, but the north is at full strength. Our main body is intact and approaching from the east. I would say that within an hour we should be able to commence operations on their neural net and whatever other defenses they have in place."

"Excellent, Kentarious. We have waited for this day a long time now. Once we are in position I want you to launch the continuous barrage we planned for."

"Yes. I am bringing up the ammo resupply ships now to be in position behind the attack ships to keep the firing going nonstop. We will breech their defenses in as many places as possible and then deploy cloaked fighters through the breeches to wreak havoc on the surface. I have a number of them loaded with nukes, once we know we can safely pass into the atmosphere and the Ess pilots have targets already assigned." Tenekaris smiled. The vision of Elior in flames was long awaited.

Alex walked up the back ramp into Thyon's ship and took his position at the console for firing the pulsar cannon. Thyon, Lorakit and the four turret gunners were already on board. A minute later Thyon took off, his two sisters' ships right behind. The encrypted channel was open for communications with his sisters, Olis, the Elastin commander, and the Admiral. They were the first phase of the attack. Thyon enhanced the sensor to detect a heat trail left by the LuQuarin cloaked fighters. A moment later it came in view on his screen, positioned only a few hundred miles away. Olis had already taken up position between the LuQuarin forces and Elior and would uncloak and be the bait. Her other troops were to her north and the Elastin group to the south.

Thyon would position himself behind them. With his magnified viewer he saw Olis ships uncloak. A few seconds later the LuQuarin ships uncloaked, all 10,000 of them and moved into attack Olis. She turned her ships to face the oncoming enemy. They began to exchange fire. Thyon uncloaked behind them as did his sisters and all three ships opened up fire taking out 10-12 LuQuarin fighters with each blast. Olis' ships to the north uncloaked and moved in as did the Elastin's from the south. They had the LuQuarin surrounded. The LuQuarin ships disbanded in multiple directions trying to avoid the firepower being launched at them from all four sides. Hundreds of explosions occurred, mostly LuQuarin fighters. In five minutes Alex had used up all the pulsar charges and Thyon was zooming in and out of the LuQuarin fighters with all four turrets finding targets. Ten minutes later, it was over. Only a few LuQuarin fighters had decided to cloak and run away. The rest had been destroyed. Olisaria reformed her battle group and Thyon, Kira and Tira headed back for a fast reload.

The Admiral watched the fast battle in the west and gave the order for the three battlegroups to engage in the south; one head on to their advance, one underneath and one on the side. The first battlegroup facing them uncloaked first and began firing into the advancing ships. They began to send out ships to try and flank the Elior attack group but were met by the uncloaking ships from the side and then underneath. The battle was raging as the forces collided in space. More LuQuarin forces were coming up from the rear to reinforce their position. As they began to join the battle they were met by Thyon's three ships blasting them with pulsar charges. They stopped their advance; the pulsar charges were blowing them apart as fast as they were close enough to being in action. The entire area of space was explosion after explosion, ships darting in and out firing at each other in passing, thousands of ships now fighting it out.

Alex was firing the pulsar charges one after another targeting the nearest enemy ship. The smaller ones were quickly vaporized. The larger destroyers and cruisers took two to three hits before exploding. Where there were once ships, was now a myriad of floating debris. Thyons piloting skills were amazing and they seemed to be connected each knowing what the other would do with every maneuver. The ship had taken a few hits from enemy fire but the shields were holding strong. The entire LuQuarin convoy halted and took up defensive positions around their command ships. With the last of the pulsar charges gone Thyon sped his ship back to where the Elior battle command ship was, checking in with the commander. He checked in with the others. The Elior were winning and LuQuarin ships were beginning to retreat, the onslaught too much to handle. Seeing the Elior were holding ground, Thyon flew back to reload again, and heard his sisters on the com would be joining him.

The Admiral was watching the space battle unfold before his eyes on the 3D map. The attack in the west had been fast, a complete victory with only a few Elior casualties. The larger battle in the south had been an intense affair at the beginning. After an hour the Elior had gained the advantage and had reduced the number of enemy ships by 40:1 over Elior losses, thanks to Thyon's three ships and the three-sided attack. The LuQuarin had stopped their advance and had taken up a defensive position around their remaining command ships. He saw when Thyon, Kira and Tira reappeared on the screen and blasted their way to a large command ship. A few minutes later it disappeared, blown out of the cosmos. The Elior battlegroups were closing in on the remaining ships of the lead part of the convoy. They disappeared one after another from the Admirals map until none remained. He saw the Elior battlegroups reassemble, the area west clear, and they were now in control of the south. Turning all their ships to face east, the remaining part of the convoy had stopped and retreated awaiting reinforcements. He sent a few orders to the commanders to shore up the three battlegroups, positioning them for a possible counter attack.

Looking up to the north of Elior painted a different picture. The LuQuarin forces had enveloped the northern half of Elior just outside the neural net with thousands of ships. They were continuing to advance, slugging their way through his northern fleet trying to slow down their efforts. He elected to send Olisaria's group and the Elastins to the north. The LuQuarin fighters had uncloaked and were trying to flank his northern battlegroup. He sent word to Thyon, once reloaded he needed his help in the north. The enemy could start an attack on the neural net and planet at any time now. He notified all the systems on Elior to be prepared and have the pulsar cannons, all anti-aircraft and ground defenses ready. He activated a fleet of ships on the planet to be ready to come out of their hiding places in the mountains to defend against any enemy craft that might enter the atmosphere. The charges for the pulsar cannons had been modified thanks to Thyon and could travel a great distance, but instead of the charge expanding a mile wide at close range they had been reconfigured to a blast just 300' in diameter. With the pinpoint targeting system on each they could pick out target hundreds of miles away and blow it to pieces. The stage was set for a major confrontation.

Tenekaris stood next to his brother after observing the battle in the south much the same as the Elior Admiral had. His anger showed as the Elior attack had wiped out the lead section of the convoy and had the rear section in a defensive posture.

"Where in the hell did the Elior come up with that many ships?" Kentarious answered.

"Based on our intelligence they are using a majority of their forces in space, brother. That would leave very few left on the planet for defense. They must be confident we won't get through the neural net. We are in position now in the north and east to attack the planet."

Tenekaris rubbed his chin. The Elior had taken a gamble and had chosen to fight in space. If he attacked the planet they would have no choice but to assist leaving space wide open to complete the move to surround the planet.

"Kentarious, give the word for all warships in the north and east to take final position and open up fire on the neural net and the planet. If they can punch a hole through it, launch our fighters with the Ess and the nukes. I want you to turn as much of that planet as you can into rubble."

Fifteen minutes later thousands of LuQuarin, Blisscrell, Thornok and Flemjot ships opened fire on the neural net and Elior. Rockets, missiles and

A Divided Universe

lasers all bombarded the net covering hundreds of miles. The first volley hit the net hard covering a wide area. It was immediately followed by hundreds of pulsar charges firing back on his ships, some exploding. The exchange continued. Volley after volley from both sides crossed through space seeking a target. Explosions could be seen as shields were breaking down on both sides. More LuQuarin ships entered the firing zone doubling the projectiles pouring down on Elior. Two hours passed and they had yet to breech the Elior defenses. These new cannons were pouring into his ships, the smaller ones gone in a flash. The larger destroyers and cruisers took multiple hits before they too exploded. In the north the advance had been stopped as more Elior forces joined in along with the three strange, unique and powerful vessels that possessed this new weapon. His hidden force of 10,000 fighters joined the battle trying to flank the Elior but had been met by a tenacious fast flying group. His fighters were dropping like flies. His brother spoke up.

"Tenekaris, we still have them seriously outnumbered. It's just a matter of time before we break through."

Tenekaris walked around the map again surveying the massive exchange taking place between the two forces. He could see explosions taking place beyond the neural net, but there appeared to be no damage. The planet looked the same as before the attack. More of his ships exploded from the strange pulsar blasts the Elior were firing.

"No, brother. Stop the attack and have our forces withdraw out of the firing range of those cannons. We have suffered enough losses and need to keep our army intact and come up with a new plan. Have the forces in the north hold their position but cease firing. If they need to pull back some, so be it. I am going to go to my command ship. When I send word, I want you to assemble the overlords and commanders of our allies for a video conference from my ship. Understand?"

"Yes, my brother and Master. I will make it so."

The Admiral was pacing back and forth in the central command center as reports flooded in from north, east and southern battles being waged. He viewed the map of the planet and the neural net. The net had sustained a great deal of damage and large holes appeared in numerous sections, the result of the LuQuarin bombardment. If not for the large hologram projections that simulated the net, the enemy would have realized the breeches. Many shields had been damaged behind the net, others destroyed along with the cannons. Hundreds of missiles penetrated the atmosphere and made their way to the ground. The real view of Elior painted a different picture. Large craters in open areas, forests and even a few cities where the rockets had hit and damaged the landscape. If the LuQuarin continued the barrage it would be only a matter of time before they realized the defenses had been broken and invade the planet. He had positioned his forces well to this point but would be hard pressed to foil his opponents' efforts if the atmosphere was penetrated with the massive forces still at his disposal. He watched the ongoing exchange, the LuQuarin ships firing down thousands each minute and his cannons firing back up. Only he could witness the true destruction taking place still hidden from the enemy. The cannons were quite effective and with their accuracy were taking out the fierce enemy ships, only to see them replaced with another one being reinforced at all times.

The firing from the LuQuarin ships stopped and he witnessed them pulling back. He gave the order to cease fire. The Elior cannons fell silent. The same occurred in all three major battle zones. For the moment the fighting had stopped. He checked with a number of his commanders and received confirmation. The enemy had backed away, now out of range, holding a position far enough away that the cannons would not be able to reach. He breathed a sigh of relief. Uncertain as to why, he set up a video conference with all generals, commanders and others to get feedback and try and plan what the enemy would do next. He found his director of engineering and gave him the order to begin repairs immediately on all shields that were damaged. He then found his munitions officer and gave the word to resupply all the cannons and to report on how the factories were doing with production of more. It was imperative to take advantage of the lull in the action. Finally, he sought out his first officer and requested a report on all casualties. He walked to his ready room for a break and to get a restoration drink. The last day and a half had been grueling and he needed to maintain his focus.

A Divided Universe

Alex was sitting in the canteen sipping an OBJ in their mountain hideaway, his son Thyon, daughters Kira and Tira sitting with him, along with Croulac and Stilzen. The table was quiet. They were all tired from the numerous engagements with the enemy and none of them had slept now in over two days. Word had come that the enemy pulled back and that the Admiral called for a video conference. They were all aware of the true situation on Elior. Thyon spoke first.

"We need to find a way to strike at the heart of our enemy, the leadership that they all follow blindly, otherwise we wage a war of attrition which we may or may not be successful at." Alex replied.

"True, Thyon, but that would require us to take out Tenekaris and all the Overlords. They are all well protected and getting to them is the problem. Plus, we are not even sure which ships they are aboard."

"Father, we need only to take out Tenekaris III. He is the architect of all of this and been in power for hundreds of years. We must also take out his brother as he wears the horns of power and is directing this war on Elior. If we take them out, the other Overlords will fight to gain control of the empire."

"That may be possible, Thyon. We know the Overlords and Lords are not programmed like the masses and do his bidding out of fear of his powers which are greater than theirs. But my son, what if the Overlords decide to continue the war with Elior?"

"That is a risk, father. At present they are following the plan Tenekaris is employing and follow his orders. What is the likelihood that the twelve Overlords could come to an agreement as to how to continue the battle and war? Without a leader or total consensus, it would be like the governments you had on Earth that rarely agreed, their own agendas taking precedent over the primary goals, which in this case is to eliminate the Elior and control the universe. It would result in gridlock. It would allow us the opportunity to attack them in a number of different ways. The LuQuarin, and possibly her allies would no longer be fighting as one unit."

A Divided Universe

"It is a bold plan, Thyon, but the question remains as to where Tenekaris ship is in the massive fleet to the east."

"There is a solution to that. We have all the stolen data of all the ships in the convoys, except for the Overlords and of course Tenekaris' and his brother's ship. Each ship they have has its' own unique identifier which we have and how we track their fleet except if cloaked. I can write a program to seek out the unknown signatures in their fleet. We would then know those are the ships that contain the Overlords and Tenekaris and his brother. With a little more math and some recon, we should be able to identify his ship."

"Ok. Then what? How do we get on board?"

"All spacecraft have exhaust ports as part of their ventilation systems. I will study the designs of their ships to see what the easiest access points would be to get us inside."

They were interrupted by the hail which signaled the video conference with the Admiral was about to start. Kira stood and activated the large monitor on the wall where they were seated. The Admiral appeared on screen.

"Good evening to all of you. It has been a trying first couple of days for all of us. We have been successful in many of the battles waged thus far, but we are taking a toll unbeknownst to our enemy. All of you know the real situation we are in, and although the damage is not yet severe, the door is open for our enemies if they decide to attack directly through the net which has been damaged in a number of areas. I am calling all our battle groups to stay closer to Elior in the adjacent systems, and forces on Elior are on high alert. Thus far our estimates show we are taking them out at a 40:1 clip which in itself is impressive. However, they still greatly outnumber us. We are repairing the shields as fast as we can and replacing the pulsar cannons lost with new ones as quickly as they can be made. The munitions supply for all fleets is still in good shape. Our cloning program has yielded an additional 402,000 soldiers, of which 10% are pilots. We needed to pull out our older version fighters which were in storage to outfit them. This will provide an additional defense force within our atmosphere. A lot will depend on the LuQuarins' next move, which I expect will be soon. We are beginning to receive signals that their infantry and ground forces are starting to come out of hyperspace, and if they breech our atmosphere, Elior may be quickly consumed by hundreds of thousands of the enemy on the ground of our home world, intent on total destruction. We will continue our attacks and counter attacks as the circumstances dictate and the theater unfolds. You all should be commended for the bravery and courage you have shown. May we be steadfast in the days ahead. Finally, I am looking for any ideas as to how we can stop their advance or turn the tide in our favor."

Alex spoke up first. "Admiral, Thyon has come up with a plan that I believe is worth listening to."

"Ok. Please go ahead, Thyon."

Thyon stood up and walked around as he went through first the reasoning behind the plan, and then the plan itself in a step-by-step process. Ten minutes later he finished and sat back down awaiting the Admiral's and others' response. The Admiral spoke first.

"Thyon, that is quite a bold plan but it does appear to be possible. How long would it take you to prepare?"

"I believe we could be ready in an hour or a little longer and take off and be in position a half hour later to commence the operation." The Admiral asked all the other Generals if they had anything to add. There were a few questions which Thyon answered to their satisfaction. The Admiral concluded by making available the resources Thyon would need along with a few suggestions. Thyon agreed to let the Admiral have Kira and Tiras' ship as they would only need his for the mission. The meeting ended.

Tenekaris had sent Eftar to let his brother know to set up the video conference on his ship in thirty minutes. He used the last hour pacing around the map on his own command ship surveying the situation and asking tech support to enlarge certain parts of the battle they had just waged. After reviewing the areas they had attacked, a grin emerged on his face. He began to make his way to his brother's ship.

Arriving on Kentarious ship he was led to the large conference room where he would speak to all the Overlords and Commanders of his allies. The room contained the 3D map of the entire battlefield surrounding Elior. Tenekaris stood at the front as the video displays came to life around the back of the room showing his twelve Overlords and the commanders of the Blisscrells, Thornoks, Flemjots and Secarios. With his brother seated just to his right he began the conference.

"The Elior and her allies have put up a decent fight thus far and their newest weapon, a powerful cannon of which they appear to have many, is quite effective on our ships. They also have three very fast ships with this cannon feature but it appears to be limited to how many charges they can carry at a time. Yes, we have taken casualties but they are insignificant when compared to the size of our forces. I have studied the last battle where we bombarded Elior hard from the north and east that apparently yielded little or no damage. That is not true. Upon review it seems the Elior have been using numerous holograms for the neural net where we damaged or destroyed it, as well as cloaking images on the surface. In reality we have weakened their defenses and done damage to the planet's surface and inflicted casualties on their forces. Out infantry and ground troops are now coming out of hyperspace and will be in position within six to eight hours. We will be making a two-pronged large attack, one from the east and the other from the north. You will amass your fighting ships with a pyramid-style head, a giant arrow with a long body where the fighters with nukes will be in the center of the shaft protected by the fleet. You will go head long into the neural net and penetrate it opening the door to their atmosphere. Once inside the nuke fighters will disperse quickly to designated targets and the annihilation of Elior will commence. The northern group will nuke the northern ice cap and cities in the northern hemisphere. If we can set off enough nukes in that region of the planet it will greatly disturb the weather on Elior and begin to block out sunlight. From the east the nukes will head south of the equator as far down towards the southern pole and set off the nukes there.

A Divided Universe

I want the equator area left alone from nukes so we can begin to land our infantry and ground support vehicles in the warmer climates. There they will establish a foothold for ground operations as we bring more troops in. They will assault any ground forces they encounter and we will greatly outnumber what Elior remain on the planet. I want this attack to commence within 4 hours. You will have two hours to gain control of the planet. The infantry will be standing by and ready to invade thereafter. Do you all understand?"

A resounding yes came from each monitor. Tenekaris continued.

"If you need additional details contact Kentarious and his staff. This is it, the time for the Elior will be at an end and we will rule the universe."

A Divided Universe

Chapter Thirty-Four
Breaking the Stalemate

The Admiral watched Thyon's ship depart, then cloak and was gone. He assembled his special crew for a dangerous task but one that might prove to change the course of the battle. He issued orders to all his Generals and Commanders and they were getting into position. On the map he noticed the LuQuarin fleets were reforming, two large battlegroups assembling into an arrow-type formation. Thousands of ships, one in the east and another in the north. He had no doubt they were preparing to attack directly into the neural net and Elior. Some of the LuQuarin infantry transports had joined in just behind the new formations. This was it. They were going to make an assault and try to invade the planet.

Lorakit was piloting the ship and carefully maneuvering above the massive LuQuarin formation in the east. Thyon successfully identified the Overlord ships and the command battleship that was docked with the Master Overlord Tenekaris ship. Behind her, the assault team was going through final preparations. Thyon, Kira, Tira and Alex formed the four small elements, intent on attacking Tenekaris and his command center. Each of them would carry a pea sized orb as a backpack after they miniaturized and departed the rear of the ship near Tenekaris location. Thyon's orb would contain three Elior master assassins. Kira had Croulac, Matt and Solaria. Tira had Stilzen, and two additional Elior assassins. Alex's orb had Olisaria with her staff, Sevarin and Solarin. The 16-member team was ready.

Thyon went over to Lorakit and told her where to maneuver the ship above and behind the LuQuarin command ship. He kissed her on the forehead and led the team to the rear to where they would exit. The twelve that would travel in the orbs vaped and were now inside the pea-sized transports. Thyon, Kira, Tira and Alex reduced their size to just an inch high, strapped the orbs to a pack on their backs, then became invisible. Thyon telepathed Kira to open the mini hatch. A moment later the four were flying through space headed to the LuQuarin ship. They flew quickly and within minutes were at the rear of the massive battleship. Thyon spotted the exhaust port of the ventilation system. With the miniature size entrance was easy. Once inside Thyon used a laser and cut three sides of the wall of the shaft, bent it inward and they passed through. Once inside he resealed the entrance he had created. Now within the inner ventilation system they flew as a group heading towards the bridge area. They all activated headlamps and four small circles of light made their way through the system.

The LuQuarin formations were complete and advancing towards Elior. The long-range pulsar cannons opened up fire at the lead elements. The LuQuarin began returning fire but were still out of range to be effective but kept advancing. The Admiral ordered up all his reserve fleets from the nearby solar systems and directed them to attack on the flanks of the massive and long lines. He had Kira and Tira's ships positioned inside the atmosphere one in the northern hemisphere, the other the east. He contacted Claudicus whose fleets were submerged just below the surface waters in four groups and told them to get ready. The new cloned group was also at the ready, and even Derek's fighter groups were told to stand by. The Admiral added pressure from space having the southern fleets pound into the defenses of the LuQuarin still residing in the south. He was down to just two final reserve groups in the west standing by. Over 16 million Elior combatants were now in place. The Admiral walked around the large 3D map showing the movements of both sides, the exchange of fire growing with each passing minute. He estimated 50 million of the enemy in each group descending down on the planet, another 30 million or more behind in a column. The battle was in full throttle now and the intensity of the exchange unlike anything ever witnessed.

Thyon led his group through the system and were now above the bridge area of the battleship and was looking down through a screened cover above the large display map surrounded by LuQuarin commanders giving orders to the advancing fleets. The four all peered down. The bridge was huge and had 80 or more technicians, attendants and commanders all busy as the battle had started. On one end Thyon spotted Tenekaris dressed immaculately. His ten-foot frame with matted down red dreadlocks stood out over the gold uniform trimmed in black. On each forearm he had a weapons band and another strapped to each thigh. Next to him was his brother Kentarious. They were observing the two large formations blasting away at the Elior outer neural net pushing closer to entering the atmosphere. The map was filled with thousands of ships now engaged in battle.

Thyon telepathed the other three who in turn telepathed to those inside the orbs they carried. They would slide through the vent and position around the map of the battle. Thyon would emerge above and behind Tenekaris and his brother on the left. Alex would be on the right, Kira the top and Tira the bottom. When Thyon gave the word Olis would vape out and use her staff to freeze time and all four orbs would have their team members vape out and take out all the surrounding attendants. It had to be done quickly. Alex had warned Thyon that the time freeze would most likely not work on Tenekaris, his brother or three of the Commanders who were dressed and identified as Lords. They slid through the vent and still invisible they took up their positions around the map. Thyon observed the LuQuarin forces getting ready to enter the atmosphere of Elior, the scene on the map looked like all hell was breaking loose. Seeing everyone was in position he took a deep breath then issued the order.

"Now!"

Olis vaped out into full-size and slammed down her staff. All the LuQuarin went still except for Tenekaris, Kentarious and three Lords. The rest had vaped out a second after Olis and quickly ran at and beheaded each LuQuarin at their stations. Thyon had become visible just behind Tenekaris and began to envelop him in the gel. Alex was right behind two of the Lords and before they could activate their shields he thrust his gauntlets into each one's lower back creating a huge hole instantly killing them. The third turned his shield up and threw a laser blast at Alex knocking him back a few feet, his own shield holding. He marched straight at the Lord, both gauntlets emitting a forceful blast pushing the Lord into the map. He closed the last three feet and thrust both gauntlets through his shield into his stomach creating a huge hole. He pulled them back out and the Lord fell. Kira, Tira, Solaria, Sevarin and the others finished off the remaining LuQuarins.

A Divided Universe

The time freeze ended and Olis stood with her staff ready to attack any possible remaining LuQuarin. She felt a blast hit her shield which knocked her down. It was Kentarious moving towards her firing a laser. Thyon finished encasing Tenekaris, saw Kentarious attacking Olis. He jumped in front of him deflecting the next charge and then released his gel at him, quickly immobilizing his movements and shutting off his use of powers. It was over in less than three minutes.

Tenekaris used his eyes and blasted a hole thru the gel and was firing wildly around the room at any intruder in the lasers path. One hit the back leg of Solarin, who fell to the ground. Thyon turned seeing Tenekaris still trying to get out of the gel using his laser eyes to melt the substance from his body. Thyon shot more gel at him filling back up the hole he had made in front of his face to fire. Sealed up again he created a deflector shield around Tenekaris so if he fired again it would deflect back at him. Tenekaris was in a rage trying to break free of the gel, as was his brother. Thyon erected a deflector around Kentarious. They were now both immobilized and if they fired they would kill themselves. Solaria ran over to Solarin and attended to his wound. The other 14 now stood around the map prepared for any more LuQuarin should they try and rush into the bridge. Olisaria went to the main entrance and used her staff to laser seal the entrance. The bridge was now secure.

Thyon stood in front of Tenekaris and his brother and spoke.

"Your days of terror are over, Tenekaris. You may speak and we will hear you through the gel, but escape is quite impossible and your powers now rendered useless."

Tenekaris glared at Thyon a look of pure hatred in his eyes.

"Who in the hell are you?" Thyon smiled.

"I am the son of Alex, bearer of the Earth Medallion and have powers well beyond yours. Now you will give the order to halt your attack on Elior."

A Divided Universe

"I will do no such thing. Even if you kill me, my forces will carry out their mission and destroy Elior."

"Killing you would be to easy. Then I will use your brother."

Thyon read Kentarious mind and found a defeated soul inside. Reading deeper he discovered Kentarious had never agreed in his heart with what his brother had been doing. The endless conquests and death he had carried out for him had left him empty. Thyon telepathed Kentarious.

"You can end this if you want to. You are not like your brother. Call off the attack now and you can take the place of your brother as the true leader of the LuQuarin. The Overlords will listen to you. Tell them the truth, that we have captured your ship and Tenekaris is no longer in power."

"But my brother will kill me." He thought. Tenekaris was watching the exchange between Thyon and his brother. He looked at the map. His forces were now inside the Elior atmosphere and his fighters with nukes would be dispersing.

The Admiral watched the LuQuarin and other forces now invading inside the atmosphere. Five nuclear explosions occurred in the arctic area and then more in the northern hemisphere. He sent a thousand fighters to engage the attackers and had Claudicus launch his northern submerged fleet with 5,000 additional fighters. He activated the sweepers and surrounded them with multiple wings of fighters. He had to contain the explosions and after effects. Pulsar cannons from the ground were blasting away at the attackers in all eastern and northern regions. The map was a melee of ships in combat. Parts of Elior were in ruins and on fire. He sent more and more of his forces into the numerous battles over the planet. The situation was getting ugly. He wondered how Thyon's mission was going. They were running out of time.

Thyon asked Kentarious again.

A Divided Universe

"Stop the fighting now, become the Master of your race and for once begin to take care of all your people that you have programmed and enslaved for centuries. Do they not deserve a chance at freedom as you have? If you do not stop this and now, I will amass a force and destroy your home world and that of all your allies. You may try and destroy Elior but you will fail there as well. My powers are beyond anything you have ever imagined. Do it now and stop the carnage and start a new path for the LuQuarin. This is your last chance."

"I will need the gel removed so I can speak to the Overlords."

"No, you will not need that. I will put you in front of the console and you will call up the Overlords and speak to them. They will be able to hear you." Thyon used his powers to position Kentarious in front of the main console. He gave a verbal command to call all the Overlords and commanders carrying out the attack. He looked at Thyon.

If I call off the attack will your forces cease fire as well?"

"Yes."

Kentarious issued the command so all his leaders could hear.

"Attention, all Overlords and Commanders. Cease fire immediately and withdraw your troops back to their original positions. Tenekaris is dead and I have assumed command. The Elior are in control of our ship and will unleash a power so great that all of you will be destroyed as well as our home world in the weeks ahead." One of the Overlords spoke.

"What is the command code then Kentarious to cease fire?"

Thyon knew there were two codes one to cease fire and the other a false code which would tell all the Overlords this was a ruse and to continue the battle. He telepathed Kentarious.

"I suggest you use the right code. If you do not I will bring the fires of hell to all your people." He watched for Kentarious reaction as Tenekaris was struggling to get free of the gel, outraged at the turn of events. Kentarious issued the command code. The map began to show the LuQuarin forces cease firing and begin to withdraw. Thyon pulled out a small communicator which was a direct link to the Admiral. He stepped back out of range of hearing and spoke to the Admiral.

"Admiral, cease fire wherever the enemy has stopped and is withdrawing. It's over."

"You made a wise decision, Kentarious."

"What will you do with Tenekaris?"

"He will be going with us and incarcerated for now."

"And when will you release me from the gel?"

"When all of your forces have withdrawn completely and are heading out of our solar system and back to your own worlds. Before that you will convene a meeting on this ship with all the Overlords and the Leaders of your allies where you will dictate a new order and the release of your parasites within your allies. Understood?"

"Yes."

"Kira, Tira, take Tenekaris out of here and transport him to our ship. I will have Lorakit get within porting distance so you can use one of the orbs and port with him directly onto the ship. Lock him up in the special room we built for this purpose and leave him encased in the gel. Sevarin, you and Solaria take Solarin and orb onto my ship as well. We have some medical equipment on board you can treat him up until we can get back to Elior. Now Kentarious, I want you to issue the command to undock Tenekaris' ship from this one and have them take it to the rear of your forces. Father, you, Olis and the others will remain here with me for the time being to insure Kentarious follows through with all instructions."

A Divided Universe

They all looked at the map and saw the LuQuarin forces were withdrawing and returning to space from their origins. Lorakit had the cloaked ship in place, relayed the coordinates to Thyon who passed them on to the others. Two orbs soon appeared, were filled and gone.

The Admiral issued the order after receiving it from Thyon. The firing stopped in all areas and the enemy was leaving Elior and the space outside of the atmosphere. He breathed a sigh of relief. The LuQuarin had come very close to landing their ground forces and invading the planet. Casualties had been severe on both sides. He summoned his commanders to get full reports from each battle group as to the losses sustained and for them to reform and be prepared just in case the cease fire failed to hold up. He wanted to hear more from Thyon, but knew Thyon had things under control and would report in when he could. Had the battle continued, well, he just didn't want to think of what might have happened. He looked at the map and saw all his battlegroups were in good position as the enemy continued to vacate back out into space and far enough away where they could no longer inflict any damage. The sweepers had all been activated, carefully taking out the ill effects of the many nuclear explosions the LuQuarin had set off. It would take at least half a day for the sweepers to complete the task and restore Elior's natural atmosphere.

Thyon told Kentarious to get on the ship's speakers and give the order to abandon ship, that a bomb had been set and would explode in ten minutes. The ship's alarms went off and the entire crew made their way to the emergency shuttles to get off the ship before it exploded. Going over to one display, Thyon quickly figured out how to lower the LuQuarin ships shields. He then gave the order for the rest of his crew to vape and orb up into his cloaked ship just above. Clamping a bracelet onto the gel he vaped and ported Kentarious up to his ship. Now on board, he had Lorakit position the ship ten thousand meters above it, turn and prepare a pulsar blast. When ten minutes was reached the pulsar blast was fired and the mighty battleship was blown into a million pieces.

Chapter Thirty-Five
The Aftermath

Thyon had Lorakit open a channel to the LuQuarin Overlord ships so that Kentarious could speak to them. He had Kentarious request that all the Overlords meet with him on Tenekaris' command ship within an hour to come to terms with the Elior for a peaceful withdrawal of all LuQuarin vessels from the galaxy. Only five of the Overlord ships acknowledged. Thyon looked at the map displaying all the ships departing the area including the Overlords' command ships. The five that had acknowledged were making their way to Tenekaris command ship. The other seven were making haste with their vessels and departing out and into hyperspace, apparently not keen on the idea of meeting with Thyon or the Elior to come to terms. The LuQuarin were divided. Thyon smiled. He had anticipated this and it would be easier to manage the five remaining and let the others go. They would soon be at odds against each other as to forming a new LuQuarin leadership now that Tenekaris was no longer in control.

Lorakit positioned the craft above Tenekaris' command ship and Thyon vaped and ported aboard with Kentarious, along with Alex, Olis and Sevarin. With Kentarious still encased in the gel, the LuQuarin guards had lowered their weapons as commanded once on board. Minutes later the five Overlords that had agreed to come on board made their entrance onto the bridge. Thyon gestured for them to take a seat at the table in the center of the room where he had already seated Kentarious. The Overlords looked at Thyon, a sense of fear on their faces. Thyon looked at each one of the Overlords gaining a sense of their position. He then started the conversation.

"I welcome the five of you Overlords here today. The time has come for change. Too many have died in the galaxies due to one man's quest to rule. Tenekaris is no more and his days of terror are at an end. Seven of your peers have elected to run away and form their own group, perhaps to carry on the days of treachery of your former leader. I can assure you they will be dealt with harshly should they pursue such ventures. It is time for a new order in the LuQuarin ways. First of all, you will reach out to your scientists and begin to reverse the inhabitation of your allies and control thereof. You will disclose to them entirely what you have been doing over the years and release them from your grip. They will once again be free to choose their own will and the will of their people. Each Overlord here will be assigned a group to meet with and begin the process. No doubt they will be angry, but we will assist you in making this change a smooth transition so that no further conflicts erupt. There is reason for all species to work together, cooperate, engage in trade and promote a good life for their people. We will be assigning an ambassador and emissary group of Elior to accompany each Overlord with this task." Kentarious asked a question.

"What will become of Tenekaris?" Thyon answered.

"He will be incarcerated for the rest of his life in a place of our choosing, which will never be revealed. You can tell your people accordingly. He will not be executed, although he deserves to be. That would bring him the satisfaction and a status of a martyr which we will not allow."

The meeting continued and the LuQuarin Overlords sent dispatches to their fleets to disperse and head home. They would remain for the next two days to complete all the terms of withdrawal and setting up a new governing body under the supervision of the Elior. They sent some of the Lords to begin the process of removing their presence from within their allies. Here again the Elior assisted as the sides met. The Admiral had come on board with a contingent of scholars and scientists to insure the LuQuarin carried out the tasks required.

Thyon went back to his ship along with Alex, and met with Tenekaris still encased in the gel. He met with Lorakit and asked if she could go down to Elior to assist with the rebuilding program and then seek out and establish a suitable home for the two. He sent a message to the Admiral that he and his father would be gone for a number of days. Now Thyon, his father and Tenekaris zoomed away into the galaxies heading for a place Thyon had discovered years ago that would make a perfect imprisonment for Tenekaris.

A Divided Universe

Traveling for five days at an incredible speed Thyon finally began to slow the ship down as they entered a new galaxy. He used the time to share with his father many of the travels he and his sisters had been on over the past fifteen years. With Tenekaris safely encased in the gel, Thyon had interrogated him telepathically a number of times but to no avail. Tenekaris refused to cooperate in any way.

Thyon slowed the ship down coming out of hyperspace entering a desolate looking solar system, whose sun was not very bright, in its' latter stages of life. There were seven planets. He headed for the fourth one from the sun. It was a dark, shadowy planet, devoid of life. A desolate place which Thyon described to his father having no genuine resources of any value. It was simply molten rock and ranges, dust and sand. It looked like a desert with mountains scattered about. Thyon went into the atmosphere, descended down to a mountain range sandwiched between two large deserts. Landing the ship, he clamped a bracelet to Tenekaris gel and the three of them ported. A moment later they were inside a large cavern that had a strange glow to it coming from illuminous rocks. The cavern emitted a strange scent, but the air was breathable. In the center of the structure were a number of stalagmites, and one in particular had a liquid dripping from it to the ground where it was quickly absorbed by the sand. With his powers Thyon levitated Tenekaris in the gel just below the dripping structure and suspended him in mid-air. He looked at Tenekaris.

"Here you will remain for the rest of your life. The gel you are encased in will act as a biomechanical suit that will sustain you until you reach your death. This planet is devoid of life and there is no reason any species would ever visit it, yet alone discover you here. I have sealed off the cavern from any known device that may detect your presence. In reality you will remain here forever, devoid of possible contact, yet alone rescue. Most of the galaxy is already charted and ignored by travelers. Since in theory you will live another 2-300 years, you will have a great deal of time for self-reflection, the death and destruction you have caused."

Thyon adjusted Tenekaris position to where the liquid drop by drop landed on the top portion of the gel he was entombed in. He went over and cut a small hole in the gel which exposed the top of Tenekaris head and hair. The first drop landed on the exposed area, followed by another drop a second later. Tenekaris tried to move his head away from the drops but could not.

"Your fate Tenekaris is a drop will land on your head every second and very slowly will begin to erode first your hair and then the skin of your skull. It may take a hundred years of more but eventually it will erode even your thick skull drop by drop eventually exposing the evil brain contained within you. That is when the fun will start for you, as the drops will slowly begin to erode the brain and you will begin to suffer. It will be very painful as time goes on and you will feel the pain you have inflicted on millions of others. It won't kill you, but will drive you into insanity. I am making a video of this and will show it to any LuQuarin Overlord who fails to cooperate in a new Universe, devoid of the evil and hate you have proliferated. Evil will not be allowed to grow and flourish as it did under your leadership."

Alex had been watching all of this and listening to his son speak to Tenekaris.

"Father, it is time for us to leave. I have set up the cavern so as to never be detected. To you Tenekaris, well I have no pity, nor will I have for any of those that try to follow in your footsteps. Perhaps your suffering will bring you enlightenment and you will beg for forgiveness. There will be no one to forgive you, and in time you will be forgotten and merely a bad piece of history in the timeline of life."

Thyon and Alex vaped and ported back to the ship and began traveling back towards Elior. They greatest evil known to the universe was now incarcerated for the rest of his living days. It would be a five-day trip back to Elior.

Chapter Thirty-Six
A New Beginning

Thyon took the ship out of hyperspace as they approached Elior. Ten days had passed since their departure and it would be interesting to see how things were shaping up. They were greeted by three warships to gain clearance before entering the atmosphere. Once clear Thyon descended the ship down to the island where his fathers home lay. Landing on the beach, they departed the ship and walked up through the dunes to the walkway leading to the home. He sent a message for Lorakit to join him there as well as his sisters.

They were greeted by Diana as they walked up onto the deck. After kissing his wife, Alex and Thyon took a seat at the table while Diana retrieved them some food and drink. It was a beautiful day on Elior, the sun was shining, blue skies and the sounds of the surf rolling up onto the beach.

Returning with a few plates of food and drinks, she took a seat at the table and spoke.

"The Admiral has asked that you contact him when you returned. I imagine a great deal has happened since you left."

"Thank you, my dear wife. But the Admiral can keep for an hour or so at least. If it was urgent he would have had a messenger disk waiting for us when we made clearance to land." A new orb appeared and out vaped Lorakit. She walked over to Thyon, gave him a quick kiss and took an open chair to his right.

"So, I take it Thyon, that you and your father have put Tenekaris into permanent incarceration somewhere?"

"Yes, my love. His evil will never permeate the universe again. How is life here on Elior?

"Well, I did find what I think is a suitable place for us to live, Thyon, and have begun to construct a home but awaited your return so we can finish it together."

"Where is it?"

"I found a tropical place similar to the one you brought me to a while back."

"Sounds good to me." Alex spoke up,

"Why don't the two of you join us for dinner and then you can head out to see your new home Thyon."

A messenger disk appeared for both Thyon and Alex. They each read the same message. The Admiral requested that the two join him for dinner in a couple of hours so he could catch them up on the many events since their departure. It was worded in a way that suggested it more of an order than a request. Alex and Thyon agreed and sent a return message. They would meet with the Admiral.

"So much for a quiet evening at home eh, father?"

"We should have surmised this would happen. Better to meet now and get caught up. Then perhaps we can spend some free time with those we cherish the most. Let's have a couple of drinks at least and listen to some good music before we have to leave." Diana issued an order and music filled the air with Alex's favorite songs. They all laughed, toasted glasses and enjoyed the moment.

Alex and Thyon ported to the Admirals command center on Elior. Sevarin greeted them on arrival and led them to the Admirals office. After exchanging greetings, the two sat across from the Admiral as he started the conversation.

"I take it you have safely secured Tenekaris incarceration?" Thyon answered,

A Divided Universe

"Yes, Admiral. I made a tape for you of his new situation that he will endure for the rest of his living days along with an audio that I added. Might I suggest you make copies of it, and if necessary give it to any Overlord who doubts our conviction to create a better universe or is not cooperating to the degree we seem fit. Also, Admiral, here are the complete plans to my ship. I am giving them to you so that we can build a number of them to help insure that the peace we have fought so hard for is maintained. My sisters and I were working on a newer ship prior to our involvement in this war and soon we will begin its' construction."

"Thank you Thyon. Your ship is truly superior and will be a great aid in keeping the peace. Now that you have returned, I can update you on the situation. The five Overlords and Kentarious initiated the steps to remove their presence from within their allies. All of the officers of the Blisscrells, Thornoks, Flemjots and Secarios that are with them have been restored to their natural beings and dispatches have been sent to the leaders of their home worlds to continue the process. The four allies of the LuQuarin have taken all their troops and equipment and are returning to their home planets along with an assigned LuQuarin and an emissary group of Elior. The plague of the LuQuarin infestation should be completely removed from their societies within a month and normal relations established. Those other seven LuQuarin Overlords that are not a part of this truce seem to be headed back to Tenekaris last sietch along with the allied troops that went with them. Until the leaders of the allies request their return that part of the infestation is still at large." Alex asked.

"How is Elior doing now after the battle Admiral?"

"Elior is doing well Alex. A majority of the damage done has already been repaired and our people have emerged out of the underground bunkers and returning to a normal life. I met with the Council while you were away. They are pleased not only that we survived the attack, but have appeared to have found a new peace with at least some of the LuQuarins."

"Time will tell Admiral. Is there anything you need me or Thyon to do?"

A Divided Universe

"At the moment no. I would like you to keep yourself available if things change, but for now the new establishment of the LuQuarins is moving along and we have the necessary people in place to handle it. I will be meeting with the Council, military leaders, our scientists and engineers daily for updates. For now, I suggest you both take some personal time to be with your families and try and enjoy life for once. If nothing important comes up, I would like to meet with you in a week and will send you a message. Now get out my office, that's an order." He said with a smiling face.

A week passed, then another. Now six months later Alex and Thyon attended their weekly meeting with the Admiral. Elior was completely back in order and the rescued humans had been indoctrinated into a new and wonderful life. The plans Thyon had provided the Admiral for his ship resulted in many new ones now built and being deployed with tactical forces in key areas to insure peace was maintained in a number of galaxies. The seven Overlords that defected were still at large and primarily taken up station at Tenekaris last headquarters. The other five Overlords and Kentarious had returned to their original home planet of LuQuar and had begun rebuilding it. Elior technology assisted in removing much of the pollution from LuQuar and new life was beginning to emerge. The biggest problem the new LuQuarin had was deprogramming an entire society.

Thyon and his sisters began construction on their newest ship which would be even faster with greater capabilities than the current one. Alex spent much of his time working with Thyon, Kira and Tira building the new ship. They were all working in a special hanger constructed for that soul purpose. Alex spoke to his son.

"Thyon. Once you complete this ship, then what?"

"Father. When complete, this ship will give us the capability to bring down the last seven Overlords if they fail to come to terms as the others have. It is time to put an end to evil."

Alex looked up at the huge ship being built, the size alone larger than any aircraft carrier from earth days and from reviewing the plans

A Divided Universe

knew that this ship would make a difference in the ongoing conflict. He looked at his son and realized that Thyon was committed to removing any evil in the galaxies or universe, his powers and abilities greater than any other creature yet known. Likewise, his sisters were committed as well. Creating a universe where all species could prosper, without conflict. But to end conflict would take force and there were those out there that would not submit to such a utopian existence. The day was at an end so Alex bade them all goodnight and returned home.

Sitting on the covered portion of the deck, he looked out at the sea. Elior weather had changed by design and a gentle flowing rain came down on the island. Sitting at the table with a beer and a shot he stared out to the horizon where the sun was setting behind the clouds listening to the rain as it fell onto the plants and trees. Diana came out, joining Alex, sitting on his lap. It was a peaceful moment as he cradled his wife in silence.

Diana sensed that Alex was deep in thought wondering where his mind was drifting after all that had taken place. He would tell her when he was ready, so for the moment she simply enjoyed being in his arms in a home she never would have dreamed of growing up. With AJ and Xia now in the academy of higher learning and Elior at peace the future looked bright.

Alex pondered whether Thyon could truly bring peace to the galaxies and universe. Violence had been met with violence in the battle of good versus evil. There was still too much unknown with the seven Overlords that defected, the new trading alliances being formed no longer under the LuQuarins' control, and then there were the Lycoats, an unknown but apparently conquering species like the LuQuarin that Lorakit said she feared even more. They would need to learn more about the Lycoats. He felt inside that the struggle would continue for many years and decades to come as it had throughout all of history. Would this time be different? History said otherwise, and even when peace was achieved in one or some parts, greed, violence and power for control would emerge in new arenas. He felt Diana shift in his lap bringing him back into the moment. For now, he would just enjoy that which he had and leave tomorrow and the future alone.

A Divided Universe

www.ingramcontent.com/pod-product-compliance
Lightning Source LLC
Chambersburg PA
CBHW021314250626
47155CB00002B/540